THE FIFTH PLANE

A Novel by

BULL MARQUETTE

BRAVE NEW GENRE, INC.

Fresno, CA

BRAVE NEW GENRE, INC.
Publishers of Books, Music & Films
6535 N Palm Ave. #101
Fresno, CA 93704
www.bravenewgenre.com

The Fifth Plane

Library of Congress Control Number: 2008937531

Marquette, Bull
The Fifth Plane/Bull Marquette
ISBN 978-0-9820474-0-8

1. Thriller—Fiction   2. Paranormal—Fiction
3. 9/11—Fiction   4. Terrorism—Fiction

Dedicated to:

Bonnie Hearn Hill, great writer, writing teacher extraordinaire, and the TUESDAYS – the best writing critique group there ever was.

Print-On-Demand, first release: October, 2008.

Chapter 1
Ten A.M., September Twelfth

"Danny Boy—"

The bird colonel — his nametag read "Logan" — was all smiles as he sat down across from Daniel Clooney, holding out a dripping can of A&W Root Beer. The world jostled, and Daniel shook his head. How anyone could drink anything on a bouncing helicopter, much less keep it down, was a mystery he didn't want to solve. The nation was at war, yet here he was, trapped in a flying coffin with a numbskull in a uniform who wanted to be everyone's best buddy.

In about an hour, if the twirlybird held together, Daniel would meet America's biggest hero since Audi Murphy, assuming the lucky schmuck was still alive. A sick thought, but if his injuries didn't get him, Osama's suicide troops probably would, no matter how much protection the FBI provided.

The colonel sat back and yelled to be audible over the noise. "How does it feel to know that you are riding on practically the only goddam piece of machinery in the sky over the whole continent?"

"What about the F-16s flying patrol all over the country?" Daniel replied. A jolt slammed his teeth together. Orders or no orders, on the trip back from Ohio, he would rent a car. "They're patrolling from every airbase that has them, I thought."

"They don't count." Again the wide grin. Daniel's father had always warned him about military big shots who came on too friendly. He had also warned him never to climb into a helicopter.

"What the hell sort of job did you say you have?" Smilin' Jack continued, taking the root beer in huge gulps. "Gotta be a big deal to let us fly on a day like this."

"Liaison Office. It's new. We coordinate FBI, CIA, and Justice. You know, cut down on duplication of effort, keep communication channels clear."

"Duplication of effort? In government?" Logan guffawed.

Daniel laughed politely, but Logan persisted, leaning forward, filling the narrow, steel-lined space between seats. Why couldn't the military make a comfortable vehicle?

"So how'd you get such a plum slot? Were you a spook?"

Daniel shook his head. "FBI. The CIA didn't want me."

"No shit?" A sip of root beer. "Wasn't your dad military intelligence?"

Another jolt, this one from the inside. Daniel's body tensed. There was more to Smilin' Jack than met the eye. His dad's profession was something Daniel never divulged.

"How do you know that?"

A shrug. "They gave me a folder when we made out the flight plan. There's a folder on everyone, as I'm sure your poppa told you."

The bird took a swooping dip, and so did Daniel's stomach. Logan yelled toward the cockpit opening. "Keep it level, McGee." The reply, unintelligible, made the colonel laugh.

Logan checked his watch. "About forty more minutes." He smirked at the way Daniel's fingertips were dug into his knees. "So why are we taking you to see the hero? Can't be security. Jesus, I heard there's almost a division guarding the hospital."

"Well, there you are." Deep breath. "Every other service branch and agency has a contingent out there, at the hospital or combing the crash site in Pennsylvania. Guess my boss didn't want our department to be left out."

A knowing nod. "One of those deals, eh?" A final gulp of root beer, and the can crinkled in the wiry hands that already displayed a few age spots.

Logan sat back again, looking almost comfortable on the hard metal. "Only problem with that story is the timing. Things are too hot to send you to make an appearance — for appearance's sake. Nice try, but your daddy should have taught you to lie better."

Daniel didn't bristle, though he wanted to kick himself for not seeing it earlier. The colonel had the atmosphere, the carriage, the doe eyes that shifted methodically. So much like his father, it hurt. Only his father never smiled this much.

"So there's something going on behind the scenes." Logan looked skyward, like a crossword puzzler trying to discover a word. Daniel turned his own gaze toward the rear of the spacious Huey. The only other passenger was one guy in battle dress, dutifully holding his M-16 across his lap on the back bench. Logan kept drilling the well, though he couldn't know it was dry. "I mean, this guy — this nobody — what's his name?"

"Frank Whitlock."

"—Yeah. He's coming back from a sales convention, probably on his second beer, suddenly the plane's hijacked, then one of the passengers calls on his cell, finds out they're all about to be toast — then this insurance-salesman-nobody gathers some bozos in the back of the plane, organizes them, they march forward, can't get in the fucking cockpit door, and somehow our boy, who has never had a day of karate in his life, kicks the goddam thing down, and they kill the bastards with wine bottles and — what was it about their necks? They broke some of the terrorists' necks?"

"My information comes from CNN, just like yours," Daniel said, pulling rank for good measure. Logan's grimace was so pained that Daniel took pity, and threw him a bone. "Only thing I heard different was that Whitlock was organizing the 'resistance' before they started getting the warning phone calls."

Logan's eyes flashed at this tidbit of new info, and Daniel kicked himself. "Well, there you are. The old fart was in on the caper."

Daniel shifted to look out of the window, but the jostling view only riled his stomach further.

"Come on, Clooney. It adds up. This old guy never flew a plane in his life, according to the records. But records can be doctored. Christ, the bad guys put the damned thing into a power dive, and Hero Whitlock pulled it out. Brought the nose up without stalling, less than a thousand feet off the deck, then lands it. *He lands it.*" Again, the insipid smile. "So where does that put Liaison Officer Daniel Clooney? You heading up there to arrest America's hero? Or give him a Black Ops medal?"

He read. With his eyes and likely thirty or forty years of training for every nuance of body language, the old colonel was riveted on any response Daniel might telegraph. Too bad he didn't realize there were none to give.

"You've got a great imagination, Colonel. It's a great scenario, and I'll bet the talk shows are onto it by this weekend." He risked another look outside. "I'm afraid my assignment isn't so sexy. Like I told you, my boss just wants us to have a presence. The Liaison office is an experiment. The lawmakers started howling for the CIA and FBI to come together an hour after the last tower fell yesterday. My boss is Gerald Sullivan, a career man, and he figures he's finally in the right place at the right time."

"Sullivan? And you're Clooney?" Logan guffawed, a little too loudly. "Well, maybe I'm wrong. They can't give real secrets to two Irishmen." His eyelids closed, leaving only slits. "But as one analyst to another, something about America's hero smells to high heaven, and I think you know what it is."

Daniel managed his own smile. "Ever think that Whitlock might just be an average American who was able to pull off something remarkable? Not everything has to be some sort of conspiracy. All the hero's told anyone is that he had a premonition about the hijacking. You've been in this game a long time. Maybe even you can admit that miracles do happen."

"Perhaps." A slow nod. Then that awful, all-encompassing grin again. "But I doubt your daddy ever told you that."

Chapter 2
Night Horror

"You're going to die today."

"You're going to die today."

The whispers were repeated, as if to make sure that Frank Whitlock understood. Voices had always come to him in dreams, but these were not the usual, sometimes inane predictions. These threats had come out of, been part of the darkness every night since September eleventh. Someone was trying to tell him something. Something he missed on the day it happened.

The death whispers always said "today." So far, there had always been a tomorrow, thank God. Was he finally lapsing into some form of schizophrenia, fulfilling Mr. Campbell's prediction uttered way back in high school English? Mental illness or latent genius, it didn't much matter. The terrorists wanted him, and they would get him. He could see that in the eyes of his protectors, though they were, to a person, professional and cheerful. He could also feel it waiting for him, somewhere out there. Almost touch it. His death would not be pretty.

Frank lay sweating in the wayward sheets, trying to urge feeling back into his legs.

"You are going to die today." The whisper echoed each time he closed his eyes. And now his blood circulation was returning, climbing at turtle-speed up his hips, pricking his fingers alive, and climbing the length of his arms, inch-by-inch, blood invading cells like tiny floodwaters, thawing flesh so strangely frozen. Waking up paralyzed in the middle of the night had been part of his life since childhood, but that did not stop him from wondering if this was how death would feel when it did come.

"It's only three." Jill climbed over her pillow and loomed above him. "Are you all right?"

"Yeah. Go back to sleep." A whiff of her cherry shampoo. He could flex his fingers now. "Did I scream?"

"No." She re-arranged the covers, tucking them in gingerly, to avoid the healing wound on his right side. "Were you dreaming about the plane?"

"No. I don't dream about that."

"I still know when you've had a nightmare." She yawned. "Sorry, I have to go in early. If you really need to talk, I'll stay up."

"No. Go back to sleep. I'm OK."

Night horrors were one thing, but the night sweats were a new addition. Shock to the body, the doctors in the hospital said. Getting stabbed by razors a half-dozen times did things like that to your system. Tiny, unquenched infections, or maybe random echoes through the nervous system that would only last a few weeks. If only the whispered threats would fade with them.

He could try to simply drift back to sleep – God knows he needed the rest – but Sam would never forgive him. So he took deep breaths as silently as he could, and tried to remember the dream. That was their code – when he woke frozen, he had received a message from Sam.

After a long time listening to the *pings* of the wind chimes on the back patio and the chimes of Grandma Landwerlin's clock in the hall, wisps of a scene began to return to the inside of his eyelids – pinpoint flashes of light, and smells pressed in from all sides. An odor of death — was he back in the plane? My God, no.

"You're going to die today."

Now the dream washed over him with full force: He saw an airplane, but not the big Boeing jet. He was a little boy again, flying gliders with Sam out on the football field. In the cold, impenetrable Texas wind – this was before they moved to California – the tiny balsa-wood crafts kept crashing straight down into the hard brown grass. Only occasionally could they catch a level wind draft, and then the wooden toys became magic, pitching up and down as they traversed the whole field, finally clacking to rest on the bleachers.

"Look at this," Sam called, and here was where things started to warp. Frank felt himself tense up, but he followed him to the end zone. "Those ants — look at those ants." Sam yelled and pointed.

A mountainous ant bed towered in one corner of the football field, an exaggerated kind of habitat constructed by fire ants. Ridiculous, Frank wanted to say. There were no fire ants back home when he was young.

He followed his brother's finger, and felt his own jaw drop. The crawling insects were not ants, but tiny human beings, clad in ancient garb, fighting a great battle with all the fervor of crazed bugs. They carried guns, and maces, and swords in their minute, muscular fists. He might have been watching a well-executed cartoon, but this scene was three-dimensional and awful. Tiny pools of bright red blood were forming all up and down the pitted dirt. Incredibly, one group of the little fighting figures wore red, and the other, black. Like ants.

Frank stood, mesmerized. He felt like a god, easily able to stop the fighting if he wished. He had only to pick up any of the tiny creatures and crush them in his fingers. What did it mean?

"No, idiot," Sam said, waving his arms, pointing past the warring bug-humans. "See? One-one-five-eight-seven. There — in the grass."

"What?" Frank feared that pulling his gaze away would break the spell. Not only could he see everything the little people did, like looking down from a blimp, but their very feelings rose on the air in grunts and wails. Each warrior faction was fanatical, wronged, vengeful.

"The numbers — the numbers," Sam insisted.

There, across the end zone in white marking chalk, someone had written the digits: *1-1-5-8-7* — as if that were the name of some strange home team.

"See?" Sam got right up in his face, excited. "Remember them." He repeated slowly, "One-one-five-eight-seven."

"Why?"

It was stupid even to ask. His big brother died when Frank was thirteen, but still came to his dreams, to show him things. Marvelous things, often horrifying, always urgent. But he never answered *why*.

At that instant, one of the tiny wooden gliders flew into view, circled the numbers for one, two, three turns, then sailed upward on the wind, and stalled. Frank had had only a couple of flying lessons when the company bought a private jet, and knew what a stall was. On September eleventh, he had used that knowledge to barely keep the jumbo jet out of one. The balsa craft slammed down onto the hard ground, hitting the chalk "5," raising a miniature cloud of white dust.

In the dream, Frank picked up the craft and straightened its wings. There on the side, letters had been scrawled in ballpoint, obviously Sam's handwriting, "k...,l,m," and some childish scribbles that looked like little birds and clouds.

"You ruined it," Frank said. "Is it the alphabet? We agreed not to write on the planes. You're supposed to use the stick-on decals."

But Sam was running away, down the field, into the cold wind that had suddenly increased in fierceness. The sign that the dream was about to end. The sky grew dark, and in his last glimpse, the tiny people on the big ant bed had ceased to move, their weapons hanging limply by their sides or at their feet. The miniatures slept and groveled in eerie sitting positions, and their feelings could just be made out — pleading whispers, perhaps prayers that seemed to also ask *why*. Frank could hear their unspoken fears: These people knew that this was just a lull in their wretched little war, and that when they awoke, they were all going to die.

Frank's eyes came open, and his stomach churned. It was always good to see Sam, even though he was trapped in that slippery, scary world of dreams. Each time Frank tried to talk to him, man-to-man, he scurried away. He never did get to ask him, *are you OK?*

That question had real meaning now, since he might well be joining Sam in the near future. Maybe his body was even getting ready for the end. The real world had been a blur since that fateful day — the roller coaster fight on the plane, the horror of the screams, the wrenching landing, the blood and the press, and the woozy hospital visit by the President of the United States.

He fought it, but for a few moments, the *big* fear reached out of the darkness: Was he still on the plane, bleeding, dying? Were these three tumultuous weeks since the eleventh only the tortured dreams of a dead man, like that farmer on Owl Creek Bridge in the Civil War? To hell with the accolades and bouquets and never-ending replays on television. Had he lost Jill?

He listened. Her breathing was regular, now. Soft. He slipped his feet out of the covers, and into his house shoes. Wrapping his robe around him, he went into the den and switched on the small reading light. The police guards would notice, so he had to work fast. In the phone book, he found the number he wanted, punched through the maze of audible choices, and finally heard the voice — too perky for this time of night — of a human being.

"Yes." Frank was careful to whisper. "I just wanted to know if KLM Airlines has a flight one-one-five-eight-seven? Yes, I'll hold."

Chapter 3
Pre-emptive Strike

Daniel was not one to be awed by the White House, even with the three layers of security checks where one layer used to suffice. For whatever reason, he considered it less imposing than the modern marble halls of CIA Headquarters in Langley. Especially under this president. Even with a war on, the clerks, secretaries, and stiff-upper-lip advisors moved briskly and efficiently, speaking in hushed spurts, smiling only politely.

He turned down a long corridor. Marine guards glared, as if John Dillinger were passing. Any courteous, business-like smiles were a thing of the past. He would have to take the dime tour here sometime, find out whose portraits these were, hanging on the wall, maybe even stand in the room where Clinton got his jollies. This was where power originated, not the CIA building, he reminded himself.

"Daniel Clooney to see Ms. Bernstein," he told a woman behind an immaculate desk. Her nameplate — *Stacy Pringle* — was positioned exactly parallel to the desk edge. She drank coffee, and centered the cup perfectly on its coaster after she swallowed.

"Good morning, Mr. Clooney." A smile, tinged with the slightest impatience. He caught a look that passed between her and the older lady ensconced in another desk across the narrow passage. Maybe they didn't like last-minute changes in the schedule. A wave, and he was in.

"Sit down, please." Loretta Bernstein's voice was friendly enough, but she did not look up from her scribbling. "We set you up for ten. Why did you need to move it up two hours? How's Gerry, by the way?"

Daniel's boss, Gerald Sullivan, ran the new Liaison Office like a man who wanted to prove government bosses could be tougher than those out in the corporate world. That persona didn't work when he ran for Congress, but it was said he had quit a fat CIA job to try his hand in politics. "He's good. Still trying to fire people. When he finds out he can't, he throws a little fit and gets them transferred to Alaska. Or Arizona."

"Now, now. I know that's not true." Gaze still glued to her writing. "Actually, I like both of those states. How long until he banishes you?" A pleasant chuckle, and Ms. Bernstein finally leaned back in her chair.

"Don't laugh. It may be next week, if the president says the wrong thing this morning." He tossed a slim file onto her ledger. "Frank Whitlock."

She picked it up, but didn't open it. "Is this about his smoking dope in college? We're aware of all that. The man's a hero, Daniel."

"And we're giving him a medal. Director Sullivan thinks that's enough. For the president's sake. He shouldn't be elevated to giving a speech to a joint session of Congress."

Ms. Bernstein squinted. Perhaps too vain to wear reading glasses. She had to be pushing thirty, Daniel guessed. She turned a few pages but did not seem to be soaking anything in. "Who said we were going to do that?"

"Not me." He crossed his legs, wishing she would offer coffee. Or a Bloody Mary. "The Director — Gerry — was told yesterday that Senator Hathaway had finally convinced the president to let Whitlock do just that. Gerry — we — don't care that it's unprecedented. The problem is, our hero is a kook."

"Do you drink coffee?"

"Love some."

She called out, not bothering to use the intercom, and Daniel was horrified to notice that he had not closed the door. Maybe the CIA was right not to hire him.

The file still poised in her hands. "When did I meet you?"

He swallowed. She didn't seem capable of focusing, and if this didn't stick, Sullivan would have his ass. "Right after the disaster?" he guessed, though he didn't remember her face. "I've been up here with Gerry a couple times – lots of people in those meetings."

"No. It was two years ago." Her smile broadened. "We were just getting the Washington office of the president's campaign patched together. Audubon Society Dinner." Perhaps she did have a memory.

"That rings a bell." It didn't. "I think I remember…"

"I don't see how. You were the life of the party. How much did you drink? Oh, yeah — you're a staunch Democrat, aren't you?"

"I voted for the president."

"Mmm. Perhaps there is hope for you, yet." Her attention went back to the file. Coffee arrived.

"Mr. And Mrs. Jennings are here," Pringle said.

"Explain the delay. Just a few minutes."

Daniel pointed. "Could you close the door?"

Bernstein nodded.

All business. "I do not know whether the president intends to let Mr. Whitlock speak. If he does, it will be scripted. We'll write the speech for him. It would give the country a lift. Any man who fights his way into a cockpit of terrorists—"

"He had help."

"Yes, but he's the one who kicked down the door — the other witnesses said it was phenomenal, for a guy pushing sixty. He's the one who took the controls and stopped the tailspin, even though he had been stabbed." Her voice was rising. "And brought the plane out of a dive at an altitude of one hundred—"

"Please." Daniel put one hand on the desk and pointed at the file with the other. "I've seen it on television a thousand times. Look at those notes. Going back to 1972. Whitlock wrote Nixon, proposing a solution to the Vietnam War."

"He was in junior high."

Daniel's fingers punched the air. "Bad habits start early. Next he wrote Ford, warning about flying saucers, claimed that the president was in danger."

Her gaze flitted across a page. "There were two attempts on President Ford's life—"

"There were three incidents. Whitlock's dire warnings came after they were ancient history. He wrote Carter saying that one of the hostages in Iran was a double agent."

"I see that." Her finger traced an entry. "But he didn't give a name. Not much of a clue, huh?"

"Like any clue from a wanna-be fortune teller. Whitlock thinks he's a psychic, for God's sake. He applied to the CIA twice, proposing that the government let him set up a mind-reading platoon. The man is bonkers." He reached for his coffee and drank.

She looked up. Perfect lipstick, cute pout. Off limits, though, if she was so buddy-buddy with Sullivan. Could she be the secret squeeze everyone always speculated about? Nah. Her eyes closed partly, her face acquiring a shrewd look. Pretty, even that way. "This isn't just about Gerry, is it? Trying to prevent the CIA from looking bad, because they didn't hire Whitlock?"

"Not hiring a kook would hardly make them look bad."

"Let's see." She picked up a pen and began rolling it between her hands. "The Liaison Office is made up of CIA, FBI, and..."

"Justice. Sort of. We have two lawyers, but everything else is still being worked out."

A smile. Why was she enjoying this? "I'm not really the one to take this to the president," she said.

Daniel sipped his coffee, waiting for the rest. It did not come. "Ms. Bernstein—"

"Call me Loretta. Since we've gotten drunk together—"

"I wasn't drunk at the Audubon do. We were just cracking jokes, horsing around, trying to impress some girls. Which did not work, by the way."

She smiled. "That much was obvious. I remember being jealous of them. The only handsome guys in the place, and those dummies were playing hard-to-get, weren't they?"

This conversation was veering from folly to nonsense. "This is serious," Daniel said, feeling his hackles rise. "What Whitlock did was miraculous. I'm still having trouble believing it. The Air Force was in position by then – he's lucky they didn't shoot his plane down the instant he pulled it out of that dive. Everything he did could not happen, but it did. Maybe he really is hooked up with gods or aliens or whatever, and they save his ass when he gets in trouble. Anything's possible."

Loretta scowled, but her eyes were saying something else. She was hard to read. Was she devoid of common sense? He stretched his hand across the desk and laid it on the paperwork.

"This file confirms that he is a loose cannon. If Senator Hathaway's favorite son is allowed to speak before Congress, the whole war effort could turn into a joke in five minutes. Then I'm fired, I can guarantee that. And Gerry. And you, and whoever else is not authorized to give this information to the president."

"Good speech." She thought another moment, scanning the memos. "Don't worry, I'll see that the Chief of Staff gets it within the hour. He's in a meeting right now."

"You can't have that file. You are welcome to make a copy of the summary on page five, but it leaves with me."

"You're interrupting me." Loretta sat up straight. "It may not look like it, but we're busy as hell around here, especially this morning.

"Once he learns what you've told me, if he announces at the news conference that Whitlock is going to speak anyway, I'm sure it will be because America needs a shot in the arm from a real hero. Certainly the Liaison Office can appreciate that." Again, that impish smile. "After the president's news conference, would you like to go to lunch?"

Daniel exhaled, like someone punched in the gut. She really was being forward, and it had taken him this long to wake up to it. A real intelligence agent would already have her lying across the desk. Could he get out to Langley and back in four hours? Thankfully, a knock came at the door before he could choke out an answer.

The door swung open. "Sorry." Pringle, again, backed up by a woman he had never seen before. "Ms. Bernstein, you told me to interrupt if something happened. We have the TV on out here."

"Oh no, what?"

Daniel stood.

"Another hijacking. In Europe. Two planes. One over Spain, one was still on the ground in France."

"Christ," Daniel blurted. "Are they American airliners?"

Pringle shook her head. "Both KLM. The police were ready, it turns out. All of the terrorists were killed, but both planes are safe."

Loretta's gaze settled on Daniel. "Did your people have anything to do with that?"

"They—" Pringle was nodding. "They said that their police had a tip from our FBI. Didn't say exactly who it came from."

Commotion out in the hall, but in the room, the news required a moment's digestion. The focus turned back to Daniel.

He met each gaze in turn, ending with Loretta's. He shrugged. "Don't look at me."

Loretta began spouting orders, calling for speechwriters. Daniel sat back down and watched her. He liked what he saw.

Chapter 4
A Shot Across the Bow

"Virgin Territory." The phrase came out of the phone like a sarcastic ghost, intent on haunting him. Frank put the receiver down. How did Maureen know he would be up this early? She wanted to order him a cake if he was coming in today. He wasn't.

She was excited — rightly so — that Richard was finally going to open up the Valley. *Virgin territory* was Frank's own phrase, though for years Richard had ignored his urgings to do just that. Now the spoiled brat could take the credit for invading the long stretch from Sacramento to Bakersfield, where high rates hung like apples on trees. Fickle and Company would pound the competition. Was Richard taunting him by this, or pressuring him to come back?

He poured a fresh cup of coffee, and gazed out the kitchen window at the police trailer that rested in the driveway. Jill was already in the shower. What a time for her career to finally take off.

"Damn," Charlie said. He sat on the couch, feet propped up, watching the latest news bulletins. "Just look what they did in Europe, catching those bastards on those two planes. Even had a shootout in the air, and they didn't so much as break a damned window. Sure makes us look like amateurs."

"You FBI guys are too hard on yourselves. How could you have known before September eleventh?"

A weak smile. Charlie sipped from his own cup. "At least the European tip came from us. Someone in Washington, I guess. Doing his job, thank God."

An involuntary shudder shook Frank. How long until they made the connection? Another gulp of coffee. The shower in the back bathroom was running, too. Ned, likely, from the sheriff's department. Or Pierce, the cop. It was hard to keep them all straight.

As he watched, the door of the mobile home swung open, letting out a female officer – was her name Johnson? The neighbors had tolerated the operations headquarters so far, but that wouldn't last. Not in this part of town.

The TV blared a new brace of headlines, repeating the Europe gambit. He still did not hear his name in relation to the KLM planes, but two more reporters had just joined the lone wolf out at the curb. Frank squinted. One was Caiten, or something, from the *Herald*.

The sound of the back shower ceased – but there was something else. He put his cup down without sipping. Some other noise from somewhere made the small crowd of reporters outside flinch. In unison, the cops' hands moved to the guns in their belts. Someone yelled, and a news guy tumbled, almost knocking his television camera off of its tripod. Frank stood, shaking with the same adrenalin rush he felt on the airplane. But this time, his head was foggy, not clear. He could only watch as the mobile home rocked, spitting out bodies clad in blue and khaki. The law guys scattered across the front yard. Charlie's walkie-talkie screeched, and the frenzy spread inside when a car backfired down the street. Reporters scrambled behind a hedge. Frank's heart pounded. Another backfire? No. Guns, of course. Charlie grabbed his arm from behind.

"Come on, Mr. Whitlock. Into the bedroom."

Frank let himself be shoved toward the hall. A man in a suit was unlocking the back door. He carried a compact, mean-looking machine gun. Two more figures paced along the back fence, one holding a device with a round antenna of some sort over his head.

"What's happening, Charlie?"

"In here." Footfalls behind. The FBI man pushed him down onto the bed, then yelled to the bathroom. "Mrs. Whitlock, we need you out here, pronto."

"My God – Frank?" She peeked out the door. Frank waved her back. Ned entered, pistol drawn, pants but no shirt.

Charlie's radio barked, "Secure. Secure."

He answered. "More back-up on the roadblocks. Call downtown." Affirmations came, while Frank caught the FBI man's eye.

"Charlie, you said 'Mr. Whitlock.' You call folks by their last name when they're about to die?"

Ned laughed and touched his shoulder. "You're only going to die if you don't get more hot water in that back bath." He holstered the gun and extracted the shirt he had tucked into his waistband.

Charlie spoke in mumbles, the radio answering, until he gave Frank a weak smile. "They got a middle-eastern-looking guy in a white sedan. A block over. Carrying enough guns for a platoon."

"They shot him?"

"He shot first."

"You sure he's a terrorist?"

The lawmen shared a knowing look, and a new guy at the door chuckled, his mouth visibly quivering. Ned snapped his fingers. "Maybe he was just out here to do someone's yard."

Charlie came closer. "We expected it, Frank. This is the pattern. It'll die down, like I told you."

Jill came out of the bathroom, hair tousled, buttoning her blouse. Frank smoothed the bedspread beside him and she sat down. "When?" he asked. "When will it die down? In a year? Five years? There'll always be some Iraqi or Palestinian looking for me." He gestured toward the nightstand. "My face is all over Time magazine, for chrissakes."

"Frank, we talked about this."

The radio crackled. "Lead bird says move when ready."

Charlie thought for a moment, then replied. "We're moving." Ned was buttoning his shirt and bantering with uniformed guys in the hall.

"Get your jeans on, Frank. They want us to take a ride downtown."

"We did that yesterday."

"It'll just take a little while. Some of the FBI guys want to sweep for bugs again."

Frank stood. "What the hell for? Ten of you guys have been here around the clock."

Charlie might have answered, but his cell phone rang, and for a few moments he was lost again in hushed tones. Frank patted Jill's leg, rose, and led her back to the bathroom.

"It's OK. You can finish your hair," he said, as tree branches scraped the frosted window, and a voice boomed, "Here. No, put it over here."

In here, out of sight of the officers, Jill started to shiver. "They got someone? Coming for us?"

"Coming for me, Darling."

"Oh, my God. They stopped him?" Her hands went over her mouth.

He nodded and kissed her forehead, then washed his hands. "I told you, they're pros. We have nothing to worry about. They'll get you to work on time. I might be downtown later, too. Maybe we can have lunch."

In the mirror, he watched her hold herself together. Brave Jill. Last night, the whispers seemed more urgent than ever. Was this the day the prophecy would true? Dying in the leather seats of some cheesy government limo was not an attractive thought. He kissed Jill's cheek, then emerged from the bathroom.

"No one's planted any bugs, Charlie. I want to stay right here."

Charlie slipped his cell phone back into his coat pocket, looking more stern than usual. "We're not going because of bugs, Frank. Have you been making some calls to the airlines?"

Chapter 5
The Morning After

It was the phone. It was the alarm. The phone. The noise kept repeating. A look at the clock. Daniel usually had his pants on, and the news, by now. No, the pager. As far as anyone else was concerned, traffic was horrible, and there was no reception. He turned over. Loretta's eyes were open. She smiled and groaned.

"My God, we're late. Oh, no. On the first date, I can't believe it. This may be the Bush White House's first real scandal," she said, giggling.

Daniel's hand went to her smooth white shoulder. "Don't forget Enron. Let's see, I'm Irish. You're a Jew. Does that make me a schick-*so*?"

She laughed outright and rose up to kiss him. "I've never done this sort of thing before. I mean — you know, without at least some courtship. My mother would kill me if she knew I was with a Catholic. Did you get a page?"

She could have said anything, Daniel thought. Like, "Let's do it again," or, "That was the best night of my life." Anything to extend the respite from the twenty-hour days. Instead, she was letting the screaming pager haul them both back into reality.

Daniel rubbed his eyes and read the text on the tiny screen: *More fun. Shooting in California. Just happened*, it began. He scrolled through, and looked at her. "A block away from

Whitlock's house. The bad guys missed. I'm supposed to call Sullivan on a secure line."

There. His name had been mentioned. She looked away, and he could not discern her reaction.

She stretched, exposing her glorious breasts above the sheet. "My goodness. If they kill Frank Whitlock, what will it do to the country's morale? God, we're both so late."

"They'll be gunning for him for a long time to come. There are always holes in a security screen. I just hope we can plug them all." He started to climb out, but she touched his back, then kissed it.

"You will."

He turned, and kissed her for a long time. "That was nice. Everything. I don't know how it all happened—"

"Yeah, right." A coy look. "You and your tequila shots."

"Gotta blow off steam sometime. Especially now." He stalked into the bathroom.

"Aren't you calling Gerry?"

A pause. He wanted to come right out and ask her. "Shower first."

"You never admitted it."

"What?" He kept his hand under the stream of water, waiting for the warm.

"You can't remember what we argued about all night? That our hero, Mr. Whitlock might be a genuine psychic? You swore you would concede the point if I went to bed with you."

She stood in the doorway, as naked as he. Black hair. Pretty, but in a girl-next-door way. Perfect breasts. Enough equipment to sleep her way to the top, if she wished. But she seemed more the brainy type.

"Oh, so that's why you finally gave in?"

"That, plus booze. Plus a little G-man charm." Now her arms were around his waist. One hand started groping. "You also told me last night—they confirmed that the phone call came from Frank Whitlock's house. *He* saved KLM flights 115 and 87, not sleuthing by the FBI. How do you get around that one?"

"If that's true, you're not supposed to know it. I deny I ever said it."

Her hand found what it was looking for. "Admit it."

"OK. Whitlock may have a gift that can't be explained. Sometimes." A kiss, and a smile. "Then again, maybe he's one of the terrorists. I don't care if you go on holding that all day."

Loretta scowled, and he pulled her into the shower.

Daniel blasted out of the bathroom, but it was too late. Loretta stood, looking sheepish, holding the phone out to him.

"Where are you when all hell is breaking loose?" Gerry Sullivan's voice boomed. "And who is the broad who answered the phone?"

Daniel could have given Loretta a more withering glance, but they were still in the early stages. Interesting. Sullivan had not recognized her voice.

"Sorry. Worked on some stuff late. Went to the bar for a drink." He was not sure how many more lies to heap on. "She's an old friend."

"Can it. The honeymoon's over and you are meeting me in Senator Hathaway's office in one hour. That's eleven-thirty. So get in the damned car. He wanted your head on a plate at eight, then this shooting happened. Thank God we stopped it. I mean it, Daniel, touch base with those California guys, so you have something to tell him."

Loretta's feelings were hurt, obviously. She pulled her dress on in jerks. He focused. "Senate office building? Who else will be there?"

"What do you care? And not the Senate offices, unless you want anthrax. He'll be in the Annex, over on E Street. By God, Clooney, if you turn your cell phone off again, you're through."

Daniel laid the phone in the cradle. God, that was close. Loretta was working with her hair.

"I owe you an apology."

"No, you don't. I shouldn't have answered your phone. It was dumb. Reflex."

"Not that. All last night, when we were looking into each other's eyes, I suspected you of sleeping with Gerry Sullivan."

"I was."

Chapter 6
The Senator's Charge

The makeshift offices were crowded. Clumps of bodies
– mixtures of Senate staffs – fighting for desk space and
computers. Wires lay all over the floor. Daniel had raced and
beat Loretta, but McNee, the senator's aide, placed him smack
between her chair and Sullivan's, anyway.

They sat, sipping coffee in a library of sorts, listening to
Hathaway beller on a phone in the next room. What if Gerry
recognized Loretta's voice after the fact?

As if Daniel had never been reprimanded, Sullivan
glanced over, confidence suddenly filling his demeanor. He
even winked. "We're not going to let this happen."

"Right."

As luck would have it, Loretta was ushered into the
room at the same instant the senator blew in from the other
door. Hathaway puffed and grunted, and chewed on his lip
while they all shook hands cross-ways. Loretta had procured
perfume from somewhere. Their gazes did not meet. My God,
her perfume. Something would tip Sullivan off.

"Thank you for coming." Senator Hathaway had the
biggest chair, and he rubbed his age-spotted face like someone
just waking. A gulp of coffee, and a glance at Sullivan.

"Mr. Director, we haven't seen each other much over
the summer. Since the president's speech."

"Yes, sir. We were putting the department together. Just in time, it seems." Both men shook their heads for a moment.

"Yes, well." Hathaway took another swallow from his cup. "Cards on the table. First of all, Ms. Bernstein, why isn't the Chief of Staff here? I just got off the phone with some jackass who said he was detained. Does this mean that the president has changed his position?"

"No, Senator. Not at all. You can imagine the load we are all dealing with at the White House."

A skeptical glance at Sullivan, then to Daniel.

"Then why does it seem like I'm being stonewalled? Give me one good reason why Frank Whitlock can't come here — hell, even tomorrow night — and give the American people a huge morale boost?"

"The president will be in Pennsylvania tomorrow night," Loretta answered.

A roll of the eyes. "Please, Madam, let's not screw around. Gerry, what will it take to get you to drop your objection?"

"It's not wise, sir--" Sullivan reached for his briefcase.

"What the hell do you mean, 'not wise?' Don't worry about a speech. My writers have whipped up two versions. God damn it, when you have a hero, flaunt it. We did with Eisenhower, with MacArthur, with Sergeant York. Am I the only one in Washington who is cognizant of history? This thing must happen."

While Sullivan fumbled through files — the one that Hathaway could look at would have been edited differently than the one Daniel showed to Loretta, more CIA idiocy the high-concept Liaison Office had not managed to go beyond — Loretta stayed in there, pitching. Almost as if she were on their side.

"Senator, the Chief of Staff's only question was – well, shouldn't this be coming from one of California's two fine lady senators instead of yourself? Whitlock doesn't even reside in your state. Any benefit to your election campaign--"

The seasoned face reddened under the white straw hair. "Frank Whitlock was born in my state, and came back for college. He's as much ours as anyone's. And I didn't think that the White House would be chafing about any election angles. I'm a Republican. They should want me to win.

"But this is not about me, damn it. This is about lifting the spirits of the people."

Sullivan finally pushed the manila folder across the desk, but Daniel was in no mood to watch him do his traditional dance around the issue while kissing butt. He went for the jugular.

"Senator, if Whitlock speaks, the Religious Right will not vote for you this year." It came out more forcefully than he intended.

Hathaway blanched, opening the folder. "Is that a fact, Mr. Clooney? You're a Clinton holdover. What insight would you have about the so-called Religious Right that is worth a spit in a saloon?"

Sullivan quashed Daniel's reply with a seething glare. "My subordinate spoke out of turn, Senator. Trust me, our objection--"

"Oh, I trust you, Gerry." A wave of the folder. "But your Democrat is mouthing off, and I want to know what his investment is here. What is it, Mr. Clooney? Are you folks already starting a slash-and-burn campaign against anything that might add to George Bush's popularity? We're supposed to be united, just now."

Sullivan's face had that verge-of-apoplexy look that usually appeared only after he'd been drinking. Loretta's eyes were downcast. How long had she been with this twerp? More to the point, on which side of the desk did her feelings lie now?

"Senator, I'm not trying to be disruptive. The reasoning — and some Republicans in the Bureau agree — is that the Religious Right abhors demons. The big hero has been a mystic all his life. He thinks spirits talk to him, or astral projections, or whatever."

Hathaway's hand came up. "You're talking about those KLM planes, aren't you?"

"Well, yes, but there's more than—"

"Stop right there. You can put your mind at ease on that. You guys in the Liaison Office may not have all of the contacts that some of us old-time committee members do. I have it on good authority--" He repositioned the folder in his lap and peered over his reading glasses. "—that those phone calls that tipped off the FBI about the European planes came from a terrorist operative, not Frank Whitlock at all."

Loretta's hand covered her mouth.

Daniel felt the breath rush out before he could reply. Only Sullivan seemed unimpressed by this new information. Daniel could guess why.

"Senator, I have not heard—"

"They did it electronically. Relayed the call to make it look like the American hero did it. They're trying to set Frank Whitlock up. For what, I don't know, but they're still running rings around our high-tech defenses." His eyebrows went up, and he looked at Sullivan.

Sullivan turned full-face toward Daniel. No message, other than that he was looking for a way to blame Daniel for something. Anything, perhaps.

Daniel pressed anyway. "Where did you get your information? CIA?"

"Perhaps. Perhaps not." Now he spoke to the boss. "I'm sorry, Gerry, but my committee is senior to your office."

"Of course, Senator."

"I'll be damned." Hathaway used the file to tap the desk. "I sort of like catching you flat-footed, Mr. Clooney.

What was all that religious poppycock you were heading into?"

Sullivan's eyes were steel.

"I was simply advising you, Senator, that Mr. Whitlock — and I'm sure he's a fine man — has a history of seeing spooks and UFOs. He's a loose cannon, whether he made the calls or not. The file should illustrate that beyond a doubt."

Words failed him. Thank God, Loretta picked up the ball.

"Are you sure of your facts, Senator?" Her gaze darted nervously between the other two. "I thought the FBI confirmed yesterday morning that the call came from Whitlock. Don't we have agents with him who would know?"

Daniel tried to catch her eye. Too late.

Sullivan's voice boomed. "And who gave you information like that, Ms. Bernstein? Has the president changed the communications officers' protocols?"

A blink. She was in trouble. Then she smiled. "Gerry, this is Washington. We hear gossip, even in lowly Communications."

Daniel watched as thoughts passed between them. Sullivan was not happy. How recently had she broken it off?

"I'm sorry to interrupt any cross-leaking." The senator rocked in his chair. "But what would be your objection if Mr. Whitlock followed a script absolutely? Hell, we don't want him rambling, anyway. In his speech, if he doesn't go into this mysterious philosophy of his, what's the harm to the image of the international coalition against terrorism?"

Daniel shrugged and pointed. "The worst will still happen. The information in that file will come out one way or the other. I'm surprised Whitlock hasn't been skewered by the National Enquirer by now."

"Are you through?" Sullivan sneered.

"He's through," the senator answered, and closed the dossier.

"The president wants to accommodate you, Senator."
Loretta clasped her hands and leaned forward. Such perfect
hands. "If you drop your insistence on a joint session being the
venue, then I'm sure we can — "

The folder came down onto the desk with a *whack!* "It's
a crying shame." Hathaway stared at each of them in turn. "A
goddam crying shame."

"Our entire approach has been to shield you, Senator.
And the Administration." At last, Sullivan was alive, chopping
the air with his hands.

He piled on the bullshit, but Daniel's attention
wandered. He didn't really want the meeting to end, just yet.
Did not want to get upbraided in front of Loretta out in the
hall. Did not want to see her walk away with this blowhard.

"— I'm sure you can appreciate that, Senator," he
concluded.

Hathaway brushed his wispy hair, his eyes suddenly
weary, jaded. "Thank you for that, Gerry. You've reminded
me that we are politicians first. But goddam it, we're also
supposed to be protecting the American people." He rose, and
stalked out.

Chapter 7
Tightrope

Suhail Farid wrung his hands together, a habit picked up from his grandmother. The grinding movement cleared his thoughts, but had also produced calluses over the years – evidence that his mind required as much flushing-out as anyone's, no matter what the neighborhood grandmothers said about him.

"You say the computer work is done?" He called the question through the screen door, into the dimness inside the apartment.

Esam Malik was shuffling with something. "We have the addresses, and can go in through the back door, Master. We wait only for your order."

Suhail's fingers clung together. "We're on a tightrope, my friend."

Below the balcony lay the tan and pungent city of Cairo. Suhail liked London better, really, except for the smells. The perfumes, the stench, the smell of cooked food — these were home.

"Nonsense." Esam pushed through the door, stirring his tea. "We have nothing to do with this debacle. They won't come for us. You have preached against this for years. To his face, even."

"I never spoke to Osama about this eventuality."

"You told him to grow up. Think like a man, rather than a petulant child who doesn't mind getting his hands dirty as long as there is a hot bath to run to."

He sipped, then squeezed his ample bulk into the chair opposite. "I sat in the same room with you when you warned Osama's cousin against a big display. That's fine. Let them reap the whirlwind. The bombs won't fall on Egyptians. Our people are not the ones having their throats slit at night by arrogant infidels."

Suhail chuckled. Even this early, Esam had broken a sweat. "My friend, you and I think alike, God be praised. But don't make a habit of talking about our colleagues in such terms. Osama is a grown man." Suhail removed his sandal, then the bandage. The toenail was still infected. "If you call him a child often enough in private, you will certainly say it aloud in a café." He gestured. "No more Esam."

Esam snorted, as all big men snort when they grow into maturity. "Bah. I will say it to anyone. To *Al Jazeera* Television, if they will put me on. Stealth and silence. That is the way. Strike the top, and all around the top. Allah knows they have enough people in place. If they had followed your plan, they would have killed people who count, not a bunch of rich Wall Street tycoons."

The big man's cheeks were red now, and a wide hand cleaved the air. He bolted from the tight chair, stalked toward the doorway, and stared. "They have set us back five years. Twenty years. The Americans have license to muck around in our alley forever, now." He gulped at the tea, and let the cup linger.

"That is precisely the tightrope I am talking about." Suhail raised both hands and drew a rope in the air. Horizontal. Long. He caressed it, followed the invisible strand out to each end. Esam watched. "Yet, if we walk on it without losing our balance, we might find opportunity at the end."

"Bah." Esam became a smudge behind the screen again, headed into the cool kitchen. Perhaps the tea was not to taste. "I suppose you will tell me that the rope came to you in a dream?"

Suhail laughed loudly, and sat back, gingerly tugging his sandal back on. "Where else do good ideas come from? You should listen to your dreams, Esam, instead of fighting sleep like the tired man who goes to a brothel."

He waited, taking deep breaths. The cool air invited a nap, and he needed more time to nudge the puzzle pieces into place.

Esam's bulk filled the doorway again. "And how would we walk this rope?"

"Assassination, as you say. As I have always advocated. Nothing has changed. Better results come from surgical movements of the knife, not broad swings. We have people in position now. They have more. We adjust their thinking, if that is possible, and we get better results."

"Where do you mean? In Israel? There is nothing new about that, Benefactor."

"Not Israel. That chance has come and gone. All it would have taken--" He drew in the air again, but now it was a twisting blade, not a rope. "I'm talking about a week, maybe even just a night or two, of surgical determination. That would make the Eleventh of September look like a lazy picnic. The leaders of America would be talking surrender to us, instead of planning war."

"One night, Master, not two. Americans are like anybody else, no matter what we may say about them. Their masses are quick to hide in their shells once a shot is fired. But explain – why the change of strategy? You have always counseled that we should avoid America. Too open. Unpredictable. Corruption of our agents – we send a freedom fighter to the States long-term, he comes back a whoremonger. Could it be that Osama and the sultan have finally asked your help?"

There was a small stool across the balcony, and Esam seemed to prefer its non-confining openness. He perched on it now, and set his tea on the railing, just able to peek over, like a fat, curious child. Suhail suppressed a smile.

"They will, eventually. How and when, that has not come to me yet. But look at it. Every move the Al Queda have made since their lucky day has been clumsy. Reality has caught up with their boasting. When they want lasting results again, they will come."

"Bah. Why should you even give them an audience? You conduct your own business on your own schedule."

Suhail nodded slowly. "Your suggestion is not without merit, my friend. But, as strategists say, this is a time when the field is open. If Osama would cede control of just a few of his operatives, I would show them how to see it through to the end."

Plenty of obstacles still stood in the way, but the last dream had possessed that undercurrent — the dominoes would fall his way, finally. Such a deep feeling had come to him only twice before, one of them was on the night before he met Farah. But Esam did not need to know this yet. Given the end result, in spite of his industriousness, he was the type who would want to grow lazy and wait.

The big man was on his feet again. "I agree. The field is open, as it has never been since 1973. With our troops, and your planning--" He stopped suddenly, looking pious. "Master, I know your intelligence network is without equal, your techniques I can only guess at. Some day, I hope you will trust me enough to introduce me to some members of that secret brotherhood."

"I have told you, my friend, that you are my network."

A raised hand. "It's all right. My goal is to serve you so well that you can do nothing but eventually promote me to

their ranks. I must admit, one thing Osama's magic trick has
done is to get my blood moving again. We must give him that.
I'll go down to the café, and see if there is an answer from the
sheikh."

"Thank you, defender of the faith." Suhail lay back on
the small couch. The cool breeze was irresistible. If growing
old had taught him anything, it was that one must not miss a
chance for a nap on a morning like this.

Chapter 8
In Stir

Jill laughed easily, sitting in the middle of the couch. Ned had the recliner, and a cop named Roby had pulled up one of the stiff kitchen chairs. Frank's gaze remained on his wife, rather than the TV re-run of *Leave It to Beaver*.

Eleven years. More than a decade of crazy swings in his own job, failing to get her pregnant, all of his bullshit, and now an invasion of strangers on top of the continuous fear of being blown up as they slept. All of this, and she had rarely uttered a complaint. She just blinked those soft, tolerant eyes, and kept their lives together. How much longer could she survive this? He took a deep breath, pretended to laugh with the others. Yes, she could take it. But could he?

"Want to go out for dinner?" Frank blurted when a commercial intervened on the screen.

Jill almost jumped. She looked at Ned, then frowned. "I don't think so, Frank. Wasn't the plan to let a couple more weeks go by? I've got a casserole to put in."

Silence. No one seemed to know what to say, but he could see she thinking.

"Hell, that's just it." Frank stood and stalked toward the kitchen. "They won't be expecting it. Christ, Orinda's not filled with terrorists. Anybody want a cocktail?"

"It's OK," Jill said quietly.

"Tell you what." The lawmen were on their feet. Ned stretched, and waved a finger in the air. "We'll bring in a pizza. My treat. Or, at least the department's."

"I don't want a pizza." Ice. Scotch. He watched as Jill gave them her awkward little signal to scram.

"Why don't you guys get one for yourselves? Eat it in the back room," she said. "We'll figure something out."

"That's cool." Ned patted Roby on the back, shoving him ahead. "We'll eat in the trailer. The guys won't let us get away without including them. Tell us if you decide. We'll go out and get anything."

"Thanks, Ned." She smiled, calling after them. "Remember, Cooper doesn't like mushrooms."

"Forget Cooper."

It was impossible to ignore the instant bond that had developed between her and Ned, but Jill would never be unfaithful. If the prophecy of the night whispers came true, maybe the humorous lawman could be a candidate for her new life after he was gone.

The scotch was twelve years old. *Laphroaig*, a gift from Senator Oben, whom he remembered fleetingly from the hospital. It bit. "You deserve better than this."

"Don't, Frank." She approached, but he took his glass and stayed out of reach.

"I mean it."

She tugged at his shirt, trying to turn him around. "Frank, it's only been a few weeks since you got out of bed. Wait until we win the war. You can't be upset this early. It may take a long time, but we'll get back to normal. We have to believe that."

He picked up the remote control and flipped through the channels.

"Relax, will you? They're even taking you back to work day after tomorrow." She sighed.

"Just for a visit, Jill. There are too many Arabs still on the streets."

"Frank—"

"I didn't mean that. I meant the bad ones. They're everywhere. We'll never know where they hide, or what they are planning, no matter how many policemen move in here."

She caught the edge of his belt. "You like the steaks at The Mountain House. I'll give them a check, and they can pick some up for us."

He took another sip. "I would rather drive to The Mountain House. Just you and me."

"Darling, it's going to be a long time."

Maybe not that long, he wanted to tell her. The whispers in the night had to mean something.

Coming back into this building was not really as bad as he expected. Cake, punch, trivial taunts and bullshit, and the same fake smiles. Not really the same — everyone, from Richard Fickle down to newbie secretaries he had never met before, had that sort of wary, giddy gaze. That look that said, *So glad to see you. Did you really kill people in that airplane? What was that like? Are you stable enough for me to stand close to you, or might you go crazy, and wring my neck like a hapless suicide pilot?*

Frank sniffed the air at the doorway of his own office, kept sniffing all the way to his desk. Maureen had covered the credenza, the little TV table, every flat surface with flowers. But even their frangrances could not mask the overlying mustiness. The office smelled deserted. Like his career. Even he, himself, smelled old. Or maybe it was the lingering Band Aids on his stomach. Or was it the smell of death approaching?

Ned leaned against the wall in the corner, attacking a piece of the sheet cake with a plastic fork. One more whiff brought back the familiar tinge of the leather of his worn chair.

Smell — that was how you could tell if something was real. He wasn't dreaming.

"Another tad of champagne?" Leonard jostled toward him, leaning over the desk to pour.

"Let the guy relax in his own office," Richard scolded from the hall. "For God's sake."

"Thanks."

Of course the office had not been locked all this while. Leonard and Buck were in here every day, no doubt. Probably fucked up the computer. They needed the files. Ned swallowed his cake and looked attentive, while Leonard sat down and slapped the spotless desktop. Paul grabbed the other customer chair.

"Come on, bastard." Paul hit Leonard's arm. "Ask him."

Leonard put down his plastic glass. "Shut up. Sorry, Frank. We were just wondering about your scars."

"My God, you louts." Richard had returned to the doorway. "The man's a national treasure. Leave his ass alone."

"It's OK." Frank leaned back. Cool leather. A shake of the head to tell Ned it was all right. A deputy sheriff, a new one, hovered in Maureen's office, peered across the hall with too much eagerness.

"Shit if it is." Richard gestured. "It's not enough these screwballs try to steal your accounts."

Laughter all around.

"Yeah, that'll be the day." Leonard slurped from his plastic cup. "They all love you, Dude. And after this hijacking shit, no way they would ever leave you. You can write every insurance policy in the state."

Paul set his own cup down, and his hands assumed an attitude of prayer. "He speaks truly. Please, please, O' Master. Would you do just that? Swallow up every account in San Francisco, and we'll do the paperwork." An exaggerated wink.

"For fifty percent. Just think of it. You don't have to fill out another sucking form. We do it for you."

Leonard pointed a finger. "He ain't kidding. The world's your oyster, Frank. We'll get your back. You make the sales calls, we'll write the policies, brush up the compliance, make the reports. Twenty meetings a day and we'll all be rich."

More laughter, except for Ned. Normal people didn't like insurance salesmen.

"My oyster, eh?" Frank leaned back. "Where did I hear that before? Oh, yeah." He shot the bird at Richard. "It was that S.O.B., right there, when he hired me." They laughed.

"Well?" Richard shrugged. "It was true, wasn't it? You were always our best salesman, even before September Eleventh."

Leonard sat straight. "I beg your pardon."

More laughs and taunts, but Frank was musing how easily these buffoons had digested the presence of a half-dozen men carrying guns. Automatically, he pecked at the keyboard, entering his e-mail password.

Paul finished his champagne. "So, enough with the small talk. When are you coming back, Mr. All American?"

A glance at Richard, then back to the screen. Only thirteen un-opened messages. Maureen had kept his mailbox clean. "That's something that Richard and I will be talking over. He wants me to wait a little longer, so I won't blow your end-of-year numbers." Laughter.

Most of the message-senders were names he recognized. Congratulations, likely. He positioned the mouse to open one that listed the sender only as "a friend."

"I'll take that challenge." Leonard stuck his chin into the air.

Paul pointed. "It's the liquor talking."

Leonard belched, and they laughed again.

"That does it." Richard waved them out over protests. Frank squinted. The font was way too small, and he had forgotten his glasses, on this, of all days. He shaded it, made the letters bigger—

He peered at the message. Flowing script rather than block letters.

"Frank?"

He read it again. No greeting. No signature. Only a simple sentence:

You are going to die.

Chapter 9
The Sheikh

The sheikh swaggered into the stuffy café a good five minutes after the whispers of the infallible neighborhood telegraph heralded his presence. Commotion outside, hails and cries of "Welcome," but the number of bodies inside were few, as if those who were unworthy knew to stay away. Esam had done his job.

Before Suhail could react, Fouad — *the heart* — Al-med burst in from the bright sunshine and announced loudly, "The bombing has started in Afghanistan."

It was not a sheikh's place to say such a thing, and with such an excited countenance that the few poor uneducated souls cowering at their tables could not guess whether Fouad approved or not. Rather than rise to cheer or curse, they remained quiet. In the old days, the master would have sent a lackey to precede him, and educate the citizens on how to behave. Sheikhs were not what they used to be, Suhail observed silently.

"My Sheikh." Esam rose, kissed the weatherworn cheeks, and led him to the table, smiling broadly.

Fouad smote the air, as if Suhail had something to do with the inevitable response from the West.

"Women and children," he bellowed. "It's the Gulf War, all over again."

Suhail took his kisses, then waved his hands, as one would calm a child. All eyes were leveled on them. "Perhaps I should have had a microphone installed at this table, Sheikh Al-Med."

The slightest of grins, but Fouad chose not to banter.

"Two." He held up two fingers. The stocky companions who followed him in now scattered to nearby tables. A couple hustled to the wall near the entrance, produced short Russian machine guns from their coats, and sat on the floor. The proprietor rushed over with coffee.

"It's all right. Thank you." Esam nodded at the stooped old man, and helped him empty his tray.

"He will give you two." Fouad leaned his broad shoulders across the table, too impatient to let the old man get out of earshot. "That's all we will risk. There are other plans afoot, you know. Your orders must be sent by tomorrow. All the phones are tapped. Waleed is going to Cuba, then a boat to Miami. God grant him entry."

Suhail did not speak, but let the air grow thick as the loudmouth dripped honey into his coffee. "Where is your master?" he finally said.

Fouad almost laughed. "Sir? Do you think I would tell? The sultan is safe, of course. But if you mean Osama, do you think I would know? He may already be with the Redeemer. Allah be praised."

"Of course that cannot be true." Suhail smiled, but from the corner of his eye, he saw Esam flinch. It was time to put this phony in his place. Suhail leaned forward, and whispered, "Perhaps you will join Allah yourself, if you do not behave more discreetly. This neighborhood sees me as a benevolent businessman. But there are spies everywhere, my Sheikh."

In the moment it took for the words to hit the bottom of the well, Esam swallowed and both of Fouad's bodyguards at the next table fidgeted on their chairs. The sheikh raised a calming hand.

"My good friend. If I didn't know better, I would fear you are on the horns of the demon of envy."

The old man returned with cups for the others, and this time the sheikh kept his mouth closed until the ancient sandals scraped away, back into the small alcove behind the bar.

"But it is understandable," Fouad continued, "that jealousy would grow when you have worked a lifetime collecting a resume of brave deeds, only to be upstaged in a matter of minutes by the greatest terrorist act of all time."

Bread lay on a plate. Suhail broke it and offered a piece. "Give me your two. You will see what deeds are great. My demons of envy are looking for a new home."

Fouad did not seem amused. He stared, and again Esam grew restless. There was a tight string between the fat man and the sheikh's bodyguards. Suhail was tempted to smile, for he felt the sheikh searching his mind like a clumsy child. Trying to discern by a nuance, or the glint of an eye. So many pompous men pretended to be mind readers. He had known only a few who — like him — had the talent. Disturbing, rodent-like men whom he steered clear of.

"What great deed?" Fouad asked through a full mouth.

"Your master knows my position. The way to victory is by neat acts, not sloppy bombast. We will take the most important man, and we won't squander human life as quickly or as foolishly."

Fouad laughed loudly enough to finally coax a smile from his bodyguards. "Bush? You want to kill Bush?" He spat toward the floor. "We don't need your help. We can do that ourselves. You know this. And it is you who are a fool. That *is* a suicide mission. It cannot be done without sacrifice. Is that why you want the Sultan's men? For sacrificial lambs?"

"I thought suicide was your specialty, Sheikh. Just when will you and the sultan carry out Bush's assassination?

A year from now? Three? And lose the momentum Osama has given us? Of course, the Clumsy One has given us nothing. It was Allah who brought down the towers. My guns are not aimed at Bush, anyway."

A snort. Fouad straightened up. "Then who? His father?"

"No. Even better. America's most beloved personage. The only man who has faced us in honest battle and lived to tell the tale."

A stare, then a growing smile. "The hero?"

"Sahib Whitlock, himself."

"Ridiculous." The sheikh's mouth worked. "In spite of your years of service to the cause, you talk like an amateur, Master Farid. My good friend, September Eleventh delivered us into what Americans would call *the big leagues*. Their hero is more protected than the president."

Suhail let silence work for him again, smiling a little more broadly bit by bit. "Then it was the sultan who sent the scout to kill Whitlock the other day? He has a bad habit of wasting lives on probes, when a pair of binoculars would suffice." At the next table, Fouad's bodyguards were neglecting their coffee.

"If the hero is such a rock in your craw," he continued, "then I propose to show you exactly how to extract it."

"You would never reach him. With all due respect, I must recommend to the sultan that he keep his men. We have history, my friend, but forgive me for saying you are too insolent. We cannot sacrifice our warriors for arrogance."

Suhail smiled patiently. The man had to flex his authority, after all. But such men did not respond to obeisance. "I will forgive insults. Once."

Once again, the hands of the bodyguards went under jackets. My God, the Al-Queda clones were living on a razor's edge. Perhaps the rumors were true – about Americans and British agents murdering people in their beds.

Sheikh Al-med gritted his teeth. "With all respect, Teacher, you will forgive them more than once. As I said, you have served long and hard, but your day is past. Even I am getting old. I freely admit it." He drank. "A new order is ready to claim the world."

For a moment, their gazes locked. Yes, this sheikh was strong. But instead of the volcanic fire of purpose deep in his soul, Suhail could see only mists of corruption.

"You are worried about security? We are already under the security umbrella. My troops will do the work. I ask only for support from Osama's side. If the police were not on such high alert, I would need nothing from him, or you. If they come with my men, they follow my orders. No one else's."

Fouad sipped again, making another feeble attempt at reading the unreadable. No, he could not pick the fruit off the tree, not with a timid mind that groveled behind sweaty boasting, like a child behind his mother's skirts. He should learn, Suhail thought, how one must quiet the ego before reaching into another's tree, then grasp slowly and firmly, like squeezing wine from a grape. Suhail smile, and squeezed a few select thoughts for him, dripping them silently through the ether, wondering if the pompous ass could catch them.

Fouad, too, began to smile. "And if you could reach this man, you would just kill him, then hide?"

"No, Sheikh. Osama made his mark because his acts were televised across the world. If he is not killed in the assault, we will take this Whitlock to a place where he can also be a television star. To reach into America's heart, and take their prized possession, then snuff it out with proper ritual, that is the way to break their spirit."

The sheikh's smile vanished, but his eyes sparkled like those of a child gazing at candy. He looked around, as if making sure his audience were listening. "My good friend, since you allow only one insult, Allah be praised, I will keep it a secret that you are crazy. You may have the men. When the hero goes down, we will celebrate the fall of a third tower. Next time, in my house."

Suhail raised his mug in a toast, and sipped. "In your house, may it stand forever." He had heard many admiring comments about the sheikh's house. He was one of those leaders who lived off of the comforts of the hard-fought victories of his own troops, then spent those same soldiers like so much sand. It might be nice to see this mansion before the sheikh was buried in it.

Chapter 10
CIA Report

Jimmy Johnson's face was the first thing Daniel saw when he entered Sullivan's office. The former basketball player always looked funny in the government chairs, his long legs sticking out a mile. But he was one you had to keep your eye on, because he sat through meetings looking sullen, until he erupted with some stinging question that unraveled an angle everyone else had missed. Daniel had learned that the hard way.

"Daniel, Jimmy wins the prize. You gotta learn to move your ass." Sullivan leaned back in his chair, thumbs tucked into his vest, fingers twiddling above his belly. A dapper man on the other side of Johnson stood up. "This is Carl Tims. CIA. I wanted you to hear this, get some FBI take on it."

"Sure." Daniel shook the hand of the newcomer. Each contact with Sullivan raised the ghost of Loretta, but the guy was a genuine spook – he just couldn't be read. Did he know? Even more irritating, Daniel had again neglected to get her home phone number. Of course he had asked for it, but other things always intervened. Ms. Pringle had so far done a perfect job of seeing that he did not get through at the office, either.

"So what's new?" Daniel took a chair. "Any line on Osama?"

"Listen." Sullivan spoke as one might to a child, and gave the floor to Tims.

"Gentlemen." The CIA man took a moment to consult papers in his lap. "Nothing conclusive, of course, but our preliminary review indicates that the miracle that Frank Whitlock performed may not be a miracle at all." A leer over the rims of his reading glasses, first at Sullivan, then he turned.

"We know that there are some big questions." Sullivan said, chewing on the end of a pen. Tims grimaced. A phony grimace. Daniel wanted to glance at Johnson, see if he felt the same way.

"Well, the biggest problem is mechanical," Tims said. "Specifically, a digital device called the *VDLM2*. That stands for VHF Digital Link Mode Two. The device is involved in ground-to-air communications on the Boeing Seven-fifty-seven. This is a new piece of equipment. Almost all of the Fifty-sevens out there use the older stuff, but as of September Eleventh, three planes were testing the VDLM2."

Sullivan nodded. "Don't tell me. Whitlock's plane was one of them?"

"No." An informed smile. "The plane Whitlock was on was the only one in the world testing the new *VDLM-Five*."

"Five?" Johnson interrupted. "What happened to Three and Four?"

Sullivan laughed.

Tims shook his head. "All I know is that the Five is a little beauty that kicks things up another notch. Not only does it allow for clear digital communication and monitoring of flight systems, like the Two, but the Five is tied into the flight computers directly. Bottom line, it allows you to fly the plane from the ground."

In this business, only rookies let their faces show surprise. But then, Tims' little bit of theater had to be aimed at discrediting the hero, didn't it? Why?

"That's been done before," Daniel said, wondering if he could induce some sort of temper tantrum. When liars concoct a story, they hate for anyone else to interject a new element. "They've been trying technology like that since the Sixties."

Tims' head turned with a jerk. "Correct. But they've never had a system reliable enough to use in a real situation. The Five is so reliable, they trust it on planes hauling passengers." He looked back down to his papers, as if to make sure he was correct. "Furthermore, the VDLM2 works off of the nationwide ground-based VHF system. The Five, on the other hand, can receive signals from satellites."

Daniel leaned forward. "Don't tell me. You recorded a satellite transmission during the flight?"

"I gave you a lay-up, eh?" Tims winked at Johnson, obviously proud of his basketball reference. Then he concentrated on Sullivan, jabbing the air with a finger.

"Add to that what Whitlock himself told your guys—" a nod in Daniel's general direction, "in the hospital. He claims to have had foreknowledge. Claims he had a dream the night before in his cozy bed at the Radisson Hotel, home of the National Insurer's Convention." Tims' voice rose and his eyes flashed.

"You should have been a carnival barker," Johnson said abruptly.

"Thank you. I think. But the only circus act we're dealing with here is Frank Whitlock, himself. I mean, get real. This guy claims to have had a premonition, and he still got on the plane."

They looked at each other, until Daniel shrugged. "Would you have preferred that he cause a scene, and claim the plane was going to crash, like that old *Twilight Zone* episode?"

Sullivan's stare was icy. "Your conclusion, Carl?"

Tims put his hands together. "We — the analysts — think it's pretty obvious. Unless we're ready to recognize fortune-telling as a scientific fact, the conclusion must be that Whitlock knew about the hijacking because he was a trained operative." He made weighty eye-contact with each of them.

Daniel exhaled. "You want us to believe that Whitlock is one of the terrorists? A plant put there to kill his own comrades, and that someone else on the ground flew the goddam thing by remote control? That our one victory on September Eleventh was a charade?"

Even Sullivan seemed alarmed. "Carl, the president can't announce that America's Hero is one of the bad guys. That's political suicide."

Tims was unruffled. "That's the only answer that combines all of the scientifically believable factors present. We don't care if it's announced — ever. But – I'm sure you'll agree – if we're ever going to catch all the terrorists, we have to base our decisions on reality. Not what they want us to think."

"What about the other planes?" Jimmy Johnson was not smiling. "The one that crashed in Pennsylvania?"

"None of them had the VDLM5. Nor even the Two, for that matter. Looks like we had some real heroes on the Pennsylvania flight."

There was something outrageous about the performance Tims was giving, but nothing Daniel could finger solidly enough to blow him out of the room. Of course not. This was a CIA scam from top to bottom. And why? What possible motive did these guys have for discrediting Whitlock? Embarrassing the president wasn't enough. He appealed to Sullivan, on the off chance that he was still a human being. "Now wait a minute. There were heroes on this 'Kentucky' flight, also."

Johnson looked as steamed as Daniel felt. "Yeah. If this were a plot, what would have happened if the passengers never rallied behind Whitlock? There was some hellacious fighting on that plane. Those two guys from Wisconsin – and the one who became Whitlock's co-pilot?"

"They couldn't all be in on it," Daniel said.

Tims' eyes were the picture of understanding. He shook his head slowly. "Of course we had innocent bystanders. Brave innocent bystanders." Eyebrows raised, but the CIA shill was obviously waiting to play his trump card.

"We know that Whitlock has a history of trying to get next to presidents. We don't know how an American like him could get sucked into a terrorist plot. Maybe he answered an Internet ad, or they told him something else was going to happen. Gentlemen, we all want to sympathize with the man, but the facts point the other way."

Johnson slapped the notebook in his lap. "Hold on. We're not even there. How do you know this suspected satellite communication wasn't a simple cell phone call?"

"We haven't nailed that down yet." The fact did not seem to bother Tims. "Along with dozens of cell phone calls that were alerting the passengers, we tracked at least one from a Russian satellite. We'll piece that one together. We just don't have all their codes."

"That's bullshit." Johnson's voice fell like a lead weight. "We have all the codes. We've always had the Russian codes."

Daniel wasn't sure how someone of Jimmy's grade could be so sure about that, but it was nice to see Tims finally squirming. "So what if the recordings are inconclusive, Jimmy?" Tims' jaw was tight. "The tapes are still under study. Would you rather believe in hocus pocus?"

Sullivan tapped for order. "Gentlemen, we can all agree that the cake isn't completely baked. But we have to thank Carl, here, for sharing some key information. I'll include it in the department's report to the president. Carl, keep us informed of further developments, especially the analysis of those transmissions to the plane. And I'll want you to stay behind for a moment."

"Do you want me to call the FBI Director?" Daniel asked.

"Not yet." Sullivan's pen traced his bottom lip. "This report doesn't leave this room. Thank you, gentlemen."

When they closed the door behind them, Daniel caught Johnson's eye.

The basketball player nodded. "It's bullshit."

They went their separate ways.

Chapter 11
Celestial University

Frank recognized the stout brick buildings, some red, others the color of Austin stone. Most seemed three or four stories tall, until he tried to focus on them. That action made them change, tower, stretch upward forever.

The University. *Celestial University*, was the name Sam had given it, the first time Frank had dreamed about this place. The wide walkways, orderly patches of grass, the ponderous stone fountains, all inspired the certainty that somehow every center of higher learning in the real world must be patterned after this mold.

"Real world." The phrase echoed in Frank's head, made him smile. He was beginning to prefer dreams, for they were the only places where he did not look around to see bodyguards following.

If this was, indeed, some sort of college for departed spirits – that was the only guess he could come up with, over the years. From back in the day when he read all those books on the occult, trying to figure out the source of his talent. Or maybe it was just a disease. He had walked these long, brick-lined paths and wide quadrangles many times, but rarely encountered students up close. Yes, he glimpsed them always on distant walkways, gaits slow and even, faces shrouded by brown cowls, like those worn in a monastery rather than a college. When he was young, he ran from those hooded scholars. Now that he was old, it was he giving chase. They never actually ran, but somehow they always eluded him.

A movement made him turn – a young boy, dressed up in a suit, was waving from the corner of a building. Sam.

Thankfully, his brother waited for him to come close, rather than teasing and running away, as he often did. Frank recognized the suit, and shuddered. It was the one Sam was buried in.

This time, his big brother let him pull very near, almost close enough to give him a hug, before he wheeled around, threw a smart-assed wink over his shoulder, and continued up a side street, gesturing ahead. Orange leaves fell from the trees, and Frank was transported back to an autumn day in Georgetown, during his own college days. Up ahead was the aging house where he lived during sophomore year. Sam leaped up the front steps, waving a hand to hurry him.

They were inside, and up the rickety stairs before Frank could take a breath. Mutely, Sam came to attention, puffed his chest out, and pointed to the crisp white handkerchief that stuck out of his coat pocket. A smile. Before Sunday School, he had always lectured Frank that you weren't really dressed up without a *snot-rag*.

Now Sam's hand rose to the dresser behind him. The room was faithful to Frank's memory – he had bought the chest-of-drawers at a garage sale for ten dollars. On top of it lay Grandpa's old watch, and money clip, a pair of dice, car keys, and wallet, just where he always placed them when he came home from class.

In a lightning movement, Sam grabbed the billfold, and thrust it into Frank's hands. It fell open. There, radiant and glistening in the foggy plastic slots, the picture of Elizabeth Khoury gazed out at him. He had carried that picture religiously, for many years after college, all through his first marriage.

Elizabeth was his first great love, an exchange student from Lebanon. The dream-photo made her appear real enough to touch. He had touched her, but her upbringing never let her commit to marriage. The same moral compass called her home after they graduated. Eventually, she returned to the United States, but the years and distance and cultures took its inevitable toll. She was married now, he once heard, to some Arab businessman who made a fortune in Styrofoam containers in Southern California.

Frank stood, mesmerized, waiting for the beautiful girl in the picture to speak to him, maybe give words of solace or love – until a stinging pain jolted Frank out of his reverie. His brother had jerked the handkerchief out, and popped Frank on the cheek with it. He pointed again at the wallet.

"You're telling me something about Elizabeth. What is it?" Frank demanded.

Sam reared back, and threw the handkerchief high into the air. It spread out, glued its edges to everything – the old wooden trim around the ceiling, the faded wallpaper, even the blue sky and orange leaves hanging outside the window. Down it fluttered, pulling pieces of the dream with it. Frank awoke in bed, his throbbing right side bathed in sweat.

"Are you OK?" Jill's voice came softly out of the darkness.

"Yeah."

He lay, waiting again for the pin-pricks to restore life to his legs. Of course he knew what Sam was trying to suggest. But Elizabeth Khoury was perhaps the only thing he and Jill had ever really argued about.

Perhaps Sam couldn't grasp the passage of time. The handkerchief had to refer to Elizabeth's uncle, some sort of holy man back in Lebanon – but the old guy must be dead by now. Especially in a dangerous country like Lebanon.

Perhaps, in the astral plane, or wherever Sam existed, he was oblivious to the brigade of guards in the trailer in the driveway. Even if the Elizabeth's uncle was still alive, and did consent to coming to America to meet him, there was no way the government would permit a complete stranger from the Middle East within a mile of this place.

When the pin-pricks stopped, Frank rolled over, frustrated again. He had come to rely on the dreams, he realized, to show the way out of this horrible mess. That was a mistake. All the books he ever read, all of his instincts told him that same thing. To retreat into that world of dreams would be the end.

Chapter 12
The Chess Player

"Does your sheikh think my plan is a joke?" Enough of biscuits and tea. Suhail purposely changed his demeanor. The mouse-like woman sitting at attention, introduced simply as Lina, shivered visibly. Perhaps she was beginning to understand. "You are the girl he brags about — the chess player, no? Tell me again why Waleed is not sitting here with me instead of you."

"Please, Honorable Servant of the All-Powerful. You obviously know that Waleed's mission to Washington was aborted. My master thinks it much less suspicious to send a woman, given the added security in the West. I have sisters in the United States. If this were a move on the chess board, it would be a sound one." She bit her lip.

"Show me your explicit instructions. Who you will contact and where?"

Her shaking finger rose in the air and touched her head.

"Ah, a good messenger must have an excellent memory. Then tell me."

Her lips pressed together defiantly, but Suhail could feel it – her resolve was like a tower whose foundation was starting to crack. He could also hear her bodyguard, grumping in the next room, but he would be no match for Esam and Muuji. Suhail fixed her with a strong eye.

"I am waiting." He gripped a pen, feigning to take notes.

With halting words, she described her route of travel. "I meet a man at a certain plaza in San Francisco. Union Square. I give him the oracle, which shows I am genuine, then reveal the telephone number you supplied my master. I also have instructions for the next phase of the sultan's operations. In code, of course. But – Allah be praised – my job is to make certain they know that your operation takes precedence at this time."

"I see. They perform a duty for me off-handedly, then go back to the real war. Is that your sheikh's attitude? What are these next operations of the sultan's?"

"It is in code, Master. I swear they do not share such things."

"I seldom use allies, Lina. And never females for true battle. It is against the Word of Allah. Your sheikh offers me help, but requires it come from his arsenal's scrap heap. Do not take offense. It is not your fault, young one.

"You mentioned a chess move. Well-said. Please understand that what happens next will be just that: a move strong enough to catch your master's attention. I am not one of his part-time agents. You see the necessity."

Lina bowed her head. He saw her paging through her mind, not panicking, but calculating. Better on her feet than some men. "My sheikh knows you have been at this much longer than he. He is impressed with your mastery of technique and your invisible intelligence resources. He told me to say this. He respects you. Any suggestions from you will be thankfully received." She let her gaze meet his again. Bravely. Bravo. But she had never learned how to hide the residue of the sheikh's contempt.

"I am proud to be a messenger. A woman can pierce their shield. The Americans, the Israelis, even certain parties in the Egyptian police, are at the highest alert level ever."

"Certain traitors, you mean. But you have not explained. What is this oracle you speak of?"

He knew women who played chess. When they were young it was impressive. When they grew up, the game pried open their souls. Made them connive and scheme even more than an ordinary woman does. He could feel her weighing each move, a glistening female soul who had already been corrupted. A pity.

She was trying to resist, but her soul was clear glass. Like the ancient combination locks he and his comrades used to practice breaking, her tumblers fell – one-by-one – into place. This was a game she had never played before, one where she still held onto hope with her shapely fingernails. In chess, surely she would have the insight to lay down her king. With her eyes, she refused once more, but her hands reached into her coat, and extracted a small box. From it, she withdrew a miniature white object and handed it over in a smooth, delicate motion.

Suhail stared at it – a puffy seashell, very small. "This is your oracle?"

"Yes, Defender of the Faith. My sheikh loves the sea."

And her master would join her in the sea soon, Suhail could have said. The Great Sea. He closed his hands around the shell. Her eyes grew wide.

"You will not need this, faithful one. Esam!"

"I will. I will need it, sir." Tears filled her eyes. Esam appeared at the door.

"Send the messenger and her friend on their way, Esam."

Lina rose, knocking her teacup to the floor. It broke. "You are merciful, *Al-Gwath*. Yes? My master swears by it."

Finally, an outright lie. Checkmate. She looked at his eyes and shuddered, and her tears finally released as she turned, guided by Esam's broad hands.

"Return after it is over," Suhail said quietly, catching his *major domo's* eye.

"Of course."

Carefully, Suhail laid the delicate shell next to the small box she had left on the table. The entire building shook, rocking the tiny crustacean on the smooth surface. Cheap Eighties construction. The Germans were as bad as the Americans. Muffled noises in the hall. Not a shot fired. Struggles with Esam were as quiet as they were futile. Then the big man's voice, and a car revved outside. The sheikh would not send pawns to meet a king again.

He sat, piecing through his dreams of last night. Much chaos. Nothing that began could carry through to conclusion. Did the imminent arrival of a woman affect the sprites that way? Still, they pointed to one person over and over. The ideal person to take the false messenger's place. His tea grew cold.

The shadows were long when Esam finally stepped through the doorway.

"Are you out of breath, my friend? Is age catching up to you so fast?"

Esam smiled in his naked way. No hidden feelings in this piece of God's work. "I am as fit as the day I was born." He patted his belly. They laughed, then a cloud crossed the big man's brow.

"This must be wise, Suhail, but why should the sheikh's people work with us now?"

Suhail reached for his cup, then thought better of it. "To refuse now would mean they have lost sight of the larger game, my apprentice. If we show strength, they must show strength in kind, or risk their army of agents finding out who is stronger. Of course the sheikh will plan to retaliate later, when he thinks we have lost our alertness. But by then, he will know the face of Allah."

"I see. Of course. Yet, the game is paused for now, is it not?"

"Ah." Suhail picked up the oracle, returned it to its box. Ceremoniously, he lifted it in the air, until Esam got the message, and thrust out a fat palm to receive it. "No need for a pause, for we have a new messenger. Esam, you are going to California."

Chapter 13
Surprise Visits

He knew the general neighborhood where Loretta claimed to live, but their one night was spent at his place, and the napkin with her address and home phone number had disappeared somewhere in his stacks of newspapers. Her secretary, Pringle, seemed to enjoy her role as a stone wall. Before 9-11, he would simply have waited outside the White House to follow Loretta home, but now even a guy with a badge could be held for acting suspicious.

Daniel put a stack of memos into his case. Why kid himself? Pringle could not keep him at bay without Loretta's permission. No, her direction. She was not his type – she had that edge. Soft edge, yes, but she was too smart, or cultured, or at least feigned sophistication – damn it, why was she even still on the radar screen?

A tap at the door, and Sullivan himself barged in without waiting for a response, ballpoint pen protruding from his lips. Indoor substitute for cigarettes.

"Chalmers is going to Afghanistan." He sat down. "Frankly, I expected you to volunteer."

"Thought about it. Decided I don't really need eight days of prancing around with some general, giving advice the Afghanis will forget as soon as I leave." Daniel propped his feet up on an open drawer. "You know we've got our hands full. This new initiative to find all the illegal Arabs who have blended into the woodwork."

A sneer. "And don't take it lightly. Secretary Ridge believes there are enough bad guys left to pull off something big. Maybe soon."

This was no time to fight. "He's probably right."

"Is that all that makes you want to stay in Washington? Illegal aliens? Or is there something else?"

Daniel checked himself. "This is where the work is."

A slow nod. "You're staying on top of Whitlock? Right on top?"

Daniel shrugged. "I've strategized with the lead guy every day since that would-be assassin got shot near his house."

"Who's the lead guy?"

"Thornton. FBI."

"That's right." Sullivan nodded thoughtfully, then stood. "You know him?"

"Not before all this."

"Will he do the job?"

"Seems competent. Why? Did we get another credible threat?"

The question seemed almost a surprise. "Nothing you haven't seen. Get more involved, Daniel. The anthrax thing almost set off a general panic. They get to Whitlock, and heads will roll. Make Thornton accountable. Don't take shit about chain of command. He answers to us. Clear?"

"Clear."

Without another word, Sullivan was on his way. Not like him – he almost seemed to *care* about Whitlock. As if Loretta had gotten to him. Did that mean they were back together? Daniel stopped him with a question. "Senator Hathaway's been quiet. Did he finally back off the speech idea?"

Sullivan leaned against the doorway, wearing a gloating smile. "He's still rumbling under the covers. Congressman Conesta supposedly has proposed that the president bring the hero out here for a rally on the mall."

"Are we going to let that happen?"

"Not a chance." The pen tapped on the door sill. "I don't want Frank Whitlock even speaking to the Elks Club in Podunk." Sullivan's eyes narrowed. "Whitlock — you've been up close. Does he have the look? The move? The feel of a bad guy?"

"He was heavily sedated when I met him."

"I'm asking your professional opinion, Agent Clooney. Again. Is he a terrorist or not?"

Daniel shrugged, refusing to be intimidated. "You've heard the testimony. The fight on the plane wasn't staged. All these conspiracy theories don't really add up."

"But Danny Boy, that only leaves the psychic shit. Don't tell me you're a believer."

"No. But if the aircraft was landed by remote control, the flyer was a piss-poor pilot. They came that close to being pancakes."

The pen jabbed in the air, hammering home the absolute truth. "The hero's a wild card, Daniel. Don't believe fairy tales. Keep me posted." He disappeared into the hallway.

Daniel drove the new route home, weaving through the snow and around the spastically shifting daily placements of new barricades and roadblocks. Something in Sullivan's demeanor told him that he and Loretta were back together. Time to get on with life.

But when Daniel opened the door to his townhouse, he could hear the television blaring. Hair stood up on the back of his neck, and his hand went automatically up under his lapel. No, he had not left the TV on this morning.

Gripping his nine millimeter, he stooped, and peeked around the door to the den.

"Hi."

The gun hovered in the air. He focused. Loretta Bernstein was sitting on the couch, stocking feet resting comfortably on the coffee table.

Still shaking from adrenalin, he managed a question. "What are you doing here?"

"I heard you called."

Chapter 14
Shrimp Cocktails

Slowly, one noose was being loosened, while a different one, made with a thicker rope, grew tighter. Frank visualized it that way, anyway, as Ned wheeled the police SUV into the driveway, past the mobile home, and up to the gate. Two cops scrambled to cover his egress.

It had been the second time they had allowed him to work out at the gym. Ned and Markham stayed with him on the rowers, the treadmills, and in the weight room. They were in such better shape. The cute little college girls, the hard bodies he used to wink at, all stood around and stared at his every motion.

The moment he stepped through the front door, Charlie raised a hand. Commotion in the backyard.

"Stay back, Mr. Whitlock." Roby waved from the picture window.

A swarm of lawmen at the back fence, automatic weapons at the ready. They surrounded a red-faced Cherie Raed, who was carrying a tray.

"It's just Cherie," Jill said, waving at her through the window. "Let her in. She's our neighbor."

"Shit," Charlie said, close enough for Frank to hear. "I thought that gate in your back fence was locked."

"She has a key."

Ned brandished his ever-present clipboard. "They're OK. We checked them out. Remember, Charlie? Husband's been a doctor here for sixteen years."

"I know."

"They used to be our best friends." Frank pulled his arm from the grip of one of the officers.

"I know." Charlie looked weary, and now all eyes were on him. "It's just that I wish they didn't have a goddamned Arabic name." He signaled. "Check what she's got on that tray."

"Shrimp cocktails." Jill moved toward the sliding door.

Frank looked at Ned. "Shrimp cocktails and beer. The four of us used to get smashed every Friday night."

"Sounds like my kind of party," Ned replied.

Charlie grimaced. "Why have they been so quiet and to themselves since we arrived?"

Jill seemed perturbed. "Come on, Charlie. You've seen us talking over the fence."

Frank followed her through the sliding door, and the commotion shifted to the patio. Cherie stretched up and hugged his neck. "You dear man." Jill distributed shrimp cocktails to those lawmen who would take them.

"We eat first," Charlie said to Frank. Not the first time.

"I didn't make enough. I didn't realize you had the entire army here."

Charlie bristled. "You never look out your window, Mrs. Raed?"

Jill laughed him off. "You should have come over two weeks ago."

Cherie crowded next to her. "Sorry, Darling. We're just hiding in our bungalow, hoping those helicopters won't shoot us when Faris washes the car." She grinned at the surrounding officers. "One of the most successful doctors in town, and he won't pay to have the car done. It was his upbringing."

Ned toyed with a shrimp. "No, Ma'am. The helicopter would radio us down here, and we would shoot you."

Laughter.

"I'm still embarrassed that we've ignored you." Cherie grabbed Jill's sleeve. "Especially since I came to ask a favor. It's finally happened."

Jill brightened. Frank watched her. Out here in the chilly sunshine, talking to a friend, she seemed almost alive again.

"What is it?"

"The Guild. They've chosen my house for the silent auction this year."

"Oh, my God. You've been trying since forever."

"I was always at the back of the list, and now this – but the board cleared it with the cops – I mean, these gentlemen. As long as parking is two blocks over. You know, where the field is. We'll hire a little tram."

Charlie took a step and got in her face, brandishing his cocktail fork. "Who cleared it? Orinda Police? We haven't heard about it." Cherie colored.

"Oh, of course you can host it," Jill blurted. "Ignore him. Besides, it's weeks away, yet. Right, Cherie?"

Delight returned to the brown eyes. "Only two. They're having it early this year."

"Two weeks, then." Jill pushed Charlie out of the way, and led Cherie to a chair on the lawn.

"Faris has been so sour since – well, you know." Frank ambled closer, listening. "He wanted to come over, too, but he was on call last night."

"That's OK."

"But he's such a dear. He's going to let me re-paper the kitchen. And Janice says they have some new crystal champagne glasses at Costco. Elegant, but cheap."

Frank smiled. "Well, that's the kind Faris would approve of." They all laughed again.

"So what's the favor?"

"I'm shopping for table cloths tomorrow afternoon. Thought you might want to get out of the house." Silence. "Jill, I don't have your eye for color."

Jill moaned lightly, and gave Ned a pleading look.

Charlie's jaw set. "It might be OK."

Cherie grabbed her hands. "Great."

The clump of officers was thinning, leaving red-smeared goblets. "We'll go with you. Separate cars," Charlie said.

Jill shrugged. "That's better than nothing."

"Well, some of you handsome men can ride with me," Cherie said. Then to Jill, "We can meet there. I have to have you."

Frank sat down at the patio table, picked up a goblet and munched the tart shrimp, gazing at the crystal pool. The cops were good leaf-dippers. He wanted a beer, but not enough to leave this seat just now. The women made happy sounds out on the lawn, and the world was letting slip the slightest whisper that things might be normal again. If only the summer would hurry.

Chapter 15
Doctor Faris Raed

"Doctor, I have Cathcart in room three." Jolie squinted over her clipboard. "Are you feeling OK?"

"Fine." Of course she could see that he wasn't. Fifteen years as his nurse, including two affairs together, each lasting more than a year, had opened the window to his soul. "Please, don't bother me for a while. I've got to make a call about a cancer patient."

"Mrs. Burry?"

"No one you know." That was stupid. She knew all of his patients. "Please, give the Cathcart boy something to read. No one for a few minutes. Fifteen minutes. Let me make the call."

Jolie was so good. But she was also a stubborn American bitch. She remained in the doorway, micro-managing, as ever.

"Faris, what is it? Your old friend who just left? Is his cancer untreatable?"

"Jolie."

She bit her lip and disappeared. Voices in the hall. Now she was pissed, but he could not listen. Faris Raed's head would hold no more. No more data. No more smells of alcohol swabs. He wanted to puke out of the window into the flower bed. Or onto the floor.

He rose to stare out. The blinds were down – no matter. Nothing out there he wanted to see. Not the new clinic building, nor the parking lot they had just had refinished. Nothing he had created with the partners. Not the bright sunshine. Not the brown hills that stood between him and the Bay.

Those things he did not want to see were once the pillars of his world. Or at least the grace notes. That world existed no longer. There were only wavering colors – reds, oranges. Undulating red stripes cast off by an angry boy so long ago. A boy. A boy with semen between his ears. And hunger and envy. So stupid. A punk who ran in the company of kids whom his mother forbade. And their old, angry, dirty uncles who fed their egos with amazing facts and plans to take over the world. My God, he had to quit staring at these blinds.

Dr. Faris Raed collapsed into the small love seat against the wall and wept. A prayer rug lay on the floor next to it. He hadn't prayed properly in weeks. Across years and oceans, and galaxies of forgetting, that boy had come back. A phantom, riding in the wake of a big fat man with garlic on his breath, he came, invisible, hiding behind the swarthy oaf's smile. Mouthing the secret code word in a deep, resonating voice with no shame. A cute phrase, full of mystery and portent. The words children use in games of war.

He would not blame the messenger. How could the fat man have ever realized that the boy was using him as a conduit? Reaching with once slender fingers through time and space, to dig his nails in? Dig in and tug. He, Faris Ali Raed al Faisal, was once that boy. And the memory came rushing like a wave – in those days, he never could get his fingernails clean.

Faris wanted water. Wished a cold bottle would magically appear and save him the test of walking through the hall, meeting everyone's eyes. He wished that Jolie were beside him, stroking his hair, whispering that it would all work out. His third wish was to pick up the phone and call the police.

Alas, when that dirty boy ceased to be, when his angry dreams gave way to a love for science, Faris had stopped believing in genies. None of the wishes would come true.

Jolie had carelessly left a stack of the thin cotton examination gowns on the edge of his desk. Faris took the topmost one and used it to wipe his face. He tried to order his thoughts. First the problem, then the solution.

Replaying it. Step-by-step. Perhaps it was not as bad as all that. He had just finished administering measles vaccine to the Barkley twins. Small talk. Mrs. Barkley was so pretty. Strolling in here, gripping her elbow. More small talk. The twins were cross. Then, when he was alone, notating the file, Jolie stepped in, wielding a handwritten message in Arabic.

"I'm sorry, Doctor. There is a man named Khalil. That's all – Khalil. Here." She handed over the scrap of paper. "He says that he used to hold the hot test tubes for you in medical school. He's a joker. An old friend?"

Faris remembered nodding, already being smothered by a fog that began when he heard the name. Jolie went to admit this person while Faris tried to unscramble the jumble of Arabic words. Once straightened out, he knew he was supposed to understand their meaning, but they jumbled again, like a snake coiling in a fire, until they grabbed the pit of his stomach and squeezed.

The big garlic man came in. Jolie spoke words. The man spoke words. Faris did not know this man, but was supposed to pretend. He remembered smiling, then Jolie left. They were alone.

They stood there in the room, the two of them, staring at each other across a gulf of culture, of purpose. But Faris did not really see the garlic man, for the boy filled his senses – a boy who came rushing out of the past like a demon from Hell, dragging behind him his crumbling stone house with no running water, and his eternal promise. His promise. The blood oath a boy makes, when he believes oaths are all that matter. Forever.

"I want nothing to do with this." He remembered pushing the words out of his paralyzed throat. "I give money. Besides the money to my aunt and uncle, I give thousands of dollars to the relief organizations, and the mosques. I never forget my hometown. I am not one to desert my people."

"Of course you wouldn't." The fat garlic man laughed, as if meeting Faris was his greatest pleasure. "Especially not your aunt and uncle, and your cousins. And Sharma. Remember Sharma? She was like a mother to you. Please God, she is so old now. She likes her tea, and her cats, and treasures the memory of her son who made such a success." The garlic smile. Another laugh, from this man who could not know anything about Mother Sharma, nor her cats.

It was enough. The threat was on the table. Thank God his real mother had come here to die. The garlic man reeled off more names, members of that small, holy group that had grown, spread its tentacles like an octopus. They reached into everything now, those tentacles of anger and stinging, and some of them were mad that Faris no longer wrote, not even on e-mail. More names. More possibilities of harm. The unspecific threats fell out of the garlic mouth and into the room, like wads of litter, while Faris and the boy watched in silence. Then the fat man was gone.

"Doctor?" Jolie knocked, and Faris pawed at his own eyes, sweeping away hot tears. Another knock. "Are you ready for Mr. Cathcart? He's been waiting a half hour."

Shut up, Faris wanted to yell. Do you wish to broadcast every one of my failings?

"Doctor?" The knob turned.

"No. I'm coming now. Two minutes, Jolie, please." His voice did not crack. The knob relaxed – not a nice noise. Rather, the sound of a prison door closing. Tears poured anew, and he could only hang his head and watch them fall to the Oriental carpet.

Jolie knew him. Why didn't she know not to close that door? Of all people, how could she lock him away with such finality?

The phantom boy was quiet now, standing in the corner, gazing through time out of hollow eyes. The garlic man's maneuver had been one of perfection. No way out.

No way out, because Cherie had finally arrived. Life was so perfect for her now. Not even September Eleventh had shaken her friends. He had become a man with his feet in stone, and the tentacles could move over him as they would. No running. They would follow, until he became like the old man who had his throat slit that cold afternoon so long ago. A traitor's death, which he and all the other boys were made to watch, so they would never forget the real power of the octopus.

"Doctor?" Jolie was the only one he could still trust, but she was married now.

"Coming."

He wiped his face. The boy stared in wonder. At his office, at his clothes. Amazing, how the boy's training had still pulled through after all these years. When the garlic man demanded help in taking Frank, the boy's instincts kicked in, as if he were still dodging in the streets with his fellows. In the camps. Artful, how he guided Faris' tongue, inventing boy's lies to turn every one of the big man's sneering thrusts. He would never have surrendered anything if the fat man weren't so relentless with so many names from the past.

A final tear coursed down his cheek, as Dr. Faris Raed straightened his tie and prepared to step out of the prison, into the sweet world that no longer existed. His boyhood wiles had successfully protected Frank. But he had given them Jill.

Chapter 16
Magic

They lay in the street lamp stripes. A thousand times before, Daniel had followed the straight, ghostly lines over the mountains of his rumpled bedspread, down across the rug, the freezing wooden floor. Tonight, they streaked Loretta's smooth back. She lay easily, head flat against the sheet, and turned toward him. Her body language said she belonged here, and if he let her be, she would fall asleep without a care. The only other light in the room was the yellow dancing fire. He was glad he paid extra for the condo with a fireplace.

"Sorry I dispensed with the formalities."

She laughed. "I guess I didn't come here for small talk."

"Yeah, but I want to know how you got in."

She raised up, her breasts enticing in the shadows. "A credit card, remember? You showed me last time."

"I did not."

"You did. You were drunk. Again."

"You must have a pretty low opinion of me by now."

"The lowest." Her hand traveled to his hip. "Why doesn't a big shot FBI guy buy a more secure lock? Some enemy spy might come in. Seriously." The hand roamed. My God, she did things even before he wished for them.

"That's why I stuck with a simple lock. Let 'em come in. I don't want to tangle with anyone who can open the really secure locks." He bent down and kissed her for a long time, then hovered over her glistening eyes in the dark. "Why do I get the feeling that you're here because you want something?"

He detected a smile.

"All I want is a little magic."

"What sort of magic?"

She pushed him aside and sat up, resting her arms on her knees, which remained under covers. He could see all of one breast – gossamer orange in the firelight.

"I guess I came to Washington for magic. Leadership, law, all the noble things. At first I thought I found it."

He caressed her back. "The dominoes fell your way because you're beautiful."

She turned her head like a coquette. "I didn't sleep my way to the top, if that's what you're implying."

"No, I –"

"Even Gerry had a spark or two when I first met him."

A still settled on them for a few moments. She was thinking. Maybe crying. The fire hissed, and needed another log, but Daniel felt her warm leg against his, and wanted it to stay there.

"Are you still with him?"

"No. I'm sure I told you."

"You told me and then went incommunicado."

She sat up straighter, her naked back immune to the cold. "Didn't you have some reason to come here? To Washington? When I got out of law school, I knew I didn't want to be in the courtroom. I wanted to make the laws. You know, write them."

"What has that got to do with not returning phone calls?"

"I'm getting to that." But she fell silent.

"So?" he said. "You were saying you wanted to run for Congress?"

She shook her head. "They don't do the real writing. I guess I thought I could make them concise. More understandable. I thought laws were like works of art. Now look at me, as political and compromising as the worst of them."

"There's nothing magical about writing bills and laws."

"There could be." She reached around and stopped his moving fingers, studied them in the streaks of white light, then kissed them. "I first got a job with Congresswoman Pilar. Late nights. Pizza parties. We were really doing a good job. I guess that first night with you threw me back into the old atmosphere. You know, back when I went along with all the crap. I didn't know if I wanted that."

"How long were you with Gerry?"

She ignored the question. "Isn't that sad? I was rude to you because of my own problems. I want out of here. I went back and forth, thinking that being with you might trap me in this town, where everything you do gets turned into a weapon against you. Then I would switch, and picture you rescuing me, taking me out of here. When I didn't call you back, I was being merciful. You don't deserve a head case like me."

Daniel moved his hand to her shoulder, and pulled her back down to the pillow. "Look, let's get on the same page. If you're not sleeping with Gerry anymore – and I'll believe you, because I want to. That's my Achilles heel. If you want me to be your white knight who rescues you from the evil Emerald City--"

"Jeez, Daniel, you're mixing metaphors--"

"Shut up. Let's have one thing straight. Frank Whitlock didn't save the plane because he is magical. OR psychic, or anything else that doesn't pass scientific muster. My job is to oversee his protection. But believe you me, I'm also trying to figure out who he might be connected to, and why. And if I don't find out, someone else in the Bureau or a local police department will. You got it? That's our job, and it will be done."

He kissed her. Realized her eyes were still open.

"How can you believe he's one of the terrorists?"

He shrugged, then fell back onto the pillow. "Maybe he's not. Maybe her works for the Company."

"The CIA?"

"Yes. And not one word out of my mouth leaves this room."

She chuckled. "Don't worry. I still like you. But you're as cynical as Gerry, goddammit. The only way he could be CIA is if we knew about 9-11 beforehand."

She leaned over him. The mirth in her eyes had evaporated. "We didn't, did we?"

"Of course not."

"You don't sound very sure."

"Of course we didn't know. I've been in meetings with a lot of good liars. Professional liars. I know the looks. The body language. This country was caught with its pants down."

Her turn to collapse, on the other side of the bed, though she extended her hand, intertwined it with his. "Maybe if the CIA had started a corps of psychics when Whitlock wanted them to, they would have had their pants up."

"Stop it, Loretta. Learn to trust the KISS theory – *keep it simple, stupid*. Whitlock's connected somehow. There's another agenda behind the scenes. Or maybe staring us in the face. Leave the analysis to the pros, and you won't go crazy."

She sighed, and he watched her naked breasts rise and fall, again in perfect position in the street lamp stripes. "OK, pro," she finally said. "But your pants are down, too."

He rolled over, on top of her. "When I'm with you, that's where they are going to stay. And at least in this case, thousands aren't going to die."

She laughed, and he kissed her. She laughed again.

"I hope your pants are down when you find out the real truth."

Red flag. He fixed her with his eyes. "What truth? That you're really sleeping with Gerry still? Tell me, Loretta--"

"No, silly." She kissed him. Deeply. Wrapped her legs around him. And sighed, as their bodies started to move together again. "The real truth," she whispered between moans, "is that people really can be psychic. Like Frank Whitlock--"

"Shut up about the hero, for chrissakes. He's too old for you." Daniel smothered her in kisses.

Chapter 17
The Wax Museum

Frank shuddered awake. He commanded his arms to move, but it was beyond their power. Too soon to have another visit from Sam, he thought, but what else? He listened to the moans of the house in the bay breeze, mixed with the rivulets of blood humming in his ears.

"Don't worry," Jill said abruptly, and flopped her arm over his chest. Asleep. He needed to piss something fierce, but could only wait while the pinpricks reclaimed his limbs. Wait and try to remember the dream:

They were traveling, Sam and he. The *BART*? Yes, first the BART, way back when the cars were new and clean, but just as he was about to touch the unsullied upholstery, the scene turned dreamy, and they were on a Metro bus, boxed in by the towers of San Francisco, and Sam was laughing at some scene in a comic book. Frank glanced at the magazine in his own hands. *The Flash.* But his attention wavered, just before he could discern the words in the little bubble above the superhero's head. He turned instead to watch Sam, wanting to drink in every chuckle, bask in that glorious, unfettered atmosphere that always followed his big brother.

It was one of their treasured trips to the city – just the two of them. The bus slowed and they climbed out the back door, but the scenery shifted yet again before their feet could hit the curb. "Come on." Just once, it would be nice to be with Sam when he wasn't in a hurry.

Their shoes never touched the cement, but landed on the smooth tiles of a darkened gallery. Eerie, mute figures loomed around them. At first, Frank jumped back – no – of course. The wax museum. "This way. The circus is over here," the words came out of the ether, and Frank followed, bathing in the memories of the sound of his brother's voice.

"I don't remember a circus in San Francisco, Sam."

His big brother pointed. They stopped in front of a scary man, arm outstretched, his features almost wooden. Moustache, top hat, crisp red coat, and a whip.

Sam yanked on Frank's sleeve, urging him on. But Frank was mesmerized. "What is he? A carnival barker or a lion tamer?"

Sam pointed past the wax figure – there, almost concealed in shadow, sat an old-fashioned railroad car complete with a cage. A circus exhibit. Frank strained to see, and for an instant, thought he could make out a huge stuffed lion behind the thick steel bars. In front of the cage, a sign read *Beware the Beast*.

Even as he read it, the cohesion of the printed words began to warp and change. Frank blinked.

Sam's finger touched the sign, and the letters froze into place, all returning to their former shape – except the last word. Frank squinted, following the moving finger: *Beware the Lady*, the message read now.

Behind the sign, the caged lion had been consumed in a fog, and Frank was seized by the certain knowledge that the mist would coalesce into the form of a woman. His knees began to shake. For reasons unknown, he could not bear to see that.

"What does it mean?" Frank heard himself scream. He turned in time to see Sam's lanky form slip through the side display. "Don't, Sam. Don't try to hide and scare me."

But Sam kept moving,, straight through a door that had opened in the black wall. A gale-force wind blasted through it, ruffling and rippling the clothes of the ghoulish wax people that surrounded Frank. Thankfully, the dream collapsed before the face of the woman in the cage became clear.

The next afternoon, peering at the new Dell computer, Frank felt for a moment that the old juices might actually start flowing again. Dave Tomkins waved him away, and recited technical terms into his cell phone, then typed in whatever directions they were giving him.

"That's it." Dave dropped the phone into his pocket and patted the gleaming monitor. "Now you can work from right here. Great to have you back on the team, Frank."

"Pretty slick." Charlie bent down to look at the screen. "Damn, this is nicer than the one in your real office."

"It is." Frank grabbed the chair and unceremoniously began pecking at the keys. Charlie did not budge, but hovered, looking over his shoulder.

"Don't worry," Frank said. "I know the rules. You check the e-mail every day. I won't stick any passwords on it."

Charlie gave one of his grim smiles. "We look first, OK? Show us every one, even the advertisements. They could always be some code. Just a precaution. You don't know what those sickos out there might try."

Frank slouched and rubbed his eyes. "Come on, Charlie. You know your guys will be intercepting and reading them at the server, before they ever get to this machine. Lighten up."

"Now how would we do that? We're the government, not Microsoft."

Jill came in from the hall and stood, hands on her hips. "It's beautiful. But you promised to put it in the spare bedroom." She laughed.

"She wants you out of her hair, Frank," Charlie said, and slapped him on the back. An instant later, a knock on the door made them all jump.

The FBI man straightened up, hand inside his jacket. Two policemen barged in.

"What is it, Ken?"

"A woman." Ken jerked a thumb over his shoulder. Ned was positioned in the back doorway, and the guys with their antenna gadget were busy at the back hedge.

"They stopped her car down the street."

Frank felt his stomach fall away. The dream about the lady in the cage filled his mind.

Ned strode in. "Are we secure?"

"Not yet." Charlie waved for him to follow.

The two of them left together. Ken nodded toward the bedrooms. "Mr. Whitlock, you want to--"

"No. I'm fine right here at the computer." As he moved the computer mouse, Jill ran her fingers through his hair, as one would to a grandfather who was expected to die soon. *My God*, he wanted to say, *I've got to get you out of here.* Instead, he drilled into the "properties" page, still not believing the thing could hold eighty gigs of memory.

At last, Charlie returned. "It's a woman. Arab extraction. Mid-forties." A grimace.

Hairs bristled on Frank's neck. He reached for Jill's hand and squeezed. "Did you guys let her go, or shoot her?"

Charlie tossed a card down onto the keyboard. "She says her name is Elizabeth, and that you sent for her."

Frank's jaw set. The card read, "Elizabeth Kismet, Realtor." Address, somewhere on Wilshire in Los Angeles.

Jill stiffened. "You sent for her?"

"Honey, stop." Too late. She was moving toward the hall and no one would get in her way. "Jill, it was decades ago."

"Who is this woman?" Charlie loomed, while Ned hustled after her, down the hall.

"An old girlfriend. I never knew she got my message. Let me talk to her, for God's sake."

For a moment, it was a battle of wills, then Charlie turned around. "Get Janice. Call for backup. Another female. They can strip-search her in the trailer.

"Jesus, you can't do that." Frank slammed the new desk with his fist. There were cops everywhere. They would search her anyway.

He got up in Charlie's face. "I may have more gray hair than you, but I'm tired of this shit. At least let me talk to her alone. In the backyard."

"Absolutely not."

"Goddamn it, I want to see her alone."

Their hug was perfunctory. Nothing like the reunion he had always dreamed about.

"You kept the 'K'."

"What?" She smiled and brushed her hair back. Still down to her shoulders.

"Your last name. It used to be Khoury. Now it's Kismet. What kind of a name is that?" He motioned toward the metal web chairs in the grass. Charlie fumed on the patio. Two men hugged the fence. Frank didn't care. She had the same light brown eyes.

"My husband is Turkish. In the old world, our families would have been mortal enemies." She laughed. "It's our running joke."

"My God, Liz, I'm so sorry they searched you like that. I've lured you into Hell."

A shake of the head. "I wanted to see you. How's Jill taking all this?"

"Better than I am."

"What did you tell Kim Binion? She called me and said you were blabbering something about my uncle. Did you have a premonition?"

"I didn't realize you had followed me to California." He laughed. "Well, that may be a lie. Seems like I heard you were out here, from somebody. Is your uncle still alive?"

"Frank—" Ned approached, carrying a soda for each of them. "Mrs. Whitlock told me to bring these. She said the lady used to favor Dr. Pepper."

Elizabeth blushed. "Thank you."

Frank leaned close. "No bad predictions. I just need to know if your uncle is still alive."

"Yes."

"Does he ever come over here?"

"He'll never leave Lebanon. Strong as a horse, they say. I haven't seen him since my father's memorial service, eight years ago. We buried him back in the homeland."

"Not Professor Khoury. God, I'm sorry."

She looked down. "He had a good life."

"Does your uncle still help people?"

She seemed surprised. He watched her face. Older now, but still enchanting. Though they only had three years, off and on, he probably revealed to her more about his gift than he had to anyone else, until Jill.

She tasted her drink. "That was nice of Jill. I wish she would come out."

Frank shook his head. "I feel sorry for her, saddled with a nightmare like me. This may tear us up, Liz. We had a good marriage, until I had to go play hero."

She might be listening, but her eyes followed one of the pacing policemen. "When are they going to let you out of your cage?"

Frank's foundations shook. Cage. The dream. God. If he couldn't trust Liz –

"It is a cage."

"My uncle has helped a lot of people." She sighed, sat back. "But I think this is out of his reach, Frank. He always said that people create their own worlds, that when they come to him, they just need a change of direction."

Frank sat back and let the fizzy drink bite his lips. "Change direction. How the hell can I do that, with the whole world on my back? They sent a guy to kill me just the other day, Liz."

"Frank, I'm so sorry. Surely you realize there are fanatics in every society--"

"Don't be silly. I don't blame the Arab people. I just wish your uncle could change time, put it all back the way it was before 9-11. Could he do that?"

Their gazes met, meshed meaningfully, then she began to laugh. "Sure. No problem. I'll write him tonight." For a few moments, they laughed together, and he watched the way she tossed her head, the way her eyes sparkled. A curse, this difference in cultures. If that never existed, they would have been married.

She sipped her drink, and leaned closer. "I'm sorry. You would have to go to Lebanon to ask. And besides, don't you remember? He doesn't help everyone who asks."

"I know. It's like winning the lottery. You told me about the ritual with the white handkerchief." The handkerchief in the dream had been the clue to everything. But in the other dream – the woman he should beware of – no, he told himself again. It couldn't be Liz.

She was staring. "Frank, I'm sorry to ask this – but did you really land the plane? What's all that about some device on the airplane? The pundits on TV aren't being very nice about you."

He shrugged. "I've quit watching. It's either some weird disinformation the terrorists are putting out, our maybe it's from our own government. God's way of twisting the knife. Believe me, the plane didn't land itself. I almost killed everyone, coming out of that dive, but it wasn't remote control."

"If they had died, it wouldn't be because of you, darling Frank. But they won't let you go to Lebanon. So what will you do?"

He looked into her eyes again, imagined autumn leaves swirling around her. This was Liz. Was there some deep corner of space and time where she was still his? Could he ever reach that point again? It would be no betrayal of Jill – this was different – but Liz, the fact she had answered his summons, submitted to a search – but all of this was bullshit.

"I'm sorry I asked you here, my dear Lizzy. I know, you always hated that nickname." He reached, and rested his hand on top of hers. Jill would probably be watching from behind the blinds, and the cops seemed perturbed. He had to do this. "Don't you remember? I've always got a plan."

"Oh, don't tell me –"

"No. Don't you tell. Anybody. Once the heat's off, maybe after we're out of Afghanistan--"

"America – we – will never be out." She blushed. "I'm a citizen now."

"You know what I mean." He squeezed again. She looked down, shy, then responded. "If things get better, I've got a couple of congressmen who act like my best friend. I think they might agree to send me on a peace mission to the Middle East."

An impish grin took over her face. "Now I do remember. You're crazy."

Her hand rose to caress his cheek. Once. Twice. The lawmen tensed, but Frank's thoughts went back to a certain oak tree, on the campus at the University of Texas.

"Even if the government--" she began, frowning. "Do you know what you mean to the people over there?"

"I doubt I'm a hero."

Her brow furrowed in thought, then her hand moved back to his. A squeeze. "You're still a beautiful idealist Frank. Forget my uncle. He's not a magician."

"You said he was."

"Oh, yeah. I guess he is. But he'll throw the handkerchief back if you show up with a hundred bodyguards, for pity's sake. He's not like other people." She laughed. "Come to think of it, he's more like you."

She opened her purse and started digging, and that brought the deputies jogging across the yard. "Miss--" the lead one called out. As if a weapon could have possibly survived their search. She produced only a small address book, quickly found what she wanted and scribbled on the back of a business card.

He held it up. "Realtor. You've got your own shop." He dropped the card into his shirt pocket, wondering how he could keep it out of Charlie's sticky fingers. "I'm impressed. My first love is a businesswoman."

Liz blushed. "I guess. That's one thing that's still better in the old country. Wives don't have to work to make ends meet." She stood up. "Better go. Alan had to work, but he's taking a flight up to San Francisco. We'll probably do the town."

Frank rose and hugged her. "I'd like to meet him sometime."

Their fingers lingered together, then Charlie stepped over and took her away. Frank waved, and stood there, sucking in the afternoon smells and the last of her perfume. No, he would never be afraid of her. Even if she appeared out of nowhere and shot him, herself, it made no difference. Her judgment he could accept. Sam's warning had to mean some other lady.

Rather than enter through the back door, Frank did the only unpredictable thing he could think of. He walked around the back corner, pulled out a key, and unlocked the side bathroom door. The one they never used.

"Hey Frank, you OK?" one of the cops yelled out.

The door stuck, but he jerked it open. Thankfully, Jill was not sitting on the toilet, but in the telephone chair in the bedroom.

"How was she?" Her gaze remained riveted on the book in her lap.

Frank detoured into the closet and slipped Liz's card into a crevice in the little metal box that held his grandfather's watch, then went out to sit with her.

"Fine. She wanted to see you. I wish you wouldn't hold a grudge."

She rocked softly, gazing into the distance. "She's still beautiful."

"Jill, you're the one I've spent all these years with. You're the one who filled my mind on the plane, when I thought it was all over."

A frown. "Ignore me, Frank. I'm trying to hang on and not flip out."

He took her hand and kissed it. "You're being perfect. It won't last forever." If he could make it to Lebanon, that wish might come true.

Chapter 18
Little Birds

The heavy winter clouds over Cairo acted as if they
would never leave. Each day, Suhail rose, took his tea and his
walk, passing by the blind man, Old Mahmud.

"How is my friend, today?"

The old man's well-scratched cane went into motion,
caressing the walkway in smooth sideways strokes. "I am
well, though the air is thick this year. Mahmud's lungs long
for the freedom of the next world." His whiny voice could
barely be heard above the rhythms of the radio behind him.

"Your lungs are too pessimistic." Suhail dropped coins
into the cardboard box at the man's feet. "Are our friends as
gloomy as you and the weather?"

"They are. They wonder if their leader will ever lead.
Their brothers are dying a thousand miles away. Arafat is
making his mark, but little progress. Mubarak is hiding in his
harem. Only Osama and the sultan seem to have the heart to
act." The cane whipped against Suhail's leg. "Their leader
does not feel dead. Is he?"

"He is not dead, my friend. Tell them that it is a foolish
creature that comes out of the den when the fox is sniffing
around. Do you not listen to that radio? Osama's men are
already decimated. And have we heard a peep from his
'legions' in America? No, my friend. Tell the troops that their

leader is a tortoise. I am always moving, whether they notice it or not."

He patted the old man's arm. "Tell them to come and give you money often. Soon, you will have so many orders to pass on, you will be a rich man."

"Allah be praised," the old man muttered as Suhail walked away.

They were not lies. Yet, Suhail knew that unpredictable impulses come from the land of the Blue People. He could not tell Old Mahmud that there would be no new strikes until the Blues gave their blessing.

Too bad Osama had no discipline. Impatient, just like an American. He had to have his party now, and all he could bite off. When the light turned, Suhail crossed the busy street. Well, the spoiled child's eyes were bigger than his stomach.

If only Osama had listened to his teachers. But so few of the young ones ever did. The knowledge of the *jinn* was there for the taking, by those with discipline. So many talked of another surprise, another humiliation that could hit the Americans any day now. Rumors. The jinn, and their realm, that was the home from which true surprises sprang.

He turned into his street. If only the human race would be silent, and *listen*. They would soon learn that there were no superpowers, no rebels. The blue people were naturally closer to God, he had concluded. They knew that there was only a fine line – the tightrope – between following the Word of God and falling into the Abyss.

In the morning, daggers of sunlight made Suhail turn over. The clouds were finally gone. A good omen, he thought, then closed his eyes and went back to the caves of his dreams, and walked along the wide viewing platform. With dream hands clutching the railing tightly, he peered down, watching the masses of Blue People. They shifted and shuffled, like a pen of nervous geese. But these creatures were not waiting for the butcher to come claim one of them for supper. Quite the opposite, actually. He, the human, was their prey.

He stared at the forms, beckoning information with his stillness, trying to wipe clean his mind, expose his goodwill, lay out an unsullied slate for them to write their messages upon.

At the moment he felt drowsiness begin to overcome him, a bolt of lightning coursed above the field of blue heads, knocking Suhail back, even as one of the strange beings – one he had met before – leaped up against the railing and spoke silently. Suhail kept still, and listened.

Another jolt, and he could hear children in the street. Suhail kept his eyes closed, barely daring to breath while he groped for the memory: The bold sprite had delivered two messages, not one. Both exhilarating, both portending happiness. A knock on the door brought him out of bed completely.

"Esam. The sight of your face is better than the sunshine." He kissed the loyal servant, who beamed and offered a paper sack.

"Incense. Long-burning. From America."

Suhail laughed, and admitted the big man. "Only you, Esam, would bring incense to Egypt from America. Didn't you know it should be the other way 'round?"

Esam smiled, but perhaps half-heartedly. "The news is bad from Afghanistan. Oh, and I brought this from the café." He produced an envelope. Formal-looking. Sealed with wax.

Suhail grabbed a knife from his sink, opened and read it.

"But this is excellent." He slapped Esam's shoulder and turned on the stove burner beneath the teapot. "An invitation from our friend, Sheikh Al-Med. He is inviting us to his estate across the river."

Esam's face darkened. "No, my Benefactor." He strolled across the room and settled into a chair. "That is bad news. I do not trust the man. Remember what we did to his bitch messenger."

Suhail shook his finger. "He will do nothing to us in his own home."

"He has waited long enough to lull you, Master. You mustn't go."

Suhail checked the tea. "I am being rude. I have not even asked you about your news."

Esam rubbed his forehead wearily.

"What's the matter, my friend? You still seem oddly affected by that little chess player. We did what we had to do, Colonel."

A grim smile. "I'm fine. Everything is set. Even though my digestion has been ruined throughout the whole trip. I went through checkpoints, through customs. I stared into security cameras. Yet none of the Americans even blinked at me. How, Master? How did you know I would be safe?"

"I am your leader, Esam. It is my job to know."

A shake of the head, then the big man continued. "Our target is thoroughly protected, but your sleeper on the inside gave us the key. The Al Queda men, too, have behaved like good soldiers. A couple of them seem smarter than the others – they would love to work for you."

"Excellent. So we are on schedule?"

"So far. Again, Muhammed is ready for a long engagement. He has three locations where we will hold the prisoner. One in the mountains. Another in the desert, and the third in what he calls 'rolling hills.' All quite remote."

"Perfect. Perfect." Suhail poured tea into two glass mugs, then distributed them. He re-read the invitation again. Remarkable, the things the Blues knew in advance. Hopefully, the signal for action would come soon, with so many things already in place. "Then I am going to see the sheikh. You are going with me, my friend."

"Bah." Esam stood and stretched. "What are you doing, Master? This is not just jet lag asking the question. How do you know you are not leading us all to Allah?" His fist clenched in the air. "I think, in this case, you should listen to your loyal servant. The sheikh and his cronies – they do not fear you so much, anymore. You perceive that. It is all Osama. No one on any street can speak without praising the rich infant and his impossible theatrics. They borrow Osama's courage. To them, you are the old guard. Mubarak – they have to wait for him to die. You – they are not forced to be so patient."

"Esam --"

"It is the talk, Master. Even with the spoiled children in America. Do not think that I agree. But protecting you is still my first priority."

"Drink your tea, Esam. Your face is a red balloon ready to burst."

The big man hit one palm with his fist. "We should be training. We should be in Sudan. The men are restless."

"The Americans have put snakes in Sudan, too. Patience, my friend. They will run for cover when we take their hero from them. We'll be back in the field soon enough. In the meantime, Kareem is doing well, teaching the recruits about explosives."

A frown, and the big man found his chair again. Suhail picked up his own cup, plus a plate of cheese, and crossed to the couch. "Haven't I brought us this far, my friend?"

A nod. His stare had no humor. "Of course you have. But please don't say a little bird told you it would be safe to have an audience with the sheikh."

"Easy, my friend. Your blood pressure." A careful sip of tea. Esam was so dense to be so brilliant. "Not a bird, though these particular agents also have the gift of flight. They told me that two things would happen today. Both glorious steps on the path. Your good news was the first. We are ready to strike. The second is this." He held up the invitation. "This confirms that my informants are hooked into the heart of this matter."

A visible shudder traveled up Esam's body. He smiled weakly, and drank. "And if our enterprise in California fails?"

"I am told we will not fail. It won't be easy, of course. Life never is. But we will eventually bring more glory to the cause than Osama ever dreamed."

"My Benefactor, no matter what flying agents speak to you, they cannot foretell the future."

Suhail laughed. "Can't they?"

A worried look. "But even if we do succeed, why would the sultan funnel resources to us?"

Suhail sat back and closed his eyes. It was good that Esam was a skeptic. He must remain sober, no matter how infallible the Blues' intelligence might seem. "I have it on good authority that the sultan is looking for more reliable performers than Osama. After we taste the sheikh's hospitality, we will eliminate him from the equation, as well. The sultan, and all of his rich brethren, have fewer and fewer holes in which to stick their money, and they appreciate dynamic precision more than resting on old laurels."

With his eyes shut, he could only feel Esam's exasperation.

"Your little birds," the big man began, but stopped to swallow his mouthful of cheese. "You're my commanding officer, but please, don't keep me guessing like this. Are these birds really men in the sultan's own organization? It's vital that I know something."

Suhail chuckled, and opened his eyes. "No, they do not work for the sultan. If that great man laid eyes on my intelligence agents, he would soil himself from fear."

"Perhaps all commanders speak in riddles, or perhaps I am stupid." Esam collapsed back on the couch, a weary blob. "I say it for the thousandth time. Your sense of timing is uncanny. You know when to move. When not to. You order us to back away at the very instant a smuggling operation or a kill seems easy. Then we find later that it would have been a disaster to proceed. You move the chess pieces perfectly, then try to tell me that all the brains reside in your intelligence agents, these shadowy soldiers I can never find and to whom I am never introduced."

Suhail began to reply, but Esam was rubbing his eyes. "I know you will tell me of compartmentalization, General. But if you can't trust me, then who? What if something ever happens to you? The Americans and British are snooping around, you know. And they do not always knock before they come in."

Suhail gazed at the tea leaves in the bottom of his cup. "If I were ever to be killed, I am confident my messengers would come and find you."

"I see." His hand returned to the cheese plate. "Allah be praised."

Chapter 19
Sullivan's New Squeeze

"For God's sake, Daniel." The voice fairly blew him out of bed. Loretta. "What are your bastards doing?"

"What? What happened?"

"Don't give me that." He heard her curse, away from the receiver. "Turn on the news."

"Loretta, my alarm doesn't go off for twenty --"

"It's Frank. They're trashing Frank Whitlock. 'Unnamed source.' That means defense. Or you guys."

Daniel groped for the remote control. "God, you almost gave me a heart attack. Why the hell do we get to talk when you decide? I've left a message three nights in a row."

When the television came to life, the familiar cartoon diagrams of the remarkable flight of the fifth plane flashed by. He flipped through the channels rapidly – and every talking head that once spoke so glowingly of the insurance man's impromptu flying prowess now gazed out, faces dark, and disapproving. She was silent now, though he could almost hear the pout.

"What are they saying, exactly?"

"They're saying that it's confirmed – some terrorist landed the plane by computer, that Whitlock is a sham, maybe even a bad guy. Congressmen are falling all over themselves to call for hearings."

"Loretta, why haven't you returned my calls? I don't even know where you live."

"I told you I wanted out of this town. Now – Christ. They're even saying the FBI raided Whitlock's old high school yesterday, looking for his records. You guys are doing this smear job good and proper, aren't you?"

"Loretta, anything the Bureau does is standard stuff. They can't do anything to Whitlock without notifying us, first." He shuddered, knowing that was a lie when he said it. "I want to see you again." He might as well have thrown a rock down an endless well. "Loretta?"

"You scare me." Was she crying? "Take that as a compliment."

"If you want to compliment me, answer the goddam phone. If Stacy Pringle screens me one more time, I'll ask *her* out."

"You're all crazy," she screamed. "It's snowballing. Some government guy in Italy is questioning whether the U.S. had some culpability in the September Eleventh attacks."

"Loretta, I want to see you. Friday night. This time, we go to your place."

"Look, do me a favor, OK?" She was weeping. "Just go into your office and find out what's going on. Please. Tell Gerry to – never mind."

Whatever was bad in this world, it was Gerry's fault, he wanted to tell her.

"Damn it, Daniel. If I fall in love with you, I'll always have to live with filthy, dishonest tricks like this."

"Would that be so bad?"

"It would be horrible."

Gerry Sullivan was fairly beaming. That CIA buffoon, Tims, came prancing in, practically on the boss's arm. Another ration of shit. Daniel tried to catch Jimmy Johnson's eye, but the basketball player sat still, hands on his knees.

"Welcome, lady and gentlemen," Sullivan began. "We've got to make this fast, because I am due in the president's office in one hour. I'm sure you've all heard the news. I'm afraid our suspicions about the remote device on the fifth plane have been confirmed."

Tims held up a dossier. "We traced the satellite signal. The real flyer had to be sitting in his car, somewhere down near the Ohio River," he said. "We're speculating they had another joystick guy ready over in West Virginia. State of the art equipment, people. We're working against pros."

Sullivan gave a mock sneer. "Now, Carl, I don't recall giving you the floor."

"Oops. Sorry." A few chuckles.

Rather than look into the gloating eyes, Daniel scanned the room. The original klatch had been joined by Leah Cummings, lead attorney, and Bill Walden, FBI rep by way of the Bureau of Alcohol, Tobacco, and Firearms. His name was being circulated as a better bet than Daniel for an under-secretary job in Treasury. And that all depended on the peacock behind the desk, who was enjoying himself too much.

"What's on your agenda with the president?" Daniel asked. "Surely this airplane story was leaked with his permission."

Sullivan's smile actually threatened to crack. After a moment, he seemed to recover, and took on his aristocratic veneer. "I don't know who leaked the story, Daniel. If I find out that she or he is sitting in this room, that person will be on the next plane to our Office in Guam. Which doesn't exist. For your information, in the Oval Office, I will be trying to plug the dyke and mend fences at the same time. We don't want the hero convicted before all the evidence is discovered."

His gaze abandoned Daniel, and he was back on the soapbox. "What you may not have heard, is that before this news broke this morning, Congressman Madison jumped on the bandwagon with Hathaway and Conesta. To a degree. He has requested secret service approval for a peace mission to Turkey, Lebanon, and Jordan, and wants to take Frank Whitlock with them as a peace ambassador."

"Jeez." Leah Cummings quit sketching on her legal pad. So far, from where Daniel sat, he could see the outlines of a dog and some flowers. "That won't fly now, will it?"

Walden drowned her out. "How long did that story breathe before the big news smothered it? Five? Seven minutes? It's D-O-A."

Laughter. Especially Tims. Jimmy Johnson smiled broadly, still not looking this way.

Sullivan rapped his knuckles on the desk. "Yeah, don't have to worry about that one. Those meddling congressmen – Whitlock must have called in his only chit. Daniel, who is the FBI guy down there with the hero? Thompson?"

"Charlie Thornton."

"Yes. I want you to activate plan Monitor. All e-mails and phone calls--"

"Are already tapped."

"If you will let me finish." Sullivan sat up straight. "I don't want Frank Whitlock talking to anybody on the phone or in person without our guys interviewing the other party first. If his e-mails are not clear, if they even smell fishy, he never gets them. Got it? If he tries to call Hathaway or anyone in government, put a fake secretary on the line and deflect him. See to it."

"Of course," Daniel said, wondering if Leah were the only one in the room impressed by Sullivan's command demeanor.

"I almost forgot. We want to welcome Jimmy back." Eyes turned toward the tall man, slumping ridiculously in the too-small chair. Sullivan shuffled papers and handed them out. "Here is a copy of his report for each of you."

Daniel managed to lean over and whisper. "How come you get all the trips?"

Jimmy smiled. "There's more leg room on the planes since the Big Day." A pause. "Not."

Daniel stared at the report's heading. Yes, Jimmy had been to the Boeing plant in Seattle.

Another rap of knuckles. "Like I said, I'm under the gun. Summarize, Jimmy. Please. Real fast."

Jimmy put his broad hands together. "Technicians showed me through the seven-fifty-seven that delivered Frank Whitlock and the other heroes. They confirmed to me that the aircraft was equipped with the new high tech gadget, the VHF Digital Link Mode Five. They also showed me readouts of the type of data transmissions they produce, as compared with other standard equipment. Wave transmissions, digitized. Identical to cell phone calls, but on another band set.

"It was over my head, but they claimed that some signals that were sent to the aircraft at the vital hour were from Cincinnati, and some from as far away as Louisville, Kentucky. Either one sender, mobile, or two. The terrorists built in some redundancy, apparently."

"So what's this about West Virginia?" Daniel asked.

A shrug. "Don't know anything about that," Jimmy said.

Tims was smug. "We're filtering more transmissions. That plane was bound for D.C. They had to have another guy on the ground en route."

Sullivan pushed his chair back and stood up. "Jimmy, did they give you a demonstration?"

"Sir?"

"You know, switch the machine on? Show you how it works?"

Jimmy waved the report. "No, sir. There is evidence that the device was de-activated before the technicians got to it. Computer chips removed. Had to be after the plane landed, and before it was put under twenty-four hour guard."

"Which was not long." Sullivan smoked his pen. "And those computer chips would have told us — what?"

"Well, it wasn't just chips. It had a newfangled sort of hard drive thing. That drive would contain the log of the transmissions."

"Conclusion." Sullivan's chest swelled, as if he, alone, had it all figured out. "Since the plane made its emergency landing at Wright Patterson Air Base, someone in the military is working with the terrorists."

"Good God." Walden slumped.

"Does that make any sense?" Daniel looked at the others. "I mean, they can't have a conspirator waiting at every base and airport, can they? How the hell did they know where he would land? Come on, people, that plane wasn't supposed to land anywhere."

"Daniel, you must have dated the wrong girl last night." Sullivan shook his head and the others broke into outright laughter. That, for God's sake, was a shot across the bow.

Daniel smiled with them. "Gerry, if Al Queda has a working agent twenty-four-seven on every air base, why don't we just throw in the towel now?"

Sullivan looked away. "Here's what I want. A thorough check of every person on duty at that airbase that night. Daniel, put that together. Jimmy, you stay on the tech guys. Coordinate with Carl on all the transmissions in the Midwest on the Eleventh. I want something irrefutable.

"Carl--" He looked at Tims. "Re-do the background checks on everyone on that plane. There was a lot of confusion after they hit the tarmac. Get Walden to help."

"Right." Walden made hurried notes. "I'll cover the domestic checks, you start on the international, OK?"

"And Leah? Have we broken any laws yet?"

The counselor looked up. A bird had been added to her artwork. "Just be careful, Gerry. This one's a hot potato. Give the commander-in-chief the wrong lead, especially with this Whitlock character, and Al Gore may win the next election." Laughter all around, but Daniel saw how Sullivan blushed. Maybe he wasn't after Loretta, after all.

Carl Tims raised a hand. "So how will the president take the news?"

A smile. "He's had all morning to listen to the sensational stuff. I'm going to play it like the objective guy. Cool. Put up a wall to protect some of the hero's prestige, but give him enough ammo to quash any congressional peace mission. I'll suggest some alternate speaking engagement to Conesta and Madison. They'll both be there."

"So you're going to let Whitlock make a speech after all? Even after all this?"

A sneer. "Daniel, am I going too fast for you? You heard Jimmy's report. The man's a fraud. Worse, probably. No chance – that speech will never happen. Good job, folks. Get cracking."

Jimmy Johnson took a sip out at the fountain near the elevator. Daniel blocked his getaway.

"Buy you a drink after work?"

Jimmy shook his head. "Got a hot date. Finally. Eight o'clock."

Daniel risked grabbing his sleeve. "I'm serious, Dude. Just a quick drink. Right after work."

Things moved in the man's mind, his eyes twitching, like a slot machine. Deciding which side he wanted to be on.

"You know where Chavo's is?"

"I've driven by there. Expensive joint, isn't it?"

"Yeah." Jimmy pushed past, a player not caring whether a foul was called. "Gotta be a special occasion to pay that much for a steak. This woman is one of those occasions. I like to hang out at the Macintosh Tavern, across the street. Meet me there at seven."

Daniel smiled and hit him on the arm. Jackpot.

Daniel was early, and sat at the bar. Experts argued on television. A fully automated landing under those conditions was impossible, one said. A woman in Illinois screamed at a reporter, telling him to leave Frank Whitlock's reputation alone. For a fleeting instant, even young Charlie Thornton made it onto national TV, making a stand in Whitlock's front yard, fighting back a throng of press.

"They're out of their fucking minds." The bartender pulled close.

"Who is?"

"All of them." A glass clinked into its rack. "First of all, you can't put a plane that big through acrobatics by means of remote control."

"Were you in the service?" Long ago, perhaps.

"Hell, yeah." He pulled his bar rag taut. "Marines. But shit, you can't trust anyone. Even that kooky Whitlock. Probably works for the CIA, himself. He don't have no five or six hours of flight training. He's gotta be the saltiest pilot around."

The old marine glanced around, like someone embarrassed at spilling real beans. He leaned over and stuck out a thick finger. "You know what they're doing, don't you?"

"What?"

"He's CIA alright. They're setting him up like a hero, then bringing him down. Then they'll send him to the Middle East. You know, Iran or Mesopotamia or somewhere, and he'll be in disgrace, so instead of killing the bastard, those Arabs will recruit him as a spy. He'll be a goddam double agent, but really working for us." A wink.

"Make a good spy novel," Daniel said, spotting Jimmy Johnson just in time. He threw down a ten. "Excuse me."

Jimmy insisted on a booth by the window. "My lady is meeting me, Dog. I don't want her standing out there getting hit on." He raised his highball and took an ample swallow. "Shit, man, we should do this more often."

"You're the one with the crowded social calendar." Daniel felt antsy. "I just talked to a guy who thinks Whitlock's CIA."

A grimace. "Yeah? Might make sense."

"Jimmy, what really happened in Seattle?"

The tall man started laughing. "First of all, you read my report, and second, what if the boss swore me to secrecy?"

"I think you love Sullivan about as much as I do."

"Point taken."

"You're hiding something, Jimmy. Why?"

He sighed. Sipped. Scratched at a dirt mark on the window with his fingernail. "Met an old friend up there. Opponent, actually. Jonathan Doaks. Forward for Minnesota, back when I played. Good shooter."

"He some big stick at Boeing?"

"Big enough. Always had more brains for math than for round ball."

"Is he a good enough friend to tell you straight?"

"Hell, I guess so. I stepped on him in a game, broke his ankle, ended his career."

"So he hates you."

A big smile, but he kept his gaze riveted outside, looking for his date. "No, we actually started talking once in a while. Got to be pretty good friends."

Daniel stirred his drink, feeling tingly, wondering if he really might divulge something Sullivan didn't know. "Are you going to tell me this Doaks guy worked on the mode-five autopilot thing?"

The smile grew broader. Jimmy was making him squirm.

"Come on, Dude. Is it true someone disabled it before the ATSB could get a look at it?"

"True enough." One more check of the door. "Even more interesting. My old friend tells me the device has never been tested, is basically a mock-up. Yes, it was removed after the plane landed at Wright-Patterson. But it was also *installed* after the plane landed. It was never on that plane during the flight."

Daniel tried to keep from swallowing the chunk of ice in his mouth. Long seconds passed. Suddenly, he felt the way most CIA field agents must feel throughout their lives – with no one to trust. Why in holy hell was quiet, professional Jimmy suddenly confiding in him to this degree?

"So why did you give everyone the impression it was active? You saw their faces – how could you leave that information out of your report, for God's sake?"

"I delivered my report exactly as I was directed to give it." A weighty look. "You spill the beans on me, Daniel, and I'm coaching in some Georgia high school next year, so hold this egg with both hands."

"I don't get it. So who landed the plane?"

Jimmy shrugged. "That old fart who lives in California, near as I can tell. You've met him, I haven't. Sorry, Old Buddy – here's Rebecca."

Jimmy stood, tossing bills down onto the table.

"You better have a reservation at Chavo's, or you'll never get in," Daniel said as he watched the lithesome, lanky woman climb onto the curb from a taxi.

"Don't sweat it, man. I know somebody." Johnson winked. "Uh, remember." He touched a single finger to his lips, and walked away, towering over the other bar patrons. The place was filling up.

Daniel quaffed one more bourbon and coke, and was reeling by the time he made it to the sidewalk. Not from the liquor, but from the audacity of whatever scam Sullivan had concocted. Who was running whom? The cards were being stacked against Whitlock, but why? How could the U.S.

government possibly benefit from that old man's ruin? How could Sullivan benefit?

He blinked, steadying himself, wondering where he left the car. Across the street, another couple emerged from Chavo's big doors, and hailed a cab. The man was Gerald Sullivan, taking long strides, a lady holding onto his arm for dear life. Loretta.

They climbed into the vehicle, and Loretta peered out the back window just at the moment it pulled away. Perhaps their eyes met for a nano-second. It was hard to tell, because Daniel wheeled around, and headed for the corner through a whirlwind of spent leaves, old newspapers and other street debris.

Chapter 20
Scene from a Mall

"What made you change your mind?"

Charlie sat, placing his coke and notepad on the coffee table. He seemed so tense these days, even though the e-mail threats had tapered off. The whispers were another story.

"It's not a change, Frank. I've said all along we would get you back to normal." He opened the phone book. "So what'll it be? Mountain House? McDonalds?"

"Forget it. Leftovers. Jill's eating with Cherie. She'll love being out for a change." The worry would not leave him. "Are you sure she'll be all right?"

A tolerant smile. "Frank, you asked that ten minutes ago. We have an army protecting her. Even the Walnut Creek police are giving us a couple of cars."

"Not really back to normal, is it?"

"Frank, Frank." Charlie grabbed his cola and stood up. "About once a week, we go over this, and you're fine. A paragon of patience. That makes me feel good. When you're nervous, I get nervous."

Frank went quickly over his idea. This was as good a time as any. "I want you to let me start protecting myself. James McNee from the senator's office has been calling. If you let me go on that goodwill tour to Lebanon, I can show the Arab people that I'm not some sort of monster."

Charlie shook his head, like a son somewhat ashamed of his old man. "Frank, that just won't work. Those guys in Congress may want to honor you, but they're using you, too." He scratched his chin. "And you keep bringing Lebanon up. They want to go to four countries, but you single out one. Your old girlfriend has relatives there, doesn't she?"

He set his cola down, and whipped out his little notebook. Frank's stomach turned over. Charlie read.

"Elizabeth Kismet. Works in real estate. You dated her for a total of two years."

"Leave her out of it, please."

"She gave you something, Frank. Why won't you show me that card? Have you heard the rumors they're throwing around on TV? Some idiot even said you had ties to the Al Queda. I'm getting worried, and you're not helping me."

"Come on, Charlie, we haven't lied to each other yet. I don't think. I'm not a terrorist."

"I know you're not, Frank, but that may not matter if the dogs get loose inside the Beltway."

Frank rose, started for his room, turned and wound up pacing in front of the government man. "Charlie, no offense, but you're all alike." He clenched his fists. "Hell, yes, I want to go to the Mountain House. But I want to go *alone*. I want to sit and drink, and swap lies with Kirby, and have a thick steak, and just *live*. It can't be like this for the rest of my life. For God's sake, let me go to Lebanon."

Jack Hillerman was hilarious, whether they were sitting around the office or on a tense stake-out. Roby had known him since childhood, and delighted telling tales to the other guys on the force about Jack's pranks in high school. They rarely believed them, and sometimes Roby wondered if his memory hadn't inflated with age.

"The you are, Pencil Boy." Jack pointed, and slapped Carmen Rialto on the arm. The phrase was originally "pencil dick," but a rebuke by one of the women on the force put a stop to that, even when no females were around. "See? Right over there. We can get you a new bra, Carmen-baby." Jack swerved the car briefly, as if they would turn into the strip mall.

"Very funny. Ha-ha," the gruff detective replied.

Roby stifled a laugh, but Captain Jewel hit the top of the seat. "Stay alert, goddamn it."

"There's the Wheel." Ned's country twang was unmistakable over the radio. Two cruisers swung left, then turned into the parking lot of the North River Shopping Mall. Down at this end, *The Cheddar Wheel* already had a line out the door.

"Poor unsuspecting chumps," Roby said. "They don't know what's going to hit them. After the shopping trip was over, Mrs. Whitlock and her friend would be dining there. Silently, he marveled at the number of cars in their convoy. They had used fewer black-and-whites on jaunts taking Frank downtown.

"OK, we have a problem." A female voice. The dispatcher. Silence.

"Well?" Carmen yelled, though he did not have the radio mike in his hand. "Finish the fucking sentence." Roby's muscles tensed on their own. Carmen jerked the shotgun out of its holder.

"Go ahead." Sheriff Bozell's voice.

"OK." The female resumed – had to be Carly – but she spoke so haltingly. "Sorry, but they're yelling at me from the other room. Captains Jewel and Moon, you are authorized to abort. Repeat, abort trip. The subject's friend will be delayed."

"What?" Jewel came forward in the seat, punching numbers into his cell phone. He had someone. "What is this? I thought we had some people with her." Someone answered, and he thanked him and folded the phone. "Can you believe this shit? They've been with Mrs. Raed all afternoon, then that fabric store out on the loop gets a bomb threat. They're questioning everyone."

"Crap," Roby said. "Mrs. Whitlock's about to go nuts. Bummer if she doesn't get to have her little outing. Why did they pick that place?"

"Wake up, Roby." Jack slowed, but none of the cars had yet turned. "We get ten of those calls a day now."

"Yeah, but at the same store we're monitoring?"

Carmen lodged the gun back into its bracket. "I don't like coincidences. She's a Middle Easterner. Just remember that."

Now Jewel motioned for the mike, and Carmen gave it to him. "What's going on up there?" he demanded.

"We're heading back." That was Captain Moon. "Just picking a different route from the one we just used."

Jewel shook his head. "Everyone up front is too damned nervous."

Roby glanced around. They crossed Orchard Boulevard, too slowly, in spite of the motorcycle cops blocking traffic in both directions.

Carmen leaned his head against the window. "Damn shame to put up this many people just to have the whole thing fizzle."

"Look out," a voice cried on the radio. "It's a goddam truck!"

Roby was up, his ass off of the seat. Two blocks ahead, a *Norman's Toys* tractor-trailer was pulling out from behind the store.

"Shit, didn't anyone block the alley?"

"Up there." Roby pointed toward the strip mall's roof. "Two guys with rifles. Are they ours?"

Jewel jerked the mike back from Carmen. "Hey Moon. Jake? Where the hell's the chopper? Dispatch, get the chopper over the mall."

An indecipherable screech, the helicopter guys answering, but Roby slapped the window. "I said, are they ours?"

Jack twisted the wheel, copying the movements of the car ahead. "This is bullshit." He found a space along the curb and turned, coaxing the vehicle up onto the sidewalk. They nudged a mailbox, but he kept going, and bodies under a covered bus stop scrambled out of the way.

"Goddam. He's in position," Roby cried. As he watched, one of the riflemen on Norman's roof knelt down behind the short wall. Jack swerved around a telephone pole. The rifle guy pointed. A flash, then a report. Roby craned to see. A cop at the checkpoint behind them went down.

"He's shooting. They're not ours. He's shooting."

Cries erupted on the radio. "Shoot the tires. Stop him."

Roby's gun came out of its holster, but he froze. Still a block ahead, the entire side panel of the huge tractor-trailer came crashing down, forming a wide sort of ramp. At least a dozen men, all carrying weapons, piled out of the back of it.

"Turn around. Get her out." Ned's voice.

"Open the goddam doors," Roby cried, and only then realized that the windows of the car to their left were shot out.

Police, plainclothesmen, deputies, all scrambled from their cars, firing, using the open doors for cover. Then a deadly staccato sound – low-pitched. A patrol car door three cards ahead splintered into bits, sending the men behind it flying.

"Christ, they've got a fifty," a radio voice screamed. Jack released the door, and Roby tumbled out. Crouching. Toward a concrete wall. Bullets peppered the sidewalk behind him. They weren't all fifty caliber. Screams from the parking lots on either side. People were running, but the form that caught Roby's eye poised and fired from behind a pillar in front of the toy store. Roby aimed, and got a shot off. Someone crashed into his back.

"You OK, Jack?"

"Yeah. They're wearing vests. Somebody sold them goddam vests. There's the SUV." He pointed.

Across the side street, the green SUV was halted, its windows and doors riddled with holes. A couple of old cars drove toward it, not away. Two men dragged a struggling form between them.

"They're fucking taking her," Jack screamed.

Roby checked his own *Kevlar* vest. Fastened. "You first."

They had made this rush a thousand times since childhood, Jack and he. Against a thousand Indians whom they left for dead in the woods. A thousand Viet Cong, and twice that many Confederate soldiers. Union, too.

"Now." Jack was in the street with one prodigious leap. Roby counted three, then copied him.

They ran, hiding behind the crippled police cars, under a spray of more zipping bullets than any simulation he had ever experienced. The horrifying one – the fifty – was silent, and he could only hope someone had taken it out already.

There were too many shoppers still on their feet, dodging between cars, screaming, going down when they were hit. Jack made a beeline toward the old cars. Two cars. Three. They were firing from inside vehicles that had obviously formed a flanking movement, once the semi opened fire. The lead one, an old pink Cadillac, was full of holes, but a barrel still stuck out, blasting short spurts at the cops off on the right.

"Watch it, Jack."

Jack tumbled down behind the very short concrete wall that fenced the lot. Bullets chipped right above him. Roby collapsed behind a car.

"I'm pinned," Jack yelled.

"Wait a minute." Another man scrambled up behind the duo dragging the woman. She was clad in a blue blouse, black pants – Jill. She kicked a foot. Still alive. The third man lagged. Roby pulled the trigger, and the man's head cracked open. He went down, but a fusillade rained onto the car, making Roby crouch lower – he lost sight of what the two men did with the writhing woman.

"Damn it," he yelled to Jack. "I might hit her if I shoot."

"Don't hit her."

But something hit Roby. He went sprawling out into the open, blood covering his hands and the pavement. He looked down. Upper arm. No pain. Why? His fingers could still move. Reaching for the gun. Reaching. He felt the metal and rolled half-under the car. More pings above him. Screams came in waves between spits of gunfire and crashing glass.

"Hold it there, Jack." He screamed it under the car, though he couldn't see his friend. "Chopper's coming."

The world blew away in wind and noise. Roby lay there, gripping his freely bleeding wound. Bullets whizzed past, skipping near him on the pavement. Looking skyward, he could see an officer leaning out of the helicopter.

"They'll follow them," he yelled again. If the bastards did get out of the parking lot. Poor Jill. Surely she had been hit by now.

Yells – some people were cheering – then a *whoosh*. One of the cars far up ahead exploded. He stretched to see around front, from under the fender. *Whoosh*. His mind rejected the slow-motion scene. The helicopter was blowing up. Coming apart.

"They've got rockets." But his voice sounded like a timid child's. He looked around, and couldn't see Jack at all. The cheers changed to screams. Roby pushed. Piercing pain in his arm, but he *pushed* as far under the car as he could get. Metal and fire rained down everywhere.

A new flurry of gunshots, then the giant scraping, crashing sound blurred everything, and firebrands darted through the air. His heart felt suddenly full. He could lift this car if he wanted. Instead of trying, he slid out, holding his arm, kicking flaming shards away from his pants legs. More shots.

A man dressed in shorts and a golf shirt approached. "You OK, man?"

"Get down. You'll be killed."

The stranger knelt, and gripped Roby's throbbing shoulder. "No I won't. They got 'em, see?" He pointed up ahead, but Roby's gaze rested on the form of one of the riflemen, draped over the side of the toy store's roof.

"We've got to stop that bleeding."

Roby pushed the hand away. Painfully – he must have sprained his ankle – he stood. The man kept chattering and picking at Roby's wound as he walked. Around the big truck, its cab fairly destroyed, the scene was right out of a war movie: smoke, curls of metal sticking up from corrugated police cars, store windows shattered. Sheriff's cars and ambulances had lights blaring, all of them weaving separate paths through the dazed throng swelling in the far edge of the parking lot. Then he saw Jack, stretched out across an oil-stained parking space.

Roby loped forward on the stinging ankle. The uniform cloth on Jack's hip was smoldering. "Jack." The odor of burning fuel. The copter had nailed the pink Cadillac. The other cars were gone. Black smoke threw rolling shadows across the lot.

"Jack."

"Leave him," the man in shorts said, then Roby saw why. The fire had not gotten him. It was the clean bullet hole in his forehead. Jack had been going to war since childhood, but this time their enemy had not been imaginary. This one shot back.

Frank knew he had to cool off, so he stalked away from Charlie, headed for his new office. The computer had been moved into the front bedroom. "I'm going to finish that Powerpoint presentation," he said, under his breath. Charlie just sat there, looking impotent. There was nothing worse than a government that said it could do everything, but couldn't. Thankfully, instead of calling Kyle out of the trailer, to hover behind him at the computer, Charlie just nodded.

Frank sighed and sat for a moment, weary of the bouncing balls on the screen-saver. Weary of everything. Did he really have the heart to bring those office jokers out here? Any classes he might give them would just bore them. A handful of them were already better salesmen. For the millionth time, he tried to imagine retiring at this age. Social security, 401k, and McNee had hinted at some sort of government "stipend." No more donations out of the blue. No more speaking fees were being offered. The editor at Simon & Schuster would no longer return his calls. Thank you, evening talk shows.

A finger hit the keyboard, and the floating balls disappeared. The flashing icon at the bottom meant new e-mail. He hesitated only an instant before breaking the rules. Kyle could read it later.

Perhaps he comprehended the message immediately, but he could only sit, blinking, feeling his body stiffen. The sender's name was gobbledygook. The message, simple and short, like all threats: "We are sorry, Frank. We will take care of her until you join us. Transfer possible. Surrender and die honorably, and your beloved will live." Frank's lips moved, reading over and over, but his voice would not come out.

"Hey," he finally yelled to no one. "Where's Kyle?"

The words were drowned by a car skidding to a halt outside. Commotion at the front door. Bodies appeared in the hall, Charlie at their head, his rasping walkie-talkie shivering in his hand.

"Shit. Fuck, Frank." The FBI man fell back against the wall. "They hit the convoy. They took Jill."

"What?"

Mouth moving. Gibberish. Then, "I was wrong, Frank. I was wrong and I'm sorry." They had his arms, pulling him across the hall, toward the bedroom. Was Jill there?

Charlie led the way, but now uniformed guys poured in. One of the cops – Pierce – got right up in his face.

"Ned was killed, Frank," he said. "But we think she's still alive. We'll get her back, Frank. I swear on my mother's grave."

Cars revving outside. Radios crackling. In the gloom of the bedroom, Frank found the bed, but Jill wasn't in it. He sat down, couldn't feel the mattress under his butt. Inside the door, a wall of blue uniforms. Frozen. Gawking.

"What?" he asked again.

"Frank, the witnesses are saying she wasn't hit. They can't be sure, but they saw her moving. We'll get her back." It was that young FBI guy. Charlie.

Frank studied his face for a few long moments, but his thoughts weren't about this world. Why didn't Sam warn him about this? Sam had always taken care of him – *why didn't he warn him?*

Perhaps he did.

Chapter 21
The Assignment

"God damn it to hell."

Gerry Sullivan's voice rolled out of his open door and over the heads of a dozen people in the hall. Quitting time exodus was in full swing, women draped in coats, men carrying umbrellas. Daniel was in the hall, on his way to check his laptop into the tech security closet.

"Holy living shit. What are they doing out there? Eating sushi and smoking weed?"

Sullivan was on the phone, obviously, and the realization seemed to hit everyone at the same moment – he was so far over the top this time, something might really be wrong. Paces faltered. Jimmy still had his feet up on his desk, but an ashen look on his face. Daniel leaned into his office.

"Who's he talking to?"

A shrug.

"Don't tell me that. Ever again." Sullivan slammed the receiver down so loudly, that it sent a visible pulse through the people who hadn't made it to the elevator. Chalmers, freshly back from Afghanistan, resembled a scared rabbit.

"Hold that elevator. Nobody leaves." The boss stood at his door, and motioned for Daniel to cross the hall.

"Come on," Daniel urged Jimmy. Better not to be in there alone.

As he moved past the threshold, Sullivan dodged him and addressed the confused throng. "Daniel and Leah in my office now. The rest of you in the big conference room. Meeting in fifteen minutes. Call home, make your excuses, but no calls to the press. Big Brother is watching."

Leah skulked in, and before the door could close, Jimmy Johnson followed, bless him. "What's up, Chief?"

Sullivan let him enter, but was already looming over Daniel, who had made the mistake of sitting down. "What the fuck is your man Thornton doing in California?"

Daniel looked up. He could break that finger jabbing toward his face. It would almost be worth it. "What happened, Gerry?"

"Jill Whitlock was just kidnapped in broad daylight. Sixteen. Count 'em. *Sixteen* policemen were killed. Two dozen injured. They said it looked like a fucking Bruce Willis movie out there." The stale odor of Sullivan's sweat lingered even after he moved back to his desk. The stench didn't matter – Daniel's stomach had fallen away. This war was real.

"They get any of the bad guys?"

"Eighteen dead. Caught seven. At least another seven got away. With her."

"How could they get out of a populated area without air pursuit--"

Fist on the desk. "They shot down the air pursuit." He wagged his finger, placing all of it on Daniel. "They had to be sleepers. They had to have help from other sleepers. I don't know how many came across the border in Tijuana, but every conceivable fuck-up has just occurred in one fell swoop, and it's on your watch, Amigo."

"My God," Leah whispered.

Jimmy leaned against the closed door. "We're in the shit now."

"That's not quite it, Jimmy. They brought war to an American city on September Eleventh. Today, they brought *war --"* Slamming his fist. "War to an American suburb." He pointed to the phone. "In a minute, that will ring, and it won't be Ridge, and it won't be Mueller. It will be *the man*. Daniel, you have been sifting through illegals for months. Every cop in the Universe has been studying pictures of terrorists. Somebody sold them bazookas, for God's sakes. How could you have let this happen?"

"Mr. Director," Daniel spoke for the record, "the protection program has been run by the FBI. As you are well aware, we have technically been on a consultant basis. Like Homeland Security itself, we have no real power. And never will until Congress clears up the chain of command."

Sullivan might be near tears. "Consultant – bullshit. When are you people going to learn? This is a fluid situation. We are a fluid agency. I don't want to hear excuses like 'they're in charge.' *We're* in fucking charge."

"No excuses." Things got worse when the blowhard was partly in the right. "They'll hold her hostage for Whitlock."

"Well," a sneer, "you guessed one thing right."

"The Bureau isn't stupid. They'll track them down."

Jimmy had one foot up on the arm of the couch, his head shaking. "Lot of hiding places in the Bay Area."

"Right again, Johnson. Daniel, the correct answer is: they *won't* catch them." Sullivan glowered, his gaze boring down. "You, Daniel. *You* will catch them. You're going out there. I want you in Frank Whitlock's living room. I want you to handcuff yourself to him. If he gets shot, you get shot. Put the fear of God into these country yahoos who lost that woman. We are going to take lemons and make lemonade."

"Yes, sir."

"This is the Liaison Office taking the reins for the first time." He opened a drawer and extracted an envelope, then tapped it on the desk. "This is our authorization. And we are going to show our muscle. This case will be solved now that we are on it. Best of the FBI. Best of the CIA."

He turned toward Jimmy. "You. Advise CIA. Get Tims here for an emergency meeting in the morning. Eight o'clock. Leah, I want you to draw up some blanket search warrants, phone taps, the works. Plead the emergency powers act. I have the president's signature."

"Do you want me to talk to FBI?" Daniel asked.

"You're not listening. I want you there by tomorrow morning. That means you're on a plane before you even get to the airport. You need a break from Washington, anyway." What was that supposed to mean? "Dismissed. Leah, I need to see you for a moment."

Daniel followed Jimmy to his office.

"Good luck out there," the basketball player said.

"Thanks. I'll be happy to be the one to go out for the grandstand play."

Jimmy's eyebrows arched. "Just don't fuck up."

The form on his front stoop huddled against the cold. Even so, he could tell it was Loretta before he ever climbed out of the car.

"Hi."

Daniel fumbled with his keys. "Why didn't you use your credit card? You must have heard the news."

"Don't kid. You made your point." She stood. "What point?"

"Not answering my calls. Turnabout's fair play. Touché. I need to talk to you."

The key clicked in the lock. "I don't talk to other guys' girlfriends. Not at home, anyway."

She held the door. "Please, Daniel. You know I'm not with him. Yes, we went to dinner that night, but that was part business--"

Perhaps his look stopped her.

"I'm not lying." She clasped her hands together, actually begging. "Sure, Gerry thought we would start up again, but I went along just to let him down with some class. Daniel, you have to listen."

He stepped inside, but left the door open. "No, I have to pack." A moment later, he heard her follow.

"Daniel, I know things should be going better between us." She watched him pull the hanging bag from the closet. "Wait. Where is he sending you?"

"California."

"I should have known. He left another message on my machine. Don't let him jerk you around."

With the bag hung on the closet door, he rummaged through shirts. "It's my job for him to jerk me around. Stop the pretense. If your destiny is to wind up with Mr. Washington Opportunist, who am I to louse things up?"

She grabbed his arm and held on until he turned.

"Don't you ever pay attention? It hasn't gone right for us because I think I'm falling for you." Her eyes searched his, dismantling his walls against his will. "Nothing fits. We're like two ships bound for different harbors. But you keep coming back to my head while I sit there in the press meetings. Even when I'm talking with contributors. I want to come home to you even thought I hate the thought of being trapped here." Her arms were around his waist now.

"I want it to be you refusing to give me secrets at the dinner table, not Gerry."

He looked at her, and dropped the shirt and hanger. They were still the same eyes. Beneath that pert hairdo, the expensive clothes, he could not avoid the fact this was a real woman talking to him – not just some trophy on the D.C. meat market.

"You keep coming back to me, too. But don't say I'm stupid for thinking it's you who has all the secrets."

Her hand rose to his face. "The way I feel about you – that should be pretty obvious."

If it was a lie, it was sweet. He bent down, and their lips touched. Then he was shoving the shirts off the bed, and they made love like two people not afraid of their feelings.

Daniel's watch was still on his wrist. "I can't risk going to sleep. I'm catching the red-eye."

"How long will you be gone?"

"Two-three days. Two-three weeks. Whatever."

She snuggled against his chest. For a while, they were quiet.

"Is this what you came here for?"

She looked up, her face wearing the streetlight stripes. "I hope so. Maybe, in the back of my mind--" They kissed.

"I should have figured Gerry would send you the moment I heard about the kidnapping on the radio. I guess I just came to see you before you left."

"Shall I pass along your condolences to the hero?"

"Don't kid." She draped her arm across his chest. "Daniel, treat him right. He's not part of some conspiracy, like those assholes on the talk shows are contending. This isn't some plan by the Bush White House to start a war and take away our freedoms."

"Loretta, I don't believe either side – the psychic crap or the conspiracy crap."

"He's for real."

"Yeah. We had this conversation."

"Daniel, he had a premonition. That's how he reacted so quickly, don't you see? He didn't have to absorb it for awhile, like they did on Flight Ninety-three. He already knew what was happening."

Daniel looked at the clock. A single flight leaving in the middle of the night, and security would probably still be crazy. He would fall asleep on his feet, waiting in line. "So he knew, but he didn't call cops? Sorry. I have to believe that there is order in the universe. Logic. Empirical evidence. You know, the stuff that keeps us from going nuts." He climbed out of bed. "And now I have a plane to catch."

She got up on her knees, keeping him from pulling on his pants. "Don't ask me to prove what science can't. But just watch his interviews. He's unbelievable, yes, but that's what makes him real, damn it. He's not rehearsed. Some people like that have to be real. We need to believe that."

"Why?"

"They took his wife," she said, her eyes brimming with tears. "He tried so hard, and they took the woman he loves. Promise you'll treat him well, Daniel, because you know his wife's never coming back."

A kiss.

"You know that for a fact? Is this *Madame Loretta*'s own premonition?"

She wiped tears, stared into his eyes. "They took her. What could be worse?"

"He could be dead."

"Well, you know she is, by now." Another kiss, and she finally released him. He made for the bathroom, but she stayed there, naked, crying softly. "Promise me, Daniel," she said. "Promise you will treat him well."

Chapter 22
A Memorial

"It is Waleed. Hold." Esam raised his hand and Kareem slowed the limousine, almost to the stopping point. "I don't trust him, Benefactor. We can still turn back."

Suhail, too, recognized the man at the head of the driveway. Skinny, dour face. The kind of man you would avoid on the street. A lump bulged under his lapel.

"This is Egypt, Esam, not Los Angeles. The sheikh will not kill me in his own house. Where is your sense of hospitality?"

"We have to get into the house, first, Master."

Kareem looked over his shoulder. Suhail nodded, and the vehicle nosed past the small guardhouse.

"Are your people in position, my friend?"

Esam blew, vibrating his own lips, and patted a small device on his belt at the same instant. "The sheikh has an army hidden around here. My scouts won't not make much of a difference, but they are here." Sweat covered the big man's brow.

"Relax." Suhail patted the thick shoulder. "As long as his men see our men. Some of them."

Waleed leaned over, and Esam lowered the window.

"Welcome, my friend." The smile took up much of the narrow face. "It is a nice day and no bombs are falling."

"Let them fall." Esam managed a booming laugh. "We are immortal."

"You will leave your weapons at the door." Waleed waved them on. The sheikh's palace was no palace, if one compared it to the monstrosities of Saudi Arabia. But for Egypt, at least in the modern era, it would do.

Four guards with rifles on their shoulders came to attention, while a fifth patted Esam down, accepting the pistol from the shoulder holster, and the smaller one from the boot. He did not touch Suhail. Waleed came trotting up from behind, and led them into the main corridor, speaking as he walked. "O' Defender of the Faith, the sheikh is happy that you honor him this way." A curt genuflect.

"It is he who honors me," Suhail said.

As they walked down an ornate hall, another guard fell in far behind, causing Esam to tense.

"Esam." Suhail tried to calm him with his eyes.

The colonel whispered, for Waleed was well ahead. "Never fear. Your prediction that the sheikh would commit an entire cell, not just two fighters, to the kidnapping, came true. Allah is with you. But it is still my job to be nervous for both of us."

Guards opened large doors, and Waleed halted, letting the guests pass into a large chamber, a room with carving on the walls, and several stylishly drawn verses of the Koran, hanging large, in scattered fashion. Sheikh Fouad Al-med sat on a large chair near the middle of the room, with no chairs for visitors in evidence. Perhaps he expected mortals to grovel, Suhail thought. If only the poor of Cairo could see this.

Their host stood for a moment, smiling, then stepped down from his raised throne and kissed each of them in greeting.

"Illustrious One." Suhail bowed.

"Please." Al-Med gestured to chairs placed around a long table in a side room. The room could barely hold the furniture, but a large alcove opened to a window. Drapes were over it, but the light coming through them was strong. The room's doorway was actually rather tight, and Suhail stifled a chuckle when he saw Esam take note of these cramped features.

If only the big man could learn to control his fear. The blue sprites had been exceedingly content when he asked them about this meeting. He even asked them what might come of his next two moves. The sprites had vibrated in their cavern valley below the rail, then conjured a rare collective voice.

"Only good."

"My condolences." Fouad bowed his head, even as a servant appeared and swiftly served tea. Guards stationed themselves just outside the smallish doorway, rifles clutched close to their chests. "I understand that two of your men were lost in the operation in California." His gaze migrated from Suhail to Esam and back again.

"Thank you," Esam answered. "Your loss was greater than ours. Your troops performed flawlessly."

A slight smile, and a thoughtful sip of the brew. "Our men do not expect to come back. The moment they step into battle, they arrive on Allah's doorstep."

Suhail closed his eyes politely. *Then perhaps we should give condolences for those who survived.*

When he opened them, Fouad's face wore a beaming smile. "General Suhail Farid, I am impressed. You did what you said you would. You snatched the pearl from the claws of the dragon. Not *the* pearl, but a gem of value, nonetheless."

Suhail raised his cup in a toast. "We will have the real pearl, by-and-by."

"And I had no idea," Fouad seemed to actually relax, and nodded in Esam's direction, "that our friend here commanded such an ingenious cadre of computer hackers.

Our people in California were quite envious. The sultan, himself, is actually amazed at your entire operation."

"And Osama?" Esam must have instantly realized his impertinence, for he lowered his gaze.

"A compliment from the sultan is enough," Suhail said quickly. Fouad did not return his smile. Either he did not know where Osama was, or wanted to give that impression.

Fouad held his gaze for a moment, then turned his face toward the window. "Our great leader has been abandoned by his people. He and a few loyalists – true brothers in the fight for freedom – are still holding out in the mountains against the Americans."

It is what you would tell the CIA, Suhail thought. Fouad suddenly tapped the table with the short scepter he had been turning in his left hand. Again, his gaze gravitated to the window. Not the window, but an alcove in the wall that was covered by black drapes.

"I have made a monument of sorts, a tribute to the frightening new warfare we find ourselves in." As he spoke, the servant returned, moved speedily behind him, and drew the curtain with a tasseled rope.

The black drapes opened, and Fouad's monument fell into the light. A chill coursed through Suhail's torso. Inside the small alcove, a chessboard rested on a small table, flanked by two cushioned chairs. The chess pieces – all of them, even the kings – lay on their sides. Not a shrine to war, but to the beautiful Lina.

"Allah be praised." Suhail took a sip, hoping that Esam's composure would hold. Perhaps the earth shook. He had assumed the chess player was one of the sheikh's lovers, not *the* lover. How could the sprites have advised him so carelessly? Another reason why the logjam that was Fouad must be removed as soon as possible.

The sheikh took a deep breath. "Does the small memorial not remind you, my friend Suhail, that those of us on the side of anti-Zionism, on the side of freedom, should not fight among each other?"

"To be sure, Sheikh. May Allah be pleased with our joint endeavor. But things have changed, have they not, since we last spoke? Pawns may fall, but Kings must attend to the real task at hand."

A blind camel could read Esam's thoughts from a distance of a thousand meters. The chessboard had shaken him. Fouad, on the other hand, seemed to be closing up, and, for some reason, let Suhail's glib diversion of subject stand. He seemed puzzled, if anything.

"Many things have changed."

"Allow me to be frank, Defender of the Faith. Osama's network is crippled. Even money cannot flow now. The warrior still marches in the field, but with a crutch. The Americans were being lulled--"

"Do not lecture me, Suhail, about things even schoolchildren know."

"I would not dream of it. But some schoolchildren think that Osama is winning the war. You and I know that it belongs to the Americans. So far."

He leaned forward pinching fingers against thumb. "They were already going back to sleep, the Americans. Sleeping while a few soldiers with their computers drop bombs, or pay Pakistani traitors, or other lackeys, to sell all of their self-respect. My plan." He thumped his own chest. "My plan, not Osama's, woke them up again. And I will keep waking them until they are too tired to go on."

"The Americans are on permanent alert--" Fouad's fist clenched. "—because Osama is winning the war so far."

"Oh? A child can pull off a surprise. But look at my operation. See what we did, with all their policemen watching. They were ready for us, and still we prevailed."

Fouad's face was crimson by now, but he folded his arms and sat back. "You have Whitlock's wife. For how long?

America is a sieve of nosy neighbors, tattle-tales who keep no secrets. So how long until they find our people? A day? A week?"

"My sheikh, this plan has worked flawlessly up to this point. We will get this Whitlock. He receives messages from us every day. Soon, he will be a puppet ready to move on our string. His death will be only the first of the shockwave of events that Bush and his cronies cannot stop."

Slow, very slow nodding. "Suhail, you criticize our people for dying so easily for the cause. Yet, you spent those warriors we gave you pretty easily. And now you come to me wanting more manpower?"

"The prize is worth it, my sheikh."

"We have spent years sending sleepers over. We have established the routes whereby we can infiltrate tens, hundreds, in the blink of an eye." He turned his heavy gaze to Suhail. "And now *you* wish to harvest what we have sewn?"

"Your generosity overflowed on this operation, Fouad. The word is out on the street, and you deserve credit for that. But I designed the strike at the shopping mall. I used one tenth the men that you proposed. Americans are not stupid. They will stop large groups. I just need a few more, to complete my plan. More importantly, I need funds."

"How much?"

"Six operations. That is all. Six projects, and we will break America's spirit. My planning is impeccable. I don't just throw an occasional grenade and then wish for the other side to surrender."

Fouad lingered over his tea, then looked at Esam. "What would you say to such a request, Colonel?"

As he always did when confronted with an actual question, Esam turned instantly from an uncertain child into a sober military man. "If the plan were poorly thought out, and the troops amateurs, I would run from it. If I were certain of my men and the plan, I would act."

An arrogant leer. "And yet, I do not know the plan. And I doubt our friend here would ever divulge it before the fact."

"True." For a moment, Esam seemed to be sizing up Suhail, as well as the sheikh. "But you know his record for achieving phenomenal results. Better, he has the wife."

Fouad lifted his cup, drank, and returned it slowly, almost ceremoniously, back into its saucer. "I know his record well, Colonel. How he operates with so few soldiers. Almost as if an invisible, rich benefactor were backing him up. There is something undefined-able at work. You will excuse me, Suhail – but if I were told the Russians, the Chinese, even the British or Americans were your godfathers, I would believe it."

"He is a master at compartmentalization--"

Fouad's hand came up. "Yet, I do not think it would be Egypt."

Suhail fingered one of the dates on his plate. "I would not work with Mubarak, unless he had a revelation that brought him back to God."

They all chuckled.

"Yes. He needs more than that." Scratching his chin. "What then? When do your secret spies report to you? How is it you can send a wanted man through American customs in broad daylight during heightened security? You can't use submarines, like the rest of us?"

"Boats are slower than jetliners. I am not a traitor, Sheikh. I work with no government on this earth." It was the truth. "Now shall we sit here trading cloaked insults, as we always do, or will you give me the assistance to stop the American empire and destroy Israel?"

"All assistance comes from Allah." Fouad returned to his tea.

Esam chuckled, seeming suddenly bold. "He will give us what we request, Master. And more." He reached forward and dared to pat the sheikh's arm. "He only wishes he were fighting at our side. Eh, my Sheikh?"

A winning smile overtook Fouad as he sat there, gazing at the table, and Suhail breathed an inward sigh of relief. For an instant, the chess player's ghost was lurking, threatening to make everything unravel, but now the predictions of the sprites was shining forth again.

"Your colonel is a mind reader, Suhail. You will have men. And funds. And you do not have to reveal your plans, other than a rough outline." He looked Suhail in the eye. "But these six operations – starting with taking the American hero – they must be masterstrokes, or we will be allies no more."

They stood. Suhail bowed. "This will happen quickly," he said. "Please have your troops in San Francisco within three days. Our meeting place near the St. Francis hotel."

"Blessings upon you and the sultan," Esam added.

Fouad, himself, took them on the long walk back to the entrance. A gracious gesture. At the door of the limousine, Suhail turned. "Make sure your television is in working order, my friend, and keep tuned to CNN."

They laughed. Guards at the door stared warily.

"Where is Waleed?" Esam asked.

Fouad shrugged. "He does have duties, Colonel. Perhaps he is washing my Mercedes." They laughed again.

As the car negotiated the curves of the long driveway, Suhail closed his eyes, happy he had spent his life in more modest houses. Stay poor and your men will trust you. A mansion awaits each man with Allah, anyway.

Still, he could feel his bones getting old. Perhaps, after this campaign, and after Israel finally falls, he should indulge himself. What soldier would criticize him? With the Jews gone, and the sultans and princes with them, Arabia should be split up among the military leaders. Those who are brave enough to fight will deserve the spoils.

"Shall we celebrate?" Esam asked. He was clearly relieved they had made the highway.

"Later, my friend. Limber up your computer troops. We must get messages to the American hero through every channel possible."

"The rat must be lured to the trap, eh?" Esam's booming laugh filled the car.

Perhaps Esam deserved his own palace. Smaller, within walking distance from his own. But the picture of the big man as court jester popped into his mind, and made him smile.

Chapter 23
The Red Cross

"I'm Police Chief Burke. We're glad you're here. Do you have any new leads?"

Daniel shook the outstretched hand. "I was going to ask you the same thing, Chief. Find anything in the bust down in the Delta?"

The stout man shook his head. Gray, where he wasn't balding. "Nothing there. Better keep moving before the reporters spot you."

The two guys with video cameras stared steadily from the shade of a Japanese maple in Whitlock's front yard.

They climbed the driveway. "That's our main thing right now," Burke said over his shoulder. "We're spending the bulk of our assets on rural areas. Probably owned by a friendly, and we've got the names of all the landowners with a Middle-Eastern background. If they kept him in a city, we figure somebody would spot something."

Officers loitering around the mobile home drifted over to be introduced. Daniel chatted, trying to get the lay of the land before he started the *big hammer* act. If these guys closed up, he would be left to twist in the wind, and Gerry Sullivan certainly would not cut him down.

As the uniformed guys bandied ideas back and forth, Daniel noticed the house. Upper middle class, but the place had been taken care of. A painted brick wall flanked the walkway, and gave protection to a small front porch. Someone inside was yelling. Burke stuck his thumb over his shoulder.

"Your FBI guys are in there. Whitlock's flipped out."

"I want to see him."

The door swung open, and Daniel recognized Charles Thornton, who looked at him and rolled his eyes.

"My God. Any news? Shit, it's you." Frank Whitlock rushed past him like an angry drunk in a bar. "Did you find her?" His face much more had color than it did in the hospital.

"Mr. Whitlock. I'm happy to see you again. No news, sorry."

"Fuck." Whitlock threw the magazine he was clinching, rolled up like a weapon, onto the front walk. "How in hell can they evade the whole government, Agent Clooney?" He jabbed a finger. "Even I could find her, if these amateur bank dicks would turn off their radios and give me the phone." He turned away, near tears.

Charlie made introductions. "Bernard Harper, Sacramento office. James Vasquez, here in Orinda." Nods. Only one man in the room wore a uniform, dark-haired, five o'clock shadow puffing out above his navy blue collar. "This is Captain Altebemakian, Orinda police. Gents, this is the guy from the Liaison Office here to relieve me of my command." A wry smile.

"Not true. Just here to supervise and spend more of the taxpayers' money." Get in the middle of it, Daniel figured. It was no time to stand around and jack off about chain of command. Whitlock collapsed in an easy chair in the sunken den. He followed, and stood over him. "Who do you want to call, Mr. Whitlock?"

The police captain started to answer for him. "That's why I--"

"That's why he's here," Whitlock bellowed. "Her name is Janice Bergstaller, and he's worked with her on dozens of cases."

"Cases?"

"She's a psychic." The captain said it, never breaking his hollow, skeptical look.

"You want to call a psychic to find your wife? I thought you--"

Whitlock whipped around. "Don't you see? She's better at this than I am. I'm psychic, but you can't be emotionally involved. Sure, give me some quiet, and I can get to first base, but then panic starts to set in. Have they already killed her? Goddam it, Mr. Clooney, can't you let me make one lousy phone call?"

Daniel scanned the other faces. Perhaps this guy was looney, but Charlie had said mostly good things about him. "Why can't we give Mr. Whitlock the phone number?" he asked the Chief.

"Because," Frank yelled.

The chief gestured for calm. "Because, Frank, for the thousandth time, she won't talk to anyone but me. She's been burned in the past."

"Shut up." Whitlock sat down again, his head in his hands.

Daniel gestured to Altebemakian. "Let's call her." Charlie frowned, but Daniel shook it off, and led him and the police captain to the back patio.

"Nice house. What's going on out here?" The question was for Thornton.

"He's cracking. It's been like trying to talk down a suicide all day."

"He's suicidal?"

"No. No." Up came Charlie's hands.

The captain leaned his weight back against the iron fence that lined the pool. "Jeez."

"OK." Daniel moved, maneuvering the two men back together. "How do we stop all this psychic bullshit?"

Charlie shrugged. "Not by feeding the monster. I recommend you do *not* make that call."

The captain stared for a moment. "Look, I'll do whatever you guys want, but this lady is temperamental. People like her--"

"You mean psychics?"

A frown. The captain had middle-aged spread, sweat around the temples, but bear-trap eyes, like all cops who had stayed with it that long. If he gave this psychic kook any credit, there might be a reason.

"People like her get rattled if you sit on them too hard."

Daniel stepped forward and got into his face. "Captain, let's assume for the moment that this swami woman really has helped you on some cases, and you didn't just figure things out for yourself. I'll bite. But don't you think it's a bit egotistical to for you to decide who this lady wants to talk to?"

"Yes, it would be." The pudgy jaw set even harder. "I'm trying to tell you that Ms. Bergstaller does not want a call from Frank Whitlock. She's already discussed the case with me."

Charlie hit his own forehead. "Goddam it, man. You didn't tell me that."

"Calm down, Charlie." Daniel made eye contact. "I'm not here to bust anybody for the fuck-up yesterday. The internal guys will figure that our." He took a step back and put his hands in his pockets. Suddenly, he could see the humor. "I know this is la-la land out here, but what the hell are we talking about?"

The captain did not seem amused. "She lives in Carmel. Works with several departments up and down the coast. All for free. Won't take a dime." He produced a cell phone and punched in some numbers. "Here. Name is Bergstaller. Don't call her Janice until you get to know her."

He thrust the device forward and Daniel took it. "Think about it, Captain. Did she ever really solve a case for you?" The phone was ringing.

The captain was matter-of-fact. "Sixteen. She finds them if they are dead. Never located a live one for me."

Someone answered before Daniel could take that in. "This is Janice."

"Mrs. Bergstaller." Where to begin? "This is Daniel Clooney of the Liaison Office. Captain Altebe--"

"Altebemakian? Is Conrad there?"

"Yes, he's right--"

"I don't know any Liaison Office."

"It's – I'm really with the FBI."

"I can't help him."

"What?" He turned. The captain gave him an I-told-you-so sneer. "Who?"

"I can't help that Mr. Whitlock. I was told to stay away."

For some reason, the face of Gerry Sullivan popped into his head. "And who told you that, Ms. Bergstaller?"

"The red cross." She paused. "Not the organization, The Red Cross, but it's some boards erected to block a path on the astral plane. Red letters on the boards. I can't read the writing, but it means I'm supposed to stay out."

"Did you say astral plane? I'm not following --"

"There are different levels. Different planes. The blockade is on the fifth level. I can't find her if I can't go there. Maybe it's my physiology – they found a spot on my lungs."

If he were standing out on the grass of the back yard rather than on the hard bricks of the patio, Daniel might have let himself collapse. Did Sullivan know he was sending him into a nest of loonies? "Mrs. Bergstaller, I don't want to seem rude, but what does a path and some boards have to do with finding Mrs. Whitlock?" The captain lit a cigarette, looking bored. Charlie looked as lost as Daniel felt.

"Because they won't let me go there. Down that path – that's where she is, and some Force is preventing me from traveling it."

Daniel could think of nothing else to say, and slowly lowered the phone.

The captain flexed his eyebrows. "Welcome to California."

An officer with the nametag, "Harper," burst through the open back door, panting. "Get in here." He swallowed. Charlie was already pushing past him. "I got him calm enough to sit down at his computer, but now there's a new e-mail – offering to exchange Jill for Frank."

Chapter 24
The Intruder

Dusk coaxed a wispy fog from the surface of the Nile, and Kareem handled the car deftly, dodging through clots of traffic. Esam shifted nervously on the seat, scanning the surroundings in sharp jerks of his head, starting the moment they left the sheikh's property.

Suhail laid a hand on his shoulder. "My friend, there will be no ambush. It is not his way. Even if it were, this is no time to be calling down Mubarak's attention."

"Of course." Esam nodded, but his breathing remained heavy. "No one followed, but where was Waleed?" He bit at a piece of loose skin on his thumb.

"Perhaps trying to woo one of the sheikh's daughters?"

Even Kareem joined their laughter. A breeze blew from the south, but Esam insisted on keeping the windows closed. Suhail wished the traffic would thin before he got carsick in the close air.

Esam wiped sweat away with his thick fingers. "You are the master at reading people, my Mentor, but I could not help feeling the sheikh's agreement to be half-hearted."

"It is not that. He simply is looking for a way to take command, once his men are committed. His confidence in us will solidify when we achieve our objective. Only then will he let his guard down."

The big man turned to face him, eyes open and childlike. He could not begin to tell a lie, for his heart was there for all to see. "Let me confess. This is the first thing we have done that seems absolutely impossible. We can fool their FBI only so many times. They know we brought men in through San Francisco Bay, and over the border, to augment the sleepers. Those avenues will be closed now. Exchanging the woman for the hero? Bah. It would be better just to get a single sniper close enough – that is your way."

"You are correct, Esam. Our task is impossible. Nevertheless, it will be done." He sat back and breathed deeply. Perhaps a nap would take away the nausea.

"But master, even if we can execute the diversion and grab Whitlock, how do we keep them from tracking us?" The pudgy hands flew up in despair. "Abdul is getting nervous in London. He is running out of servers to tap for the notes my guys send. He wants a warning, so he can move before the computer trail heats up. We can risk only a few more messages."

"Esam, you have always told me your men leave no computer trail."

Kareem turned off the wide avenue into the alley. Boys with a soccer ball and big brown eyes stood and stared at the limousine.

"Of course there is no trail. But there is always a trail to the practitioner of a certain level."

"How many more messages?"

A grimace. "Let Abdul move. He suggested Glasgow."

Suhail shook his head. The blue beings insisted on harmony, and that came from steadiness. "To move an operative would not be wise. The British are watching as carefully as the Americans, you know. Abdul is clean."

Esam leaned close enough for sweat to flip onto Suhail's jacket. "There are too many transmissions going out. We know the FBI is getting them, too. The men want to know exactly how Whitlock will get the instructions of when and how to move. And if he does get them, will he move?"

The car glided to a halt. "We are home, Defenders of the Faith," Kareem said over his shoulder. "Your servant has delivered you through the dangers of the Cairo streets."

Suhail chuckled. "You are truly fearless, Kareem."

The air was miserable, but instead of reaching for the door, Suhail leaned closer to Esam. "Tell your troops two things. First, remind them that this Whitlock is smarter than they think. Do not underestimate him.

"Second. Their instructions have not changed. The woman is to be bound and gagged and delivered to a location that they will scout out, and which you will approve. When the time is right."

"Yes, sir. But I am more curious than they. Do you truly have someone on the inside besides that simpering doctor?"

Suhail smiled, and looked away. They climbed out. The early evening breeze blew warm, and Suhail strode slowly, enough so that Esam loitered at the bottom of the stairs with his impatient look. Children filled the alley, tossing toy soldiers with rag parachutes, watching them float down to the asphalt. A miniature invasion force in the failing light. Men at either end of the block rose from their stools. Two more darkened a doorway.

"Salaam," one called, and Suhail waved a greeting. Loyal troops. Truck motors ground away on the larger thoroughfare, and a single dog barked in the distance. A lonely sound. Perhaps he was that dog, for his was a lonely quest. These men, even the children, would follow any order he gave, but none of them understood the magnitude of what was at stake. Still, this was home. The only place in this dimension where he could seek solace.

"Benefactor, let me see you to your door, then I must go." Esam caught up with him. "It's getting dark, and I have calls to make from the cafe, eh?"

"I appreciate you, Colonel."

At his door, Esam's hefty hand paused in space, and Suhail immediately saw the problem. The door was not fully closed.

Too fast for a man his size, Esam yelled back down the stairs, and produced his pistol, then kicked the door in.

Though he should have stayed put, Suhail followed. With a rough swing, Esam whipped aside the black curtain that covered the pantry. It fell back into place, but in that fleeting moment, they saw it was empty.

Footsteps on the stairs.

"Close the door." A figure filled the bedroom entrance, pointing a handgun.

"Waleed." Esam hissed the name.

Cushions lay strewn on the floor. The drawers of the dresser below the television were pulled out. The entire apartment had been ransacked.

"Wait," Suhail whispered, and closed the door behind them. An immediate knock.

"Hold," Esam yelled over his shoulder. "You are outnumbered. Put the gun down, Waleed."

A twitch of the eyes indicated that the sheikh's servant was making a stand.

"Are you crazy, Waleed? Your employer made an agreement with us." Suhail raised his hands. "Please. Esam will shoot."

"And so will I," Waleed said quietly. "Your agreement is void. Where do you keep your notes? Your communications? Where is your computer?" The man's eyes moved in concise twitches, from Esam's gun, to Suhail's eyes, then back.

"You will find nothing."

"I found nothing." A deep breath, watching Esam more intently. "Your operation will now be under the sheikh's control. Esam, you are welcome to join. You may still command."

Esam took the slightest step forward, and Waleed jerked.

"My friend." Esam used a kind tone. "We have been adversaries a long time. Guns, eh? Playing dead man with trucks loaded with explosives when we were young – that was more fun. Why end it this way?"

"Because you are a fool."

Pounding on the door.

Suhail flinched, and the intruder's weapon waved in his direction. "Get back." Waleed's left hand was not visible. Holding onto the bedroom doorsill. Or hiding a grenade.

Esam straightened. "I am a fool. I should have shot you just then. You owe me an explanation before you die."

More banging. "Esam?"

"General, are you all right?"

"A moment," Esam bellowed.

Perhaps Waleed softened. Perhaps he realized he was no match for the big man. He actually started to whine. "You are a fool if you do not know what he is." A nod toward Suhail.

"He? He is the greatest general the freedom movement has. And your master is the biggest jackal. I choose to work for the cunning lion."

"He's not a lion." Amazingly, he lifted his gaze from Esam and stared directly at Suhail. "He's a witch."

"What?"

"You know the Koran. '*And there are certain men who fly for refuge unto certain of the genii, but they increase their folly and transgression.*'"

Suhail felt his blood turning to ice, but only because Esam was not pulling the trigger. This night would come out correctly, for the Blue People had so promised. But was that a splinter he saw appearing in his colonel's aura?

Esam cocked his head with a half-smile. "Well-quoted, Waleed. You are a man of God. Let me usher you to him."

"Listen to me." Desperate, short breaths. "You said yourself that his operations always succeed. Why do you suppose that is, you giant oaf? Your master is an unholy magician."

In moments of action, no one thought more rapidly, more perfectly than Esam. Now, however, Suhail watched the big man's wheels turning slowly. His own heart pounded, but he spoke quietly. "Shoot him, my friend. He has violated your commander's base."

A weak smile. "Waleed, your diversion is nonsense." Esam's pistol rose.

"It is truth. The sheikh has known it for years. The sultan. Everyone knows it but you."

"And how could such smart men believe such rubbish?"

"Damn it, Esam, don't argue with him." But the gun remained poised.

"Because they have their own witches who warn them about monsters like this." Incredibly, the nuzzle of the intruder's pistol moved from Esam's direction to Suhail's.

"Put it down, Waleed."

"Esam, shoot."

"Monsters, Colonel." Waleed's gaze remained on Suhail now. "His *jinn* are *shaytans*. Therefore his works are unholy. Come with me and work for the sheikh."

"You are crazy," Esam's voice boomed, but his eyes blinked slowly. He seemed in a daze.

Knocking. "Colonel Malik? General Farid?"

"Wait, I said." The big man was actually sweating.

Waleed's gun rose, his face contorted. "It is the duty of every believer to kill monsters--"

"Esam," Suhail said it softly. The time was now. He looked straight ahead, mentally sending a signal, calling the Blue Forms. Blinking. Once. Twice.

A loud crash echoed behind the pantry curtain.

Suhail cried, "Esam, it's a trap."

Like lightning, Esam fired his gun. Deafening blasts. Waleed danced, disappeared into the bedroom, but Esam spun around, pointing his weapon, emptying his rounds into the black curtain. A loud *crack,* and the outer door flew open. The room filled with bodies and smoke and the smell of sweat and iron-tart blood.

Suhail felt himself sink onto the couch. A man ran out of the bedroom. Kareem. Kareem was unhurt.

"He went out the window." A tug on Esam's shirt, but the big man kept coming toward Suhail. More shots – in the street. Followed by yells.

"You are hit, Suhail." The fat hands pressed a towel against his shoulder. A moan came out before Suhail could stop it. Another blast of gunfire.

"The police..." Suhail could only manage a whisper.

"There was no one in the pantry." Esam's voice was soft, understanding. He was the colonel. The colonel had disobeyed orders, but his hands were sure, caring.

"The police are coming. We will take you to the emergency hospital. Saud and Rafiq will clean up. It was an intruder, and Saud's name is on the rental."

"You are unhurt?" Suhail managed to ask. "The children downstairs? Are they all right?"

"We must hurry. Your wound is not mortal."

Hands lifted him, carried him down the stairs. The car was running, but Esam paused before closing the door. "Put those bodies in the other car," he called to someone. "Wash down the curb. Mohammed, you follow, and protect our rear."

Then all was black for a moment, and suddenly, Kareem was whipping the vehicle through the streets. "The doctors will ask questions." Suhail's breath came with difficulty, because of the unrelenting, stinging pain.

Esam pressed on the towel. "Not the hospital, Master. The clinic you built, Allah be praised. The police know nothing. Under God's mercy, this is my fault." He yelled to the front. "Abbas. Did you call?"

"They know we are coming."

Street lights flashed by. Must not lose consciousness. Suhail felt the urging, a silent calling. They would drug him, and he might forget.

Deep breaths, and Esam whispered prayers. When they stopped, he watched the blurs hustle around him, until they installed him in a beige-colored room. A doctor, dark skin, refined face, cut through his shirt with scissors.

"His shoulder may be fractured, too."

Esam was backing out of the door. "You will be all right, Benefactor. They will have you as good as new. I will send my messages."

"Good."

Nurses arrived and went about their preparations in silence, each declining to look him in the eye. An intravenous bottle was hung. Good. He had messages to send, too, before sleep overtook him.

The room grew dark. Allah be praised, the Blue Beings were quick enough. In the lightless cavern, they hovered before him as he gripped the railing weakly.

"Faithful servants. You know your target," he sent out the words silently. "Give to the infidel this message: *You are going to die.*"

Should he explain? "I must sleep, good friends. Be patient, and I promise you will soon have a taste of this heathen's life force."

Under the eaves of the great cave, a blue sphere rose and flew away. In the beige room, a man with a paper mask was saying something. He was a friend. As were the Blues.

Yet, as Suhail closed his eyes and whispered a final prayer, he could not shake the question. Why had they not warned him of Waleed's treachery? He would not go back to ask. Now was not the time.

Chapter 25
Silent Auction

"Howard Brown? Who in hell said he could come here?"

Charlie bit into a wing. Kentucky Fried Chicken Boxes littered the table, but most of the officers had taken their plates and moved out onto the patio. He spoke between crunches of crust.

"Your boss. Sullivan."

Frank sat at the end of the table, staring into space.

"Damn it. Sorry, Frank. Howard Brown and his UBC crew are not coming in here, I don't care who gave authorization. When did it come?"

"A couple of days ago."

"Shit." Daniel leaned toward the hero. "You're not ready for this, are you?"

Frank wiped his hands. Mashed potatoes on his plate lay untouched. "No, I'm not. But if it publicizes things so that even one person spots Jill--"

"Publicizes?" Daniel glanced at both of them. "Frank, if you had any more publicity – God, year-old babies in China know about the kidnapping."

The hero's expression did not break. "Mr. Clooney, not one request I've made has been listened to, so if I can't get out of here to look for Jill, I'll damned well talk to anyone I want.

Howard Brown is world-famous. He might get something
done."

"Frank," Charlie began, then said no more.

Daniel leaned back, looking up at the deepening blue
sky through the high windows, up above the drapes of the
dining room. It was a nice house. A well-to-do home of a
successful insurance agent. Clumps of the famous Bay fog
were beginning to roll in. Would Loretta answer the phone
tonight?

Noises outside. Daniel sat upright. Scuffling? No
knock, but a key clicked in the front door, and the lawmen
stood automatically. Milton, who had come out of FBI
retirement to beef up the local office, rushed in first, flanked
by Chief Burke, and Roby Thompson.

"Got something." Milton nodded, drawing Daniel into
conference. He gestured toward Chief Burke with his
clipboard. "We've been conducting the second wave of
interviews."

"Got a bogey," Burke said.

"Where? Who?"

The chief unsnapped his gun, and Roby followed suit.
A gesture. "Goddam neighbor behind us. Dr. Raed."

"Oh, fuck." Charlie tensed.

"No way." Frank yelled it, though his mouth was
finally full of food. "Leave Faris out of this." He stormed
around the side of the table. "They're old friends. Just because
Cherie--"

Daniel raised his hand. "I thought we cleared them."

Burke continued to whisper, even though Frank stood
right there. "We did, from *their* interrogation."

Roby faced Whitlock. "Frank, the doctor met with a
bad man a couple of weeks ago."

"Bullshit."

"Frank, please." Daniel grabbed Roby's sleeve to stop
their drift toward the back door. "What bad guy?"

Burke again, "Two weeks ago. One of the office nurses said a stranger came in without an appointment. Said he was a family friend, but the nurse will bet the farm he wasn't. She's got a history with the doc, I guess." A meaningful look.

"Your doctor buddy been sleeping around, Frank?"

Frank shrugged. There was that crisis three years ago. Faris had seemed – different – since then.

"The doctor was a basket case after the visit. The nurse tagged the same guy from Milton's book of photos. Positive. He's a terrorist." Burke punctuated the sentence by drawing his pistol from its holster.

"What are you going to do, John?" Frank stepped into the middle of them, crowding toward Burke. "Shoot him? Just because Jill was going shopping with his wife?"

"Frank." Daniel gripped his arm. "Your face is red. You gotta calm down." He motioned. "Go back to your bedroom with Officer Pierce. We're not shooting anyone." He frowned at Charlie, who was fingering his own weapon in its shoulder holster. Then to Milton, "Keep them alert on the roadblocks." The retiree nodded and slipped out the front door.

Pierce nudged Frank into the hall.

"What's the plan?" Charlie said in a whisper.

Burke strode through the patio doorway. Word had gotten around, and every picnicking cop had abandoned his or her plate. He spoke quietly. "Jenkins is coming from the other side. We'll go through the back gate." They collected on the patio.

Charlie nodded to Daniel. Was that a smirk? "It's your show."

Daniel extracted his own pistol and led. The team out on the next street was ready. They were barely off the patio when a shot rang out.

"Goddam. Who's the shooter?" Daniel bent over, running toward the gate that separated the two yards. Some followed, while others merged with the thick bushes along the back fence. Roby and Burke hunkered down behind Daniel at the gate.

"It came from the house," the radio on the Chief's shoulder reported.

"Do you see anything?" Burke demanded.

Daniel snapped his fingers. "Tell them to hold their fire." An engine revved on the far street.

"The armored car is here," said Burke's radio.

Daniel pushed his weight against the wooden gate and peered over. A surreal scene greeted him. A woman lounged on the diving board over the pool, her dress hanging down, her bare foot playing carefully in the water. Clouds flitted above her in the failing light, making her seem a goddess in a garden, immune from any noise, or whatever battle lay ahead.

"Jesus." He gripped the latch. "Charlie," he yelled to the side, "get a couple more." He motioned for them to follow. "Roby, there's a woman on the diving board. Get her out of the way."

"She may have a gun," Burke warned.

Daniel crouched and pushed. Several steps down the walk, he addressed the goddess. "Ma'am, go with the officer back through that gate." Roby duck-walked toward her, but she was oblivious to warnings. The pool's surface rippled, lit from below.

"Down." Daniel reached a back wall, and slid beneath the picture window. Charlie crowded behind him and a pair of unfamiliar cops.

"Door's open," the radios echoed each other.

Through the window, Daniel saw a crack of light at the front door. "Goddam it, I didn't say to go in." Hugging the wall, they tried the back door, and entered.

"Careful. No crossfire," Charlie whispered to the forms already pouring into the living room.

Pistols held high, Daniel and Charlie led the search down the hall, nudging each door, then slamming in, keeping low. First, a sitting room – no, it was an office. Desk and television – FOX News guys in a heated argument, on mute. Bedroom. Single bed. Guest room?

"Oh, no." One of the cops had leapfrogged them.

"Check the closets," Daniel ordered. Across the wide bed, in what was obviously the master suite, a man lay. Arab or Jewish-looking. The spread was soaking up blood. A black handgun lay against the man's hip. The air was hazy, illuminated by the lights outside the window. Ripe smell of gunpowder.

"Damn," the cop said. "Did his wife do this?"

Daniel shook his head and pointed at a paper on the floor. Charlie shoved his hand into a rubber glove, felt the silent body's pulse, then picked up the note.

"Listen to this." He read. "Tell Frank I am sorry. Tell him they have chosen a terrible path, but they still have honor. They will not violate Jill. Do what they say and they will not violate Jill."

He looked up. "Fuck."

"Closets are clear."

Daniel strode out slowly, his gun still hanging in his hand. On the patio – more ornate than the Whitlock's, with stone urns and a fountain – he holstered it and walked around the pool's deep end.

"Keep those goddam reporters back," Chief Burke instructed some patrolmen.

Roby stood on the textured decking, looking helpless. "She's zoned out."

Daniel knelt near the goddess, a moving statue on the diving board. The light from below made her foot black, delicate, splashing languidly, causing shadowy ripples to flee on the surface.

"Mrs. Raed?"

She was muttering. "...silent auction. Caterers on their way--"

"Are you Cherie Raed?"

"— tell them he's busy. He'll be on call tonight--"

"Mrs. Raed, would you come off of the diving board? We need to ask you some questions. Did you hear a shot a few moments ago?"

At that instant, the front gate swung open, and bright lights intruded. There was a scuffle.

Burke rushed forward. "Goddam it, I said keep them out."

The woman on the diving board looked at Daniel, a hoarish blue light reflecting in her eyes. "Let them in. They're here to set up the tents for the auction..."

Chapter 26
Broken Equipment

It's a trap. The words reverberated, closing in to suffocate him. Suhail's eyes jerked open. The world was beige, and his beard was covered with saliva, his forehead with sweat. Mediciny taste, as if a pool of Novocain had collected under his tongue, but he knew this was not the dental office. Murmurs in an adjoining room. Modern-looking computer-like consoles sat on a shelf above the bed – their screens dark.

He closed his eyes, sinking back into the events of the night before – or had he slept for days? For the first time since he was a child, at least in this world, he felt afraid. It was a trap. He could try to lie to himself, but the Blue People had let it happen, with no hint of a warning.

Flashing faces, long, hollow, and merciless. All night long those blue ghouls had hovered like vultures, crowding in, filling the spaces between his feverish fantasies. Vultures, not comrades in arms.

He fought sleep, flexing the fingers of his right hand. One by one, he catalogued his meals of the last few days. His words. His actions. Had he transgressed some promise to them? These blues were not his friends, but impatient jackals trying to entice him to make the leap over the railing. Would his eternal companions be that heartless when he joined them? Forever? The thought sent a chill through his being.

"There you are." Doctor Aziz stood at the door, wearing a gray tailored suit. He waved, and a nurse rushed in to take Suhail's blood pressure.

"With your permission," she said, and smiled sweetly.

Aziz reached for the machine on the shelf. "I apologize. This monitor is not working. But after surgery, your heart seemed as strong as a camel's." He smiled.

"Thank you a thousand times, Dabir. Allah be praised that he gives such talent to someone like you. My hand – I could not move it last night. Now even my shoulder does not hurt."

A shake of the head. "It will. That is the morphine. I want you to lie quietly, General, for a day more, at least. The nurse will give you something to squeeze, to exercise the arm. But don't over-do it."

"So he is ready to re-join the fight?" The booming voice belonged to Esam. He entered without invitation, holding a bouquet of flowers aloft. "They are from Farah's mother."

"Ah." Suhail felt tears form instantly, but held them. "I have neglected her. We must have her to tea, soon."

"And how do you feel?"

Suhail smiled, though such little exertion taxed him. "Fine, until Dr. Aziz began begging me to buy him new equipment."

The doctor laughed.

"Keep begging," Esam said. "He has friends with money."

Aziz looked at the nurse, prompting her to nod and relinquish the clipboard she was notating. "I'm sure you gentlemen have business to discuss."

"No problems with the police?" Suhail heard himself blurt out.

Aziz did not break stride, but gestured toward Esam. "He spoke with Captain Bahour." The nurse took the flowers and they left. Esam hovered at the bottom of the bed.

"They took Saud into custody, but released him this morning."

"Waleed? Dead?"

A shake of the head. "He had accomplices. One of them, one of ours." He turned and sat on a bench against the wall. "Omar."

Air rushed out of Suhail's lungs. "It is my fault. Somehow, we have been clumsy, but that is due to a failure with my intelligence agents." Indeed. How many had died in California? Mostly the sultan's men, but that should have been a warning. The Blues would not conceal something like this. Were there other forces at play? "Omar was a prince, at heart."

Tears glistened in Esam's eyes, visible even from here. "You are a great leader, because you take responsibility. The fault is mine. I knew Waleed was up to no good."

Suhail closed his eyes. Sleep tugged at him. "You are loyal, Esam. You tried to warn me."

"The blame is not yours, my general, but the sheikh's. They were looking for your notes. Osama's men are following orders and not revealing the Whitlock woman's location. So far. If they do--"

"Your meaning?" Esam's words were not making sense.

"Benefactor, they were trying to take over your entire operation. That means they are desperate."

"Mmm."

"And they will keep trying."

Suhail blinked. Esam was standing.

"You need to sleep, Master, but we must strike soon. The sheikh is not finished with us. If Whitlock dies, he wants Osama to take the ultimate credit."

"We will...strike...avenge Omar." He heard himself slurring. But not until the Blues explained their treachery? "Bah," he said aloud without meaning to, " —those creatures are like jackals--"

"Jackals?" Esam looked to Dr. Aziz. "Suhail, you must sleep. I have only one question."

"Question?"

Esam leaned close. "A thousand pardons, but Master, you have always told me that ideas come to you in dreams. Dreams, little birds, shadows, they are just figures of speech, no?"

Suhail's eyes flew wide open. "My friend, my friend," he stuttered. The sudden movement re-awakened the shoulder pain. "I am no witch," he said, focusing, trying to put the sharp stabs in a box, "– it is Waleed who has bewitched you with his trick to get away. People who cannot understand strategy explain it away as witchcraft."

Hands motioned for quiet. The pudgy face looked ashen. "Of course, Master. I was a fool. I almost got us both--"

"Enough -- Put your computer troops through a dry run. But watch out for Mubarak's spies--"

Suhail heard his own voice fade, then whispers, and heavy feet. Must rest. Sleep without the insipid audience of Blues. For all their power, perhaps a turning point had been reached. There were sayings, warnings about the Blues' treacheries. Old Amal used to sing songs about them. He was too weary to try to remember just now...

Chapter 27
Orange Star

"They could still be mistaken. Just because he resembled a picture? It might have been someone else. A cousin. An idiot salesman."

Billy Pierce lay snoring softly on the living room couch. The only lights were from the bright floodlight the police had erected in front, streaming unhampered through the high windows, and the stubby yellow walkway lights along the patio's perimeter. Someone was smoking a cigarette out there.

And the fire. Frank had put a few small logs on. The fireplace formed one side of a compact conversation pit. Daniel memorized the layout. He was starting to like this room.

"We all do that, Frank." It was his first time to sit with the hero alone since the hospital. "You know, try to look for other ways it might have been. I investigated a murder when I was fresh out of the academy. A woman. I really sympathized with her husband. Nice guy, really torn up about it. All signs pointed to him. Statistics pointed to him. Still, I argued the guy's case to people, much better than his high-priced lawyer. Then the S.O.B. confessed."

"Faris Raed did not confess."

"You read that note, Frank. I let you, even though it broke the rules. That and the bullet are the best confession you can get."

"Then they made him do it. Somehow. But why Jill?"

Convenience, Daniel might have said, but two dozen law enforcement officers were hardly a security slip. Like Waco, the perps just had more firepower. Frank rose in the dark, moved, and became a shadow in the kitchen.

"What time is it?" Daniel asked. The reporters had been gone for some time. A clink of ice was followed by pouring.

"Two A.M." The shadow returned, stepping into the nook carefully, as if the man in his fifties felt like a seventy-year-old. "I always thought they slept together. At least once."

"Who?"

"Faris and Jill."

A clue? "They couldn't get you, Frank, so they tried the next best thing. Now they send you notes trying to set up a switch. Vague directions, because they know we're listening. You haven't hidden anything from us, have you?"

The ice tinkled when he shook the glass. "Kyle reads all my e-mails. Regular mail, I rarely see. Pierce, there, answers the phone, and you're starting to sound like Charlie the asshole."

"Charlie's not so bad."

A chuckle. "Maybe not, but my wife is in a locker somewhere, and all the brains in Washington can't track down where the notes are coming from. I'd be better off throwing you bastards out and calling Bill Gates."

Daniel laughed. Perhaps for the first time since his arrival. "Frank, you might have something there."

The fire popped, as if to hush them. They stayed silent for a while. Daniel had a hotel room, but this recliner would do fine. Perhaps Loretta would hear the news and understand why he didn't call. She would be waking up soon.

"You scare me, you know?" Ice. Did he often drink this late?

"Why?" Daniel asked.

"Because I had a dream about a guy in a den of lions last night. Your name is Daniel. I think it means I should trust you."

"Tell me about your dream."

"Why? You don't believe in that shit. I think that's how you put it."

"You weren't supposed to hear that. I believe in science. My girlfriend believes you, though. Please. Tell me your dream."

"No."

"Was it the same kind of dream you had the night before the big day?"

Frank stretched his feet out. A policeman in the backyard threw his cigarette down, like a wounded firefly. "Who came up with those rumors about me on television? You know, about how I might not have landed the airplane?"

"How would I know?"

A long pause. "I just had a feeling you would."

"Did you really do the flying, Frank?"

"Hell, I had an air traffic controller and two pilots talking me down. A goddam eight-year-old could have brought it in."

Daniel wondered where, and how much he could press him. The truth lay here somewhere. "You had the good sense not to stall the plane, and you were bleeding to death at the time. Pretty incredible."

A silence. Fire hissing peacefully.

"Daniel, I'm through trying to prove it. But something makes me want you to believe it. Didn't you talk to the other guys who fought alongside me? The real heroes?"

"How can I believe that you dreamed about something seven hours before it happened? That is right, isn't it? You said you woke up at three and had already had the dream?"

Another silence. "They're going to crucify me, aren't they, Daniel? I heard it – the guys on TV were starting to go on the warpath, then Jill was snatched. That's the only reason they stopped. Please level with me."

He took a large gulp of scotch and answered the question himself. "Pretty tough to go from toast of the town, buddy-buddy with the President, talk about speeches to the U.N., Congress, everywhere all the way to this. Fucking McNee will not return my calls. They're whispering that I'm involved with the CIA, or the terrorists, and Jill..." It sounded as if the scotch was taking hold.

"Frank, please."

"She's ten years younger, Daniel. She can still have a life." There might be tears next, but the shadow only breathed deeply. "If they really think I'm a villain, why worry if I disappear? She should be sitting by this fire, instead of me."

The fire answered him with a *pop*. Daniel believed – like Loretta – that it was already too late for Jill Whitlock. But this might be his only time to find out what Frank really knew.

"Are you part of some CIA plot, Frank?"

No answer.

"How long did you work for the CIA?"

"I didn't. They wouldn't hire me." The shadow pulled his feet in and leaned forward, elbows on knees, his drink a blurry orange star in the firelight. "But I expect you know all that. They keep files on all the crackpots."

"Does it take a crackpot to board a plane you know is going to crash?"

The shadow shook his head. "You don't know shit about it, Daniel. I had a dream. It came back to me when I was in the line to board. I felt something would happen, and when they closed the doors of the plane, those dreams from the night before were ringing like bells. I knew I was in deep shit, I just wasn't sure what would go down. Sure, I saw shadows of a hijacking, but for all I knew, they might have been warning me that I might have had a heart attack. That's the way *psi* works – it's all in the interpretation, and when your own life is on the line, that's when it's hardest to read the signs."

The statement was too obtuse. "So what good is being psychic when you see something in the future, but you don't really know what it is? Is that what you're saying to me?"

"What good is it?" Frank gave a quiet laugh, and swirled the orange star. "I reacted more quickly than anyone else, didn't I? Something happens, a human's first response is, 'hey, I'm OK, nothing's really happening.' To me, I had already lived it, so I got my ass down the aisle, grabbing big, tough-looking guys to help me as I went. If I had waited five more minutes to be sure, hell, *two* more minutes, we would have been Pennsylvania all over again."

Daniel sat back. This guy was nice, even if he was guilty of something. "Sorry to be so hard on you, Frank. I just thought seers could really foresee the future."

"I tried to explain that, but the congressional committee heard only what they wanted to. Are there real seers? Ones that can really see everything, and whiz through the astral planes like an Olympic swimmer in water? Yeah. I'm convinced there are. I've even heard of one. But I'm a little leaguer compared to those guys."

A drink, and the star tinkled, now dull white. Pierce snorted and rolled over on the couch.

"I like you, Frank. And your story's tight. My inability to make the jump into fantasyland won't change the fact that we are damned well going to find your wife. I hope you believe that."

The shadow seemed to be studying the empty star, turning its solid insides round and round. "I believed before. Not now. Except, for some crazy reason, I'm supposed to trust you."

If he was ever going to break, it might be now. More pressure. "Frank? If you foresee things, why didn't you get a warning about Jill?"

"I did. Just interpreted it wrongly. I've been telling you guys, interpretation's half the ball game." The shadow stood up.

"Did you ever perform ESP experiments with a CIA operative named Gerald Sullivan?"

"Don't know him." He started up the steps.

Daniel fired again. "What did that woman, Elizabeth Kismet, tell you when she was here?"

"I told Charlie already. Read his report." The shadow was bound once more for the kitchen.

"There are too many weird twists to your situation, Frank. If I were a Hollywood movie writer, I might jump to certain conclusions. Just like the press is doing."

The shadow paused at the kitchen counter. "Some friendly advice. Stick to your day job. I'd love to stay for more sharp-shooting, Daniel, but if I did, I would need another drink. I will let you in on one thing, though."

"Yes?"

"I'm getting tired of waiting for you guys to find my wife. I've got a plan."

"A plan. You have to tell me, Frank."

"Later. There's a sleeping bag in the back room, if you're going to stay." The shadow glided toward the hall.

Pierce grunted again. Daniel eased himself back in the easy chair, watching the sedate flames and replaying the man's answers. More riddles than solutions. If Frank were CIA, he would deserve an Oscar for blowing smoke. Then again, if there were a way to sense future events ahead of time, perhaps Daniel felt it now. In his stomach. And it didn't feel good.

Chapter 28
The Anchor Man

Other than five thousand nights watching Howard Brown on the evening news while growing up, Daniel had seen the nation's father figure only once in the flesh. At an embassy party, and he had been too intimidated to introduce himself.

The UBC anchorman was quick to condemn the frisking of his crew in the driveway, but managed a smile when he walked over the threshold.

"What an entourage," Roby grumped. "He could do this with three people instead of fifteen."

"Frank didn't get any sleep," Pierce said to cops scattered through the living room. "Hope the big cheese doesn't go too hard on him."

Roby sneered. "How would you know how much sleep he got, Rip Van Winkle?"

Daniel shook his head. "His magazine show is nothing but zingers. He'll have something up his sleeve. If I give the signal, we hustle these clowns out of here, cameras first."

Frank brightened visibly when Dennis Rook, one of his fellow "instant" commandoes from flight 3456, walked through the door. The two survivors hugged.

"Boy, you Californians live the good life, huh?" Rook spoke in a New Jersey twang as he surveyed the back yard. He gripped Frank's shoulders. "What about your wife? Any news?"

"They're looking. Through the whole west coast."

"Fuckers. I hope Bush kills all of them."

"Gentlemen," Howard Brown interrupted, "your reunion is exciting, but save some of it for the camera. Let's sit over here."

The anchorman obviously liked the conversation pit as much as Daniel did. Lights and camera were already set up.

He began in a friendly enough manner, Daniel observed.

"Frank Whitlock, we wanted to talk to you, to help the American people catch up on what you've been doing. And we've brought your comrade-in-arms, Dennis Rook of Jupiter, New Jersey, so you two can recall the events of that fateful day when you and your fellow passengers won the only victory out of five battles that were fought on September Eleventh."

Rook patted Frank on the back. "He was our leader."

"And we'll get to that," Brown said, his head cocked pompously back. "But we must start with two other traumas that you have suffered, much more recently, Frank. With your permission. Of course all of America shares your agony about the kidnapping of your wife, Jill. But there was another incident last night, wasn't there?"

Frank looked pale in the monitor. "Yes, sir."

"May I ask when did you discover that your friends, Dr. and Mrs. Faris Raed were part of the plot to kidnap your wife?"

"I didn't," Frank said simply.

"Pretty impressive, here in person," Pierce whispered.

Daniel had to agree. It was gratifying how Brown dwelled on Jill, reading letters of condolence from viewers, and repeating the president's early vow that the kidnappers would be tracked down.

"With your permission, Frank." Brown extracted a new set of notes. "The nation knows the basic story, but would you mind helping us through a play-by-play, in your own words, of how that terrible flight transpired?"

Frank seemed so weary, but Brown led him through it, sensitive enough not to demand an accounting of which of the "instant commandos" – the brave citizens who had helped Frank storm the cockpit – had killed which terrorist, as if that could be determined in the melee. Instead, the veteran questioner focused on those frightening moments in the cockpit when Frank – with the terrorists already subdued – scrambled through weightless air and brought the airplane out of a deadly belly-over, an act that even seasoned pilots lauded as "improbable." Frank answered the questions in halting, clipped sentences, looking more and more miserable.

"You did have some pilot training, didn't you, Frank?"

"Yes." The hero managed a smile. "But I've said this in interviews before. My boss decided several years ago that we would increase our efficiency if we bought a plane and a couple of the salesmen learned to fly. I passed the ground test, and had four or five hours of practice in the air. Then my boss changed his mind. Too expensive."

Brown gave one of his fatherly, clarifying scowls. "Now this was in a light plane, correct? A single engine plane?"

"Yes, sir."

"And you've never had training in a large, multi-engine jet? Not even in one of those infamous simulators, like the terrorists used in Florida?"

"No, sir."

Howard Brown sat back, his face contorted into a sort of shrewd grimace. "And yet, Frank, you expect the American people to believe that you actually took control, brought a modern airliner, whose autopilot had been disconnected, out of a dive, and successfully landed it on your first approach?"

"Oh, Christ," Daniel whispered to Pierce and Roby. "Here it comes."

Frank kept his cool. "That's what happened. I had help, of course."

"Help?" Brown ruffled his notes. "What sort of help, exactly?"

"Well," Frank was thinking, then speaking, "Benny Epps, the guy I called 'Wisconsin--'"

"Oh, yes. Wisconsin. His two cousins died in the fight. He got quite a book deal." The anchorman smiled weakly.

"He's a monster." Dennis Rook chuckled. "You don't want to mess with him. I saw him in action. But, Mr. Brown, I think I see where you're headed with this--"

"If you don't mind, Mr. Rook, I wanted to know what help Frank is talking about."

Frank exhaled, puffing his cheeks out. The bright lights illuminated a trickle of sweat dripping from his temple. He pointed over his shoulder. "And this guy, of course. Behringer, LaClede, you know the names of the other commandos.

"Once I had it level, Wisconsin helped me look for an autopilot. They told me later that we found the right switch, but the hijackers had smashed the connections, like you said. You know the rest. The radio was destroyed, too, so the others got air traffic control on their cell phones, and begged the F-15s not to shoot us down."

Rook jumped in. "Then Frank sent me and others to go through the plane, looking for anyone with pilot experience, calming people down. He covered all the bases."

Brown scowled. "But they found no passengers who were pilots, did they. Frank?"

"No. The fighter pilots and the controller talked me down."

"I see."

Brown pulled out an eight-by-ten black-and-white photo. "Ever see something like this, Frank?"

"What is it?" Pierce whispered.

The hero's face darkened. "I think I saw that on television."

"Then you know what it's for, don't you, Frank?" Brown's chest seemed to swell to huge proportion. "I won't bore our viewers with the technical name, but this is a very complicated device that enables an operator on the ground to actually land a plane by remote control. Is that what really landed your plane, Frank?"

"This is bull." Dennis Rook was on his feet. "Pure bullshit." He pounded his chest. "I was there."

"Mr. Rook, please."

Rook's hands joined in supplication. "Frank, please tell him he's full of crap. Don't let them do this to you."

"Language," the cameraman yelled.

"I was there. Frank piloted that plane."

"Frank? Is what Dennis says true? Were you truly an instant commando, or were you part of some other operation?"

Frank fixed Brown with a cold glare. "Sir, I don't know how to fly an airliner, but it responded. If someone else was flying it mechanically, they were making the exact movements at the same time I made them."

"But, Frank." Brown leaned forward, everybody's best friend. "You said it yourself. You don't know how to fly a plane that large. There was no autopilot active. How could you bring it out of a spin so quickly, when the nation's best pilots doubt they could have done it?"

The goddam device wasn't even installed until the plane landed, Daniel wanted to scream, but didn't.

"I asked it."

"I beg your pardon?"

Frank's hands hovered in the air, illustrating his actions. "I braced myself under the seat. The hijacker had been subdued, but was still buckled in."

"Was he dead by then, Frank?"

"I don't know. I just braced, feet on the pedals, and reached up and around him to take the wheel. I asked the plane how to turn it, how to push the pedals, so we could pull out."

For once, America's most trusted man seemed caught off guard. "I'm sorry, Frank. Did I hear you correctly?" Pause. "You asked the plane *itself* how to fly it?"

A shrug. "Well, I know physics. I could have figured it out eventually, but there wasn't time."

"I was hanging onto a door in the galley," Rook interjected. "The world was coming at us in the window."

"Frank, you *asked* the airplane?"

"Yes. I focused. I didn't really ask the plane, itself. I asked the situation. In times of ultimate stress, that's what you have to do. The universe has the answer. You've just got to knock through all the interference and preconceptions. You know, get in touch with reality, and the answer comes. That's how I righted the aircraft."

Daniel caught himself smiling, imagining Frank saying these things in front of a packed Congress.

With a jerk, Howard Brown confronted the camera. "Well, there you have it. Though the CIA refuses to confirm or deny anything about International Airlines Flight 3456 on September Eleventh, the FBI does confirm that it removed a remote control device from the aircraft thirty-four hours after it landed at Wright-Patterson Air Force Base.

"Furthermore, UBC News has learned from reliable government sources that Flight 3456 was actually landed by someone – whether friend or foe, we can't be sure – using that remote control device.

"On the other hand, and you heard it here, the hero of the almost doomed flight, Frank Whitlock, says he landed the plane by 'asking' the craft how to land itself. I leave it to you, America, to decide what really happened. This is Howard Brown in Orinda, California."

"Goddam it." Dennis Rook was back on his feet. "You're full of shit, Brown. You sandbagged him." Lights still on, cameras rolling. "Don't you understand a fucking thing? If the country's best pilots say they couldn't have saved the plane in person, how could some yokel terrorist do it with a fucking joystick? Huh? You tell me, Brown."

Howard Brown stood, removing his lapel mike. "Mr. Rook, please calm down. I just report the facts." Daniel seriously doubted that Rook's speech would make the final cut.

Sullivan was not one to return calls unless he was pissed at you, so Daniel felt himself relax a bit as he made a highball, using the dinky bottles from the honor bar. Tonight, Charlie had the duty.

He dialed, and for once, Loretta answered.

"My God, I've been thinking about you. Has it been horrible?" she asked.

"Pretty tough. He's hiding it well, but I'm afraid the hero is disintegrating."

"I was going to ask--"

"No details. Sorry, doll, but this is an insecure line."

"Is he a nice guy?"

"Very. I don't know what to think. I've seen a lot of people stand pressure. But this – we'll see."

"Think he's a fraud?"

Daniel sipped his drink. "Jury's still out."

She paused. "I was in a meeting this afternoon."

"Yeah?"

"Ashcroft is considering whether to bring charges against Whitlock."

"Ridiculous. He doesn't have anything concrete. Does he?" Daniel said it, unsure why he sounded so convinced. The thought had been nagging him lately: Jimmy Johnson was a professional. Why would he have spilled classified beans about the remote device? Too many parts of this equation still didn't add up.

"I'll guarantee you that your boss, Mr. Bush, won't snare many votes by arresting the hero while his wife is still missing."

"Believe me, everyone's aware of that."

Silence.

"I've been thinking about you."

"You said that. Thanks for saying it. The feeling is mutual." The phone rustled on her end, and he pictured her on her bed, changing positions, and wished he could be next to her.

"He knows about us."

"Who?"

"Gerry. Today, we chatted in the hall. He asked me how you were. I never told him I was seeing you. Did you?"

"Of course not." Another sip. "What did you expect? He's in the CIA, for god's sake."

"It's getting pretty depressing here. Today, I had to draft letters for the president's signature. Going to parents of soldiers who have died in Afghanistan."

"Ouch."

"They killed that journalist."

"I heard. Still, it's going pretty well, isn't it?"

"The war? Yeah. Amazing, how well. I'm still worried."

"Afraid of more terrorist attacks in the capital?"

"Afraid of Gerry. I've know him long enough to be afraid of what he might do. I think I want you back here for protection, then I realize he might just sabotage your career." Her voice was so soft.

"Forget him." He should also warn her about what to expect on Brown's show tomorrow night, but he wasn't in the mood for another argument.

"I'm serious, Daniel. When we were standing together in the West Wing today, he had that look."

"I told you to forget that look," Daniel said. Another sip of bourbon, and he settled down in the pillows. "What are you wearing?" he asked. After a moment, she laughed.

Chapter 29
Computer Troops

The city center of Heliopolis was not that familiar to Esam, but he felt a nostalgic freedom walking through the side market streets. He could be a boy again, tugging at his mother's shawl, arm-in-arm with his friend, Hani. Smells attacked his sucking nostrils, and he reveled in them. Wallowed in naked sunshine, recalling the odor of crispy *schwarma* hovering on spikes above pits of leaping fire, waiting for the butcher to carve off a workingman's lunch. Just like these hanging before him. For the first time in years, it seemed, he felt almost carefree. Like a citizen rather than a rat flitting from one dark hole to the next in too much haste. To hurry was to ignore life.

He entered the strange café and felt another rebirth. The room was light, filled with sun from open windows and smiling faces. The opposite of Suhail's favorite haunt, always so dark and dowdy, full of morose, cadaver-looking men.

Abdul Assam and Abdul Saleh beckoned from a table against the wall. They smiled.

"My friends." Esam kissed them. "You look like two schoolboys sneaking away for lunch instead of the premier computer hackers of the Orient."

Assam pointed at Saleh. "He is not of the Orient. See his blue jeans?"

"My robes were dirty." His was a mocking tone. They laughed.

"Ah, youth." Esam passed his hand over their steaming cups of tea, ordering one for himself. "What are you both doing with your youth today? If I had not called, would you be looking for wives?"

Now Abdul Saleh did the pointing. "Not he. He is through looking since Hooda took his shoes."

"Shut up."

Esam laughed. "Why would a young woman be interested in your filthy shoes?"

Assam shrugged, and flipped open a small notebook. It was no insult. These two were often scribbling figures or formulas, and showing them to each other, even while they stayed with the conversation. At first, it irritated Esam, then he realized they were insufferable geeks. "I wore them only once. Now she thinks that if I let her keep them, I am interested."

"You'll be dead." Saleh wagged a finger. A sly wink to Esam. "Hooda's father once spoke to Assam about her older sister, Salma. He ignores things like that." Back to Assam. "Some people take a nod as a contract, idiot."

Assam seemed about to taunt him in return, but changed the subject. "Colonel, we were just talking about relocating. We think that if you moved us to Istanbul, there would be enough server routes to allow us to hide our origin indefinitely."

"Why not Rome?" Esam had been waiting for this. He turned icy, as command often required. "Are you afraid the Americans will come knocking at your door? It will be much easier for them in Rome. Or Istanbul."

For once, Assam started to scowl. Good. If these two computer geeks had some spirit let them show it. The landlord brought the new cup, and they were all quiet until he left. "Colonel Malik, don't insult us by thinking we wish to run. Mubarak's merchant class cannot keep up with the times.

Almost any place in Europe will have better broadband support than we have here."

Esam sipped, and held up his hands. "I am accusing no one of anything, young soldier. Your language tells me you are still infected with notions of class warfare. Remember your roots and honor them. This--" He glanced around the shop. "—is a land of opportunity."

A look passed between them. Esam reached across, tapped the notebook that Assam always kept nearby. "You never keep our schedule in your book, there, do you?"

Assam snapped to a sort of attention. "Of course not, Colonel." He tapped his temple. "We keep those up here."

"Things may change." Esam held the warm mug in both hands, gazing above it, surveying the other customers.

"The messages? You want them altered? Are there new plans?" Saleh seemed agitated.

Esam turned his mug back and forth. "Tactics may change. That is none of your concern. But I have new messages today, and will have more soon." He took a slip of paper from his shirt pocket and slipped them between the pages of Assam's notebook. "You must transmit them immediately, and let me know, using the river drop, if you do not succeed in delivering them."

"Of course, Faithful One."

So trusting. Such bright eyes, these young goats. But perhaps the kids were growing into rams. "I still don't see it. Why don't they just pull the plug on the man's computer?" Esam said it to the air. "Are Americans so addicted to their machines?"

"Yes, I think so." Saleh had just the right irony in his voice to bring their smiles back. He continued. "Sahib, we are not frightened. But someday, we may be forced to relocate – under your direction, of course. They are trying to track us down. We can see them monitor the messages, and they throw bait back at us. It is almost comical. They cannot penetrate our decoys."

"Yes, but perhaps Whitlock, himself, never sees the messages, anyway," Esam said.

Assam shrugged. "Colonel, General Farid assured us the infidel is reading every one of them. I wanted to ask about that – how could he know, unless he has someone on the inside? And how long until his insider discovers your inside man?"

Esam fought to contain his anger. "Abdul Assam, you know never to mention our insider to General Farid."

"Of course, my Colonel." Both boys were bristling at everything. Not good.

"Yes, Saleh? You have something to add?"

"No, sir. It's just that both you and the general have exhorted us to find ever-new ways of delivering your messages, which we have done so faithfully. But we are of the new generation. Yes, we follow orders, but we also have a drive to innovate, to use the new knowledge our fathers never had."

"Be careful," Esam said so loudly that heads turned. "There was nothing lacking with your fathers' knowledge. Faith and obedience are the ways to Allah."

"Yes, sir."

The youngsters bowed their heads, and Esam let them think for a moment. Thinking for yourself was like a disease that the computers carried. Wars were not won by iconoclasts.

"Istanbul, eh?" He laughed, to break the tension. "What would you like there, a spacious flat full of musky Turkish women?"

Weak smiles. He could only hope that they did not read him – these two would never be allowed to leave the country. But Saleh's face showed new excitement. "Something else, Son of Omar?"

"Colonel, you would never regret it. Here, we are known too well." Saleh fairly jumped, and words began flowing out of his mouth, while his face turned crimson. "The university is overflowing with rumors. A professor at school was arrested. He may tell things, because I am certain he does not have the cause in his heart."

"What is the professor's name?" The question seemed to shake the boy.

"Please. He is fine. Not important. We only went back to pay a visit last week. He asked questions about our software business, and then--"

"You must tell me this man's name if he is a security risk."

"Please, Sahib." Saleh glanced over his shoulder, cheeks red to the bursting point, as if suddenly wary of the people in the room. "Professor Saba. Computer Sciences. Please do nothing to him."

"That is for someone older than you to judge. And what is this talk about Istanbul?"

Saleh motioned. "Assam has cousins there."

"Ah, yes. I forgot that we are working with a half-breed." Esam laughed, then reached to pat the boy's forearm. "Don't worry. You will achieve your goals here, and later in life, will have enough money to travel where you wish. And it will be an Arab world."

He clapped his hands. This brought the landlord, and so more tea was ordered. The day, the fresh smells, the new path that was taking shape – Esam reminded himself not to be too hard on them. They had no idea of what was to come. His master was still Suhail, and a commander showed his troops power at all times. In an instant, he changed his grin to a frown, and lowered his voice.

"These messages now. Then, by the start of next week, you will receive a series of three new ones from me, and the exact timing of their release. You must have your channels arranged, and clear. My instructions will be succinct. Even if they seem strange, even counter to what I have told you before, execute them exactly." The two exchanged a meaningful glance, but he held up a hand. "No, don't try to guess what the plan is. With the general, it is always the unexpected. Neither of you is new to the cause, so don't forget how crucial absolute silence is."

"Of course." Saleh stared into his cup. "But are we part of the next great strike, Colonel? It has been long in coming. Is this the operation--"

Esam snapped his fingers. "Do not let your mind wander from your orders. Ask no more questions, or you will find yourself in another branch of the freedom fighters."

Assam buried his face in his hands. "Allah be praised."

Saleh raised his cup. "We will be ready when you call, Defender of the Faith."

Esam finished his drink and stood. In turn, he gripped the hands of each boy between his own larger, rougher ones. "My faithful twenty-first century soldiers. Godspeed to all of us."

Chapter 30
Blackmail

"Did you see Howard Brown tonight?" Daniel was surprised Sullivan had answered his phone at all.

"Saw it." The gloating note in his voice confirmed it all. "Old Howard Brown to the rescue. I've been friends with Howard for years, you know. Better a news anchor as hatchet man than Bush or Ashcroft. What about you? Did they edit out any good parts?"

"Sorry, didn't have time to watch," Daniel said. "We've been planning for tomorrow's raid all evening. But I saw the taping. I know Frank has no more credibility."

"Oh, come now. There are enough nuts out there who will always believe his ESP malarkey – too bad if I'm stepping on toes. You almost sound sorry for the guy."

"He's a good person, Gerry."

"He's dirty. Get that through your head. We just gotta find out which terrorists he's connected with."

A pause. What if Frank were telling the truth? "Sure. But that airplane remote control thing doesn't hold water."

"Technology, my boy. Are you leading the operation tomorrow?"

"Gerry, we're on a cell phone, remember? FBI has the lead."

"God. Not Thornton."

"No. New guy who just flew in. Carpenter."

"Will Carpenter? I've met him. Good man." Why did that commendation bring Daniel no joy? "Good luck, Daniel."

"I'll tell Charlie you said hello."

"You do that."

He kept the television on "mute" and extracted the bottle of bourbon he had bought. He didn't want to drink all of it, but it was a hell of a lot cheaper than the honor bar liquor. With a drink in one hand, he dialed the phone again. If there was a God, perhaps she missed the interview altogether.

"Hi. Thanks for picking up. Got an early wake-up tomorrow, and just wanted to hear your voice."

"I've been crying for an hour." She sounded far away. "Since the interview. Old Howard finished him. Why did you let him destroy Frank, gut him like that for all the world to see? Why, Daniel?"

"I wish you wouldn't say that --"

"Why not? You're there aren't you? Gerry sent you to push his agenda, and you're being a good little lapdog, aren't you? Come out and tell me, Daniel. If that's where your heart lies --"

"Stop it, Loretta. You're mad at me for the actions of others. I'm trying to find Frank Whitlock's wife. It wasn't me who sent for Howard fucking Brown. Besides, the public won't desert Frank so easy."

"That's not all I was crying about. I had lunch with Gerry today."

Daniel peered at the blue of the television through the tumbler of whiskey. "Oh? Sounds like you're seeing a lot of him."

"Don't say that. Nothing happened. Except that he's trying to blackmail me."

"That's crazy."

"I can go back with him, and keep my career alive. If I don't, I'll be looking for work elsewhere. Not in the White House. Not in Washington."

"He doesn't run HR for the White House. What could he possibly have on you?"

"Doesn't have to have anything. One word is all he needs to say. He's connected."

"Come on, Bush likes you."

"So what? The president won't know about it until I'm already gone. Daniel, he scares me."

"Ignore him. You're with me, now. He's all talk."

"No. I came home today, and my house had been broken into."

"Shit. Did you call the cops?"

"No. When Gerry and I first hooked it up, we joked about him being in the CIA way back when. He supposedly had an alias, named Monroe Louisiana."

"So?"

"A window was forced open. On my bed was a map of Louisiana, with a circle around the city of Monroe."

Daniel exhaled, already inventing ways to get back at the bastard. "I'm sorry, Loretta. I should be there for you. But keep the map. If other people knew his alias, then we might do a little blackmailing of our own." A stupid thing to say over the cell phone. Besides, this wasn't the time to stoop to Sullivan's high school-like mentality. He had to be sharp – just a few hours from now.

Silence.

He used the remote to switch off the television.

She finally spoke. Wistfully. "It doesn't matter. I've been wanting to get out of here anyway. I hate people who set conditions in a relationship, but here it is: My condition is that I'm leaving. You have a career here. I'm not asking anything, but Arizona is sounding better and better to me."

In the background, there was a soft buzzing that seemed strange. Whoever was eavesdropping was being sloppy. "Fuck Gerry," he said, loudly, so it would be clear on the tape. "You know what I would do to you if you were here?"

"Daniel, stop. No more phone sex. It just reminds me how far away you are."

He whispered, giving his voice its most seductive timbre. "If you're leaving Washington, babe, you're going to have to get used to phone sex."

Chapter 31
The Source

Go to the Source. It had been a long time. Suhail mused, propping his feet, trying to feel relief – but the breeze was unseasonably warm.

"Would you like an orange drink, Master, before I leave?"

He started. "Muuji. I thought you were already gone. Yes, I would love one, if you insist on being my mother."

"If I were your mother--" the voice faded into the unlit kitchen, and when Muuji returned, he also held a bottle of pills, shaking them. "You mother would not let you forget your afternoon dosage, Defender of the Faith."

Suhail read the directions for the twentieth time. Medicine was a foreign substance. Like British oil workers in the desert. The body should heal itself or not be healed. Had not the human race survived before the invention of all these new poisons?

"Thank you," he said, and washed the capsule down with the sweet liquid. "Where is Esam? I expected him yesterday."

Muuji clutched his own shirt, as if about to rend the buttons apart. "Master, he is busy. Something about the computer messages. He thought it would be wise to cease transmission for a day or two." The young man turned pale – he had said too much.

"Stop them? Interesting. I remember giving no such order."

"I'm not sure, Master Farid. Perhaps I heard it wrong."

Suhail smiled. "Don't worry. And say nothing of it. Send for Esam. Perhaps he had good reason. An army does not flinch just because the top general is wounded."

"Yes, General. I spoke out of turn. I am a fool."

"You are truthful, and a sparkle in Allah's eyes, Muuji."

He sipped the drink slowly, listening to the sounds in the street below. Children calling, a truck unloading at the market in the corner. Esam seemed surrounded by a cloud just now, but Suhail had only himself to blame. He had stayed away from the Source for too long.

Weeks? No, in the name of the Redeemer, it had been months! Too caught up in the excitement of planning the end game against the Americans. Another wave of Osama's sleepers jailed on America's west coast, it was reported, but Suhail's men remained untouched. It would not remain so forever. The Source would rejuvenate him.

He slammed a fist into the cushion. A detour. The kidnapping of Whitlock's woman was the detour, a cheap diversion. Why had he never realized this before? The Blues were shifty. Ask any holy man – but their messages had always been so true to him, he had never really believed it. A mistake. In that other, vast world, he should trust only the Koran, and The Source.

But was it really the Blues who first sanctioned the wrong kidnapping? Suhail buried his head in his hands. No – Esam. The big man had come back, saying the sleeper could only deliver the woman. My God. A circus trick. A chance for a clean kill was muddied, just because the fat man was nervous, in a hurry. The Blues never really sanctioned such a long, drawn-out diversion, though they were quick to go along with it.

His breaths came quickly, on their own, and he fought for calm. He couldn't blame Esam, for he, himself, had been too blinded by jealousy to see the thoughts tucked menacingly behind those blue countenances. Fool. When an operation hit a major obstacle, it must be aborted. Instead, he had gone along, slavering to make a bigger splash than Osama.

Too far into the folly now. Since he had started this kidnapping, he should at least – no!

Suhail hit the cushion again, biting on his tongue. How to pick the jewels out of the shit? There was no way to win this game without a visit to the Source, but how could he hope to gain an audience with such mistakes marking his soul?

He breathed, loudly and labored, at first. The stay in hospital had done him no good. The shoulder still occasionally hurled lightning bolts through his very being, but he would not take painkillers, only antibiotics. After a protracted struggle, the noise of his own lungs, as well as those from the street, faded into darkness. He opened his eyes and stood – as one never injured at all – with his hand on the railing of the great cavern.

He felt himself smile. The gift was still his. This ominous, tainted, underworld felt like home. On the vast floor below, the smooth blue vessels shifted. Were they saying "welcome?" Or "beware?" Or both? One thing was certain – they knew his wish already, for it floated above their heads like a murmuring mist.

With a careful hand, he gripped the rail and walked the rocky ledge above them for many meters, holding on, attempting to quell his nervousness. His only solace was the rule, and he kept repeating it to himself: they MUST grant his wish, and deliver him to The Source. But the power of his journey was not his to control. It must come only from them. Their power. That was why he must be ever so careful. Their treachery was tangible in the air.

It was a trade of convenience. He forfeited his own heavy earthly energy into their vapid waves of tittering below the ledge, while they returned the gift with a jolt of their airy lightning. He told himself to quit analyzing. Even so, he fairly jumped out of his skin when he noticed a Blue Being striding beside him, walking exactly as a man would walk.

"Old Friend." Not a voice proper, but a wave of feeling that washed over, leaving Suhail giddy. The strange, long face smiled at him. "You have finally returned, Man of Allah." The feelings continued.

Suhail steeled himself. "Stop your flattery, Prince of Afrits," he yelled at the lanky form. "And do not invoke the name of Allah unless you are prepared to do God's work, and not tricks for your own ends."

Suhail's strong, disciplined emotion made the afrit retreat a short distance. "Of course, Suhail Farid. We are happy to see you among us again."

"I am not among you, but separate." To agree with his kind was to put oneself at risk. "I am alive and well in the world Allah created. So come forth. Do you sincerely wish to do his work?"

A wave passed through the teeming forms below, like a sigh of yearning. "It is what we live for, Master Suhail. But so few travel here to invite our service."

More flattery was being slotted, like artillery shells being shoved into hot guns. Suhail felt it, but he had the vibration now, and barked out commands. "Then serve. Take me to the Sand Advisor. The Source. I require immediate answers."

"Of course, Suhail of the Amber People."

A wave of lightning slipped out over the Blue masses, illuminating the tops of the cavern with an azure vapor, and the Afrit Prince was gone. Suhail leaned against the rail, wanting to hold on, avoid the rush that he knew was to come—

Another flash of blue lightning, and the teeming, agitated, spherical bodies below him started to swirl, and his fingers let go of the railing. His body was carried aloft, toward the rocky, oozing cavern ceiling, up and above the mass of thirsty blue monsters, then forward, through the interminable tunnels of the jinn's world. Suhail closed his eyes, said a prayer, and didn't open them until he felt his feet touch the hard sand. When he did, the vision that filled his gaze also filled his heart – he had come home.

The Advisor of the Sand, an aging man – he might be perhaps seventy or even ninety – sat smoking a hookah only three meters away, his body resting on a worn rattan settee. The room he lived in was made of stone, but smooth. It was a cave, or a sturdy stone house made long ago. Suhail had never ventured outside on his visits here, so he couldn't be sure.

For a moment, he could only watch, stunned at the memories that began to flood his mind. He had spent a lifetime here, at the feet of this holiest of holies, but when one left, the Source's magic made one forget almost everything, save the memory that you were here for a few moments, and, if one were pure, the answers to one's questions.

It was like remembering artifacts of childhood: the old man's heavy stone table, threadbare Persian rugs, his antiquated brass weapons, polished and leaning against the wall. A certainty returned, as it always did: he was standing here, peering into the house of a seer of another time. Long ago, maybe even hundreds of years.

"My Master." Suhail fell to his knees, clasping hands together, then prostrating himself, as if at prayers. "If you would grant me your wisdom."

The hookah gurgled, and a pungent smoke settled on the floor around Suhail's head. The Sand Advisor stared past him, with old cataract'd eyes. The pipe stem left yellow-brown lips, and the Source coughed. "And have you already sought for these answers yourself, my son? Are you lazy?"

"Great one, it is I, Suhail Salim Farid, and I need counsel only because I have been fool enough to stay away from your wisdom for many months." He looked the Advisor straight in the eyes, but could not dissect their glazed quality. The old vizier obviously possessed sight, but would never react to any of Suhail's movements.

Another gurgle of the pipe. "What are these questions?"

Brief. Not an iota of ego, Suhail reminded himself. He remembered the sting of coming to this man with a mind full of boasting and notions. Only humbleness was permitted here.

"Should I release the woman or kill her? Will we be able to trade for her husband? What will do America the most harm, and the freedom fighters the most good?"

He collapsed back to the floor, as if speaking here were an experience of heavy gravity. From that lowly position, he twisted his head up and watched.

A puff of smoke. Calm hands covered with calluses and cracked skin. There seemed to be article of a game of sorts on the table – wooden pieces on a flat wooden plank.

"These are not your questions, Sahib Farid. You mean to ask only, what is Allah's will?"

"Of course, Master, for that is all that matters."

"You will not be able to trade her without difficulty."

"More difficulty than--"

A hand rose, though it was held in a direction ninety degrees from Suhail. "By difficulty, I mean that you are locked in combat with a mortal enemy. You will not succeed unless one of your enemies helps you."

Suhail pushed up and sat on his heels. "I will not work with infidels, nor ask their help."

The Advisor's gray eyebrows raised. He laid the hookah stem down and rose. As he shuffled toward the room's bright opening, Suhail glanced around. A bladder – full of something – hung on the wall, and below it, a smooth wooden staff lay as if it had fallen to the floor. The Advisor didn't reach for it, but looked this way and that, never setting his gaze directly on Suhail. "If an infidel fights beside you against your enemy, he is your ally, even if you deny him honor. Die in battle together, and Allah will judge you together, whether you like it or not."

The words hit Suhail's heart like sharp darts.

"But there is one more question, isn't there?" The Advisor leaned against the hut's doorway. Outside, the sun appeared to be setting over a flat plane of sand. Closer in, a lone camel stood on a tether, humbly chewing a branch of scrub.

"Will Esam betray me?"

"He already has."

Suhail felt a shudder. Yes. He already knew that. A question had been wasted, and he felt his face flush with embarrassment.

The Advisor extended a hand out into the open air. "I sense you are disappointed," he said. "Don't be. Everyone betrays everyone else, eventually, for we are all bent to our own causes." Another weighty look. "It is the same with the *Blue Jinn*. Their cause is not the same as yours. So beware, my son."

One did not have to breathe in this realm, but the feeling that rocked Suhail back on his heels was that of losing breath. Or perhaps his soul had been knocked from his body. That was the question – the real thing he wanted to know, but had not been able to voice.

"But my alliance with the Jinn – that is what makes my leadership unique –" Suhail felt his own voice fail. Useless to argue, for he had always known this truth, too.

"Grieve not for petty betrayals," the Advisor continued, with the faintest hint of a smile. "But to betray Allah, now that is a sin."

Suhail swallowed. His last question, he had asked before. "Will I find enlightenment in this life? Will I ever be given audience with one of the immortals?"

The old man turned, and shifted back toward his chair, wearing a wisp of a smile on his face. "Those answers are the same as they have always been, Suhail Salim. Allah grants enlightenment to him who opens his heart.

"And He grants audiences with the immortals to those who are meek. Such an audience comes when one least expects it, and such a meeting cannot be lobbied for. When it happens, the pure of heart are ready. But you know this rule."

"But how can I remember?" Suhail blurted into the air. "The purity of your world is hard to hold onto back in that hurricane of sin that my people live in."

The Sand Advisor returned to the pipe, placed the stem between parched lips, and the hookah gurgled. Now, a true smile. Suhail already knew that answer, too. The purer his heart, the more he might remember –

Suhail's eyes opened with a jerk. Children laughed in the street below, and the wind chimes sang on the next balcony in the warm afternoon breeze.

Chapter 32
Guns at Sunrise

Fog flitted above the already crowded freeways, but thankfully, it was high enough not to cause problems, and the convoy was outward bound, the right direction to go at this hour. Daniel couched a paper coffee cup between his hands, trying to wake up. It had been over two years since he had been on an actual raid, and he hoped this would not be another Waco, where they lost all the bad guys, and hostages, too.

"You know they are heavily armed," said Will Carpenter, as if reading his mind. Everyone had been reminded that this guy commanded the FBI's premier SWAT team for two years, and he was the sole person standing up in the back of the van, seeming to disdain the motley grouping of police and sheriffs' deputies he had been stuck with. The rest of the FBI forces across the country were drawn too tight to have it otherwise.

"Shit," Billy Pierce said during a lull. "I hate these operations. It's too easy for them to plug the hostage. How do you get surprise on a goddam farm?"

"That's why you're staying in the rear, Officer." Carpenter had obviously learned his version of tact on the SWAT team. "And that's why we're going in the dark. Just watch out for booby traps." He peered out the small rear windows. "My guys can get closer than you would believe, except for booby traps."

Daniel propped one foot up, and looked across to Sheriff Bozell. "You say you know the property?"

A nod. The man's mind seemed a steel trap compared to Police Chief Burke. "North end of the county. I was a deputy up here, before I moved down to Contra Costa. Used to be a Japanese family. Vineyards. Then some Syrians moved in. Called themselves Syrians, but we knew one of them was from Yemen. Wasn't that big a deal at the time. Had a bunch of kids and no furniture. Head guy also owned a convenience store."

"Christ," said Pierce. "Hope we don't shoot any women and children."

Carpenter looked disgusted. "Don't."

Naylor, one of three FBI guys who had come from D.C. with Carpenter, was yelling from the van's passenger seat. "OK, Commander, we're getting onto the farm road. Team Alpha is three miles. Beta is suiting up. They've spotted one lookout."

"How far from the house?" Carpenter bit his lip repeatedly. "That means we have to neutralize him. And if he's got a radio, it could be trouble." The van suddenly swerved, forcing him to brace against the wall.

"Stop. Stop," Naylor screamed.

In one motion, Carpenter unlatched the back and they all swarmed out. Daniel's boots hit the pavement. He tossed his coffee cup to the road's shoulder, and they swung out to surround a large gray sedan in the opposite lane.

Daniel pushed up behind the sheriff. Naylor was asking questions of the terrified driver.

"What is your name?"

"Podolsky." He was pale, lit by a large flashlight beam, and his outstretched hand shook so noticeably that his driver's license slipped out of it and fell to the road.

"What are you doing here?"

"Going to work. I own a jewelry shop in Fairfield. Far West Street."

"Oh, yeah." Sheriff Bozell elbowed forward. "I've been in your store. Couple of years ago."

A weak smile. The wide eyes focused from one lawman to the next. A cop tapped a back window.

"What are these cases you have all covered up, back here?"

Mr. Podolsky cleared his throat. "Rings. Jewels. I take them home every night. But please don't tell anyone. I'm buying a safe in three months." He kept looking around, perhaps searching for another friendly face. Daniel watched. If this guy had been lugging valuables home in his car for years, was he always this frightened?

"Pop the trunk," Naylor said.

"Forget it." Carpenter stepped into the middle of the gathering, shooing the others back toward their vehicles. "It'll be light soon."

The driver accepted his license, and fumbled, preparing to start his car again. Daniel stared at Carpenter. Wondered what he was really thinking. Then he pushed past the senior officer, leaned into the window, and grabbed Mr. Podolsky by the shoulder.

"Give me your cell phone," he demanded.

"Clooney, get your ass in the van."

"Wait," Sheriff Bozell said. "He's right."

Podolsky was more panicked than ever, and handed his cell phone through the window. "I don't have many numbers in my directory. My family--"

"Can it," Daniel said. "I'll return this to you later today."

"Clooney. You're out of line. Give the man back his phone."

"I'll take that." Bozell grabbed the phone, put it in his own pocket, then pushed his own girth up in front of Carpenter's height. "Agent Clooney's right. Just a little insurance." To Podolsky: "I'm sure you're a hard worker. Just go to work and we'll return this later."

Daniel jogged past Carpenter's hostile gaze, and climbed back into the van.

"Jewelry," Pierce said under his breath. "He's going to work a little early, ain't he?"

After a short, bumpy ride, they pulled up on a gravel road, well hidden from the surroundings by a cluster of hills and trees. When they got out, Carpenter waved them up a path and took a radio from a patrolman's hands.

"What's the status on the lookout?" he asked.

"We've spotted two." The whisper came between crackles. "Moving into position."

"I'm watching Cherry," another speaker interrupted. "He's inside the perimeter."

"No night vision on those guys, right?"

"No equipment besides rifles. Automatic."

"Ten-four." Carpenter handed the radio back, and glanced at Daniel through the murkiness. "There will be casualties," he said, his mouth tight.

"Ho," the radio voice said. "They're running. Lookouts are moving."

"Fuck," Carpenter said. "Something tipped them." Instantly, they were all jogging, quick-time. Daniel tried to keep his footing in the darkness.

"Get the forward guys down," someone whispered into a radio.

"Go. Go."

They crested a hill just in time to see the yellow flashes of a weapon through wisps of fog. Loud reports came an instant later.

"Crap." Daniel crested a hill, and headed for the cover of a pile of ancient fence posts. More gunfire.

"Yep, an automatic," Chief Burke said, well behind Daniel. "Not quick enough. If she's in there, she's gone."

In the small valley, the lone farmhouse was flanked by what looked like cars or machinery. Flashes from the windows. Bangs. Daniel extracted his pistol, and stooped, leap-frogging with Pierce and Bozell, winding up behind a birch tree. In faintly increasing light, he thought he saw a form lying on the ground in front of the house. Friend or foe?

"Gully," someone yelled. Daniel turned in time to see a cop tumble into the ditch to one side. With effort, he jumped over it, then flattened out in the grass. Suddenly, all farmhouse windows flashed awake, and a deafening roar echoed against the hills.

"Concussion grenade." Charlie's voice, off in the grass to the left. Another flurry of shots, then it was over. Moving bodies swarmed the lawn. Daniel leaped over a fallen tree trunk, then up the rise.

Two black-suited men wearing flak jackets galloped toward him. "Not here," one cried. "Down the creek." They were past him, but Daniel wheeled and followed.

A bullet whizzed past, and he rolled.

"Where?" one SWAT guy asked.

"Trees." Daniel pointed toward the thickets on the far side of the creek. Dawn was coming quickly, but he still had been able to spot the barrel's flash. He dove behind a large rock.

Far up the rise to the left, another team member stood and sprayed the thick underbrush with fire from a small automatic. Shots answered from below, and the SWAT guy went down.

"There are two of them," Daniel yelled at the crouching men. In unison, they fired toward the woods, though they were still at distance.

Then all was a hail of bullets. Flashes came from the bush. SWAT members swarmed down the hill in force. Bullets whizzed overhead, and a helicopter approached from the south, a man leaning out, firing with a rifle.

Then one of the perpetrators moved, becoming visible under a tree just before he buckled and tumbled into the gravel of the creek bed.

Another shot, and his comrade crashed out of the brush. Daniel braced and aimed, but the guy wasn't charging – he was down.

Carefully, the SWAT guys picked their way down the hill. Daniel waited until he saw them talking near the fallen bodies, then turned up toward the house. Near the structure's back steps, a lone woman sat in the grass, tears streaking her face. She wore American jeans, but her head was covered by a Muslim-type scarf. Her hands were cuffed, but the two female SWAT members who flanked her had let her keep them in front rather than behind.

Sheriff Bozell dodged through the milling bodies toward Daniel. "Not here."

"Any sign she was?"

"They think so. Carpenter has the Orinda guys looking through the debris."

"How many did we get?"

"Five. All Middle-Eastern, by the looks. of them." Bozell hiked one foot up onto a tree stump. "By God, they weren't going to be taken alive." A nod. "How many got away down there?"

"Two down. That's all, I think."

"They were freedom fighters," a voice said. They turned. The woman blinked at them.

"What?" Daniel asked.

"Do not think badly of them." Tears kept coming down. "It was their duty."

Bozell crowded in. "Was it their duty to kidnap an innocent woman?"

Daniel waved him back and squatted near her. "Was Mrs. Whitlock here?"

Tears came until she closed her eyes. A nod.

"Where did they take her?"

"I don't know."

Billy Pierce walked up. "She was here." A gesture toward the house. "Her shirt. I recognized it. They got out in a hurry."

Daniel rose and faced the sheriff. "That Russian. The jeweler. Put out an all-points bulletin."

Bozell blanched. "Shit." He motioned, and a deputy followed him to one of the cop cars that had materialized on the long driveway.

Carpenter was yelling orders, loudly instructing seasoned cops on how to protect a crime scene. Two ambulances rumbled up the dirt road from the fence line. Daniel ignored it all, walking slowly out into the pasture. His father had taken him hunting on mornings like this. Those were the only times the old man really seemed alive. Certainly the only times he seemed to relax, tramping through the weeds, calling over his shoulder for Daniel to fetch the fallen birds. In a strange way, Daniel had always associated sunrise with the sound of gunfire.

Chapter 33
Meeting in the Bedroom

"Oh, Christ, it's a fucking circus." Charlie's hair was pasted on his forehead with sweat. Daniel climbed out of the black-and-white first. The milling bodies at the farm were a picnic compared with the throng of onlookers outside the Whitlock house.

A man wearing knee-length shorts and a sky-blue shirt accosted them in the middle of the street. "Are you guys cops?" he asked, but did not wait for an answer. "I've seen you hanging around. Here. Deliver this." He wheeled and pointed at the second house on the side street. "In case you want to know, I live there."

Daniel took the stapled sheet of paper.

"Mr. Clooney."

"Mr. Thornton."

Reporters shifted, like a gaggle of geese, away from the uniforms at the curb. "Can you tell us what happened in Solano County?" "Do you have new leads?"

"Mr. Clooney, did someone tip them off?"

Daniel waved and they jockeyed through to the driveway.

"What does it say?"

Daniel pried open the staple and read. "Regular bitching."

An elderly lady held a plate of brownies near the mobile home, refusing to relinquish it until Frank came out. "The neighborhood has a schism," Daniel said. "Some want the hero out, some are more forgiving."

Inside, Whitlock and a cop were involved in a tug-of-war over a suitcase.

"Come on, Frank. It's not definite."

"Let go" The hero looked madder than Daniel had ever seen him. "Daniel," he pleaded, "they called and said I was going to testify before Congress. Charges may even be filed, and these assholes won't let me start packing."

"Officer." The man's nametag read *Soto*. "Let him pack the case."

Frank jerked it away, but instead of rushing down the hall, he looked up. "You missed her. By an hour? How long? Is she alive?"

"An hour," Daniel said. "A day. I don't know. The trail is hot, Frank."

"Is she alive?"

"I don't know. They're chasing a lead now. I'm sorry."

"That's not good enough, Daniel." The hero seemed an inch away from being frantic. He looked down at the suitcase. "Lose any agents?"

"One. So far."

"Sorry to hear it." Frank stalked into the hall.

The living room was filled by a throng of milling cops, and but the noise of the angry neighbors outside had grown louder. "We've got to get some order here," he told Charlie. "See where we are. I want Whitlock to hear this, too. Get reps from each branch back in his bedroom in ten minutes, OK?"

"Daniel, please don't." Charlie was wiping his face, and sweaty hair with a towel. "That's better done downtown, with Sullivan on a conference call. Without Frank."

Daniel pointed. "We'll do it by the book tomorrow. Right now, my way. Ten minutes. In Frank's bedroom." His own cell phone bleated, halting any argument. He picked his way through the living room crowd and moved onto the patio.

"I was hoping you would answer." Loretta. "Heard the news. You OK?"

"Yeah. Sleepy and pissed, but we're getting closer."

"Do you think she's dead?"

"She wasn't a while ago."

"Well." She sighed. "I'm sorry to call with more problems, but Gerry was here last night."

Daniel exhaled. She might as well have hit him in the stomach. "Darling, I'm afraid you're going to have to make up your mind."

"Daniel, I already have. Nothing happened. I stopped him at the door. But he's going to take it out on you. I just feel it."

"Take what out? That he's an asshole?" It was noon. A policeman emerged from the house and set sacks on the patio tables. Sandwiches.

"Us. Daniel, he'll fire you or send you somewhere awful. He didn't say it in so many words, but I read between the lines."

"Too late. He's already threatened you. He'll have to back off or I'll have his job, if he so much as looks cross-eyed at me."

She was talking, but Daniel's attention was drawn through the picture window. Will Carpenter entered the front door, looking like a man with a mission. As commander, he belonged at the hospital, or debriefing the lead SWAT team, not here. Frank stepped out of the hall, and Carpenter stopped him. Together, they turned back in the direction of the bedrooms.

"I don't care," Loretta was saying. "For a while, the intrigue and chaos were fun. Now I'm tired of all this. And

Gerry. Why can't you convince them that Frank's telling the truth?"

"Loretta, why do women fall apart just when their boyfriends are where they can't do anything about it?"

"Is that what you are? My boyfriend?"

Inside, no one else had left the living room.

"Daniel?"

"Sorry. There may be something going on."

"I gave notice to my landlord today."

"I'll call you back."

Charlie, Roby, and a few others finally moved when Daniel walked past. He got to Frank's bedroom first and opened the door without knocking. Carpenter looked up with a jerk.

"What's up?"

"Nothing," the SWAT commander said. "Just filling him in." Frank looked ashen.

Daniel stared, looking for reactions. "What about the Russian?"

Carpenter scowled, but answered. "We found him behind his shop. Bullet through the head."

"Robbery?"

"No. Cases still in the car."

"Trunk?"

"Empty."

"Then he was a mule. Since when do they use Russian mules? Any witnesses?"

Frank interrupted. "He says she was in the trunk."

Carpenter scowled. "That's not certain, Mr. Whitlock."

Frank shook his head. "She was there."

Charley entered. "We're here. What's the plan?"

Daniel paced. "Where's the computer clown? Get him in here." He moved toward the bed. "You all right, Frank?"

No eye contact. "Fine."

Daniel faced the others. "Best guesses, gentlemen. You first, Will. Where is Mrs. Whitlock?"

With his flak jacket hanging open, Carpenter seemed about to bluster. Instead, he said something coherent. "The trail led through Fairfield. Two ways to go, we figure. Across to Marin, or up north. We have lookouts on all bridges, and roadblocks in Fairfield. But we're still at least an hour behind them. Ukiah and Chico will be blocked, too."

Daniel turned toward Kyle, who was just coming in. "Any messages on Frank's e-mail?"

A shrug. "Same stuff. Repeating. They want to exchange Jill for Frank. First one suggested Frank shakes us and takes BART into the city. Next one said Silicon Valley. Amateurish stuff. Not even up to the level of Dirty Harry. Can't tell if it's terrorists or hackers."

Daniel nudged Frank. "Hang in there with us just a little longer. We almost got her."

The hero's face went through a gamut of expressions, all of them winding up in weariness. "Will you let me pack a bag if they subpoena me in Washington?"

"That won't happen for a few days," Carpenter said. How did he know? Daniel didn't like the tone of his voice.

One of the cops raised his hand. "The neighbors are going to court over the noise."

"Fine," Daniel said, still watching Frank, who was studying the floor, his eyes shifting nervously. "That's why we have to calm the reporters. From now on, all news conferences are downtown. Is that clear? Now let's work on finding Jill."

With murmurs of assent, they began to file out. Though he had seen only a couple of ransom situations up close, Daniel recognized the signs. Frank was going down. Today was the topper. A nervous breakdown might be next, but somehow, Frank seemed capable of something else. It might be wise to fit the hero with a GPS tracking device, the type that parolees wear. He wondered how Frank would take that suggestion.

In the middle of the hall, Carpenter nudged him. "It's going to be bad," Carpenter said. His eyes projected shrewdness.

"What is? When we find Jill?"

"No. When they rake that poor schmuck over the coals in Congress. Your boss was telling my boss that the Attorney General is following leads that might result in conspiracy charges against America's hero. He deserves a better fate, don't you think?"

"My boss?"

"Yeah. Director Sullivan. He's keeping us in the loop."

"I see." He put a finger into Carpenter's chest. "You're the S.W.A.T. commander. Here on the ground, it's my show. Understand? You don't talk to Whitlock without asking me first. "

Carpenter shrugged, looking snide. "I just think he deserves a fate more honorable than jail. Sure, I'll stay out of your way. But I'm here. Orders of the FBI and the A.G. So you stay out of mine, too. Deal?"

Daniel got in his face. "We lost a guy this morning. Too bad that house wasn't empty when we arrived, eh? Even better, too bad we didn't check that guy's trunk. Wonder who decided that?"

Carpenter wasn't fazed. "You think you're in the loop, buddy. You're not."

"We'll see about that." Daniel headed back to Frank's room. He figured Carpenter was correct, but maybe there was still time to figure out why Sullivan would want things to go awry out here in California.

Chapter 34
A Change of Strategy

Standing before the small mirror, Suhail maneuvered it to get a better view of his wound. The stitches had left small holes, but the red and white stripes had faded to an angry pink. To invade the body is to disrupt the energy field. Waleed had struck a larger blow than he imagined.

Even so, he felt better. His bowels had ceased roiling, and an appetite for minced beef on *baladi* bread had returned. He would have Muuji bring some from the café, or better yet, go down and order it himself. Of course, that might depend on Esam.

Esam – the very name evoked despondency. A deep breath. Suhail realized that he was in mourning for a friend who was still among the living.

Talking in the hall. Heavy footsteps. When he opened the door, Esam's beaming face peeked above a tall loaf of French bread.

"My Benefactor. How well you look. I have brought a feast. Time to regain your strength."

"Please come in, Colonel." He suffered the kisses. Esam always carried a weapon, but the Blues had seemed so confident of today's outcome. "Esam. I should have you drawn and quartered. Muuji said there was some problem with the computers."

"Bah. Muuji." He began unloading groceries. "Vegetables. Olives. What can your Colonel prepare?" The smile.

"I was just craving a sandwich."

Esam pried the lid off of a container. "Yes, but first, *hummus*. Muuji talks too much. But he did tell me you were not eating enough."

Suhail opened an orange drink. "Today, that has changed."

"Good. Good. Because the war goes on. Hussein told you about the FBI?"

"Yes. Is the woman well?" Suhail motioned, and headed out to the balcony.

"The Infidel's wife? Yes, but during your unexpected – ordeal – your faithful servants have been forced to work on their own. Good training. That is why I did not--"

"In the name of Allah, Esam, you are thrashing about the balcony like a wounded camel. Sit."

"Bread?"

"No."

The big man spoke with his mouth full. Sloppy. This was not respectful Esam. "We had to make some changes."

"Oh?"

With his haste at the bread, Esam's stress began to show through. "You will be happy to know that our men in California fought to the death."

"How many?"

"Two of ours. Five of the sultan's troops. Eleven escaped. It is unprecedented. Osama's large sleeper network is paying off."

Suhail shook his head. Careful. "Such is Osama's training. You know that, Esam, so why didn't our men escape ahead of the threat? Were they listening to martyrdom drivel from the others?"

"What were they supposed to do?" When the mouth got empty, he spread *hummus* and ate more. "The Americans were tipped off. Perhaps the sultan has double agents. Every side has double agents."

"Not ours, Colonel. We have never used traitors."

"True, Master. Your troops are the exception. Somehow you have always known when a link grew weak --" Almost comically, he choked when he said the words, until he recovered, red-faced, and rose. "Olives," he said, too loudly, and swept his bulk into the apartment, still talking, indiscreetly. "But there are dialogues. Always negotiations between sides. If you can glean useful information while consorting with the enemy--"

"We do not consort with enemies."

He emerged with a tin of olives, blustering. "Master, you know these things. Like soldiers during the Iran-Iraq War. They were opponents, but could lay down their arms and chat during *Ramadan*."

Suhail refused the olives, but took another sip of orange drink. "Esam, please do not tell me we have been talking to our enemies during my recovery. And you – you have been talking with Waleed? The same cretin who invaded my home and shot me?"

Another cough seemed to herald another choking spasm, but the big man recovered. "How – I told no one of my meeting with him. I was not followed. Master, how did you guess?"

"Perhaps you are no longer trustworthy with a gun, that you miss him at such close range?"

"I was distracted. He had a booby trap, though he denies it, set to make that noise in the pantry."

"He told you the noise was made by something entirely different, I'll wager. Waleed has been filling your head with ideas, eh, my friend?"

"No." Esam twisted the bread in his hands, shredding it rather than eating.

"When you met with him, why did Waleed not kill you? The truth, Colonel."

"I agree--" Esam began. "Of course the sheikh must be removed. But why not use his resources first? They have an army we wish to use. Our army is smaller, but better. They simply want the same thing – to use us. Reciprocity."

Even knowing ahead of time that his old friend would do this did not ease the pain. "What resources, exactly?"

"This is the plan, and it is bold." Hands waving. "We will attack in force. We will assemble one hundred freedom fighters. One hundred, Master! They will never expect that. The greatest invasion force on American soil in a century. And from within! Think of how surprised they will be."

The air fell silent, except for girls singing in the street below. This was the second blow, and Suhail felt it in his gut, more powerful than the gunshot. Above, in the sky, a jetliner climbed into the air. For an instant, they both watched it.

"I have to give Osama his due." Esam seemed to have become absolutely reverential.

"Of course," Suhail answered. "Why doesn't Waleed fly a jet into Frank Whitlock's roof? That would be his idea of a surgical strike."

"Master, don't you see? As a military commander, I must recognize when conditions of battle change. Of course your plan was superior, but I have been there, within blocks of the man's home. I have seen the patrol cars swarming."

"So the sultan and the sheikh will field one hundred martyrs. What then?"

Esam slammed his fist down on the small table, sending two flies fleeing from the *hummus*. "We attack. They will not expect it. They will know we are serious. Their hero will die."

Now they could hear the rumble of the jet. Suhail closed his eyes. Let Esam surmise that he was acquiescing. Instead, his thoughts went back to the murky hovel of the Source. The Advisor spoke of meekness. Why not let Esam have his new commander? The sheikh would spend him soon enough. A just punishment for intentional blindness.

But that would be giving up, wouldn't it? If Osama's tactics prevailed, if the sheikh and the sultan kept at their childish games on the backs of the true brave hearts, then all of Islam might as well surrender to the Israelis, because that path led, ultimately, to nuclear war, or worse. Even Osama had to know that he, Suhail Farid was the true heart of the war against the West. For two decades, his tactics, not Osama's had kept the fight alive. It was not time to give up, but time to teach the sheikh a lesson. Esam, too. He opened his eyes.

"Well?" The man's lips quivered. "Is it not a masterstroke? Can you communicate the new plans to your secret spies?"

"My secret spies…" He meant only to think it, but the words came mumbling out. "Tomorrow, Esam. You will have my answer tomorrow."

"Of course, Master. You have to strategize, too. But I must tell Waleed no later than that. He already has men traveling through the western states. And the secret route from Mexico." Esam stood, bent over, grabbed both of Suhail's hands and kissed them. "Don't worry. Of all the cities of America, Arabs will be safest on the streets of San Francisco."

Suhail nodded. "So one hundred will die to make the exchange?"

The big man flushed. "They are martyrs, Sahib. Down at the Café Al Haq, they revel in stories of the days when you risked martyrdom daily."

"I may have risked it, Colonel. But I didn't seek it. One does not win battles by dying before his enemy does."

Esam was on his feet, but peering over the balcony. What was he not saying? He cleared his throat. "Master, there is only one thing – because there is an emergency."

"What emergency?"

"It seems they must speed up the timetable, to avoid the newcomers getting caught. I must return now, not tomorrow, and tell them whether you approve of the plan."

Their gazes met. His executive officer had crossed to the other camp while he was gone. And this massive raid was folly. The words of The Source came back. A pure heart could take advantage of any folly. Esam was waiting, expecting his general to fly into a rage, marshalling whatever argument Waleed had given him next. But Suhail would play his own game, not theirs.

Suhail sighed, feigning thought. "The one hundred sleepers the sultan claims to have?"

A fat fist cut the air. "Already in position. When we strike, that is, when you give the order, they will attack, and the American people will have their second September Eleventh." Esam fairly slobbered with excitement.

"I give my blessing," Suhail said. "That is all I have to say." Esam leaned forward, kissed his hands.

"My master, you will never regret this. I will make the arrangements." He exited in a lumbering flurry.

Suhail fingered his own phone in his pocket – the secure one. A small change in plans was necessary. The Sultan wanted a sacrificial bloodbath, that he would call a victory. Allah willing, all of his men would die, while Suhail's survived. The Sultan, Sheikh, Waleed and even Esam would never expect that outcome.

Chapter 35
The Believer

"Loretta, are you crying?"

"No. Not yet, anyway. How are you?"

Her voice took him by surprise every time. New York and Virginia, mixed together in some exotic way. He thought of a lawn chair, and a beach – Rehobeth, maybe – and kids. Somehow, being at Frank's today had left him with a sense of how fragile it all was.

"Well, I feel like crying," he said, trying to make a joke, "because I'm almost out of whiskey."

"Don't drink alone."

"Plus, you're not here. If you were just right here on this hotel bed."

Silence. "Well, you almost redeemed yourself. Thanks for hanging up on me last time."

"Sorry. Gerry sent a new lackey down here. I think he's trying to convince Frank that glorious torture and death at the hands of Al Queda would be superior to rotting in some Club Fed prison."

"My God. But I thought you almost recovered his wife. Doesn't Gerry want to win?"

"You tell me. He's your former boyfriend, and so far, every leak in this operation traces right back to him. Why is that?"

Silence.

"Never mind," Daniel said. "But speaking of him, what's going on back there? No more threats?"

"Oh, sure. I've got one in my hand. Found it in my mailbox when I got home."

"What is it? If it's in his handwriting, we can get the bastard fired."

"Not his. It's a police report, not a love note. Hartford Police. I went to prep school there. Seems they caught me for possession of a gram-and-a-half of hash. I got probation. After two years they expunged the record."

"You never told me you used to be a druggie."

"This paper says I was. Looks authentic. Aged. The photostat's fading out, the whole nine yards."

"And you had to deny it to ever get past the White House FBI check, right? So he's going to show it to them?"

"Idiot. It's not real." A catch in her voice. "I can't keep doing this."

"You're saying he dummied something up? Loretta, that can be traced. We might have him, by God."

"Oh, Daniel, don't waste your breath. He'll be five steps ahead of us, and have five Hartford cops on the payroll."

"And a judge? I don't think so--"

"Oh, stop it." Now she was on the verge of tears. "Don't you see, I want out of here. Can't you ever listen?"

Daniel rolled off the bed, and paced. On the news channel, scenes of the farmhouse they raided flitted past. Sun angle too high. They would never have shot birds in the middle of the day.

"Didn't you hear me earlier, Daniel? I told the landlady I'm moving. All that's left is to tell Mary Ellen at the White House."

"Don't let him do this to you, Loretta. Don't fall apart while I'm three thousand miles away."

She was breathing hard. "Then come get me. Please."

He pictured the last time they did it. Lying in her arms. "Loretta, we barely know each other. How do you know I'm the one?"

"Instinct, as you said. That's how people fall in love. And save airplanes."

"Good God." He heard the words come pouring out, though perhaps they were not all intended. "Our future together is not some referendum on Whitlock's psychic abilities. Life is starts and stops, not epiphanies. You're in love with some dream about me being a white knight. I would rather you love just me – the flesh and bone one."

Again, she was quiet.

"Sorry. That was a low blow--"

"Daniel, there are such things as heroes." Oh, that voice. So silky. "I'm glad you didn't get shot, my darling. I'm just sorry you don't believe."

Chapter 36
After Dinner

Trace Markham was the sole deputy loitering outside of the trailer. A patrol car – manned — sat at the curb, and the roadblock on the side street had been moved in noticeably. Daniel parked next to it, and sauntered up the drive.

"Where are the reporters?"

"They'll be back," Markham answered. He nodded. "Got tired of being scooped by announcements downtown. Rest of the gang are having Chinese food in the trailer."

"What about the house? No one keeping Frank company?"

Markham scanned as they chatted. Nice to see that good training might pop up anywhere. "A couple. They're having Chinese, too. Man." He shook his head and spat into the bushes. Tobacco. "That duck is getting queerer and queerer. Every time I spoke to him today, he just grunted. Like we're the ones who grabbed his wife."

Daniel made a mental count as he moved toward the gate. "How many in the trailer?" he called back.

"Three."

"What?"

A shrug. "Your man Carpenter brought orders for a special detail – he took five uniforms out on some search."

"He did what?" Daniel's muscles tightened, all over. "On whose authority?"

Markham's voice raised. "Don't look at me, man. You FBI guys are all chiefs and no Indians. He had a paper--"

Daniel wheeled, considered calling Sullivan, and stormed through the front door. Inside, he felt some relief, because Charlie and a couple of others sat at the dining room table. In the conversation pit, Frank was building a fire.

"That cold, Frank?" Daniel asked.

The hero only glared. The conversation pit was dark, lit only by the flames. Outside the back sliding door, two cigarette fireflies stood guard. Two there. Three here, and three in the trailer. But Charlie's shift was ending. They would have six, maybe eight – enough to handle a couple of cars full of explosives, if it happened now? Silently, Daniel re-counted. But their only automatic weapons were out in the trailer. He would grab Charlie before he left, ask about Carpenter's mysterious orders, but first he poured a glass of water.

"There's some scotch up there," Frank said.

"No, thanks. When we have something to celebrate, I'll get drunk with you, Frank." He could feel control slipping away. If he challenged Carpenter, he would get some whining excuse. And Sullivan wouldn't back him up. And if he knew his boss at all, some other G-man or CIA would show up and deplete their resources further. He was watching a hit in slow motion, and didn't have the connections to combat it – or did he?

"It's a date." Frank settled into the plush loveseat, already armed with his own highball.

Daniel took his customary place opposite the hero. "I don't know if she'll be all right, Frank. I hope so." He got comfortable. "I do know one thing. You've got to quit dwelling on it. You shouldn't have sent the counselors away. They know how to help you through this kind of shit. Don't you have a priest you like? Or something?"

"Preachers and I eventually get into arguments. Do you think they might find her tonight?"

The hairs on Daniel's arms went suddenly electric. "Is something bothering you, Frank? You get a message I don't know about?"

"Kyle reads my e-mails now. Ask him."

"Why don't we talk about something to get your mind off of it? Politics? You Democrat or Republican?"

"Independent."

"Great. You vote for the man."

"Or the woman."

"Of course. Well, I'm a Democrat. My family would kill me if they knew that I voted for the man. Don't you think Bush is doing a great job? I mean, considering?"

The hero grunted. "No matter who's in the White House, they always miss the big picture. It's bigger than Israel and Palestine, Muslims fighting Hindus, or Jews fighting Muslims. It's primordial, for God's sake. It's all a great chess game. Bigger than a million Superbowls. Biggest game in the Universe, and the press – even Howard Brown – has no clue. No reporters on the sidelines." He raised his glass in a mocking toast.

"Scotch?" Daniel asked.

"No. Just soda. Gotta keep clear tonight."

Another jolt climbed Daniel's frame. Something was going on. In the next instant, the front door opened, and Daniel sprang to his feet, gun drawn.

Billy Pierce loomed in the entryway. He took in the scene immediately. "I think he's planning to shoot you, Frank." The hero stood up.

"You're giving me a heart attack, Daniel," he said.

"Sorry." Then to Pierce. "You alone?" Daniel holstered the pistol.

Pierce raised a pillow. "You guys go ahead and solve the world's problems. I'm going to close my eyes for a few minutes." He headed for the easy chair on the other side of the living room.

Frank remained on his feet, his look sullen. Daniel eased back down onto the loveseat. He remembered this antsy feeling – one of his early jobs with the Bureau, the Maynard kidnapping. Twin boys. He and Joske searching house-to-house. They and the two cops, all of them, were suddenly at each other's throats, right before they found the right place.

"Tell me what's going on, Frank." He meant it as an order, not a request.

Frank headed for the kitchen counter, and Daniel whispered a prayer for him to refill his glass with the real stuff. The hero seemed to think twice, then retraced his steps, to Daniel's side. He held his hand out. "Here. I'll give you something, but you have to pay for it."

"A business card. I can't see. Whose is it?"

Frank pressed it into Daniel's hand. "I thought I could use it, but now… You pay by making a bargain with me."

Already tight, Daniel's stomach felt like it would explode. Whatever was up this weirdo's sleeve, things were about to come to a head. "Yeah? What bargain?"

"You have to go to Lebanon."

"What?"

"I thought I could, but that's all blown. You have mobility. Take a vacation. Now. Within the week. I want to be reunited with Jill."

Daniel slipped the card into his inner coat pocket before it could be taken back. His hand lingered, making sure his gun was still in its holster. "Frank, things don't work like that. We're still operating on alert level. Why can't you help us, instead of always talking in riddles?"

In the firelight, Daniel saw Frank rubbing his eyes, wearily. The hero turned, headed for the hall of bedrooms, but stopped at the top of the conversation pit. "Tomorrow is going to be a long day," he said over his shoulder. "On the back of that card is an address in Lebanon. It's in a small town north of Beirut. Or east, I don't remember. An old man lives there.

Go alone. Around the back of his house is a walled courtyard.
Take a white handkerchief – a clean one. Throw it over the
wall of that courtyard. If someone throws it back, then go
home, we're both fucked."

Pierce was already snoring softly. Charlie and the
others were cleaning up in the kitchen, close enough to listen,
but none of them were. As if Franks' words were meant only
for Daniel. "But if the handkerchief doesn't come back over in
a few moments, go stand at the front door," he continued.

"What for?"

"If the door does open and the old man invites you in,
then I want you to ask him to reunite Jill and me. Ask him to
let us both live. On Earth. None of this 'we're immortal' shit. I
want my life back. At least some of it. Please. Just do exactly
what I said and don't go telling anyone else. Before or after.
That's the deal."

"Oh. So this is the address of one of those Aladdin
genies. Is that it?"

Frank took a breath, backtracked, came to Daniel's side
again, whispering. "I always wanted to use my gift, you
know," he said, ignoring Daniel's attitude. "People like Janet
Bergstaller, they actually go into the other world and help
people who have died. Help them realize that it's OK. They
usher them into the arms of their departed loved ones. Now
that's an instance where psychics can make a difference.
Taking the terror out of death. I should have learned to do
that. All these years. I've wasted my talent. Do you know what
it feels like to face the end of your life and realize you've
wasted your talent?"

The hairs on Daniel's neck were at attention. "You're
talking about tomorrow being a long day, Frank. Are you
getting a premonition?"

Silence. "Just do as I ask. Go to Lebanon, as soon as is
humanly possible." Almost too quickly, he made it across the

den, the wide living room, and disappeared into the darkness of the hall.

Daniel listened until his footsteps faded. A grand chess game, Frank had said. Maybe he was right. They had moved the hunt for Jill downtown, and up here, Carpenter was cutting back on the forces. Sullivan had fixed it so that Daniel would have to offer more than just instinct to requisition new reinforcements. He was running out of moves. Maybe he should just go back to Washington, and look out for Number One, try to save what was left of his love life.

It seemed his eyes had been closed only a moment, then he felt someone shaking his shoulder. "What the hell—"

"Garcia, sir. The sergeant thought you might need to hear this."

Daniel fumbled to his feet, and walked behind the man, past Pierce's snoring, through the front door and out into the East Bay chill. "Where?"

"In the trailer, sir."

A few muted lights exposed a man sitting at a small console, wearing earphones. In the far corner, a cop was sacked out, still wearing his shoes. The FBI had installed these machines, but Daniel noted that the recorders still sported cassette tapes, not the newer mini-discs.

The listener looked up and jerked off the phones, beckoning to Daniel. "Quick. Put the phones on. Don't know how long it will last. It's from Whitlock's bedroom."

Daniel went down on one knee, and when the headphones pushed into place, he could hear whispers. They grew louder, then died, alternately. Frank's voice. "What's he saying?"

"Shhh." The sergeant gestured.

Daniel focused. Louder, the words barely taking shape.

"Sam. Please come to me. Sam, I never ask this. Can you hear me, Sam? You have to come to me tonight…" Then an inaudible stretch of whispering. "...I need some sleep. Sam? It's Frank. Please be listening..."

"Shit." Daniel took off the phones and stood. "You getting this?"

A nod. "We're recording everything. Sounds like he's finally gone round the bend, huh?"

Daniel shook his head. "Unless there's a terrorist named Sam. Shit. I thought I might head back to the hotel, but not now. I'll be back down by the fireplace if anything changes."

Chapter 37
The Lone Jackal

Ibrahim al Muhlif had ridden this street on his bicycle
every day since his return to the United States in February,
ever since he had deciphered the code in the book from Cairo,
on that joyous afternoon when he learned his mission.

Now the neighbors – it seemed a district of gray-haired
people – waved when he passed, and the only time he was
stopped by the police, he was able to show them his valid
driver's license, and his ID card from Diablo Valley College,
where he was now a straight-A student.

He remembered the way his heart stirred when he
discerned just who his target was, and absolutely rejoiced
when General Farid, himself, called with the special
instructions. Mercy of Allah, his mission would not include
what he feared most: strapping a gasoline bomb onto himself.
Of course, Waz had told him a hundred times that Suhail
Farid was not that kind of commander, but war was war.

Only a few times had he come this way in the dark.
Enough to know patterns. Until the master's phone call, this
path would not have been necessary, yet this was why they
made preparations for all contingencies, no? It had taken an
hour to run his gas tank dry. So he left the car at the campus, a
poor dumb student.

Ibrahim usually came this way on his bike, anyway. He
slowed down, braking carefully so the vehicle would not

squeak, finally stopping in front of the house of the man named Simmons. Frail. Fond of raking leaves, even when they were hard to find on the lush lawn. Children living in Chicago, the old man had said, on that warm afternoon when Ibrahim stopped to drink from his hose and chat. A kindly man. Perhaps the Almighty granted dispensation for some Christians. No strange cars were in evidence tonight, just the faded Lincoln in the carport. The lights inside were always out by midnight. He was on time.

A few meager conversations were not the entirety of their relationship. Ibrahim always gave the Simmons his widest wave, and even stood on the bike's saddle a couple of times as he passed, making them laugh at his spectacle. All part of the ultimate plan that must play to perfection.

Ibrahim knocked loudly. When the door first swung open, Old Man Simmons' face was scrunched into worry. Then, a moment of smiling when he recognized the cyclist. Followed by a paleness, when his gaze came to rest on the small gun.

"I need your car," Ibrahim said. "Tell your wife to come into this room, and there will be no trouble."

Mrs. Simmons emitted an aged, breathless whine when she entered, started to protest when the old man fetched his key chain, and opened her mouth, readying a genuine scream. Or so it seemed. Ibrahim shot her first, the remarkable silencer turning the blast of a thirty-two caliber into a sickening *zip* of air.

Now they both lay there, in the arched entrance to the darkened living room, and Ibrahim waited, trying to quell the pounding of his heart. But the world crashed around him when the telephone started ringing. Once, twice, before he realized it was not some blaring angel of death. Three times. Four – then a click. There must be some answering machine on it. Was it their children in Chicago? A neighbor across the street? The pounding of his heart when he pulled the trigger – that was nothing compared to this.

Long minutes. Standing motionless in the darkness. He dared not move to turn off the kitchen lights back there. Only one curtain parted in the living room – the one at the Bay window. A *blast* – shrieking – no, again, the phone. Who was calling? Didn't they know old people went to bed early? He clutched the Lincoln's keys in his fist. His only escape, if the red and blue police lights appeared.

Again the answering machine saved him, but he wished he could hear the message, to make sure it wasn't a nosy neighbor. He chanced it – moved swiftly into the light, and made the kitchen dark, too. Then to the door to the carport. With shaking hands, he un-did the three locks. Old people. They thought more locks meant more security.

Deep breaths. Ibrahim shook himself, even slapped his face to come out of it. Remember his mission. Replay the steps. Regain focus – that's what General Farid would order at this moment.

This moment – his moment had come, hadn't it? At last, after all the training, he would become part of history. He had memorized the face of Frank Whitlock to perfection. But how Master Farid proposed to make him come, willfully, to Ibrahim's waiting car, had not been told to him.

He recited the words he must say when the evil man climbed into the back seat. "The game will be very hot by then," Waz had told him in knowing whispers, that night at the pizza place. "Stay calm. Master Farid will control Heaven and Earth around you. With the help of Allah."

The odds of Ibrahim reaching the rendezvous unmolested were not great, but the police, so ever-present in this part of town, were not his first concern, Waz explained. The sultan's men would be there, too, and perhaps reach the hero before Ibrahim, for they were many. If so, they would learn of his true talent: using an automobile as a weapon.

"Never think about the problems that might arise, for they are infinite in number," Master Farid had said more than once. "Your focus will trump all of them, if it is acute enough." Ibrahim breathed deeply. His entire being would be focused. In his hands lay the future of Palestine, perhaps all of Arabia. Allah be praised!

Suhail drew the blinds, and ordered Kareem to shut the children up, and to have the alleyway barricaded. Ensconced atop the bed, with the candle burning, he entered the waking dream.

"Blue sprites, here is your message. Prince of all Afrits, come with me to the cavern floor, down the path that is bordered by the holy gardens. Enlist your minions! Enlist the very *shaytans*, if you must, but inhabit the smoke, and guide his steps. Come with me to the precipice and gaze down into the infidel's world. He is one of the few who can follow his heart, and you are the only one who can tug the strings.

"Come, sprites. Sublime, and possessing a speed greater than any steed, hark unto your mission. Energy will come of it! A grand bouquet of longings and tart desires, the fruit of your cousins on Earth, that will be your harvest!

"Oh, faithful Jinn, sprites who constitute Allah's second worthy congregation, fly to the mind of this man. Cause smoke to waft upwind. Lead him to my humble servant, and crack the shell that my enemies seek to place around the world, and make that crack wide enough to admit my righteousness and power." In the corner of the room, the gathering bluish smoke began to coagulate – into a form that resembled a man. Sweating and blinking, Ibrahim thought his slamming heart would explode. The blue, cloudy form began to move, and he looked away.

His watch alarm beeped loudly, but there was no need. This was the darkness that held no sleep. Hours had passed since his heart threatened to burst from his body, like that monster in that American space movie. Ibrahim looked at his watch, and peered through the side of the living room curtains. Dawn was breaking. The keys tinkled in his hands. With every passing car, his heart leaped. A visitor or relative of the Simmons? The phone had rung only those two times. Something told him that, with the sun, it might break the peace again.

He forced in the cleansing breaths. For perhaps the thousandth time, he made sure the pistol was loaded with fresh shells. Soon. Soon he would enter the annals of the history of all freedom fighters. And if he executed well, Master Farid would inform his family that he was forever a hero. And if the worst came to pass, the angels would welcome him with riches beyond his wildest imagination.

Enough of things material. Now was the time. Ibrahim silently said goodbye to the old antique cabinet, the porcelain trinkets that sat so forlornly on the glass shelves, the portrait of some old couple on the living room wall, the goose-shaped salt-and-pepper shakers, his companions during the long night. His hand wrapped around the doorknob, and he waited, peering through the lace curtains, while a car, then two joggers passed the head of the driveway. Finally, with a deep breath, he stepped out to meet his destiny.

Chapter 38
The Closet

Was there a moment when he could act? Tell the cops when to strike? Frank felt supremely impotent. She might already be dead, he told himself for the thousandth time. Wouldn't he know? Wouldn't Sam tell him?

He loved her too much – when someone was truly close, it might take weeks. Sure, he knew what he had to do, had heard the voices a hundred times in the last three nights. He even made a promise to the big black shadows, and knew they would be crowding around as he fell into slumber, knew they could read his every thought. But this was his only chance to play his ace-in-the-hole: Sam.

He tossed and turned, fighting not to rise and go confess everything to Clooney. He was kidding himself to think the bastards would keep their end of the bargain. It would be like *The Godfather*. The moment he climbed into a car with them, piano wire. The end.

But if the fanatics kept their word, then Jill would be safe here in this bed tomorrow night. As for himself, Frank wasn't afraid. Whatever happened, Sam would be there when it was over.

"Let me go. I'm tired," he yelled. Sam's lithe body stood next to the bed and he kept tugging. "Goddam it, I don't want to play the night game," Frank complained, amazed to recognize the voice he possessed as a child.

"Shut up," Sam whispered, in his own voice of childhood. "You blasphemed. Dad's just in there on the couch." Frank shook from within, amazed to hear his brother speak – but the demands of the dream outweighed his surprise.

"I'm not going in the closet." Frank's feet hit the cold floor, and this time, he was determined to hold his ground. Ever since that cruel midnight when Sam told him that the bad *lazoon* lived in there. It was a stupid jest, about a stupid puppet-like animal off of television. Nevertheless, Frank had not been able to shake the image. This time, he would not be coaxed into the stuffy, close cubicle between the heavy, hanging coats and the clothes stacked haphazardly on the floor.

"It's not in there," Sam said with no emotion, obviously referring to the lazoon. "It went away to the islands and it won't be back for a long time."

"You're lying. How could you know?" Frank hated this.

"Come on. Just a minute." Sam pushed insistently on his back. "There's a surprise in there, and then we'll go through the trap door."

Sam was a devil, to always remember what Frank liked. Some nights, they descended into the cool dirt beneath the house, where their father had dug a makeshift wine cellar. They would sit for hours, picking up the bottles, trying to avoid the fatal *clink!*, and read the labels, making up stories about how Napoleon used to drink this stuff, even if it were dated 1942, their dad's oldest vintage, his pride and joy.

"If it's a bad surprise, I'll kill you."

"It's not. Hurry."

"I swear. I'll scream until Dad wakes up."

Reluctantly, with the hairs on his neck standing up, Frank crawled into position, nudging beneath the soft cotton dresses and Dad's greatcoat that smelled from the mothballs stuffed into its pockets.

"Lie down." Sam still crouched in the slit doorway.

Frank did so, cramming some of the old clothes into a sort of pillow. He caught his breath. Someone was lying next to him!

"Is – is that you, Sam?" His heart raced, and slobber started to come out through his lips.

"Mmm." The body answered. Was that Jill's voice?

"Jill?"

He pulled closer, so very slowly. What if it weren't? What if it were only the body of some old, dead man? That thought came from somewhere, but then he moved the rags and old jeans enough so that he could lean over and sniff the covered-up hulk. Her perfume! But wait – the terrorists would not have a supply of her perfume.

A consuming dread washed over him. "Jill? Are you dead?"

A long pause. "Who is it?" Yes, that was her whisper!

"Jill, my darling." He was no longer a child, and his hand caressed her leg automatically. It was folded up under her, in a fetal position. His fingers ran along it until he could grip her rump. He would have reached over, all around, until he could cradle and protect her, but the sleeve of a sweater or something was passed under his armpit, preventing him from reaching farther.

"Careful." Sam's voice came out of the darkness. He was right. Don't break the spell.

The curled-up body jolted. "Frank? Frank, is it you? Oh, my God. My God." She seemed on the verge of weeping. "Are you here? Did they get you, too? I didn't want them to get you—"

"Shh. Quiet, Darling."

"Where are you, Frank? I can't see –"

He fought against the clothing, but could pull no closer. "Jill, I love you. Remember that. I love you forever."

She fidgeted, trying to change her position, and he made one last, great lunge, cutting himself on the sharp strands of the ropes that bound her – then a bright light burst in, filling the closet. Fearing it might be the kidnappers, Frank jumped to a squatting position. He could see Sam, smiling, holding open the trap door. Light poured in from the wine cellar, and where Jill lay, now there was only a pile of soiled clothes again.

Sam was moving, and Frank was too terrified to do anything but scramble through the hole after him. "Where did she go? Sam, for God's sake, where's Jill? Did Daddy put floodlights down here?"

Instead of plopping down into cool dirt, he found himself draped over the big ottoman in the living room. The orange couch! The old leather chair! Bright sunshine glared through the large front window, illuminating his childhood living room as he remembered it. Every picture on the wall. The old plaque he had made in cub scouts. But outside somewhere, a shadow passed, and the doorbell rang.

"Run," Sam yelled from his perch on the coffee table. It was always their game, scrambling to the far recesses of the house, hiding from whatever "evil" salesmen or paperboys might be ringing that bell.

"Can someone get that?" Mom called, unseen, from the kitchen. Mom's voice – he had forgotten that wonderful sound.

Sam thudded to a halt. "Oops." He had already started getting his growth spurt and now towered above Frank. A shrug. "I guess we'd better go."

Sam led the way bravely, the responsible big brother. At the front door, he no longer had to stand on tiptoes to peek out through the little peep-hole.

"Aw, crap." His words fell like a lead weight. Frank was taking in the smells of this house he remembered so well. "You'd better look."

He stuck a knee out, and helped Frank hoist up to squint through the aperture. The face that stared blankly back from the sunny day outside turned Frank's blood to ice – it took a moment to realize – No, none of this was real – this face belonged to the present: the FBI agent, Will Carpenter.

Frank slipped, crumpling down to the floor, his arms groping, reaching around Sam's legs and holding on for dear life. He would never let go. "Is it going to be OK, Sam? Please tell me, will it be OK?"

"I hope so, little brother. I hope so."

For the first time in Frank's memory, Sam didn't sound sure.

Chapter 39
The Exchange

Sunrise was only a promise, but Hadeel Al-Wazn was thinking only of sunset. Of all nights in history, he thought, just to see the sun go down tonight would be glorious. His shoulders stiffened as he turned the car onto the off-ramp. The police had started parking at exits, watching everyone who passed, stopping whomever they wished.

"In the name of Allah, keep quiet."

Muslim slapped the dash and grunted. "Our blood is high, Waz. The martyrs of Osama Bin Laden do not go into battle with sleepy hearts." He reached back and high-fived Ahmad's hand – a gesture from American movies.

"We will be together in Heaven soon." Ahmad leaned forward, and hissed the words, too close to Waz's ear. Shivers crawled over his back.

"We will do our job," Waz answered firmly. "Allah will choose who dies and who lives." He stepped on the brake, squealing the car to a halt. Traffic on Northside Drive was heavier this morning. Allah help them if it became bad enough to throw their timing off.

A rush of blood, a shudder of the heart, and Ibrahim revved the old Lincoln to life on the first try. Half a tank of gas. Thank you, Mr. Simmons. Nine blocks to drive, and he would count every one of them out loud. Only the curved road, Orchard Street, had places where he might not see the police in time. Allah, be merciful. "One." His blood ran warm, and he was careful to pause long enough at the stop sign. "Two." Traffic was heavy, but he would find room to run. "Three." A glance at his watch. In nine minutes, the United States would get its second taste of the real world.

Daniel toweled his face dry. He should tell Frank goodbye, but it had been a late night. Maybe he could bring Loretta back down here to meet the guy. Pierce was making coffee.

"Heading out?" he asked. "You can knock on his door. He's usually up by now."

"Back to the hotel. Then a meeting downtown. I may be outta here."

"No shit?"

"Yeah, I'm sure we'll chat again. Nice working with you guys."

"Same here. Hey. Any idea when it might get normal around here again? You know, just a security guard at night or something?"

Daniel straightened his tie, using the oven window reflection. "Beats me. They say there's a war on."

Pierce kept rinsing a mug. "Shit, we already blew up Afghanistan. My wife and I have tickets to Hawaii. Hope to hell they get it finished soon."

Outside, Markham chatted with a female officer Daniel had not seen before. "This is Loretta Feliz." She smiled.

"I like your name. First time on this duty?"

"No. I was here a couple of weeks ago. Been on vacation."

The trailer door lay wide open. Inside, a small TV blared headlines about a bombing in Israel, but a coffee-drinking cop was arguing with someone unseen about a basketball game.

"Well, I'm glad you got a break," Daniel told her. "Someone needs to go in there and give poor old Billy a few days off."

Markham spit into the hedge. "Screw Pierce. Always bellyaching." At the curb, a lone cameraman yawned, equipment resting at his feet.

"Be seeing you guys. Keep the old boy honest." Daniel shook their hands again, and started down the driveway's incline.

A squeal of tires froze them all in place. Radios in the trailer crackled to life in the same moment. Along the left roadblock, an officer seemed to think twice about holding his ground, but then retreated to the lawn, gun drawn. The racing patrol car blew past him, nosed into the Whitlock driveway, almost barreling over Daniel before it screeched to a stop.

A cop leaped from the trailer. "They say to protect Whitlock."

Charlie bolted from the car's passenger side. Officers poured out of the single-wide. "Condition red."

"What?" Daniel stood his ground.

Pointing. "Two blocks over. A neighbor says some Middle Eastern guys took over a house. We sent a patrolman, and he hasn't called in. A team is headed there right now."

The words were barely out of his mouth when gunshots split the air, from the side street.

"Christ." Charlie ducked into the trailer.

Daniel squinted. "Can't see anything."

Then the world was flying, tumbling. He was chewing dirt in the flower bed. "Mortar!" someone cried. Daniel reached for his gun. No pain, so far, but he could see stars.

"Look!" Markham was somehow over by the gate. Daniel traced his pointing finger. A gaggle of men were coming down the side street, whooping like wild Indians. Five. Nine. He counted instinctively. Automatic weapons. He lost count.

"Stay down." Markham fired his gun. Automatic fire sprayed the wall. Daniel ran, crouching, across the lawn, through the hedge, for the side gate.

To the right, policemen at the roadblocks went down. A glance behind. The trailer lay smoking, the back of its metal superstructure ripped away. Grappling through the iron gate. Backyard cops were rushing to take places along the brick wall.

"Incoming!" voices cried. An explosion literally blew paint flecks from the eaves of the house. Glass crashed. Daniel glanced back. Some intruders knelt in the streets, firing their rifles. Cops fired back. All of the people at the roadblocks were down, and more strangers were pouring from the house a half-block away. Tires screeched, and a car issued more shooters. They wore jeans and black ski-masks on their heads.

Daniel turned and loped toward the rear of the house. From nowhere, Roby appeared, pushing a clip into his own automatic rifle. Two more cops – one male, two females – followed him.

"To hell with that," Daniel said. "There are too many. Let's get Whitlock and run."

Roby motioned, just as a new wave of bullets slammed the front wall. Another explosion on the front lawn shook trees. Roby was down, and popped back up. "He's on the patio."

Daniel looked just in time to see Frank, strolling through the back gate, as if intending to make a social call on the deserted Raed house. "Frank," he yelled. "Fuck, he's smoking a pipe." He waved to two cops hunkered down by the pool filter. They were aiming, firing through the house. "Guys. Let's get him to safety."

Both rose and scrambled just ahead of bullets strafing the bricks. The terrorists were in the house. Daniel stepped out, fired through the splintered picture window to cover them, then ran. The lady cop slithered through the gate ahead of him. Whoops and screams filled the air.

"Frank!" He kept running, but the hero was nowhere in the Raed's back yard. Radios screeching. Deputies in hedges, firing, as if the leaves protected them. Bullets came from every direction. "Fuck, we're surrounded." Toward the Raed's front gate, through a haze of gunsmoke mixed with aromatic tobacco. He had never seen Frank smoke before.

"Frank." Past the patio. The boarded-up door. Through the side gate. Two shots clipped limbs above his head. Daniel fell back behind the tree's thick trunk.

In the early hours, when the light pricked at his eyelids, Frank lay still, opening himself up. For two nights in a row, the whispers had altered.

"Remember your pipe. The smoke will make you invisible. Walk toward the sun. Toward the sun! She will be waiting. Your loved one will be waiting."

The first time, he thought it simply meant he had switched from paranoid depressive to outright crazy. Then it seemed to fall into place. These messages really were meant for him. He wished he could ask Sam about them.

He rose and dug through his old cedar box. The *meerschaum* pipe lay there still, a relic almost untouched since his "intellectual" days back in college. Plus an aging pouch of peach brandy tobacco he had bought a few years ago in a fit of adventure, but never opened.

Before the others began stirring, he showered, remembering the day he had married Jill. Soapy drops cascaded off of his arms with import. The suds seemed to be saying goodbye. That crevice in the plastic door, where mildew was quick to form, the one Jill always complained about – he would never see it again. As he dressed, again his wedding day came back, and how he pulled on his tux, hungover from the bachelor party. Like today. But this party would be a funeral. He chose a black turtleneck, just in case they put him somewhere drafty. Plus, that color would show blood less, if they slit his throat.

He was ready. Pipe bowl filled. Crazy, perhaps, but that mattered so much less, now. Jill was probably already dead. They thought that, even if they didn't say it. Cops, FBI, all of them. Except Sam and the strange voice that had been coming to him ever since the first. He paused one moment more, sniffing unlit tobacco, letting the memory of the dream filter back – his legs up against hers – Jill. Lovely Jill. So warm. Thank you, God, for letting me know her.

As he lit the bowl, one puff, two, three, her sweet image was replaced by the leering face of Carpenter, through the glass of the front door. His presence in Frank's dream needed no explanation. This was it.

"Walk. Don't run," Carpenter had ordered only a couple of afternoons ago. First five minutes he had ever met the scumbag, and there he was, looming over him, assuming the identity of God with his terrifying instructions. "If you screw up, your wife is dead."

A heavy pause, but there were footsteps in the hall as the bully waited for his reply. "You know they're going to kill me."

So evil. He remembered the beady black eyes from that afternoon, the same ones staring through the peep-hole in the dream. Beady eyes and no expression. Ice in his veins. "It's either you or her. Go through your neighbor's yard. Stop for no one. No thing."

The FBI would be ready, right? The others barged in before he could ask it. They had set up an exchange, and now they were going to double-cross the terrorists, right? Perhaps they just wanted him to be a convincing decoy, so that's why they didn't tell him more, right? That's what Beady Eyes was doing. He had to believe it.

He puffed. The whispers promised he would be invisible, so he puffed, clenching the pipe in his teeth like a sophomore philosophy student, and he walked.

He walked. Billy Pierce stared, and talked to him, but no sound came out. Heart racing. Only when he crossed the back lawn and the sounds of shots ripped the air did he become awake. Smells of Cherie's flowers. Stale chlorine of the pool. Look at no one. Do not talk or stop. *Walk.*

He stepped briskly through Faris's front gate, heading directly toward the sun. A car screeched to a halt. Its driver waved frantically. Shouts everywhere. Explosions, but he could not look back. He might be back on the plane, fighting for his life. Yells in English, Arabic. This had happened before. He broke into a run. Was Jill in this car? Was the FBI shooting?

The driver stretched to make the back door fly open. Bullets whizzed above them. Frank dove into the back seat.

"Where's Jill?"

"Shut up." The man grimaced, face full of hate. A fist, and Frank saw stars. He crumpled to the wide floor of the car's back seat.

"Wait." But his mouth was bleeding.

"Stay still or your wife is dead."

Screaming. More shots. Peck-peck on the metal in the rear. Bullets. He waited for the cops to block the car, for bullets to rip them to pieces. He waited the eternal, screaming seconds for it to be over. But the driver was speeding, past the yells, too fast for the bullets. The FBI had not double-crossed the bad guys. The bad guys had double-crossed him.

The ring of a cell phone. Waz almost jumped out of his skin. "What is that?"

Muslim pressed the instrument to his ear. A curse.

"No communication," Waz bellowed. "You're disobeying orders." Eyes back on the street ahead.

"Shut up." Venom filled Muslim's eyes. "Yes," he said into the phone. "Now."

"Are you crazy?"

Muslim pulled his pistol. "Turn it around. Change of plans. Almost no resistance."

"What? I have my orders."

The pistol came up and jammed painfully into Waz's jaw. "You will follow Osama's orders. The sultan's orders, is that clear? Turn around and drive to the target." His teeth were clenched. "They have taken the house. There will be no exchange. The Americans were ready for nothing." A laugh, and a smiling glance back to Ahmad. "We are killing them like flies on a shaft of *schwarma*."

"Allah be praised." Ahmad yelped and hit the roof.

Through the windshield, the abandoned gas station came into view. "Here is the station. What are you talking about?" Must be careful. "Put the gun down, the commuters will see it."

The pistol only came across harder, pushing Waz's head against the window. Muslim was halfway over the console. "Are you a woman? We follow Al-Awati's plan. If light resistance, we take the whole neighborhood. They want it back, they have to come get us. Americans fighting for their own land. That is worth dying for. Turn around or you will not die with honor."

Al-Awati was supposed to be a military genius, but these two were short, when it came to brains. Or honor.

The light turned green. "What about the code word? Did he give it? Did Master Farid approve the change?" Waz stepped on the gas, sending the car lurching through the intersection. Muslim looked away in dismay.

"Shut up." Ahmad grabbed the back of his head. "Turn around or I will kill you myself."

So Suhail did not approve. Waz wheeled the vehicle into the abandoned gas station.

"Shaytan!" The gun hurt his jaw. "I told you we were not going here." Pressing.

"You idiot. I am only turning around. Look at the traffic." They swerved. The gas pumps were taped up, but Waz headed for the empty corridor behind that used to be a car wash. Both entry and exit were placed behind concrete walls, invisible from the street. The sultan's men had agreed to dump Jill Whitlock here. But none of them knew of Ibrahim's mission. No sign of his friend yet.

The cell phone screamed again, and Waz's heart jolted. He thought it was the sound of the bullet blowing through his brain.

"What?" Muslim screamed. Ahmad had his head forward. The gun sagged to Waz's neck. "He is in the building. Or another house. We are coming." He dropped the phone, his face crimson with rage. "The house is on fire and they can't find Whitlock. In the name of Allah." He cocked his gun, looking back at his partner.

"I'm going around back. Less suspicion." Only an instant more. Waz wheeled into the dilapidated car wash, saw the curve of the metal ramp he was looking for, gunned the engine, and expertly twisted the right front wheel up onto it, throwing both men back in their seats.

Now. His right hand crossed his lap, dropped down, pulled the thirty-eight from his belt, turned, and fired one bullet expertly through Muslim's jaw, going upward, then whipped around and pulled the trigger again. Ahmad's eyes were open. Full of amazement, until the light died. His aim was luckier than he could have dreamed – the hole, just above the nose. The car came to rest, and Waz prayed aloud that no one had heard. He was on the hard pavement, racing around the front, then pulling both bodies out through the passenger-side doors.

With a bit more ceremony, for she was female, he popped the trunk and hauled Jill Whitlock's writhing form out, dumping her onto the cement a few feet from the fanatics. By the time he stood up straight, another vehicle – this one a monster, almost too wide to fit into the far opening – nosed in, then toward them. Ibrahim smiled from behind the steering wheel.

Frank Whitlock staggered out at gunpoint.

"Get in the trunk," Waz ordered the pale man.

"No. I die right here unless I see my wife."

Waz grabbed his collar and jerked him to the side. From above the wide duct tape, Jill Whitlock's eyes blinked frantically. She grunted, struggling against her binding.

"Let me at least kiss her."

Waz shook his head. "Tell her goodbye, hero." Ibrahim came from behind, and they shoved him into the trunk.

Waz controlled the car. Getting back onto the street must be orderly. Normal. He glanced at Ibrahim's huge vehicle in the rear-view mirror. It filled the driveway.

The young savant smiled, slumping down in his seat. "Those two? What did they do, Hadeel?"

Sirens wailed. Cars honked, trying to move out of the way of two fire wagons that roared up from behind. Waz guided the vehicle onto the highway entrance. Good. So much confusion, they were stopping no one.

"They disobeyed the Master."

Three bogeys were running, screaming frantically after the huge sedan the made a sweeping left turn, racing away. Where was Frank? The men took a stance, and fired their guns, but the car was gone.

"Tough luck, boys," Daniel said under his breath. "Sometimes you get left behind." Now the men in ski masks fired in different directions, and cops behind trees and mailboxes shot back. Daniel propped up against the stone balustrade on one side of the gate and took a shot. They were running this way.

From the house next door, two unmistakable shotgun blasts sounded. One of the bad guys went down. The other two ducked and fled toward the house across the street.

Daniel looked back into the Raed's yard. After an instant, a new explosion ripped the Whitlocks' flaming roof. The shock of it made him turn, take a few steps toward the front walk. Automatic fire to his right. Daniel felt a thud. His arm stung, and he stumbled through the hedges into the neighbor's driveway.

Down on one knee, he looked up. There, at the mouth of the driveway, stood an incredible sight: An emaciated man in some sort of ceremonial robes. Purple scarves, and solid, tinkling gold figures embroidered on some sort of velvet, seeming to fairly rain jewels along thick strands that hung down to scrape the pavement. On his head, a gaudy, gold-sparkled head piece, part hat, part crown. The bizarre man looked down at Daniel, smiling like a benevolent, insane grandfather, and Daniel realized he had smeared blue makeup all over his face. Some ancient psychopath, picking a time like this to parade his Halloween costume.

Another explosion behind. Crashing glass, and something fell into a swimming pool. Daniel looked around. Bullets ticking in the trees, whining down the asphalt. This was a hundred times worse than any simulation the FBI ever threw at him. His arm hurt now, but he had to save the old guy.

"Get--" No. He squinted. The bizarre figure was running – no, gliding – away, down the street. As if his long robes hid skateboards beneath. Daniel staggered toward the neighbor's porch for cover. Steps shaky. Pepper fire out in the back. Windows smashing, tinkling. From inside this house, he heard the shotguns speaking. He crossed the porch, and the front door slammed open.

"Mister."

They were not cops, but two teen-aged boys, pale-faced and shaking, each clutching a hunting gun. So suburbia bred more than one type of hero.

"You boys, get down," Daniel commanded. At the end of the street, where it intersected with Northwest Avenue, an armored troop carrier had rolled up onto a lawn. Men in fatigues were advancing from it. National Guard.

"This way." Daniel waved. The teenagers followed, carrying their guns, stumbling, wide-eyed, watching every direction. Bodies of bogeys and cops lay scattered on the street.

"Are they gonna kill us?" one of the boys asked.

"Nah," Daniel answered, hustling now, waving at the Guardsmen. "See? The cavalry's here."

Two Guardsmen aimed at them, until one stood and waved them down the street, toward the safety of the armored vehicle.

Chapter 40
The Leper

Sheikh Al-med seemed more subdued than Esam had expected. His eyes partly closed, head heavy, resting upon his arm every few minutes. Perhaps he had not slept.

"The news is bad." The simple statement clarified what Esam had feared. The hero was missing, but the army raised by the sheikh did not have him.

"The Americans have Frank Whitlock," Waleed said flatly. "They had an escape plan we did not anticipate." He sat across the marble table, eyes darting, transforming from friendly to piercing to blind fury every few seconds. A madman who might do anything, even if unbidden. Esam regretted giving up his sidearm at the door. Were they looking for a scapegoat?

"But surely," he leaned forward. "Waleed just told me. You do not have reports from all of your operatives? They may have him. They just went under cover."

Waleed slapped the table. "They don't have him."

Al-med opened his hands. "Stop fighting like women, you two. Nothing is confirmed. We are a long way from the operation. It will take time for confirmations." His gaze wandered. This was the sheikh's way of being angry. Esam shuddered, thinking of the chessboard set up on the small table in the alcove. He avoided looking in that direction. "Your men may have him," the sheikh quietly.

Waleed's glare intensified. Esam folded his own hands and rested them on the table. Whatever happened, he silently vowed to snap that rat's neck before any guns could be raised.

"This was a joint operation, My Sheikh. If anyone has him, they are *our* men."

Lips drew tight. "You are aware of my meaning, Colonel. Suhail's men have him. Those are your men. You know them."

Esam reached for his pocket, and Waleed tensed. Only a small pad of paper came out. Making notes was a soothing exercise, even though he immediately ripped up any he made, for security reasons. He drew a line, and made that line fork into two.

"I may not know them, Sheikh. General Farid's greatest strength lies in his compartmentalization. His mind, in fact, works in two great segments. One shut off from the other. I can tell this from years of watching him. I fully believe that if you tortured him, he would not give up the names of his spies."

He circled one path on the fork. "I ran, and still run, military operations." Tapping the other line. "This is his intelligence unit."

The sheikh followed the pen, dark eyes sluggish, sleepy.

"It is a formidable network, I assure you. Of it, I know next to nothing. How do you think he became a legend with such a small number of operatives, compared to yours and the sultan's?"

A weak smile. "I had thought his fame derived from the brilliance of his top commander."

Esam let himself chuckle, but Waleed glowered even more ferociously. "This is camel dung." His gaze whipped back and forth, chastising them both. "Forty-five men dead. Another two dozen in a foul American prison, where the guards will let them be picked off, one-by-one, by murdering gangsters. This is not a joke." An accusing finger came across the table. "Suhail is a traitor. You work for a treacherous snake."

This was too much. Esam rose. "He is not--"

"He is an evil man. Allah protect us from his satanic designs." Waleed's face flashed purple, veins bulging from his neck. His left hand remained riveted somewhere down at his side. A pistol. Or a knife. "When will you understand, you fat fool? Suhail has no intelligence network. He consorts with devils."

"You will die for that slander."

"I said, *Enough*." Al-med rose, at the same time he gestured for them to regain their seats. Esam refused.

"My Sheikh. Would you sit here and listen to calumnies against your own teacher? This should be a festive meeting." A polite wave in Waleed's direction. "Yes, Whitlock is gone, but we have done the impossible, nevertheless. War in an American suburb – their residential areas are sacred, you know. It is the third tower. Their government cannot stand this sort of blow. Bush will be thrown out."

Waleed looked toward Al-med, likely to see which way the wind blew. He copied the sheikh's scowl.

"Who cares if Farid's secret spies have him?" Esam pressed. "We still have him. And I'm sure in the next few days, we will hear of his untimely death."

The sheikh spoke through gritted teeth. "Osama does not want him killed in a few days. He wants him dead now."

Perhaps Waleed's expression lightened a bit. "Sheikh, they will release the prisoners if we take action against American tourists. They will have to trade with us."

Idiot, Esam wanted to scream at him. Just as Suhail always contended, they threw ten men at a job for one, hoping for death, then when five got captured, they bellowed and whined about it.

"We will decide on those strategies when the time comes." Al-med rested his chin on both hands. "Esam, I want you to listen to someone wiser than I. Wahab," he called out.

A door opened, and a guard leaned in.

"Bring in the Leper."

Esam's blood ran cold. Was this it? He had heard the name before, but where?

Instead of an armed warrior, the guards admitted an old, stooped man who moved across the marble floor under his own power, but with difficulty, carefully placing the point of a tall waking staff down on the slick surface before each step. Rather than drawing close to the table, he chose to sit on a solitary chair some distance away. This was set up beforehand, Esam realized.

"Colonel Esam Malik, this is the Leper."

The old man bowed his head. "I don't really have leprosy, but my parents did." His laughter shook every part of his frail frame.

"Of course." The memory came clear now. He was a mullah, or holy man of some sort. The crazy man he had heard about since he was a young boy in Alexandria.

Al-med was watching, and spoke quietly, "The Leper is here to explain something to you." Esam felt tingles up his back.

"Do you know the difference," the old man began in a small, high-pitched voice, "between a good *jinn* and a *shaytan*?"

Esam saw where this was going. "Stop right there, sir. I will not believe that General Farid is anything other than a skilled strategist and master spy." He turned to the sheikh, but the Leper kept speaking.

"A thousand pardons, Colonel Malik, but you did not answer my question. Do you know the difference?"

"I have read the Koran, if that's what you mean. I do not busy myself with tales of the *blue jinn* and other such childhood ghost stories."

The Leper rapped the floor with his stick. "An entire people who exist in the cosmos and worship Allah as devoutly as you or I are not just childhood notions."

"Thank you for the lesson."

"Do you know what differentiates them from each other?"

Esam relented. "No, Mullah. Or whatever you are. How could I know details about creatures I can't see?"

"I thought so. Here is the answer. Some of the *jinn*, who make up one-half of the *Thaqualan*, the beings with souls, some of them have heard the word of the prophet and worship Almighty Allah. They are part of Islam. But there are also dark *jinn*, the *kafirs*, the *shaytans*. The *shaytans* are the beings in the service of your master, General Farid."

Esam knew he should be careful, but this was too ridiculous. A glance toward Waleed. "And how would you be able to know such a thing, Mullah?"

Another rap of the stick. "Because all of the signs are there. The *jinn* will fool, will play pranks, and will gather information for the right practitioner. But that information must be used for good. Only the *shaytans* can be harnessed to divine secrets that are used to kill.

"That, plus I and my colleagues have asked the question of our own *jinn* acquaintances. Your master has his own master. And it is the Evil One."

Esam shifted, glancing again at his nemesis. "Waleed, I will stoop to ask you for help. Because you, at least, are a warrior. I know you despise Suhail, but how are we to believe this?"

Waleed scowled. "I warned you before, Esam. Even ten years ago, I warned you about the things I had heard. Farid is a good strategist, yes, but too good. Everyone knows that."

The sheikh seemed finally awake. "Colonel, the Leper is a respected authority. If you are to remain a warrior in the service of Allah, you cannot remain blind."

Breaths came with difficulty.

The sheikh leaned over. "Esam. My son. You, yourself, are a tactical genius. The men respect you. You have been loyal to Suhail, as you should. But have you been loyal to yourself?"

Esam stared at the Leper. Another scrawny neck he would like to break.

"Each time you told yourself that Suhail gained intelligence through legitimate means, you believed your own lie. Your path here," the sheikh leaned forward and tapped the stick figures Esam had sketched on the outside of his notebook, "is one that stretches through Hell."

The Leper braced against his staff, nodding silently. Esam wiped his own forehead. "I will find out whether Suhail has the hero. Is that what you wish?"

The sheikh licked his lips. "And where he is held. Even an infidel like Frank Whitlock should be executed by the nation of Islam, not by Satan."

Chapter 41
Back in Washington

"All I want to know," Sullivan stood behind his desk, hands on his hips, "is what the living fuck you were doing out there. Ordering room service and holding your dick?"

Daniel sat, determined not to take the bait. God willing, he could catch this bastard in the parking lot, later. Jimmy Johnson crossed his long legs and stared straight ahead.

Fists on the desk, Sullivan leaned forward. "Well? I'm giving you a chance to weasel out of it, Daniel. Pass the buck to those jackasses who let two dozen of them come across the Canadian border. Or the policeman who stopped one in Sacramento, but let him go because he was a 'nice guy.' Or the fucking Coast Guard who missed a whole boatful of them coming down the Delta and putting in at Stockton. Go on. Tell me it was someone else's fault."

"Gerry, I'm not falling into your trap. You know the set-up. The FBI ran the show, but they never flinched when I gave an order. I take responsibility. I wasn't creative enough to imagine a frontal assault of the magnitude they executed. I expected a platoon, not a whole division."

"A division?" Sullivan looked over, as if Johnson could help him. "Now he's bandying military terms about." Back to Daniel. "You're goddam right you're responsible. Governor Ridge is taking heat about this. He may have to resign. And guess where that heat funnels down to?" Fists pounded the paper-littered surface. "It goes here."

He pushed his chair back and began pacing. Not usually a good sign. "Well, we're not through. I'm not letting them close this office when it's the best damned idea the government ever had. Homeland Security is a joke, and always will be unless they follow the model that we've been pioneering." Still walking, he completed a circle around both of them. Ceremoniously, he made eye contact, and buried one hand in the other fist.

"We're taking control of the whole shebang," he said. "The FBI has three targets picked out. Whitlock's got to be tucked away at one of them."

He shoved a notebook aside, and half-sat on his desk. "Sorry, Daniel, but Will Carpenter drew the assignment. He's already there, anyway."

"Carpenter's dirty, Gerry."

"Shut up. Your instincts haven't done much for us so far."

"I said he's dirty, Gerry. Or did you already know that?"

"I said shut up, Mister, before your foot fills even *your* big mouth. And we don't talk derisively about our colleagues. Period. Carpenter will get the job done, while you're redeeming yourself. Sheikh Omar is reportedly in Pakistan. I want you to fly over there and ramrod our participation. We may save your career yet."

No mention of Daniel being wounded in action. Thank God it didn't penetrate to the bone, but the Bureau would have given him a couple of weeks off. Nothing in the Liaison Office Charter about stuff like that, much less Homeland. Jimmy remained a sphinx, no doubt present only for the sake of documenting the meeting.

"How long is the assignment?"

"This is Monday. I want your ass on the ground and in harness on Friday. Pakistan time. Our guys say if it doesn't happen within another week, it won't happen. The Pakistanis want a couple more days to move their own guys around, so you'll arrive at the point of action."

"Moving guys around?" Jimmy finally seemed awake. "Or buying time to play us double?"

Sullivan shrugged, never taking his gaze off Daniel. "Just be there, OK? Carly's booking the flight. Briefing materials will be on your desk shortly."

Jimmy rose, but Daniel stayed put. "Can I see you a minute?"

"Sure," Sullivan answered after a slight hesitation. Jimmy closed the door behind him. "I can bet I know what this is about."

"Look, Gerry, I wound up getting involved with a girl you used to know. It's nothing personal."

"She doesn't want to be involved with you anymore."

"Let her tell me that." He scooted to the edge of his chair. "But that's not important enough to bother you about. This is about harassment. The kind of behavior that gets people fired, no matter how high they rank."

Sullivan had yet to look up. He opened a new file. Daniel extended a hand to stop the page from turning. "You're getting in over your head. Faking documents under color of authority is a felony."

"Take your hand away, Clooney. That sore arm won't serve you in a tussle."

Daniel came out of his chair. "Gerry, you're not listening. I'll run your precious errand to Pakistan, but only because I don't think you're stupid enough to try to set me up." He leaned his weight on the restricted file. "But if you ever threaten Loretta again, I'll bust your ass back down to boy scout. And if you want Johnson to take notes, bring him back in. I'll repeat my promise."

Sullivan pushed back, a person above this fray. "Would it change anything if I told you the little Kike is an agent for the Moussad?"

In spite of its absurdity, the remark made Daniel pause. "In your dreams," he said. "Then you could write off every soiree you ever had with her."

"Already have. But it's no joke. We're checking her out."

"That means no." Daniel walked to the door. "You're so full of shit. The CIA was smart to get shed of you."

"Did they?"

Daniel sat, still not bonding with the feel of his office. Away too long. If Frank Whitlock could sense the future, perhaps he could, too. This place was festering, and something was about to change.

It took a while to piece through e-mails and advisories on his computer terminal. Then suddenly, he was calling Loretta's office.

"Ms. Bernstein's office. This is Stacy Pringle."

"Hi, Ms. Pringle. Long time, no talk. This is Daniel Clooney. Will your boss take my call?"

"She's in conference Mr. Clooney. Would you like her voicemail?"

"No. Just tell her I'm back in town. Please." He hung up before she could recite any reasons not to pass on the message.

The Langley air was crystal, for a change, the trees possessed of lush leaves. He decided to take a walk, but when he pulled his sunglasses from his suit pocket, a card fluttered to the plastic rolling pad beneath his chair. At the same moment, Jimmy Johnson appeared at the doorway.

"Come in."

"Didn't have a chance to welcome you back."

"I haven't even been home yet. The director's welcome was enough."

"Pakistan, eh?" Jimmy slipped in and closed the door behind him. "I don't think I would go, if it was me."

Daniel finally brought the card off of the floor. "Why not?"

"Kidnappings. Bombings at churches." His eyes held a meaningful look.

"What, did he have you arrange a hit on me while I'm there? Or are you afraid I'll actually catch a criminal for a change?"

The tall man leaned back, propped against a chair, half against the wall. "Just a feeling. I was just going to ask you if you wanted to grab a date and maybe catch some dinner with my lady and me tonight."

Daniel waved. "Same girl? Keep the door closed." The travel department came on the line. "Carly? Clooney. Just talked to you. Can I change my flight going over? I need to be routed through Beirut." He tried to read the address on back of the card. English, but a weird hand. "Leaving tomorrow instead of Thursday. OK. Call me back."

Jimmy stared. "Are you crazy? There may not be any stuff going down in Lebanon right now, but that doesn't mean there won't be."

Daniel smiled. "I'm aware of that. Do you know CIA's head of station, there?"

A shrug, but for once, the tall man seemed put on the spot. "We don't have a station to speak of. Not since the Gulf War. Some people in and out, of course. I might know somebody."

"You have to hook me up. Bodyguard. The whole nine yards."

He shook his head. "They're bound to be busy with all this shit, Daniel."

"Jimmy, you owe me a favor."

"Bullshit. I did you one." From his jacket, the tall man pulled a folded piece of paper and tossed it onto the desk. Daniel flattened it out. It bore a neat scrawl of a simple Georgetown address. Loretta's.

"Thanks. But look, if I'm about to get kakked in Karachi, you owe me a dying wish."

A grimace. "So, double date or no?"

"Nah. Sorry. Not dating anyone just now. That's why I figured, what the hell, might as well leave tomorrow."

In his apartment, he checked the tiny markers he had left. A toothpick dug into the side of a drawer, socks and silverware arranged just-so, a small box of cash at the back of the kitchen utensils. Yes, someone had visited. The landlady pleaded ignorance.

He called Loretta's home number. Did not leave a message. Dinner would indeed be alone. With Jimmy's sheet of paper in hand, he did a drive-through, finding her townhouse on the second attempt. A glance at his watch. Too risky to check the front door just yet. This part of town was nice, but far from posh. The buildings stood close together, and hers would be split into several flats, or else she would have a brace of roommates to pay for it. On paper, the address was 1535-C, so it was likely the former.

Several blocks down the street, he found a delightful shopping area, a product of trendy refurbishment. Pizza parlor. Bars with pool tables. A couple of snooty restaurants. Keeping his eyes peeled, he parked, bought a polish dog at a small storefront, and strolled toward her house, careful to stay on the opposite side of the street.

An old couple emerged from the building, walking their dog, but many residents going in and out of other houses ranged from mid-twenties to mid-thirties, it appeared. Seventy percent employed by the government? Eighty?

Darkness took hold. He finished the hot dog and sat in a bus kiosk, wondering if she were already in the building. Wondering if he were crazy enough to stop in Lebanon. Tensions between Sharon and Arafat were high, and the word on the street was that it was just a matter of time before Syria marched through to the northern border of Israel.

He could figure out which one was hers, go around back, and look through the windows. A light mist had begun falling, but before he could act, he saw her. The form was a couple of blocks away, carrying an umbrella, but something about that electric walk made him catch his breath, and seemed to answer the question of why he had come, anyway.

Before he could strategize, he was walking rapidly, crossing the street. When she saw him at a distance, she hesitated, seeming ready to bolt down an alley, then kept coming.

"Hi."

Her legs kept moving, so he fell in alongside her.

"Heard you were in town. How's the arm?"

"Better. I have some antibiotic gunk they make me put on it a few times a day."

She stopped. Still a block from home. "What are you doing here?"

"You have your magic wall up. How can I defend your honor if I don't know any fresh details?"

"About Gerry? Don't bother. He's left me alone since I gave my notice." She resumed walking.

"Wait. You told me about the apartment. You quitting your job, too?"

"What do you care?"

They crossed the quiet side street, and he grabbed her arm and pulled her around. "What kind of talk is that? I do care. We need more time, Loretta. You don't have to self-destruct just because the rest of the world is."

She did not speak. Just stood there breathing. He tried to kiss her under the umbrella, but she pulled away, breaking into a faster pace than before.

"Jesus. Come on."

In three long strides, he was in front of her. "What's gotten into you? Gerry may be blackmailing you, but I'm the good one, remember?"

Her frown did not alter. "I wasn't counting on you for revenge, Daniel. You're the one staying in D.C."

"So why are you pissed at me?"

Her jaw set. "You let them have him." She dodged, and bolted down the walk again.

For a moment, he literally could not move a muscle. "Who? Whitlock?" he called after her. By the time he caught up, she was climbing the steps to her own building. "Are you nuts? I let them have him?"

"Well?" She looked down from the middle step, as one might glare at a child molester. "Isn't that what you went out there to do?" She raised a hand to block his reply. "Don't worry. Your precious boss didn't spill any beans. I'm good at putting two and two together. Remember?"

A single step up, and she twirled, striking out again. "What I don't get is why he signed you up to lure me away, if he really wanted me back." Arms folded. "But I guess that's not too hard to decipher. Jealous maniacs never want something until someone else gets it."

She turned again. Colors floated before Daniel's eyes. The mist felt like a greasy film on his eyelids. He still moved quickly enough to grab her coat, brushing her firm buttocks in the process. Yes, he still wanted her.

"You can't go yet."

"Let go, Daniel."

"You have to tell me what he said. About Whitlock. Exactly."

"I told you, I figured it out." She glared. "He didn't even mean to say it. It was the night he threatened me. Whitlock's picture was on TV, and he said something like we'd all be better off if they got him. A few days later, voila. You were his man on location. Mission accomplished."

Daniel sputtered, gazing upwards, past her, at the two windows open on the second floor, in spite of the rain. A Moussad agent wouldn't be spouting off like this.

He pulled her around, jerked the umbrella away, and took her forearms. "What brought on all this bullshit, Loretta? Two days ago, you said I was the one. When I was lying there in the hospital emergency room, you were the main reason I wanted to get through this. I got shot trying to save the guy, for God's sake."

She started to weep, tears mingling with raindrops. "This isn't real," she said. "I'm afraid. For Frank, but for me, too. I wasn't afraid, because I thought you were on my side. I thought *we* were real."

"We are real, babe."

He had her against his chest, holding tight. She wept for another minute, wiping tears that reappeared from the sky. "That first night," she said softly. "Tequila shooters. Did he pay for them?"

"I paid. I'm not his monkey "

She looked down at the steps, and pulled her arms free. "How can I believe that?"

His hand under her chin, he made her look up. "He's sending me on some wild goose chase to Pakistan, either to catch some Al Queda guys or conveniently disappear. But I'll be back."

"Don't go." A whisper. She wiped her face.

"I have to. He still has the cards, and I have to beat him at his own game. When I come back, I'll follow you. Arizona, North Pole, wherever. I think we at least need to try."

"When do you go?"

"Tomorrow. Going early, so I can check out a lead in Lebanon. Loretta, I'll be back."

She wiped her cheeks again, and climbed the steps. Slowly now. She stopped at the door and did not look around.

"Do you want to come in?"

"When I get back."

She seemed to take a breath, then pivoted and stumbled down to his level. For a long, glorious moment, she kissed him. "Call. I'll try to answer the phone, OK?"

He nodded. The rain grew heavier, and he heard the apartment house door latch behind her.

Chapter 42
A Young Soldier

Muuji thanked God that he had been sent on this errand. It was one thing to be the Master's pet, to watch Kareem sneer jealously, meeting out his harsh punishments, but knowing that with Muuji, there was a line he dared not cross. Even so, the Master's bizarre behavior of late gave him room to worry.

"It's the poison from the bullet," Kahder claimed. "Waleed dips his bullets in cow dung before he goes into battle. All of the sheikh's men do, because they belong in the heart of Africa, not in God's country."

Muuji ignored their exaggerations. But he was careful not to speak of the Master's new quirks. His long spells of gazing at the walls, incoherence, sometimes even when he walked.

He reached into the refrigerated case and gripped the bottle of goat's milk, lingering to feel the cool, blowing air. A chat with the shopkeeper, Mr. Qalqil.

"How is your sister, Yasmine?" the old man asked, his eyes sparkling. "I hear she is almost ready to marry."

"She is well, thank you." Was the master getting old, like this toothless old bugger who fell asleep at his counter more often than not? Did fighting lions age? He enjoyed Mr. Qalqil's questions, but stayed too long, and had to run, holding the bag out at arm's length.

"Slow down, you moron," Kareem yelled from his doorway. "You'll hit the bottle on something."

Muuji ignored him and hustled upstairs. Suhail sat on the balcony, drawing pictures in the air with his fingers, his newspapers neglected on the table.

"I have it now, Muuji." A great smile. "The piece of the puzzle that is missing. And you may drop it into place."

"Am I going to America?" The words spouted out before he could catch them. He was ready for war. Tired of the new tension between Esam and the others. Tired of the police lolling through, asking for cards and passports, when this alley used to be sacred ground. "Am I to be a soldier at last?"

Suhail was suddenly cross. "America is step one. You will be a sword for step two. Put a harness on that imagination and listen." He gestured, and Muuji sat in the chair opposite.

"You have been trained in firearms, yes?"

"Yes, sir."

"And there are no better teachers than Colonel Malik and Abdullah."

"I can use a pistol as easily as a rifle. I like the long rifles more than automatics. They use too much ammunition."

The Master changed moods again, and laughed. "You are a boy after my own heart. Precision makes the world, not random slaughter. Picture this, my son." He leaned forward, sketching the air again, eyes too intense to meet. "In one second, America's greatest hero is executed, for his crimes against Osama's freedom fighters. Executed like a criminal, for all the world to see. Do you have it in your mind?"

Muuji nodded.

"Then, a moment later, or perhaps an hour, but the same day, mind you, a second event takes place. The assassination of the Prime Minster of Israel. Do you have it?"

Another nod. "It would be miraculous."

Suhail laughed.

"But Master, when I was young, someone shot the prime minister of Israel, no? It did not lead to a collapse."

Suhail reached out to stroke his head. "Brilliant boy. It takes more than one blow to make a stubborn ox fall. Infidels can be strong, too. You are wise not to underestimate them.

"That brings the point. Pretend you are President of China. Or Russia. Or France. You act like you are friends with America because you have to. But what if the great Satan were humiliated? And their lapdog at the same time? Once you found that the greatest nation cannot protect its own people, and that we – the new leaders of the world – can do as we wish, whenever we wish, then wouldn't you, President Muuji, think about acquiring new friends? Stronger friends?"

Muuji did not hear the end of his speech. He was shaking. "But Master, Israel puts guards around their Prime Minister. Am I to be a suicide bomber?"

"You know that is never my way, Freedom Fighter. We will infiltrate you through Gaza. We will place you within range of the Prime Minister, himself, with your trusty rifle."

Instead of inspiring happiness, the glow in Suhail's eyes filled Muuji with dread. "But how? I have heard that they are smart. They change the schedules of their leaders. How can you be sure where he will be? Will I have to lie in wait for a year?"

A rough tap on the side of his head. "I will tell you where he will be, and when," Suhail said sternly. "And I will bring you out alive. How long do you care to wait to become immortal? Are you truly a soldier of God?"

"Of course. Yes, sir."

The Master stared into space, and Muuji resolved to ask no more questions, but then he could not stand it. "But, Master, is your intelligence network really that good? Colonel Malik says--"

Suhail gave a wave of dismissal. "Colonel Malik is not privy to my intelligence. He is a great leader, but between you and me, in confidence, he is too superstitious. Tell Abdullah he is to take you shooting tomorrow. At the camp near the trees."

"Yes, sir."

Muuji ran, slowed, glanced back up at the balcony.

"Where is Abdullah?"

Salma sat inside the door, painting her porcelain cups. "He is gone. An hour. Two."

Muuji kept moving, rounding the corner so that she did not think of a chore to give him. Must have time to study this. Suhail's favorite café was behind him, but he would head for the other one, a full kilometer away. Kareem said that Colonel Malik went to that one more often, now.

Imagine, sending a single sniper after a target as guarded and unpredictable as the Israeli Prime Minister. Of course, he had seen the Master in action. But some said he was too confident. Could that be true?

Muuji's pace slowed, and he scolded himself. The others were louts and conceited slobs. Always pushing him to the back, laughing and winking at him like a bunch of buggers. Only the Master had treated him like a man. What right of his was it to question the plans of such a wise man, the person who deserved all of his gratitude?

The green door of the new café came into sight, and something prevented him from turning around. Esam might scold him for his questions, but he was surely the only one who could explain that glint in the Master's eye.

Chapter 43
Through the Back Door

Loretta had read every book by Ian Fleming, all of John LeCarre. Gerry's weakness, or perhaps his strength, was that he confessed early that he was a spy. He was also prompt, so the doorbell would ring at any moment. She leaned against the couch, wearing the beige dress he liked so much.

That had been her own dream once, being a spy. But life and earning a living had reduced that dream to a weak fantasy. Tonight would be different.

Daniel would not approve of her plan. Even with all his "field sophistication," he might end everything if she had to go so far as to "ride the wild Gentile," as Gerry put it. But Daniel's life was worth more than their relationship. Americans did not send their countrymen into death traps, but Gerry was capable of anything.

Down the street, a car door slammed.

The Palm was his favorite bistro. She catered to his every whim, gave him every sign. He expected it later, she could tell. Thankfully, she did not have to steer the conversation eastward. When the oysters arrived, he did it himself.

"So what do you hear from our friend, Danny?"

"Not as much as you imagine. Why did you send him to Pakistan?"

"That's where he's needed. After he fouled up--"

"You mean you didn't tell him to let Whitlock slip through his fingers?"

Gerry exhaled, daubing his napkin at the corner of his mouth. "You know better than that, my dear. Daniel hasn't progressed past letting his feelings interfere with duty. Like someone else I know. But let's talk about just exactly where things stand with the two of you."

"Do you think Whitlock's already dead?" Step one, keep him off guard, and pretend her interest in Daniel was nearing zero at the same time. He would have listened to the phone taps. He knew there were strains.

An oyster was poised on the end of his fork. "What? Who can guess? If I know those Arab bastards, he was probably dead before they had him in the trunk."

Truth bumps skittered along her arms. She kept a straight face and sipped her manhattan. "Is that how they took him? The trunk of a car? How do you know?"

Gerry gulped, perhaps more than oyster. "I don't know. Had to be. It's the only way in a crowded city like Orinda. We had roadblocks on every street corner after the battle." He stared. "We were talking about your lover. Is there something amiss in Camelot?"

Stay the course, she told herself, and ignored his sneer. "I think Frank Whitlock is really psychic. Do you?"

He took a swallow of scotch, and pronged another oyster. "These oysters are from Nicaragua. The chef started ordering them at my request. Better eat your share. Of course he's psychic. So what?"

With her own fork, she went through the motions. "Then why did you do all that to him? You and Danny?"

"Because, my lovely." A slurp. "There are good psychics and there are bad ones. The bad ones are those who won't play ball with us--" His glass tinkled the point. "—in *exactly* the way we say to play ball." He motioned for another round.

Daniel was his agenda, and he would surely throw a tantrum and quit talking about Whitlock, but so far, she was stroking his ego just enough to get in the back door.

She scrunched up her nose in puzzlement, like the sort of weak, dumb broad he liked. "But why would a psychic have to do things your way? If he can see and hear all things we can't, why wouldn't your people just use some of his information?"

Munching again. It was like old times, and without much help from her, he was already too comfortable. "Because goofballs like that are unreliable. You ask them to close their eyes, go into a trance, and bring you information about X. They come back with shit about the whole alphabet. Did you know--" His gazed roved around the room, as it always did. Gerry was always on duty. "— that if you stage, say, a hundred remote viewing trials--"

"Remote viewing? That's where they can see objects and people from incredible distances?"

"Exactly, my dear. You are, as ever, well-read. I was saying, out of every one hundred remote viewing runs, they might be dead-on five or ten times. Sixty or eighty times, they come up with all sorts of multi-dimensional crap and rebounds from their own sordid little lives. You can't take that stuff to the bank."

His eyes were steel. He used the napkin with ceremony. Professor Sullivan was in full voice.

"Five times out of that hundred, the inimitable psychic will come back with some crap about UFOs watching our remote viewing target. So don't counsel me about who should call the shots. They're looney, the lot of them."

He dipped. He chewed. She followed suit. OK, Daniel was innocent. But was America's hero?

"Daniel seemed to suspect that Whitlock was connected to the terrorists, somehow. You don't think so?"

He swallowed. "Not a chance. They wouldn't have him any more than we would."

The salads came.

"You got me off of the subject," Gerry said. It took more liquor than this to sully those eyes. "We were talking about lover boy. Is it over between you two?" His voice lowered to a velvet whisper. "Or did he send you here, to tease me and find out if he's walking into an ambush?"

Loretta's stomach clenched. "Daniel wouldn't send me. He doesn't want me anywhere near you. Are you sending him into an ambush?"

A bad smile. "Wouldn't dream of it, chick. But there are all kinds of ambushes going on in Pakistan. Hope our boy keeps his nose clean. I know you're trying not to answer, but I think you just did. You two are still together."

Loretta's energy for cat-and-mouse had suddenly dissipated. "Look, Gerry, are you going to have Daniel killed when he gets to Pakistan? Or not?"

Gerry hovered over his drink, and his expression did not alter one iota. "What do you mean, when he gets there? He's there now."

She heard herself reply without thinking, "Wasn't he going to Lebanon, first? Wait, Gerry--"

An oyster stuck in her throat, and before she could take it back, he whipped out his cell phone and punched numbers.

"Espinoza?" he said into it. "I need you to look up the itinerary for Shadow Boxer. I'm going to need phone logs, too. In fact, get me head of Beirut station on the line right now."

"Excuse me." Her most withering look had no effect on him, so Loretta took her purse and rose. The books, and Gerry, had emphasized it a thousand times: a good spy always selects an emergency exit in advance. She had one—the door next to the women's restroom. It led through the kitchen, but the alley door was always open, she had been assured, and she could get to a cab rather quickly. How she would reach Daniel was still a problem, but the White House operators were equal to any intelligence agency in the middle of the night.

Breathing heavily, she rounded the corner, and passed the restrooms. *Employees Only*, the sign read. She gripped the knob. The door wouldn't budge.

Instantly, as if a real spy's instincts kicked in, she backtracked and ducked into the ladies' room. She would never make the front door. He always had them seated so that he could watch it.

The water ran cold, but she splashed it on her face. Stupid. She was out of her league. For all she knew, Gerry had paid off a busboy, or the whole damned staff. There was no way out.

The pompous devil had found his place in life. He could wield absolute power, and still be invisible. Her chest heaved, and she fought back tears. For the first time, perhaps, she wanted Daniel totally, and forever. And now, because she was such a smart-mouthed amateur, she may have just signed his death warrant.

Chapter 44
Transport

In the night, perhaps on the strength of Loretta's kiss, it had all made so much sense. No one had found a direct link between Frank Whitlock and the terrorists yet. Now the trusting old boy had rolled out the red carpet – for Daniel. There was no telling what this Lebanon connection was, and the hocus pocus with the white handkerchief, but somewhere out of all the confusion, he could feel pieces falling together.

Why had Frank chosen him? The answer was obvious, perhaps. Maybe Daniel was the first lawman not to look at him like he was crazy. Thank you, Loretta. He had learned to suffer loonies without even knowing it.

As the flight progressed, though, and the Atlantic fog below refused to clear, the real truth seemed to crash in as harshly as the high altitude sunshine. Frank Whitlock was certainly already dead. If he were one of the bad guys, and his kidnapping was a sham, he could have run his own errand in Lebanon. Elizabeth Kismet's business card flipped limply between his fingers. Then again, who knew? The guy listed on the back could be a hit man, and Daniel could be falling right into Frank's twisted notion of revenge. The feeling of being a target was not one Daniel relished.

At the end of the shorter flight from Rome to Beirut, through bleary eyes and a gut full or homesickness, he gazed upon the stunning figure of Roshanna Rainey, the inside person that Jimmy had contacted to pick Daniel up. She was tall, herself. Merely a secretary, Jimmy claimed, though she moved with the bearing of someone with more extensive duties.

"So how is Jimmy?" Roshanna led him through the few lines leading up to the baggage ramps. Travelers at the Beirut airport seemed even more wary than their harried counterparts at Dulles.

"He's OK. We've had our hands full. I'm sure you have, too."

She smiled, and nodded toward the man he had been watching, behind and off to one side. "Don't sweat him. That's Tariq, our driver. He'll keep us out of trouble."

"Good." Daniel hoisted the strap of his bag up over his shoulder. "I would rather not get kidnapped until I land in Pakistan."

The touch of her slender black fingers sent a chill over Daniel's shoulder. "The people here are nice. Just follow our advice, and your little stopover here will be a pleasant one. You were going to tell me about Jimmy."

"He's fine."

She stopped him. "Let me be more specific. How is Jimmy's *sex* life?" She laughed, and he could feel himself redden. With a jerk from behind, Tariq moved next to them, lifted Daniel's bag, and led them outside to a car where a very young man – perhaps a teenager – accepted a gratuity, and opened the doors.

"That's all you have? One body guard?" Daniel asked quietly.

"No."

"Any way I could get a sidearm while I'm here?"

Her first sour look. "No. Get in."

The car jostled through narrow streets. Exhausted, Daniel fought to keep his eyes open.

"Well?" Roshanna asked suggestively.

"That's a tough one to answer, especially since we just met." Daniel tried to keep his eyes on her, but there were so many places along the road where snipers could have their way. "Were you his girlfriend or something?"

A delightful, high laugh. "He didn't tell you? I'm his wife."

"What?"

"Well, we're in the process of getting a divorce, but that's been going on for five years."

Daniel heard himself sputter for a moment before he could form a sentence. "Jimmy's a great guy. I've only known him a few months. I think he's dating, but I'm telling you that under duress. The brotherhood of men, and all that."

Another laugh, and she squeezed his arm. "You are such a bad liar. You could never work for the CIA." Then a yell to the front, "Isn't that right, Tariq?"

"Yes, Ma'am." His accent sounded perfectly American.

Daniel took a breath. "What else is new?"

"So what is this big bad mission you're on? Jimmy was very mysterious, which usually means you're just some traveling salesman. FBI, right?"

He nodded. "Before they made the Liaison Office."

"Well, the Lebanese have been showing some great cooperation with the FBI agents you guys already sent. So what is this new thing you're working on? Somebody spot Osama Bin Laden on the shores of Tripoli?"

"It has to do with Frank Whitlock." Her gaze narrowed, and he decided to play it straight. A glance at Tariq, who had slowed the car, tooting on the horn in short bursts. Daniel watched the throng of people alongside the road. Asia. He had been in Dharan before, but never here.

"Quit staring at him." Roshanna nodded toward the driver. "He's got a better security clearance than I have. Jimmy thinks your man's dead by now. So do I."

"Maybe." Daniel produced the card, and pointed to the address. "I need to see this guy. Tonight, if humanly possible. My boss will throw a hissy if I don't get to Pakistan by the day after tomorrow."

She scowled. "This is an address?"

Daniel shrugged. "That's all he gave me." She handed it up to Tariq.

"This town is ten kilometers northeast of Beirut," the driver said, looking into the rearview mirror. He held the card up. "I know this avenue. But is that 'red statue?'"

"I think so."

"Statue of what?"

Daniel pulled it from his fingers. "It says it is the street directly north from some plaza. House on the corner. Red wooden statue in front of the entry."

An American-style shrug. "We can try, but that town's off limits."

"What?"

"He's right." Roshanna settled back, and began perusing the landscape herself. "Until further notice, we have to register any law enforcement or U.S. government visitors with the local police. FBI agents are restricted to Beirut, unless accompanied by Lebanese police or military. No exceptions."

"Shit." Daniel shoved the card back into his jacket and wiped his face. "Does this car have an air conditioner?"

Tariq only laughed.

"Is that where we are going? To register me with the police?"

Roshanna kept her gaze on the traffic jam that had materialized around them. "Not necessary. Jimmy told me you were just taking a vacation day here."

Considering its history, and the current state of affairs, Beirut seemed a quiet town. No longer the *jewel of the Mediterranean*, perhaps, but modern buildings pushed into the air, complete with construction cranes. Quaint plazas and passageways suggested this land might hold its enchantments in hiding, like, maybe, Mexico, if it weren't for the unmistakable bullet holes that still pocked many buildings.

At the hotel, the American "unofficial" residence took up three floors. Roshanna introduced him to Leo, who showed him a restroom complete with shower, and who fed him English biscuits and coffee, demanding that he stay awake until sundown, or the jet lag would fell him. Leo wore no coat, but a starched white shirt, no tie, and his eyes were altogether too bright. Likely some ivy league prick who had found his career here, and would no doubt be the first on the roof if the helicopters came to get them.

"Where is Roshanna?"

"Oh, she promised to be back at dinner," Leo said. "Can you tell me more about the Whitlock case? How did they spirit him away with so many people watching?"

Though he felt refreshed, in the manner of being run down by a truck, Daniel recoiled. "Whoops. Don't know how much of that I'm supposed to discuss. Security levels, you know."

A nod. "Don't worry about me. Do you think they had someone on the inside?"

The first face that popped into Daniel's mind was that of Will Carpenter. The second that old man in the Halloween costume. He blinked, and yawned. "Shit. Did they say anything about taking me anywhere tonight?"

An insipid look. "Where do you want to go?"

"I'm following a lead."

Leo seemed suddenly bored, and there was a commotion out in the hall. He stood. "Well, I've got a few things to do. Please excuse me. Feel free to read any of the magazines or books over on that shelf. Make yourself comfortable, but try to stay awake. I promise you'll thank me tomorrow."

He exited the small office, leaving the door wide open. Two middle eastern men were talking animatedly with an obvious staffer. Leo erupted into Arabic, and appeared to try to settle their argument for a while, then gave up and moved off down the hall. The pilgrims remained, looking puzzled, taking turns leaning into the office and smiling. Each time they did, Daniel's skin crawled. He selected a *Newsweek* that he had read two weeks before, and sat on the couch. When he woke, the windows were letting in darkness, and Tariq was tugging on his sleeve.

"Come on, Señor," he said in a mock accent, and laughed. Leo leaned against the doorsill, looking a bit older and less business-like. Daniel blinked, certain that he detected the odor of bourbon.

"You ran our boy here on quite a little goose chase this afternoon." The Ivy leaguer raised a hand and began chewing on a fingernail.

"Who, Tariq?"

The young Lebanese smiled broadly. "I remember going all over that town when I was a little boy, and never found the statue. It was invisible, I think."

"You didn't find the house?"

Tariq plopped down in a chair. "Yes. You can choose between a little tourist shop with a blue statue of some Babylonian goddess, or the red bull statue in front of this house. But it was hard finding much red left on it. The old fool has it standing out in the rain."

"A bull? Why would there be a statue of a bull?"

"Ancient Sumerian symbol of productivity," Leo answered, going from one nail to the next. "It was sort of a thank you to the gods, and a prayer for more cattle."

"You did all that this afternoon? I should have gone with you. Will it be easy to find it again?" Daniel rose. So did Tariq.

"Yeah, but I don't think you'll like it. The man who lives there is a holy man. His type won't talk to foreigners."

"Holy? You mean a mullah? A cleric? Whitlock didn't say anything about that."

"Just what--" Leo interrupted, "did Mr. Whitlock tell you?"

Daniel felt himself flush. His head pounded, and the dread was back. This was a fucking dead end, and he didn't have the heart for Pakistan. Sullivan had effectively taken him out of the hunt. "What he told me was a smoke screen. Something about this guy fixing problems. I'm looking for a connection with terrorist groups. As you might have guessed."

Leo raised his eyebrows and shrugged. Tariq's head shook slowly. "It's possible, but that kind of guy doesn't usually mess around with the mundane."

Daniel straightened his coat. "What are you talking about? I thought certain mullahs were some of the bad guys."

Tariq waved his hands in front of him. "You don't understand, Mr. Clooney. He's a holy man. Sort of like what you call a witch doctor. A mystic. Very weird. When you're sick, and no real doctor can help, they take you to him."

"Better chuck it in," Leo suggested.

Daniel glanced out the top of the window at the dark sky. This holy man was his only card to play. If he listened to reason, it ended here. "No. Tariq, if I pay you, will you at least take me there?"

A glance at Leo. A resigned look. "Come on."

Through a couple more checkpoints, then into a small room where a man behind a counter seemed to know they were coming. He gave a couple of clips of ammunition to Tariq, then shoved a silver pistol in Daniel's direction. "They said you know how to use it." It was a simple revolver, a thirty-eight, but not as small as a special. The kind gangsters gave to a stoolie they were sacrificing to the cops.

"We'll try to be back before midnight," Tariq explained as they belted up in the car. "Here are the ground rules. You don't speak Arabic, do you?"

"A few words. Want to hear them?"

He shook his head, and they pulled out onto the street. "It's dark. We can't take this car down the street where the house is at night. Most decent people will be asleep, but if anyone speaks to us, especially if they are in a group, you let me answer. Got it?" An intense look.

"Sure."

"And when you knock on this guy's door, you do it quietly. If it's loud, then all of his neighbors will pour out into the street. This guy is one of those queer ducks the people like to gossip about. But he's a fixture, and if they think some foreign devil's trying to harm him, I may not be able to get us out of there."

"OK." He resisted the urge to tell Tariq about the ritual Frank had dictated. If the old man threw the handkerchief back at him, would he have the balls to knock, anyway? "Where did you learn your English?"

"University of Illinois," Tariq said. "We moved to America when I was fifteen."

"You called him strange. Does that mean dangerous?" It was a rookie question. "I mean, what else did you find out about him."

"That's the whole shot. Didn't want to get the druggist suspicious."

"Look, tell me straight." Daniel exhaled longing to close his eyes for a minute. "Are the streets full of guys hunting Americans?"

"Sometimes." A wry smile

"That reassures me, Tariq. Thanks."

Chapter 45
The Arrival of Horses

The small town boasted two bulky skyscrapers that towered into the air some fifteen and twenty stories, respectively. Others of lesser height loomed as stumpy, unlit shadows behind them. Tariq guided the car left and right, through a queasy, jolting maze, until he pulled up directly onto a walkway.

"This is the plaza." There were closed-up shops, but Daniel could see nothing that differentiated the street from any other.

Across the way, two vendors stopped boxing up their sidewalk tables and accosted them, zeroing in on Daniel.

"Laa. Laa," he said, refusing the scarves that were being thrust up toward his face. "No."

Tariq came up behind them, and uttered a rebuke of some sort. As Daniel backed away, the young guide produced a few bills and gave each one of them some. "That's to stop them from talking about us to their friends," he said when he caught up.

The light of a storefront fell behind them, and within a few steps, they were plunged into the Arabia that Daniel had always imagined, growing up. Short and squat buildings crowded the lane, so narrow that he thought he might touch both sides if he stretched his arms out.

"*Salaam*," a voice said from somewhere below. Daniel's stomach churned and he was sweating, but could see no form in the shadows. Tariq answered with a short sentence that had *Allah* in it.

"Is this the famous *Casbah*?" Daniel asked in a whisper.

"No. Shush."

They went straight, then twisted and turned up a different avenue. "Stop." Tariq's shadow looked this way and that, and then produced a small penlight, which he used to study a tiny hand-drawn map. "This way."

The light went out, and Daniel let the man keep touching him, pushing this way and that on his back, indicating the direction they must take. "There's a store," Tariq whispered. A wave indicated a building with big dark splotches that might have been windows, but that was far from certain. The shadow pointed across the street. "That's it, over on that corner."

"These people have electricity. Why don't they use it? Is everyone already in bed?"

Tariq exhaled. "Maybe they're morning people. Or maybe they just like to sit in the dark and think. Like real humans do. The young people who like to party do it downtown."

Daniel shut up, letting a clump of bodies shuffle past in the dark, chattering in staccato singsongs. When their sound faded in the lane, Daniel's ears seemed to come alive in the flood of silence that poured in, punctuated by the hum of insects, the distant barking of dogs, and a soft murmuring that issued from a closed door of a house on their side of the street. The cracks around the door wavered with inner candlelight, and he thought that there could never be such a peaceful scene. What must it be like to live in that shut-up enclosure?

"There," Tariq insisted.

No moon was evident, but perhaps starlight was mixing with the glow from nearby cities. Daniel could just make out the rather largish structure, with a smooth wall stretching out behind it to the right. Was that the courtyard?

"What are you going to do?"

Daniel shrugged. "Just follow instructions, I guess."

"I'll be over in front of that boarded-up store. If you get into trouble, yell. Remember, knock softly."

Tariq dissolved into the darkness, leaving Daniel on pins and needles as he squinted to memorize the location of the correct front door. Finally, he took a breath and walked in careful strides to the wall on the side. The handkerchief he had bought at Dulles Airport lay in his pocket, still unwrapped. The cellophane covering came off with a crackling sound that seemed to spur more chattering shadows into motion, going from and to nowhere. Daniel slammed back against the wall, panting, hoping Tariq had things under control.

Without thinking, he raised the handkerchief to his nose and smelled it. Fresh and stiff, the odor reminded him of Loretta's collar, that first time he removed her shirt. What the hell was he doing here? Any of these shadows could take him without a sound, and Tariq would stand there until he noticed a body lying in the dirt in at dawn. Unless he were one of them. Daniel stood on tiptoes. The wall must be eight feet high.

On the first attempt, the cloth came fluttering down against the wall, and he grabbed it just as it hit the ground. Now it had to be dirty. Daniel shook it, and though Frank had insisted that improvisation was not allowed, he reached down, felt for a small stone, and wrapped the cloth around it. This time, it went over, a speeding miniature ghost.

Breathing hard, Daniel waited. Nothing. Then a slight scraping sound. A metal chair on bricks? A minute more passed, and Daniel realized he might have made it to step two. Hands out ahead of himself, he groped his way back around the corner. Tariq had hidden himself well. Following Frank's instructions, Daniel positioned himself in front of the door, and waited again.

Seconds passed. Then minutes, and the darkness was a greasy highway for all the doubts in the world to come barreling down. Above, a gloriously starred sky seemed to mock him, a wounded pawn in an impossible, fuzzy war, trapped down here in this pocket of shadows. Why should the universe care about him? Obviously, it didn't. Every one of his recent actions, from winning Loretta, to protecting Frank, had been stunted at the last instant.

Perhaps failure was genetic. He thought of his father, and the frame-up, if that's what it was, that finally drummed him out of the service. Good men seemed to have a hard time of it in this world. Not Gerry Sullivan. The gods laid down a path for raving assholes only.

The interminable silence grew louder until it was, itself, noise. Pulses of tension pressed between the plaintive dogs' warnings, and voices came from doors. Were they talking about the stupid American standing there in the dark?

At the very point Daniel was considering yelling for Tariq, and trying the knob, a latch clicked, as loud as a rifle shot. His breath caught as the front door swung open, illuminating a strange world. Inside, an elderly woman, gray hair coiffed, attired in an expensive looking dress gave a sort of bow, then retreated into the mass of light, apparently resuming her chore -- laying down plates at the place settings of a large banquet table. Two blazing electric chandeliers and a host of lamps lit the old lady from all sides, as if she were on a movie screen.

Daniel blinked, and even shielded his eyes to make the transition. Seeing no one behind the door, he cleared his throat. "Is this the home of Mr. Khoury?" By reflex, he gripped the handle of the pistol in his belt. If an ambush were coming, surely it would be soon.

The woman raised up, five-feet eight-inches or so, a grandmother, but almost too lithe for that. Her hair was somewhat unkempt, blackish with tinges of brown and gray at the ends, as if she had once decided to dye her hair, then thought better of it. In America, he would guess her to be sixty. Here, fifty, maybe. "Please come in." Her eyes were clear. Attractive.

"You're having a dinner party." Daniel held his place. "I'm disturbing you."

"I have time." Finally, a wisp of a smile.

Daniel took a step. "Thank you. I'm sorry, but I was told that if I threw the handkerchief over the wall, and the door opened, Mr. Khoury would see me."

"Mr. Khoury sees few these days. Is there anything I can help you with?" The smile grew.

Daniel squinted to read the card, though goodness knows there was enough light. "Sandaleh. Sandaleh Khoury. I need to speak to him, and only him."

Her eyes grew sly.

"Look, ma'am, cards on the table. I'm looking for a terrorist cell, actually. A friend of mine – who might even be under suspicion of being connected to terrorists – referred me to Mr. Khoury. If you'll just lead me to him, I won't take up your time. Are you Mrs. Khoury?"

As he talked, Daniel had drifted into the room, closing the door carefully, and using his peripheral vision to scan for possible ambush points. The only thing that stuck in his mind was the unsettling view of a side room he passed just inside the entry, off to the right, its door only cracked. Any number of assassins might be concealed in that room's darkness, but the impression left in his brain was that a miniature electric train set occupied the room, extensively laid out on a large table.

She shook her head, and started to laugh. "I'm afraid I wouldn't make Mr. Khoury a good wife. Not at my age." Her laughter grew louder.

"Nonsense." Daniel decided to try one spurt of flattery, even though the jet lag had him on the verge of dropping, and this place felt dirty, in spite of the bright lights. "You seem very young. Surely Mr. Khoury is in his sixties, by now?" Without thinking, he sank to the couch behind him.

Another laugh. "Try seventy-eight. A victim of gout, I'm afraid. He was diagnosed with cancer last year, until I talked him out of it."

"You speak perfect English. Please, is he here?"

A scowl. "You've made two mistakes, visitor from the night. First, you didn't introduce yourself. Second, given the course of our conversation, you are supposed to ask me my age."

"Oh? Sorry. My name is Daniel Clooney." He stifled a yawn, hand still in contact with the pistol in his belt. "And how old are you, ma'am?"

A slight bow of the head. "I am three thousand, two hundred and twelve years old, as of last July. Pleased to meet you, Mr. Clooney. My name is Khulud."

Any comfort Daniel was starting to feel melted away. His hand was starting to ache on the pistol grip. "Then years in Lebanon must be very different, Mrs. Khulud. I'm here on serious business. We are getting reliable intelligence that another attack is being planned. People will die. Surely you don't want innocent people to die?"

"Of course I don't. And it's not 'Mrs.' I buried my last husband some two hundred years ago."

It occurred to Daniel to stalk outside and wring Tariq's neck. Or maybe it was Jimmy – was this a put-up job that they were recording, so they could laugh about it later? "Khulud, I would love to stay and be the goat for your jokes, but I have a war to fight. If I can't see Mr. Khoury right now, I'm afraid I must be going."

She put down the last plate and moved quickly, more fluidly than a woman of her age should have been able to. Before he could flinch, Khulud was seated on the sofa next to him. "I see, Daniel. But what could old, dying Sandaleh tell you that a three thousand year old woman could not?" She chuckled softly, and her hand brushed Daniel's arm lightly. Almost like a lover's touch, it seemed to take the steam out of him.

"Your house. It's beautiful. The lamps."

"Why, thank you. Light is such an unappreciated luxury. You know, the word luxury comes from the word for light."

"Are you a linguist of some sort?"

Another bow of her head. "I have lived long enough to learn many languages."

Though the abode appeared smallish from outside, now he could see that another room was connected to this one in the corner, L-shaped, stretching into shadows. By contrast, it was lit only sparsely, and he thought he could just make out the shape of a cross on the far wall.

"Are you Christian, or Muslim?"

She smiled, coyly, almost. "I am older than either of those religions. I thought your friend told you. Not older than Moses, perhaps, but my people raised me in the ancient ways."

"So you're Jewish?"

A girlish sigh. "No. My parents were very strict, and their beliefs pre-dated the religion of Abraham." She grew suddenly intense. "How many horses brought you here?"

"Horses?" Daniel recoiled. For the shortest instant, the look in the old lady's eyes had seemed that of a madwoman.

The room fell quiet, except for a soft hissing, perhaps a gas heater. Outside, the barking dogs were still making their reports to each other. Silently, he marveled at the brightness in here, and how the windows were shaded so tightly that none of this light escaped out into the dark street. Were the insides of all of the homes like this? Khulud's eyes were peaceful, her dress homemade, yet elegant at the same time. Elizabeth's relatives were just like country folk in the states. This woman was no terrorist.

"Yes. Just before you arrived, I could have sworn I heard an entire team of horses pull their carriage up to the door. A sound I used to relish, for it meant visitors, distractions."

"You're not making any sense, Mrs. Khulud."

She laughed easily. "That is my curse, I fear. But I am not prone to hallucinations. It seems there is a reason you are here. A reason that I cannot ignore."

"I'm sorry. I'm wasting your time."

"Please, sit back down." Her gesture held him in place. "You threw the handkerchief, and the door opened. You can't leave until your wish has been granted."

Kindness filled her eyes, but the statement was somehow scary. Daniel strained to hear any movement in that dark room. He pulled out his notepad. "My wish? It's really Frank's wish. I just have questions."

She interrupted, studying him politely. "Do you know how much like your grandfather you are?"

He shrugged. "I'm sure there are similarities. Genetics."

A smile. She pointed at his pen and paper. "I'll bet he used one of those. He probably took notes, too."

"Sure. But I'm usually sitting in front of a computer. I've almost forgotten how to write longhand."

"Ah. It doesn't matter." She sat back, hands around one knee, like a teenager resigned to entertaining her company for a while. "Did you know that if you could see a movie of everyday your grandfather lived, and his grandfather, and fifty grandfathers before him, that you would be amazed to see how much like all of them you are? Toys change. And tools. But humans do not. And the hand motions are almost the same for a computer as they are for scraping fat off a goat hide." She laughed heartily.

Without knowing why, Daniel felt his heart quicken, and he was suddenly wide awake. He slapped the pad against his palm. "I didn't come here to talk about goats, Ma'am. And I don't care about reincarnation or whatever you're selling. A man has been kidnapped in America. A friend of Elizabeth, Mr. Khoury's niece, and I'm trying to save him. His name is Frank, and that is his wish, that he be saved."

Khulud squinted, his words apparently hitting home, finally. She gazed at the well-lit table, absently flipping the colorful scarf from around her neck into the air. "But that is a wish only you can grant, impatient Daniel. Your friend did not cross my threshold. You did. But my party begins soon. You must state your own wish. That is the way, in this house."

Daniel was flustered, fidgeted with the pen. "My question is to find out what his connection to the terrorists is. Frank, I mean. He could not have done what he did alone. And is Mr. Khoury connected to bad men? No offense--"

Her eyelids closed, until she was peering at him through slits. "Your wish is to know if this friend of yours is for real?"

The words stopped him. No, that wasn't it, but it was. "What's in that front room? A toy train?"

The elegant woman's eyes widened, and she laughed her comfortable laugh. "Toy train? Did you have a toy train when you were young?"

"Yes. Is that what you have in there? Is it Mr. Khoury's?"

She reached out, and stroked his hand softly before he could move it. Her touch was soothing. "You come from a hopeful society. Let's go look at your toy train."

Something about the glint in her eye – Daniel had the unmistakable feeling that she knew about Frank, maybe knew a lot, but was playing coy. He tried to form new words, but that shining look, her simple smile, had the effect of stopping his tongue. Without another word, she rose. So did he, and followed her toward the front of the house. Her movements were lithe, easy. The scarf traced patterns in the air. She was more like a young girl leading a friend to play than some ancient, gray-haired woman. Nevertheless, he tensed as they approached the room.

She reached the door first, and pushed it open wide. Daniel's fingers dipped into his pocket, wrapped around the weapon, though he kept it hidden from Khulud. She paused, then stepped in when she realized he didn't want to go first. Daniel blinked, his eyes making the transition from bright light to darkness, yet the expansive diorama on the large table was illuminated with muted glows. His blood turned to ice.

A picture – a three-dimensional photograph, not a train set – hovered in the air in the middle of the room. "My God, it's a hologram, right out of Star Trek," he said automatically.

Before them lay a perfect image of the buildings and streets of a modern city. It wavered in the air, like a bright photographic slide projected on a cloud. The motion disoriented him, made his footing feel goosy. Yet it wasn't just a picture, was it? The miniature structures seemed anchored into the very wood of the table. The concept of some special effects studio in Hollywood came to mind, though Daniel had never seen one in person. It was like a movie set – part physical models, part projection, though he was damned if he could tell where real left off and illusion began. "A movie. It's a three-D movie," he cried into the darkness.

"Not a movie." Khulud seized his hand, pulling it away from the gun. She interlaced her fingers with his. "Don't let go of me whatever happens. Your wish is being granted."

Chapter 46
Wishes

Daniel strained against the old lady's surprising grip, trying to keep his knees from buckling entirely as a wave of nausea swept over him. He staggered, looking above, behind, for any light that might be the source of the remarkable video projection, but she pulled him closer, and when he saw the tiny cars and taxis cruising on the road around the tidal basin, he was overcome with a sense of dread. This was no cartoon, nor a film – somehow, this was real life he was watching. Washington, D.C., from a plane ten thousand feet in the air.

"Satellite," he bellowed automatically. "This is a terrorist cell, and you have satellite pictures we never dreamed of." Was is possible that the terrorists had leapfrogged American technology?

Khulud's strange, musky perfume enveloped him – she was suddenly close to his face, breathing into his ear. He couldn't recoil, for he didn't have the strength to pull his gaze away from the wonderous sight floating before them. "That's right," she whispered. "Don't look away. You are seeing reality, the four-dimensional Earth, as viewed from the fifth plane."

"What?" Gasping.

"Don't avert your gaze," she commanded again, and squeezed his arm. "Watch the silver bird."

The scene suddenly blared with light, as if the sun had risen on this miniature Washington. He could see the individual trees, trucks, fire hydrants, moving people. Trash and leaves blew in the gutters, and the landscape tilted and swayed. "The goddam floor's giving way," he screamed.

Another squeeze. "Concentrate on the silver bird, and you will stand straight."

A meaningless promise, but he held onto it, and saw the shiny glint off of the tiny flying thing, and focusing on it suddenly detached him from everything except her hands. The silver hawk flew high above the phantom Washington. At first, the bird's wings flapped. Then they became rock-stiff, and so did Daniel's legs. He was mesmerized, watching the smooth flight through the air, until the creature suddenly dove, like a seagull for a fish. Its sides became metallic, and it grew in size until it transformed into an airliner, gigantic, and now Daniel was flying too—

"Hey, help me Khulud," he cried – but from the corner of his eye, her placid stare was the only answer – it was too late, anyway. He was plummeting through the air, and she was coming with him.

His entire field of vision was sucked downward, falling toward the plane – but just as they were about to slam into the metal exterior, he blinked, and woke up to a frantic, riotous scene: Khulud was by his side, standing in one aisle of an airplane – and Daniel was only inches away from a man's tortured face. Frank Whitlock!

Flight 3456 – there were the pilots lying dead, the throng of bodies in the galley, Frank's 'instant commandoes,' the average Joe Six-Packs he had coached into an attack plan only moments before, according to the transcripts, were locked in hand-to-hand combat, faces wrenched in agony, screaming, fierce eyes, spouts of blood shooting through the air like a gory Hollywood movie. The fighters, as well as various limp bodies tumbled through Daniel's field of vision. The airplane was bucking like a bronco.

"Stop – Stop it. Please," Daniel cried. His heart slammed against his sternum, but a jerk from the woman forced him to re-focus.

A terrorist sat in the pilot seat, wide-eyed, pressing down on the throttle, obviously trying to kill the craft's speed. Frank Whitlock kicked his hand away. One of Frank's commandoes swung a wine bottle at the terrorist copilot. A miss. The bad guy stabbed with something. Then a tackle, and a twist of the neck. Bodies were flying – they had suddenly become weightless. Still, they continued their struggles in mid-air, throwing futile punches, grabbing, twisting.

Screams echoed through the tight space, and Daniel's stomach clenched. Daniel could see Khulud, watching the scene as he was, though her eyes were calm, as if she witnessed such horrors every day. It seemed that she and he were pressed against the first class bulkhead, but he could feel no physical contact with it. A group of instant commandoes fought two terrorists in twirling space, reaching, kicking for footing.

There was Frank, again, climbing the side of the cockpit like someone on a ladder. He gripped the pilot's chair – the dead terrorist was still strapped in it, staring vacantly into space – with amazingly sure movements, Frank braced against the floor, pushed on the pedals with his feet. In this horribly awkward pose, he had to peer around the dead body for vision. He gripped the wheel with one hand, while the other shoved the throttle all the way up to the 'high' setting.

Bodies crashed to the floor. Frank was bringing the wheel back slowly, and Daniel had a moment to breathe. Whether it was a dream or hypnosis, he could study the hero's face, close-up, pimples and pockmarks and razor scrapes – blood oozed from the numerous cuts the bad guys had inflicted.

This wasn't the sullen, housebound Frank, but a stronger, dashing Frank, his eyes burning with defiance and purpose. The terrorists lay among, and atop crewmembers and some of Frank's instant fighters. Now Frank was barking orders to those who could stand up, wisely telling them to go through the plane, seeking other terrorists, asking for volunteers who had pilot's licenses. The terrorists had cut him, and someone was wrapping his arms with a shirt-cloth, while another pair of hands worked at patching the pilot's headset back together. It wasn't working. Instead, a flight attendant gave him a cell phone.

Blood dripped, making a scarlet patch on Frank's shirt, and the passengers who had not passed out in the smashing descent stared wide-eyed, many of them whimpering, holding their heads in pain. Now Frank was chattering into that phone. There were no other pilots on board, someone reported. Daniel watched Frank's eyes. The news only seemed to ignite more defiance in him. Daniel felt a rush of caring for the old guy. He reached out, intending to touch Frank's shoulder, but a squeeze on his other hand made him look up.

He felt nauseated, wasted, and the old Lebanese woman was studying him. "My God, Khulud. Is this some high-tech simulation? Or did someone film the hijacking?" he asked between heavy breaths.

"Shut up, the silver bird is still flying. Now you know your friend told the truth. He was not one of the bad men. Most people on this earth would be happy with one wish, but you are an American. You lied to me – you have more than one wish."

A shake of her hand made him look back at the scene – the silver bird was indeed airborne again, bobbing and swooping above the city. The creature spread its wings and fluttered to a landing on the windowsill of a house. Daniel stared in awe. Night had returned, and they were looking over a woman's shoulder.

It was Loretta, with Gerry Sullivan leering through the door with a look in his eyes that made Daniel feel even sicker than he already was. The ex-lovers were arguing, but words would not come clear. She let him in, and they roved from room to room, his hands reaching out in supplication. Then in threat. He grabbed her.

"No. Stop it, you bastard," Daniel yelled.

"They can't hear you," the woman whispered into his ear.

Even while his lover tried to pull away, Daniel's gaze was captured by the furniture in Loretta's bedroom, which he had never seen in person. It looked like a college girl's apartment, hodge-podge pieces, nothing matching, stuff she must have bought at garage sales. But in the corner, a red lacquer cabinet stood out, adorned with Chinese characters along its sides. Sitting atop it, a tray of almost the same color, filled with bottles – not liquor, but expensive perfumes. The only extravagance in view.

Loretta backed up, close enough for Daniel to touch her, but something prevented it. Gerry had her hand, and was not letting go.

"No," Daniel repeated.

Loretta struggled, but Gerry slapped her, and forced her back onto the bed. She was crying.

"Gerry. I'll kill you," Daniel screamed.

Amazingly, Gerry's head lifted, as if he had heard. Loretta reacted, grabbed a lamp, and smacked it across the Liaison Director's forehead. Gerry sprawled to the floor.

"Is this real?" Daniel asked, but when he looked down, his feet were no longer standing on Loretta's wooden floor, but walking on a dirt road. The crisp smells of early morning dew-laden grass invaded his nostrils. "Where are we?" He looked up to see the woman walking beside him, her arm no longer interlocked with his.

"This must be your last wish." she said quietly. "My soup may be boiling over."

"Hey, Danny--" A new voice turned him around. Bending over in the middle of the field, his father – as he looked a long time ago – was patting the side of their hunting dog, Luke. A shotgun lay across Dad's arms, broken down.

"Isn't this the best?" his father asked, and stood up straight, looking around to survey the landscape. "Isn't this the best morning that could be?"

He had forgotten that his father had said that, a dozen times, describing a dozen mornings. Daniel was free of the woman, and there was no resisting it, so he ran. Ran like the world would end if he did not give his father at least one hug. But the old man saw him coming, and the thick grass beneath Daniel's feet turned to sand, and the surrounding cedar trees fell away, taking his father and Luke with them.

"What happened to my wish--" he started to say, his heart pounding in the new, moon-like landscape. The only signs of human life were a pair of structures – a shack and a trailer – standing forlorn in the middle of some desert – Afghanistan? Was the woman about to show him Bin Laden? The time of day had changed, too – he guessed it was just after dusk, or before sunrise. From behind the hut's door came murmurs – they sounded like the prayers he had heard walking along the street outside Khulud's house.

Daniel scraped the sand with his shoe, as if that act would ensure that this scene would not also vaporize. He turned completely around – the old woman was nowhere to be seen. When he moved, he noticed a deserted SUV, parked off the road behind the shack. With some horror, he realized this really could be a terrorist camp – through some trickery or drugging, Khulud might have delivered him right to the bad guys. The sounds inside that shack were the voices of killers getting ready to come out. He felt for his gun, and prayed she had not taken the bullets away.

Out here, in the middle of nowhere, in a foreign land, he figured he didn't stand a chance if he ran. His only option was to strike first, so he crouched, and settled his hand around the knob of the hut's door as silently as he could. He brought the pistol out and braced to make his move. Then a gust of wind blew sand into his eyes until the darkness returned, the murmuring prayers ceased, and he could no longer feel the structure's rough wood.

Blinking. The sky dimmed, replaced by shadows. He was indoors, again.

"What the hell are you doing to me?" The room came into focus, but it was dim – her concert of bright lights were nowhere to be see. The only forms were partly lit by the harsh fingers of lights that pricked through closed blinds. Beneath him, a cool leather sofa. It felt familiar, luxurious. Now he remembered. He was back in the office in Beirut, where he had gone to sleep that afternoon. He rubbed his eyes. So it had all been a dream.

Then a movement in the shadows next to him stopped his heart. The woman, Khulud, was standing next to the couch, her flowing dress brushing his arm.

"Are you real?" Daniel asked, when he could breathe again.

She touched his hand. "I lost track. Was that three wishes, or four?"

"I don't know what they were. Of course, my father, but those other places--" Daniel's voice shook.

"You came for help. Sandaleh took your kerchief, so it was my duty to answer the questions in your heart." She stood up, glided to the center of the room, and raised one hand. As if she had hit a switch, the security lights outside turned off, throwing them both into pitch darkness again. "You won't find me again, young man," she said quietly. Dreamily.

"Come back, Khulud. I'm not sure what the questions were."

He said it too loud, because chairs started scraping somewhere outside, down the hall, and the room's door slammed open. Roshanna stood there, dressed in sharp business attire, backlit by the glare of morning light.

"So there you are, sleepy-head."

"Where--" Daniel got to his feet. The woman had disappeared. "I had a strange dream. Damn. Did I sleep through the night?" He reached for his backpack, and started stuffing his notebook into it. "Hell, did I miss my flight to Pakistan?"

"You ain't going to Pakistan, my dear. There's been a change of plans."

Daniel looked down. The bottoms of his shoes were caked with dirt and sand.

Chapter 47
The Desert Lion

The morning breeze whipped at Suhail's newspaper, as well as his feelings. There it lay, on a back page, a modest mention of the assassination of an Italian minister who had been too supportive of Israel. Kareem had passed his first test as a commander.

He read the last paragraph over. Again. *One perpetrator captured.* He sat back, grinding his teeth. He needed to be in the field. Yemen was closed, now, and the Sudan was iffy, but there was still a facility in Libya, as well as those two here at home that the police had not violated. Yet the Blues were refusing permission.

Next to the newspaper lay a crumpled note, its message scribbled in a hasty hand. The sort of note he would never have received under Esam's command.

One freedom fighter captured, it began, echoing the headline – *Is there money to pay off an official? Can Abbas' family expect any relief?* Did the new generation know nothing of hardship? Did Osama have to put up with such whining? No doubt Esam had always filtered such problems out, saving his general from the worry. But had he sent boys to do a man's job? A man did not insist on payment for every job of the heart.

But that wasn't the problem, was it? The Blues had been crystal clear in their blessing for this operation. How had it strayed so far from perfection? What force was clouding their messages so much as to make them unreliable?

Voices rose on the street below. Esam, himself, was working his way from one storefront to the next. Let him come. Suhail sat back down, and returned to the paper. It would be essential that he recount each step with Kareem, starting with the guns in Albania. A leak? Perhaps. But why then were they not all killed? The mistakes in the real world mirrored the miscommunications with the Blues.

"Master." The big man appeared on the balcony, offered his kisses. For the first time, he had not knocked before entering. *The traitor is more dangerous than ever – show no fear,* the Afrit Prince had warned in the Cavern of the Jinn only last night. But how could he ever begin thinking of Esam as a traitor?

"Congratulations are in order." Esam gave a ceremonial bow. "The street is full of your praises for the successful strike in Milan. 'Old Suhail,' they are saying. It is just the start, eh?"

Suhail offered a chair. "That is much praise from a son who has strayed. If you had been with us, Esam, there would likely have been no casualties. Kareem's men would have gotten away without a trace."

"Casualties? I heard only of the arrest."

"Minor. He will recover."

Esam looked rested. And possessed of a new shrewdness, though it was shrewdness he wore on his sleeve. "Was the fault one of execution or intelligence?"

He was fishing. Suhail ignored the question. "I have faith in Kareem. He will learn, as you did, Colonel."

"I'm sure he will." A sigh. "Master, the man on the street is usually smart, but not always. The talk in the cafes is that Frank Whitlock burned up in his own house."

A look. Suhail nodded, pretending to consider the possibility. The pudgy eyelids blinked. "What they don't realize is that Hadeel and Ibrahim's bodies were never found. The Americans have no reason to hide them. On the contrary, they would have bragged about two more kills."

"Logical." Another nod.

"Master, where are they keeping him? The sultan still has men out of place, exposed. Or they will be, very soon. We need to kill the hero, complete the spectacle, and move on to the next mission."

Suhail's hackles rose. Making demands was a new talent for the big man. "The sultan loses more than half of his men because he usurped our plan, and decided to stage World War III in an American neighborhood," he said. "Now you tell me he has this great, anxious concern for the survivors. Impatience, Esam. We learned the wages of that vice when we were young together."

Their gazes locked. Esam's customary fear, uncertainty was still there, yes, but it had been joined by a new recklessness. The disease of fame had finally filtered down to him – from Osama to the sultan, to the sheikh. It was a diseased soul Suhail was beholding. A pity, when he had once been only fertile sincerity.

"Bah." Esam rose and stomped into the kitchen. "Why can't you take my advice just once, Master Farid? Dump his body in Hollywood or Union Square, and free us up to go on. Your men are tied down, too." He was back at the balcony door, a can of juice in his hand. "It is Hadeel, isn't it? Give me the com-link and your codes. He listens to me. I can make the arrangements for you. Your soldiers need not die, if that's what you're worried about."

Suhail stood, an action that made Esam flinch. "Colonel Malik. To give you access to Hadeel is to sign his death warrant. I am amazed that after a lifetime of *my* training, you have adopted the sultan's sloppiness in a matter of weeks."

Esam began to bluster, but Suhail waved him down. "Please. We are old friends. Let's not pretend. Go and tell your new masters that I will give the American hero up only when they release twenty of Osama's best warriors to me. To report to me and work exclusively in an assassination that will destabilize Israel."

The big man lowered his drink. "Master Farid, this is madness. As your friend, I counsel you. Even if the sultan agreed, the troops are too indoctrinated. They would never give you allegiance." He thought for a moment, then began to plead. "Master, you have never been prey to ego. It is such a little thing to admit that Osama possesses the momentum, the leadership right now. We can be part of the picture. An important part, as always. But we must learn to *follow*."

Show no fear. Not so easy, since the emotions pouring from the overweight commander were more violent and festering that he could have anticipated. Suhail stepped through the door, heading into the apartment. The Blues were watching, he could feel, so he *willed* a silent plea for help into the cosmos. He couldn't gauge what the traitor – Esam – was capable of just now.

"I will not follow schemes that come directly from that movie star, Osama. My operations will go on as I planned them. And without his help. Freedom fighters from everywhere will think twice about him, when they see that it was I who took the hero. And they will see that very soon."

Esam stepped toward the door. Perhaps he was not here to assassinate his former commander after all. In the same moment, Suhail sensed a *ping* flying through the air. The Blues had sent reinforcements. Suhail remained on attack. "I have sent Muuji on his first real mission. You will hear of his success, as well. Very soon," he said.

Esam looked dumbfounded. "Muuji? You sent Muuji?" In another instant, his lips grew tight, and he paused on the threshold. "I'm sorry, Master, but your request for twenty troops will never work." He closed the door again. His hand clenched. Released, then clenched again, until he lowered it into the jacket pocket where he usually retained a small pistol.

"I'm afraid I must insist," Esam said, his face dark, menacing. "We need the method of communication to Hadeel, and the codes. I must take them back to the sheikh now. I'm trying to hold this liaison together, but Master, please do your part." He was almost begging, but his hand was still in the pocket. They both knew what that meant.

Suhail seethed. "You must do your part, as well, Colonel. Do not enter my door again."

Immediately, a low, vibrating rumble started – from nowhere, at first. Or maybe beneath their feet. The noise grew, becoming awful – the unmistakable growl of some huge feline beast – and it seemed to take form, finally projecting from behind the pantry curtain.

Esam's body jolted, and his hand emerged without the weapon. The growl gained power, repeated, became a roar. Esam could only stare at the curtain, until he turned back to Suhail, lips trembling, and spitting foam for just an instant. Esam slammed the door open, taking great gasps as his feet pounded down the stairwell.

Suhail stood in the middle of the room, breathing deeply until the beast's grumble faded. He looked up. "Thank you, my loyal friends," he said to the Cosmos. Then, wearily, he turned back to his chair on the balcony. Later, he would send another racer, with instructions that Esam not be allowed to sleep tonight.

Chapter 48
Gerald's Exit

Frank knew it was the middle of the night. He was not sure how he knew, behind the blindfold, in the tight little enclosure – a closet. Had to be. Perhaps it was the cool. Or the smells. On the third morning, his sinuses were so clear and the dust on the closet floor so grainy, he could only think of the desert. But which one? Nevada? California? Arizona?

The kidnappers were surprisingly business-like. Because he gave them no trouble? His ears told him there were only two. That seemed strange. He asked for Sam to come and tell him where he was, he didn't feel the least bit sleepy. He was still waiting for them to take his picture holding a daily newspaper. Would they ask for ransom? Release of the prisoners being held in Guantanamo? Or just a videotape of his throat being cut?

It really didn't matter anymore, did it? When he saw Jill lying there, eyes sparkling, he knew that his job was done. Nothing else made a damn. Thank God these devils had kept their side of the bargain. They had at least a degree of honor.

His ears perked up – in the distance, the unmistakable wail of a coyote – his friend from last night. Indeed they had to be in the boondocks. Likely, when reinforcements joined these two, that's when it would probably happen.

He took several sharp breaths, and tried to turn over. No, the place was too tight. About the only movement he could manage was banging one foot against the wall. Were they oblivious to the fact that middle-aged bladders couldn't wait?

He thought of Andy Warhol. Fifteen minutes of fame. Frank had a new formula. Take fifteen minutes of terror, add six months of fame, then top that off with a few days of living hell. He closed his eyes, confident he had had a larger dose of each than most ever would, and that the hell would soon be over.

Even in her impeccable clothes, Roshanna could move quickly. "How did you get security to let you in?"

Daniel wiped his eyes. "Huh? I told you, I passed out and had a dream. Why didn't someone come get me?"

She stared, skeptical. "Daniel, who really let you in? Tariq? He called earlier. Said you sent him a note that you wanted to stay in some lady's home. The security password was scribbled on the note – so he just figured you knew what you were doing, and left. Is that all this was? A joyride with some lady?" She helped him up, and led him out and down the hall.

Daniel shook his head. "You don't know the half of it," he muttered.

They passed the equipment room, and the same aging sergeant-type who had given him a pistol in the dream held his hand out. "Your firearm, sir."

"What?"

Daniel pulled the gun out of his belt and exhaled, trying to put memories in order. "Did I really go last night?"

"Come on," Roshanna demanded, "don't horse around. You're worse than the tall boy."

"Clooney?"

"Yeah?"

Leo held a stack of files in one arm, blocking their path toward the garage. "We expect a report when someone runs an op from here. I didn't see your name on the log, either. Who let you in?"

Roshanna waved him off. "Leave it be, doll. Our boy's stock is trading, and we have to get him on a plane before the Lebanese government finds out."

Leo sputtered, but let them pass.

They climbed into the back of the same car he had come in. The driver was a mature, sour man Daniel had never seen before. As they entered the road, he looked at the peaceful countenance and tried to speak quietly. "I keep asking, Roshanna, but you never answer. What the hell happened last night?"

"Whatever it was, it's above my security clearance, sweetheart."

"So where am I going? What was that about my stock?"

"Back to D.C. My ex wouldn't tell me why. I'm guessing they're either gonna give you the gate, or a nice fat raise. Flip a coin, doll."

"Damn." Daniel slapped the seat and the new driver jumped. "I need to talk to Tariq. Find out what he saw."

"He's gonna be seeing stars." Roshanna smiled the smile of a woman who knows how function in her environment. Any environment, likely. "I think his story about some lady with a note is bullshit. Probably him that had the hot date, not you. Prep school trash, that's what he is."

A car met Daniel at Dulles. That had never happened before, and it merged with his utter weariness to make him wonder – had life become one long dream? Or nightmare? The driver was a sharp young marine. Maybe there was a war on. Daniel knew better than to ask him the news, but caught him checking his rear-view mirror more than necessary.

Jimmy Johnson's office lay unoccupied, but he spotted a gangly arm in the conference room and stepped in. The table was filled with stacks of paper, and Jimmy hovered, one long finger on one pile, saying something to Leah Cummings. His voice was barely a whisper. Not his work voice.

"Hi gang."

"Oh, shit." Jimmy grinned.

"Woo-woo. The new boss caught us fraternizing." Leah blushed.

"What?"

He looked down the hall at Sullivan's closed door.

"Go on down," Jimmy said. "He's still here, and I think he wants to tell you himself."

"Come in, hotshot." The voice, more friendly than usual. Daniel entered to a scene of Sullivan animatedly stuffing items from his desk into a single box. When he finally looked around, Daniel found himself grappling the end of the couch to keep from fainting. Sullivan's right temple was covered by a substantial bandage, out in front of which trailed the red and brown streaks of a bruise.

A grimace. "The little kike did it," he said. "She flipped out on me. Be advised. For you, it's just a matter of time."

"Is that why you're quitting?" Daniel managed the question, even though his ears were ringing.

Remnants of one drawer were dumped into the box. "Not quitting, and you know that. Good luck finding Frank Whitlock. I imagine he's sleeping next to Jimmy Hoffa by now."

"Since when do Arabs use cement overcoats?"

An insipid smile. "Don't get too cute. I may be in a transition phase, but I'm not a bridge you want to burn. I'm a survivor." The clipped machinations continued. "This is your office now."

"Thanks for the hand-off. How long will Liaison last, do you think?" A good successor would ask for a briefing on the top issues, but there were other fish to fry. "But then, you never really left the CIA when you ran for Congress, did you?"

A pause. "You're guessing." A narrow look. "You always guess before you have enough information to make it a decent one. That won't go when you're in the top slot. You wanna pitch in the big leagues, wise up."

"Well, let me return the compliment." Daniel sank to the arm of the sofa. "You're a good actor. You really do believe in psychics. You fooled me."

A picture came off the credenza. "That's classified information."

"Sure. Everything's classified. Then let me try a hypothetical. What if I had saved the flight instead of Whitlock?"

A slim file barely fit, then Sullivan started wrestling with a tape dispenser, stretching wide strands over the box corners. He tapped a fat stack of folders. "Familiarize yourself with these, first. Secretary Ridge will want a briefing on every one of these guys before the week is out."

More tape. "Hmm. But you pose an interesting question. If it were you, Danny, you would be the greatest hero in the nation's history. Speeches. Book deals. Four or six years from now, a U.S. Senator."

"Then why in God's name did Frank have to go through all this?"

The credenza door came open grudgingly. Sullivan peered in for a moment, then raised up and counted out his reasons. "Number one, he had enemies. Number two, that's classified."

"Please don't tell me he's been CIA since way back when. Frank's too nice to run with your kind."

A look. "You run with my kind." A chuckle. "We would never let someone like him into the CIA."

"Then why--"

Sullivan stared down his sizable nose, a sort of final, unctuous pulling of rank. But for Daniel, a few more puzzle pieces into place.

"You shit," Daniel said. "He wanted to start a psychic cadre in the CIA, and you already had one, didn't you? But of course, you guys wanted people you could train and control, not people like Frank."

This smile was cloudy. "I like watching blind FBI hogs turn up acorns. Why don't you take the test again? Could be a real job in your future." Back to his packing.

Daniel kicked the desk. "Gerry, there's a war on, sure, but you just couldn't stand to let someone else have a little glory."

Perhaps Sullivan drew up into himself. "Damn right there's a war on. But there's another, bigger war raging behind that one, Bucko, and we sure as hell can't risk losing that one."

"Another war? Our psychics versus theirs?"

"That's classified."

"Fuck." It was all Daniel could come out with.

Sullivan was packed. Two boxes in the corner had not been closed. He gave them a cursory glance. There was still something left, but Daniel didn't know how to get it out of him.

"Do you believe in fate?" Daniel asked.

"No. I just hate coincidences."

"Then you really got screwed, didn't you? Five billion people in the world and Frank's the one who gets on the plane."

"Look, pal, I didn't keep him out of the company. That was before my time." He tossed a small magnifying glass onto the blotter. "You're still a young punk. That's for when your eyes start going. From me to you." He picked up his box. "Someone will come for the rest."

Daniel rose and blocked the path to the door. "Do you know where he is?"

"Whitlock? No."

"But you helped him get kidnapped, right?"

A small shake of the head. Eyes darting. He was being careful. "No."

As if the blockade meant nothing, he came on. Daniel feigned a step aside, then grabbed one arm, twisted, and swung. Sullivan must not have expected it. Knees buckled, the box went flying. The heel of one of the boss's hands came around in a karate thrust, but Daniel blocked, then jerked the first arm up behind and behind his back, and shoved him against the wall.

He moved close to Sullivan's ear. "I'll open up that hole in your head that Loretta started if you don't tell me where he is. I'm not bluffing."

A grunt.

Daniel pushed. The pain would be considerable, now. "I mean it, Gerry. If I say we were fighting over a girl, they'll believe me."

Sullivan gasped, whispering with difficulty. "They gave him an option, he took it. We don't control the bad guys. It was going to be a hit, but more of theirs were going down that ours. Double-cross, but we both profit." Pressure. A weak yelp slipped out from deep in Sullivan's throat. "They're planning some sort of execution ceremony – that wasn't part of the deal, so we've been looking for him, too."

A shove, and Sullivan collapsed over the sofa arm. Daniel paced, keeping an eye on him as he rose. The former director was panting, measuring the distance between them. Then he shrugged, and stooped to reassemble the contents of the box.

"I'll give you one round, Clooney. That's it. For the little kike. Next time, we play for keeps."

"Fine by me."

Sullivan opened the door.

"Gerry?"

A pause.

"I'm going to find him," Daniel said. "If your boy Carpenter or anyone else interferes, they lose everything. Pass it on."

A grimace. "Go on. Be the next hero. Go get him if he's still in one piece. Just keep him quiet about things he knows not of, or you'll disappear, too." Daniel gritted his teeth, and Sullivan held up a hand. "That doesn't come from me, Danny – it's from higher up. A lot higher."

Daniel watched him to the elevator. Jimmy loitered at the door to the conference room. "That sounded like fun," he said, when the doors shushed together. "Come here, I want to show you something."

The other offices were dark. Jimmy's empire of paper had been stacked into six piles. He pointed at the tallest one. "That contains all the hot leads. Carpenter has them on the front line. Most of them point to the Eureka area, or the Oregon border."

"Will Carpenter?" Daniel slammed his hand down on the stack. "Then these are out. Eureka's just the kind of dodge that bastard would pull."

Jimmy scowled. Daniel fingered through the other stacks. One was flat, consisting of a single report. "What's this?"

Jimmy scanned it. "Another unlikely. Couple of Middle Eastern guys seen abandoning a Lincoln Navigator – brand new – in the desert near Baker, California. Rented six weeks ago, they extended the contract with a bad Visa card."

Daniel sat down. "Who filed it this report?"

Reading. "Eric Ramos. He's the top dog at our office in Barstow."

"Do you know him?"

"No, he's FBI. But he did talk to me on the phone before he faxed it." Jimmy pushed back from the table. "He worked for Sullivan in the private sector years ago, he said. The aluminum company. They had a falling out and he got sent out to the boonies."

"And he wound up going into the FBI in Barstow?" He put his finger down on it. "This report. We start here."

Jimmy's jaw dropped. "Why?"

"Because you're an idiot."

"No, I'm not."

"Yes you are. To split up with a girl like Roshanna, you have to be insane."

Chapter 49
Raid in the Desert

They planned all night, scanning through the several odd leads that might be. Might be. For some reason, Jimmy was agreeable, and did not piss and moan each time they started over. Perhaps the tall freak understood how desperate Daniel was. Time was running out for Frank. But Daniel kept returning to the Barstow lead. Rural area, the woman had said. Somewhere no one else wanted to look. A risky piece of driving all the way from the Bay Area, but something was *right* about it.

Before dawn, with Jimmy threatening to go for coffee or go home, Daniel called Eric Ramos, chief of Barstow FBI Station, and woke him up. It was two a.m. there, and at first, he denied any knowledge of the report he had filed. Finally, he seemed to have his wits about him.

"That's bullshit. Just some assholes on their way to lose their money in Vegas."

"How can you be sure?" Daniel asked.

"An experienced agent's intuition, Director Clooney. Something I used to use in another life, until a certain superior busted me for it. And you know what? I don't give a shit."

"Hold on to your pajamas, Ramos. That stuff's over. I need your help. Have their been any, and I mean *any* other suspicious things your guys have seen or heard about? We're under a time deadline here."

"I bet." A pause, followed by a belch. "Jesus. Couple of ragheads nearly started a brawl at the Impossible Strip Club. A few days ago, up near Interstate Fifteen. No biggie – one of them just couldn't take any ribbing from one of the place's drunken regulars."

"Impossible What? Where is that?"

"Look, sir, since nine-eleven, we've had every well-meaning yokel in the desert call us when they see an Arab or a Jew driving down the highway, so don't jump to the same conclusions. That's my advice." Another burp. "The Impossible's out in the middle of the desert. Cold beer and air conditioning."

"This was a strip club? Muslims aren't known for going to strip clubs, are they?"

"Well, I'd never have given it a second thought, except that one of the desert rats claims he saw a gun when he followed them into the parking lot. We just sent their license number to the police in Vegas and San Bernardino police. Another SUV – rented, I think we found out – in Fairfield." There was a long pause, and jaded man's voice changed. "Shit. That's up near San Francisco, ain't it?"

"When do you go to work?" Daniel asked.

A grunt. "Eight. Standard. Maybe nine, now, sir, since you kept me up on official business."

"How many guys can you round up?"

Across the table, Jimmy seemed suddenly aware of Daniel's thought process. He stuck his two wide hands up, waving them while he shook his head.

"Huh? Six. Eight if I call in the retired guys."

"Well, listen to me, Ramos. You get to work at nine o'clock and get those agents lined up. Call San Bernardino to watch your store, and don't tell them why. Tell them you had a picnic and all the guys got food poisoning. Do you understand?"

"Food poisoning?"

"It's a cover story, trooper. I want your men outfitted and ready to go by ten. I'll be there as soon as I can. Tell no one. And I mean that, Ramos. Don't screw up." Daniel set the phone down. Jimmy's face wore a look of dread. "Can we call Carly to get some airline tickets?"

"She's doesn't come in 'til nine. And I'm not buying into any hair-brained schemes. You want to fly to California, we got a jet. You're the director now, remember?"

"Yeah, but there are eyes watching every government jet. Pack your kit, Jimmy, and not one word to your friends in the Company."

A long exhalation. Jimmy looked straight ahead. "I got long legs. It's hard for me to sleep on airplanes. One peep out of you, and you make the flight in the toilet. Is that clear?"

Daniel nodded, and could not suppress a smile.

The long day turned longer. Almost the entire flight to Las Vegas was spent weighing the consequences if he were wrong. It might mean he was not Acting Director anymore. A smart man would have gone home, or knocked on Loretta's door and tried to clear things up. Was she injured? She probably had a black eye, at least, if his bizarre vision with Khulud continued to prove true. And what made the president have acted so quickly, and given Sullivan his walking papers?

Carpenter was the wild card here. And Carpenter had connections sanctioned by Sullivan, so he would have no problems going up against the new director. It might not take the traitor long to see through the cover story Daniel left. But some of what Sullivan said had to be true – maybe Carpenter thought he knew where the hero was, but the terrorists had double-crossed whatever traitors were mixed up in the labyrinthine scheme.

From the plane, he called Loretta, during one of Jimmy's bathroom breaks. Yes, she was still employed, Stacy

Pringle assured him, sounding an iota friendlier. No, she was in New York, with her seriously ill mother. No, there was no number she was authorized to release.

A second call – this one to Ramos. Apparently a self-starter. He already had a guy track down the owner of the strip club, who remembered the two free-spending "camel jockeys."

"And this is something they never told me," Ramos's voice was actually excited this time, " — that jackass owner told me one of those yahoos came back to the club a second time, just a couple of days ago."

"Bingo," Daniel said into the airline cell phone. "They're there, Chief Ramos. Don't go yet, but stay on task."

Jimmy passed out the minute he returned from the john, and slept through the drink service. At McCarran Airport in Las Vegas, he shuffled down the walkway like a groggy giant. "I don't know what the fuck I'm doing. It's almost happy hour at the MacIntosh." The puddle jumper they boarded for the hop to Barstow did not improve his mood.

"I'm driving back, man, and you're going to sign off on it." He fell asleep again.

Ramos met them, himself, and drove them to a garage below a county facility.

"I sent three on ahead, with instructions to canvas any patrons of the Impossible Strip Club," the aging agent said. The handful of others he promised were joined by an off-duty police officer, a young guy named Packard.

"He any good?"

Ramos gestured with his shoulder. "He's the cousin of Castro, over there. Worked on a SWAT team in LA for a couple of years."

They drove in three cars. Civilization ended at the Barstow outskirts and the desert took over.

"Shit. I didn't know we flew all the way to the moon," Jimmy said.

Daniel's eyes stung. As it had on the way to Lebanon, the certain feeling in his gut had started to fade.

Jimmy might as well have read his mind. "One thing I'll say for my new boss. If this is a dead end, and we're three hundred miles off the mark, and if old Will Carpenter finds our boy up in the Bay Area about dawn-time, I'll be telling tales about you in Langley for years."

"Right."

"So, dude, you'll go down in the CIA annals either way. It's win-win, Daniel."

"Shut up."

They rendezvoused in Baker just as the sun was dropping toward the far-away ocean clouds on the horizon. Ramos's forward men filed out of their vehicle. Conflicting responses to the photographs the agents showed the strip club regulars. But the lone middle eastern man who had supposedly paid a second visit had driven away in a tan Lincoln Navigator, rather than the dark one they drove on the night of the near-brawl.

"Shit, does every Arab insist on riding in luxury?" Jimmy said.

"What does that mean?" Daniel asked. "They abandon one, get another, then a third--"

"No evidence the first one was tied to the last two," Ramos said.

"Maybe they like 'em for the global positioning," the cop named Packard quipped.

"So," Jimmy interjected, "best case is they're still around here somewhere. Get the license plate?"

"No, but it was new," another of the forward guys said. "We have queries ready to go out to all the rental places and dealerships on the West Coast. This one might have been purchased, you know."

"Not yet," Daniel said. "We stay absolutely quiet for now. So," he paced, partly to keep awake. "Sorry, Ramos. I got your guys fired up too early. What say we spend the night here and call out your helicopter in the morning?"

Jimmy shook his head. "Helicopters make noise."

Ramos put his hands on his hips. "That's our best bet. Cover more territory."

The leader of those who had gone to the club, Clarence Williams, puffed out his cheeks and looked down. His skin glowed copper in the setting sun. "All this betting talk."

Daniel examined him. "Got any better ideas?"

The agent's cheeks gained color. "No. Unless you really like to gamble."

"Fuck." Jimmy Johnson whipped around and began to amble away. "Don't ask him that. He does."

"Explain yourself, Williams."

The veteran put his hands in his pockets and rocked on his heels. "Lots of losers in that club. The guy who saw the Navigator claimed he saw that car sitting out in the desert, then in the parking lot of the Barstow Walmart, then – hell, he saw it every time he looked up. Pretty drunk, so we moved on to someone else."

Daniel drew close. "If he was so drunk, how come it feels like you're giving him some credence?"

Williams shrugged. "He might just want some attention. That type, you know? A real desert rat. Shuns company, but starved for attention."

"You didn't answer my question. Where was the desert sighting, or was it nebulous?"

"That's one he was most specific about. It was on an abandoned road thirty, thirty-five miles out."

Daniel's head raced, but the cell phone on Ramos's hip buzzed, and the station chief walked away from the conversation.

"So? What's your call, Williams? Do we waste our time on a lead like that?" Daniel asked.

A shrug. "The club's owner knows the drunk. I wouldn't have mentioned it, but something about him stuck in my craw ever since we left the place."

"Great." Jimmy threw his hands up. "Women's intuition strikes again."

"Call the owner and find out how we can reach this guy," Daniel said.

Ramos approached. "Afraid not. Party's over. Just got off the phone from Washington. They want five of us up in Eureka by dawn."

"Shit." Daniel stomped a foot. "Will Carpenter."

Ramos grimaced. "That wasn't Carpenter – some guy named Rincon. Managing the recovery operation, he said."

"Why now?" Daniel sat on the car's hood. Take five away, that left four. Plus Jimmy and himself. Bad odds if they ran into a whole platoon of terrorists. "Did you confirm you would come?"

A nod. "It was an order. They said Secretary Ridge signed off on it. They think they have the hero located."

Daniel looked at Jimmy, fully expecting a new cluster of curses, but the ex-basketball player only scuffed his feet against the pavement. "You outrank Carpenter. He's got a lead, you've got a lead."

Ramos grunted. "A piss-poor lead versus Ridge? You know which one I have to take."

"You can catch a flight from Barstow to San Francisco or Eureka tonight?"

"We have a government plane. On loan since September Eleventh."

Daniel looked around. The other agents had slowly clumped around them. Any terrorist on the lookout could spot them a mile away.

The basketball player swung his arms, as if warming up for a game. "You can't go out if the airport's closed."

"What?" Ramos asked.

Jimmy shoved his hands into his pockets, acting thoroughly uninterested with his own idea. "This has to be a good-old-boy town. Surely you know the manager of the airport. He can just close it until we've flushed out Clooney's rattlesnakes tomorrow morning."

He kept looking off in the distance, and probably didn't see Daniel smile.

They sent Packard and Clarence to the barfly's house. Completely unreliable about details, he still gave them the name of a neighbor who had lived in the area for decades. The neighbor died two years ago, and that was why the man was surprised to see a visitor to a vacant house. There was a single-wide trailer on the land, too, near the spot where the new SUV had been parked.

This information was irresistible. Daniel abandoned any idea of waiting until morning. After one miss in the pitch dark, they found the property.

"The SUV is there, right next to the trailer. About twenty yards from what looks like an old prospector's shack," Clarence said. He stood up in the shallow flood-wash they had found at the edge of the property, and peered through night vision binoculars. Darkness sat heavy on the sandy landscape, and the stars above were magnificent. "Light in the trailer. None in the shack. Probably filled with snakes. They like to do their hunting at night."

"Doesn't matter," Ramos whispered. "Gotta cover the shack, too. No warm spots? Cigarette?"

"Nothing but dark. Sure, some wavers, but that might just be hot sand."

Jimmy looked down at Daniel. "I'll take the shack."

"It's yours." Daniel nodded to the station chief. "If this is going to be a dud, it's my job to lead the big group. Take Packard." The LA guy flashed a grin. "We get in position, away from the dirt road then wait, and watch. Somebody comes in, fine. But they're not driving that Lincoln out of there."

Midnight arrived, and still there had been no discernible movement. They started, moving in from the south. Before Jimmy and the youngster drifted toward the shack, though, a shudder seized Daniel. There, against the cool desert starlight, the little house's form struck something deep inside. He had seen this place before, tasted the same salty-sandy grit in his teeth, heard the same shushing starlight. In Khulud's vision. He grabbed the chief's sleeve. A nod.

"You sure?" Ramos whispered.

"Yes."

Jimmy shrugged, and traded places.

Daniel followed Packard to the side of the shack, and crouched under a boarded-up window. By then, he was shaking, his stomach so tight, it threatened to reject the lousy hot dog he ate nine hours ago in the Vegas airport.

For a moment, he was paralyzed, transported back to the dark street in Beirut by the unmistakable drone of murmurs that came from inside. Mumbled prayers. Frank was here. They should signal the others, but the distance was too great, and any sound -- Besides, how could he risk agents' lives on a vision? A glance at Packard, who gave a strong nod. He heard the chanting, too.

They would have to move now, but he had to remember how. He smelled the night sand, felt the rough wood with its prickly chips of paint, and fought not to be sucked into eternity by that soft singing. Time to forget about

Frank Whitlock. This was just another hostage. Time to be logical and definite again. A leader. The next world would have to wait. This one was his. Daniel tightened his goggles, and waved.

The sky blazed with flash-bangs. Packard blew through the door. Far away, Daniel heard glass break in the trailer.

Zip. Zip. He was in, and Packard had taken the man with the rifle. Another door. The young cop was fast. He gripped the knob and jerked it open. Daniel leaped into the doorway.

Two men in chairs. One moved, eerie green-white in the night vision goggles. Slow-motion, smooth. Something in his mouth, his hand – eating. The other one, frozen in place. Blindfolded. Daniel aimed, but the motion of the Eater was unstoppable, deliberate. He dropped the thing in his hand and brought an object in a wide arc to Blindfold's head.

Zip. Zip. Daniel's nine-millimeter flashed just before a loud *bang* exploded the night. Both men on chairs went down. Someone pushed from behind, and Daniel tumbled forward, slamming his chin on the concrete floor. The taste of blood. And sand.

"Clear. Clear." Packard yelled.

Footsteps. Then someone had a light.

"It's him. It's Whitlock."

"He's alive. He's out, but he's alive."

Daniel stood, brushing filth off of his palms. "Is he OK? Find out if he's OK," he demanded. He kicked at the thing that landed near his shoes. A pomegranate.

Williams was bent over Frank's body. "Grazed him. I see bone. It may have punctured through to the brain."

"Goddam it," Ramos' voice roared in the outer room. "The fucking ambulance probably took the wrong road."

Jimmy Johnson nudged Daniel. Through the goggles, his green face wore an impish grin. "If this was Carpenter's barbecue, he would have had the ambulances here on time."

Chapter 50
The Man in the Pantry

They led him outside to do his business. Quiet tonight, and through a crack in the blindfold, Frank fancied he saw dust rising from his shoes in the starlight.

"Hurry up, Mr. Frank." The voice of the other one. They had slipped once, two days before, so he knew the louder guy's name – Waz. But he dared not speak it.

A hand helped him over the step – wooden. He prepared to duck, curl up, and resume his position in the cramped closet, where insects skittered over his back each time he was just falling asleep. This time, though, they did not take him to the right, but angled the opposite way.

"Careful, Mr. Frank. There is a chair." They turned him around, loosened the wrist bindings, then re-tied his hands behind his back. Was this it?

They shuffled, whispering in their tongue. Arguing? Then a door closed. He waited, drops of sweat tickling under the blindfold. Waited. So tired. He had humiliated himself at first, crying and begging for a bullet instead of a slit throat. They laughed. Now he was sitting up. It would be the throat.

So goddam weary. Where was the adrenalin that created a whole new world for him on the airplane? Where was Sam?

An electronic beep sent him out of his skin. They were somewhere. He was alone, and there were at least two rooms in this place. More beeps – a cell phone? Their words were hurried, clipped. Could not tell which one was speaking. Then silence. Maybe a long silence, for he jerked his head back. He had been sleeping, sitting up. A sound – door opening?

"Are you resting, Mr. Frank?" Waz. He walked closer, feet scraping. Maybe they were tired, too. Frank tensed and waited. The scrape of a chair, and Waz sat next to him. The other one still far away, doing his chants.

"Are we OK?" Frank whispered, and realized they had left him un-gagged for some time. A record.

"We are OK, Mr. Frank. Today is a travel day. Did I tell you that you are going to be a television star? We leave at sunrise. Here." A finger touched Frank's chin, and he jerked, his heart slamming into high gear.

"What?"

"Please." Waz laughed softly. "Calm down, my friend. Do you like pomegranate? We must eat before the trip." The hand again. It shoved seeds into Frank's mouth, and he bit down. Tart and sweet. A feeling of relief, of pure ecstasy, pulsed through his glands. He could hear Waz eating, too.

"Thank you."

"You are welcome, my friend. Here. More."

The ritual repeated. Frank chewed voraciously. Sometimes Waz leaned over, their shoulders touching. The other guy still chanting. Could he ask his name? No. What if Waz was lying? Trying to make him relax? That other guy was the key. If the prayers stopped and he went outside, good. If he came in here, all bets were off.

Then the world swayed. A yell. Thunder – scuffling, and he yelled, "No--" But his voice only echoed into a bottomless well into which he was falling. For a long time.

Then the light slowly began to return, though his teeth still pressed together from a headache like he had never felt before. Slowly, he pried his eyes open to see they were back on the football field. Frank looked down, and panicked. He was wearing his uniform, and had to hustle to get up to the line of scrimmage in time. This was his second year in the Pop Warner football league. Wide receiver. Blood pumping through powerful arms, smells of dirt and sweat. He was young again.

The other boys crouched into position. Red Cobb. Whitley and Bo-re-gard. A glance to the sparsely populated bleachers. Was Linda out of school yet? Of course, she would not be here to watch him, and he didn't like this game for some reason. The quarterback began the count – old Oscar. God, so long. But Frank kept standing, watching a seagull arc over the high press box. He knew what would happen next: As ever, the bird would sail on the cool air, then twirl in such an unprecedented motion. Oscar counting urgently, but Frank would not be able to move, and the ball would snap, the play collapse into mid-field, and Uncle Carl would come running from the track, wide-eyed, and grab his jersey, and jabber – rattle out words that finally melted together, saying that Sam was in a car wreck while out driving with Richard Polk. He never should ride with Richard. Mom always told him to stay away from Richard. He should never ride with Richard.

"Is he OK? Is Sam OK?" Frank asked, over and over.

"It's not good." Uncle Carl the policeman with tears in his eyes.

Then Frank looked up, and the seagull twirled like birds should not be able to twirl, flashing into the afternoon sun. They were on the line again. "Hut!" as if Oscar and the others never even looked at their wide receiver. The play was on, but Frank could only watch outside the foul line, over the track. Sam stood there, beckoning. But where was Uncle Carl?

"This way," Sam urged. The yells of the players faded behind them. Across the track, out onto the grass behind the end zone. "Hurry." That was Sam, always frantic. But at least he was speaking. Such a welcome voice.

They reached the hurricane fence, and Frank froze in his tracks. Sam unlocked the long gate. He had done that before, but only when the dream was over. This time, he swung it wide open, and wind began to blow.

"Come on."

"What? No." Frank dug his cleats into the grass.

"Come with me."

Wind blew Frank's hair. "No, Sam, you said I couldn't go through the fence."

For a moment, his big brother looked angry, but the hard expression faded, and he walked over, reached out and gripped Frank's shoulder.

"Little man," he said, though by now Frank was the taller of them both, "you need to, this time."

"No." Frank blubbered. He was almost a teenager, and the girls in the stands would see him crying, but he didn't care. The wind came fiercely now, like a hurricane. "Don't make me go beyond the fence, Sam. Not yet, Sam. It's not over yet, is it?"

"Just this once." Sam wrapped his arm around Frank's shoulder. That smell. This was Sam. "It'll be OK. I promise."

Holding onto the strong hand, staggering awkwardly forward on his cleats, Frank let his brother lead him against the wind, and through the gate.

Aswan Abdullah fairly danced along the walk's edge. "It's happening, General Farid. Israel is starting to buckle. They are giving back land. Even the Gaza. Isn't it exciting news?"

Suhail smiled, but wished the chatterbox would be quiet. "Yes, Abdullah. The first real progress in years."

"Will the Syrians move now? Do you think? Muhammed, son of Habib, says the Saudis are going to throw out the Americans in just a few weeks. Is that possible?"

"Patience, Sergeant Major. When the last part of the enemy's spirit is broken, we won't need armies, Syrian or otherwise."

"But when--" The words stuck in Abdullah's throat, and hung in the air, and Suhail could only stare at him, until they turned the corner and he, too, saw the lone police vehicle at the far end of the alley.

"Be calm, my friend. It's a friendly." But Abdullah's eyes only widened more.

Above the apartments, a klatch of sunbirds flew, headed southeast, tinges of blue shadows on their wings. A worrisome omen. Suhail set a course directly for the stairs, but a few of his men lingered at a lower door.

"Go to the café, Master," one of them whispered, but Suhail headed for the stairs.

Screeching tires turned him around. One, two, four more police cars pulled up, skirting around the first. A man in uniform hopped out and began directing traffic around them. Suhail walked backwards.

"Get inside, General." The skin on Fahd's face was drawn tight.

"General Farid!" Men in uniform swarmed from the cars. They wrested a prisoner from a back seat. Friendlies? Esam was the one who knew the police. They brought the man forward, and jerked his head up by his hair. Kareem. "Do you know this man, General?" the officer asked. "He is accused of planning a terrorist act."

Suhail stood, flat-footed. The grocer's children hugged the wall, eyes wide. "Let him go," Suhail demanded. Who had not been paid off?

A revving engine made him look once more to the main street. Another car. Doors opened. Esam. Waleed.

"General," Esam called. "It is our duty to arrest you under orders of President Mubarak. Suspicion of conspiracy to commit terrorist acts."

"Fools." Suhail's lungs were devoid of air, so his rebuke came out as only a whisper.

He started to pivot, but a policeman strode forward. "This man is guilty," he cried. He took one more step, raised a gun. An explosion split the air, and Kareem collapsed onto the pavement.

Must get up the stairs. To the pantry. Suhail leaped, two steps at a time. "Prince of Afrits," he cried.

"Master Farid."

Above, women retreated into apartment doors.

"I'm sorry, Master Farid."

A noise, but too loud for him to discern its source. For some reason, Suhail found himself lying down, the molded metal stairs right in front of his face. The pantry. Keep moving to the pantry. Up there, his apartment door stood ajar. Did someone break in? He entered. Wind blowing through the window. The French painting was off the wall, furniture turned every which way.

"Esam, what is happening?" he called out, suddenly thinking the big man might have passed him on the stairs. No answer. "Esam, have you been in my room? Did you forget to pay the officers?"

He staggered, against a wind that seemed impossibly strong inside these walls, moving instinctively toward the pantry, even as the room sank into sudden darkness. *Afrit Racer*, he thought loudly, *come to me from your void. Shield me from the infidels* – noises on the stairway below. They were coming. Suhail's thoughts stopped when his fingers touched the velvet curtain's edge, and someone else jerked it open from within.

A man stood there, framed by shelves of bean cans and canisters of flour, sugar, jars of spices. Large man, gray hair at his temples. As Suhail stared, the face acquired focus. A face from television. CNN. AL Jazeera. It was the American, Whitlock.

"What are you?" Suhail cried. "Is this treachery? What are you doing here? Did Hadeel bring you? Hadee—eell!"

"Come in." The American hero spoke calmly. Not words proper. More in the language of the afrits. "Please come through the curtain. Your pain is over."

Suhail studied that face. Wanted to call Esam to climb up and look, too. It held no malice, that face. There was no window in the pantry, yet the wind blew even more strongly from within – as he watched, the shelves of foodstuffs, pots and pans transformed into the stone walls of the caverns – he knew this world well. He had crossed into the land of the Afrits. But how was it that the American came with him?

"I don't know if I'm ready for this," Suhail said finally. "It is not what I expected."

The American smiled. A magnanimous smile. Devoid of gloating. "I know," he said. "No harps and wings. No virgins. Just wind. Come. There is a park, just outside this cave. Your family is waiting for you."

Chapter 51
Invitations

"The doctor said it would be all right." Roby set the shrimp cocktails down, one in front of Jill, then Frank's. "But I'd go easy. These things give me heartburn."

"Thanks." Frank smiled, for the tangy sauce smell mixed with that of the roses and orange blossoms, paint and fresh-cut planks. Familiar. Good memories. Sunlight on the pool's surface. Life was good, even if it seemed he observed it from a much greater distance, now.

The whine of an electric saw drowned out his next request. The rebuilding of the house's center section was in full swing. When the grating noise faded, he yelled after the retreating lawman. "How about a beer?"

"I ain't your nursemaid, Frank. You know that's off limits. I'll get one for the missus, though." He winked.

"He knows I don't drink beer--" Jill began, softly, then realized the gambit. She smiled, her eyes somewhat dreamy. She only played with the prawns, sticking her fork in first one, then another.

"Aren't you going to eat?"

"Not hungry."

The screaming saw shut them both up again.

"They're just right," he finally said, crunching the cold meat. "Want something else?"

"Mmm."

He should tend to the pool sweep's hose before dark, but it felt nice just to sit here. The cops would run up and take it away from him, anyway. In the corner of the yard, Deputy Vecchio stood on tiptoes, craning to see into the Raed's property. Then the Tambray's. Too bad for them all. No skinny-dipping in this neighborhood for at least another summer.

Jill still played with her fork.

"What are you thinking about so intensely?"

"Nothing." Finally, she dunked a prawn into the sauce. "I just thought we might invite Elizabeth and her husband up here sometime."

"Elizabeth Kismet?"

"Yeah."

He chewed this one slowly. "That would be nice. Will you sit with me at the interview on Friday?"

A grimace. "You know I hate being on TV, Frank."

"I'm going out. Want to go out?" Jimmy threw the hanging bag over his shoulder.

"Sure, *you* want to. You've had enough sleep, asshole. It's eight-thirty at night here," Daniel said. His back felt stiff. One day in the Barstow wasteland had turned into three, and a hurricane of paperwork. "I swear to God I'll shoot the next Internal clown that shoves a form in front of me."

"Aw, quit whining." They stepped off the escalator, and headed toward the line of taxis. "You FBI guys get old before your time."

"We have more paperwork than you. Aren't you dropping by the office before you go home?"

"Don't juke me, man." They stepped out into a sultry Washington night. Air rich with diesel. "I ain't even going in tomorrow. If they ask for me, tell them I got California dysentery."

Daniel stared at him. "I can't believe my ears. There's a war on. Israel about to go up in flames. Troop movements in Iraq. Ten thousand illegal aliens we can't find, and if we don't, our careers are over. You and me, buddy boy. You want the new boss to do everything?"

Jimmy rolled his eyes. "Sure there's a war on, but I just do one battle at a time. There's something else on, my man. It's called life. I would love to go back to the office. You know it. But the Macintosh is nowhere near Langley."

They waved the basketball player to the first car.

"Hey, Jimmy?"

"Yeah?"

"Good job down there."

A shrug. "You went shooting. I went trailer shopping." The cab pulled away.

Daniel took the next one, and had trouble explaining his destination. Not Langley. Not his own place. "Turn," he directed, finally. The car careened out of the market street. "Stop here."

They were still a block from her house, and the bag was heavier than ever. Pringle claimed she was coming back from New York today, so he took the chance. He wasn't sure which apartment, but the one he assumed was hers still had lights on. Hopefully, she hadn't moved out yet.

One buzzer still bore the label "Bernstein," but before he could press it, the front door creaked open. Short sleeves, khaki shirt, jeans, and tennis shoes. She looked at him without smiling. Great. A dark smudge, obviously a bruise, lined her cheek near the hairline below her temple. Not a black eye, *per se*.

By reflex, he retreated down a couple of steps. "Hi. Still here?"

"Got back a couple of hours ago. I'm here."

"Good timing. Going somewhere? Out for a run this late?"

"I was thinking about it."

"Darn. When you opened the door, I was hoping it meant you were waiting by the window for me, forgot everything else, and rushed down when you saw me on the walk."

A smirk. "What are you carrying? Did you think I would invite you to move in?"

They both laughed. She was keeping her distance, but it wasn't all bad. Daniel decided to keep it light.

"Don't know. I heard your apartment might be vacant, soon. Want to show me around? Maybe I'll make a bid."

She shook her head, wearing a skeptical look, and picked with her fingernail at the ragged paint on the door. "Premature. I talked it over with someone. Maybe I'll stick around a little longer."

"Oh, I forgot. He's OK."

"Who?"

"Frank Whitlock. The bullet just chipped his skull. Already out of the hospital."

"That's good." She looked down, and in the harsh streetlight, he took the darkness in her cheeks for blushing. "I heard it was close. You OK?"

"Close enough. Want to go out for a drink? Actually, I need a bite to eat. The airlines ain't what they used to be."

She thought about it, swinging the door so that it hit her foot repeatedly. "You look like a high school girl," he said. "So innocent."

The smirk again. "I always figured you for a pedophile. I've got to go back up for a sweater."

"Great."

But she remained, staring. "I guess I should invite you in."

"No." He protested too quickly. "But I'm curious. Do you have more than one bottle of perfume?"

Her eyes narrowed. "A few. Like any girl. Nothing that expensive."

"Where do you keep them? The bottles of perfume?"

"Why? Did Gerry write some sort of report on my apartment?"

"Gerry's out of a job. Just tell me, please."

"On top of a cabinet. Why, did you buy me some in California?"

"What color is the cabinet?"

"Red."

He gestured with his chin. "Go up and get ready."

She stared another moment. "Daniel, are you getting weird on me?"

He sighed. "I don't know anything, anymore. I do owe you an apology, though. For caring about my job so much that it prevented me from kicking Gerry's ass in the first place."

"Not your fault. I decided to stop looking for rescuers and fend for myself. You have your hands full, already."

"Maybe we would make a good team--" He said it, but she had already vanished back through the doorway. Daniel leaned against the rail. There were two decent restaurants down at the intersection. An Irish pub and a *trattoria*. Tonight, the Italian place felt right.

A noise. She was holding onto the door, sheepishly playing with the chipped paint again. "Do you have your credit card?"

"Of course. This one's on me. Might even stick Uncle Sam with the bill. I'm a director, now – but that story's more dinner talk." He laughed. He should kiss her now, but her body language told him she wasn't quite sure. Yet.

She faced him squarely, hands on her hips. "That's not what I mean. I saw you from the window, and dropped everything and ran down the stairs. I need to borrow one of your credit cards to get back into my apartment. You know, like you showed me."

He pulled out his wallet, but her lips were on his before he could even open it.

THE END